ALWAYS BEEN MINE

Also by Elizabeth Reyes:

Moreno Brothers Series

Forever Mine
Sweet Sophie
Romero
Making You Mine

5th Street Series

Noah
Gio
Hector
Abel

Fate Series

Fate
Breaking Brandon (Fall 2013)

ALWAYS BEEN MINE

The Moreno Brothers #2

Elizabeth Reyes

Always Been Mine

The Moreno Brothers #2

Elizabeth Reyes

Kindle Edition

PROLOGUE

Valerie still couldn't believe she'd actually stooped to spying. Even with everything Alex Moreno had put her through, she was furious it had come to this. She switched the channel on the car radio and glanced at her watch: 9:45 pm. Her fingers tapped the steering wheel. With a deep breath, she stared at his empty driveway. Where the hell was he?

For as long as she'd known Alex, their relationship had been complicated. This past month and a half had been the exception. They'd been inseparable, and things finally began to feel serious. She'd practically lived at his place the past two weeks. A few times she thought he hinted that she should.

When she'd finally returned home Sunday, he stopped calling and returning her calls. Just like all the other times, he disappeared on her again. There was an entire month of calls just before bed, then first thing in the morning, then two weeks of, "Don't go, stay with me." Then nothing for four days? Was he kidding?

All the other times he'd done this, she'd let it go. He'd always reappear eventually with some lame excuse, and like a sick little puppy, she was so ready to jump back in his arms. Well, not anymore.

She should have done this a long time ago. Valerie fidgeted in her seat, rubbing her hands over her thighs. Her head told her she'd better be ready. The truth was coming out tonight one way or another. The truth she'd known all along, but she couldn't bring herself to face it. Deep inside, she'd always known Alex Moreno was not a one-woman man.

She'd lusted over him all through high school. Even then, she'd known he was way out of her league. As the gorgeous high school jock, he had girls all over him. He'd gone out with her just for fun, and she was okay with that. As the years passed, he stayed in her life off and on. But he never stuck around for too long.

She accepted it. All this time she told herself it was because she was too busy with her school and career to get too caught up in anything serious. The real reason was always in the back of her mind. Just the thought of pushing too hard and losing what little relationship she did have with him scared her more than she'd ever admit. She tried many times in the past to make a clean break from him, but she was never strong enough to stick with it.

Well, she had to be strong now. She couldn't take it anymore. Not after the month and a half they'd just had. The pain of wondering where he was and who he was with finally outweighed the fear of learning the truth and ending things for good. She owed it to herself to find out once and for all if his heart was as invested in this as hers, or was this all just a game, a game he'd continue to play for as long as she'd allow it?

Even with her head telling her to expect the worst, that she would finally get the closure she needed to walk away for good, her heart was still holding out hope that there was a compelling explanation: that he felt for her what she'd always felt for him.

Valerie glanced around the dash of her roommate's car. They'd swapped cars all week so that he wouldn't recognize her sitting up the street. All week she chickened out in hopes that she'd hear from him and she wouldn't have to go through with this. It was Thursday now, and all she'd gotten so far was a couple of pity texts saying he was crazy busy and he'd call her soon.

Headlights brightened the dark street. Valerie sunk in her seat. Alex's truck drove by the car she hunched down in undetected. She sunk so low she wasn't able to see if he was alone or not.

Scooting up just high enough so her eyes were over the dash, she saw him walking around his truck and toward his front door. *Alone.*

A glimmer of hope danced in her heart. Maybe he *was* just busy. She sat up once he'd gone inside and stared at her phone. He was home now, done for the day. So why wasn't he calling her? Could these past six weeks really have been all in her head? Had she just imagined his increased affection? She couldn't be *that* delusional. *Could she*?

He said he cared for her, that he couldn't stop thinking about her. How could he go four whole days without so much as calling her? Didn't he miss her, damn it?

The street lit up again as another car drove closer. It slowed as it passed her and then stopped in front of Alex's house. Valerie held her breath. The door opened and out came pair of long legs. Attached to the legs, a girl in her early twenties in short shorts and a snug tank that read UCSD climbed out. Valerie watched as the girl opened the trunk and pulled out what was too big to be a purse.

Her breath hitched. Every time she came over lately, Alex had been insistent that she'd bring an overnight bag. *The bastard!*

Valerie could feel her blood pressure spike, her chest constrict. This was it, proof of what she'd known all along and no two ways around it. She watched as the girl swung her long dark hair over her shoulder and made her way up Alex's walkway. Valerie's eyes stayed glued to her. Her pulse throbbed in her ears. She blinked away the tears that blurred her vision.

Alex was at the door before the girl even got there. He was waiting for her! Valerie felt her heart shatter. She'd known it all along, and yet she was in no way prepared for the acute sting of it. She squeezed her eyes shut just as Alex placed his hand on the girl's shoulder. She couldn't bear to watch.

Valerie opened her eyes in time to see the door close behind the girl. She let out a shuddering breath. Her mind raced, considering the best way to handle this. The hot tears streamed down her cheeks. Even though she'd thought of the possibilities, she'd never actually planned what she'd do if she caught him so red-handed.

She picked up the phone and called him. Of course, the call went to voicemail. Hearing his voice in his greeting only enraged her further. Without giving it another thought, she shot out of the car, slamming the door behind her.

Brushing the tears away, she sucked in deep breaths to try to calm herself. She stalked toward his front door as she tried desperately to compose herself. So many choice words came to mind that she wanted to scream at him. The two most blaring were, "It's over!" It really was, for good this time. Never, in all the horrible scenarios she'd played out in her head over the years, did she realize how unbearable the pain would be. The thought of him with someone else didn't even compare to actually seeing it.

She rang the doorbell then immediately knocked. After only seconds, she knocked again. The door opened, and even though it had only been days since she'd last seen him, she still had to take a moment to take him all in. The man was unreal. He stood there all six-foot-three of him. His dark heavy lashed eyes stared at her, startled.

"Valerie, sweetheart. I wasn't expecting you."

"Of course not." Her voice broke, but she kept it together. "New houseguest *this* week?"

He shifted in the doorway, and she caught a glimpse of the bitch sitting at his dining room table—the table they'd eaten the breakfast they'd prepared together just that Sunday. The very table he'd reached across over and over, claiming he couldn't keep his hands off her.

Valerie felt her insides tearing apart. Something had ignited in her: something terrible she'd never felt in her life. Alex stepped outside, closing the door behind him. "No, babe. I know what you're thinking, but I can explain."

He tried to grab her hand, and she jerked it away. "Go to hell, Alex! I've had enough of your lies."

She stormed away, feeling ready to go into hysterics. The image of the girl sitting at his table, of him kissing and doing things to her …

"Valerie, wait!"

Her high heels clicked loudly on the pavement as she picked up her speed. He caught up, stumbling as his bare feet stepped on something that apparently hurt. The fact that he'd been so comfortably barefoot with the bitch only incensed her more. He took her hand but this time held on tight enough that she couldn't pull it away.

"Baby, listen to me." He spoke right in her face. "She's a tutor."

Valerie let out a sardonic laugh. "Wow, Alex, the lies wearing a little thin finally?"

"No, she really is."

"Is that supposed to make it better, Alex? That you're fucking a tutor?" Valerie screamed.

She'd lost it. She was moments from having a royal meltdown, and she had to get out of there because it wouldn't be pretty. She yanked her hand away and rushed to her car. Alex followed her.

"I mean she's *my* tutor, Val. I didn't want you to know."

Of course he didn't. He caught her again just as she got to the door of the car, but her arms flung around like a crazy person. She didn't want to feel any part of him on her ever again. "Get away from me!" Her high-pitched scream froze Alex momentarily. She must've looked as crazy as she felt, because he stared at her without saying a word.

"Do you care about me at all, Alex?" The taste of salty tears and bitter mascara seeped in the side of her mouth. She could only imagine what a mess her face was. He still stared at her wide-eyed. "Do you at all?"

He took a step forward, his face as genuinely pained as all the other times he'd given her excuse after excuse. He began to reach for her again. "Baby, of course I do. I—"

She flung her hand up, slapping his hand away from her. "Then stay away from me! Don't ever call me again."

"Valerie, don't—"

"Please, Alex!" She opened the door to the car, got in, and locked the door. The window was open, and he stood in front of it. "Promise me, Alex. I don't want you to call me ever again."

His eyes darkened, and his eyebrows pinched. "No."

"I *need* you out of my life!" She cried. What she needed was her sanity, and at the moment, she felt robbed of it. Never in her life had she felt so incapable of controlling her emotions.

She struggled with the ignition as Alex began to try to explain his ridiculous tutor story again. Valerie pressed the button to close the window.

"Valerie, listen to me—"

He was still talking when she began to pull away from the curb, nearly taking out his legs.

How she'd ever get over Alex was beyond her, but nothing was worth feeling this kind of pain again. Nothing. She drove away, sobbing. Alex Moreno had shredded her heart for the last time.

CHAPTER 1

One year later

Anticipation was something Alex Moreno had experienced many times. He'd mainly felt it after not having seen Valerie for days. It was usually a welcome feeling. The excitement was well worth it in the past. But this anticipation had been building for weeks, if not months. Damn it if it wasn't beginning to get annoying.

What he was feeling now made no sense. For the third time, he wiped his sweaty palms with a napkin and threw it in the trash. He just didn't get it. The anticipation was to be expected. He hadn't seen her in over a year. The nerves that accompanied it were what he didn't understand. What the hell was there to be nervous about? He'd never been nervous about seeing her before.

As the maid of honor and cousin of the bride, Valerie Zuniga was obligated to be at all these events. Alex had had plenty of time to mentally prepare, and he thought he was. Sure, it had been more than a year since he last seen or spoken to her. It still shouldn't be that big a deal. He'd see her, they'd catch up, and that would be the end of it.

He strolled around his parent's backyard. The knot in his stomach was firmly attached and building from the moment he woke up. He tried to concentrate on the final touches. The backyard had been completely transformed. The tables and chairs had arrived early in the morning. A massive canopy almost enclosed the yard in its entirety. Professionally decorated tables with expensive, elaborate flower centerpieces sprawled throughout the yard. His parents didn't mess around when they threw a party. To them, this was huge.

His younger brother Angel would be the first of the siblings to get married. The Moreno's were going all out and sparing no expense. This was only the wedding shower. The wedding was still months away.

Alex glanced around. Everything was pretty much set. Romero and Eric, Angel's two best friends, were setting up the bar. Alex figured since they were Angel's best men in the wedding, he'd let them handle one big thing at this party. What could be more fitting than the bar for those two.

Angel stuck his head out the back door. "You guys ready? We have people arriving."

Eric gave him the thumbs up while Romero continued to obsess over the way the kegs were placed.

Alex walked over to them. "That's enough, Ramon. What are you doing?"

Romero had always gone by his last name. Alex only called him by his first name, Ramon, when he wanted to annoy him.

"You don't know about this." Romero didn't even look up as he kept shifting the keg in the barrel of ice it sat in.

"I run a restaurant with a bar. You're a bouncer."

Romero stood up. "I own a security firm."

Alex loved ribbing Romero. He was the only one of them that hadn't attended college. Instead, he worked as a bouncer at several bars and did some private investigating for a few agencies until he saved up enough to start up his own security firm. He'd actually done well for himself. At twenty-two, he already owned his own business. Even Alex had to admit that was pretty impressive. Of course, he'd never tell him that. It was too much fun clowning him.

"You have two employees." Alex tried not to smirk.

"There's four now, ass. And I'm looking to hire more in case you're interested. I'm gettin' real busy."

"Really?" Eric asked. "I didn't know business was that good."

"Yeah, and I'm branching out now. I just got my PI license. You're looking at Private Eye, Romero."

"No shit?" Eric smiled, impressed. "So you get to spy on people and stuff?"

Alex rolled his eyes. Leave it to Eric to ruin his fun. Romero started telling Eric about all the gadgets he'd recently bought to track people, and Alex lost interest. He turned to see people entering the back yard from the kitchen door. Alex frowned. They were supposed to be coming in through the side gate. He glanced at the side gate. That's when he saw her.

He felt the air sucked out of him. His heart did a wild gallop, and he swallowed hard, trying to remain composed. It amazed him how different she looked from a year ago. She was still the same Valerie he'd known since high school. Delicately petite and blonde, yet there was something different. Even as small a woman as she was, her entrance was enormous.

Alex thought of how busy she'd been a year ago, working on getting her real estate license. She spent most of her time studying for the state exam in tattered jeans or shorts. He remembered her honey-blonde hair constantly in ponytails and wearing t-shirts. *His* t-shirts.

Now she stood there in a sexy little ivory skirt suit. The only color to her outfit was the soft pink lace camisole under the jacket. Her golden locks were in a glamorous updo with strands that fell perfectly around her face. The wisps of hair accentuated her high cheekbones. Then she smiled with those full lips he'd never been able to get quite enough of. *Beautiful*.

She wore her signature very high heels. He watched in awe as she walked across the yard to greet Angel and his fiancée, Sarah. It always amazed Alex that not only could she walk in those big heels she did it with such elegance.

Valerie's posture was as perfect as ever. She'd always exuded confidence. That was just one the qualities that first attracted him to her so many years ago.

He was aware that he hadn't taken his eyes off her since she walked in. Fully aware, and he didn't care. His eyes roamed her body freely from top to bottom and back up again. He'd expected it would be pleasant to see her again. Pleasant didn't even begin to describe what he was feeling now.

"Damn, is that Valerie?" Romero asked.

Alex stiffened. Even after all this time, he didn't like anyone else looking at her that way, especially Romero's dumb ass.

"She brought a friend, Romero." Eric pointed out. "Maybe she'll put a good word in for you. You damn sure will need it."

To his relief, the only person Valerie had walked in with was her roommate, Isabel. After all this time, he'd actually lost sleep the last couple of nights over the possibility of her showing up with another guy. He wasn't even sure why. It had been so long. It only made sense that she would be seeing someone now. It really shouldn't bother him. He was long over her.

Alex had only met Isabel a few times. She was much taller than Valerie and attractive in an exotic yet inhibited way but a bit too uptight for his taste.

Romero took one look at her. "Not my type."

Eric laughed. "Since when do you have standards?"

"I'm a businessman now, Eric. I have a reputation to uphold." Romero glanced back in Isabel's direction. "Plus she looks soft. I need a woman that can handle all this."

Romero pointed at himself with both hands from the top of his head to his feet and smiled smugly.

"You wouldn't be able to handle her. Trust me." Alex said, still staring at Valerie.

He couldn't take his eyes off her, not that he was putting any effort into it. He watched as she and Sarah laughed about something. Angel left the girls and walked toward Alex.

"Shots all around," Romero pulled out a bottle of tequila and four shot glasses.

Angel laughed. "Are you crazy? It's not even three."

Alex finally unglued his eyes off Valerie. "None for me."

"Nah," Romero shook his head and continued to pour the shots. "This is horseshit. I had an entire weekend of Vegas planned. At least give me this."

Alex rolled his eyes. The moment Angel had told those two knuckleheads that he wanted them to be his best men, they started planning the bachelor party. A week later, Angel announced he didn't want a bachelor party and flat out refused to talk about why, just said it wasn't happening, period. Romero was still bent about it.

"Dude, Angel has to be presentable at least for a few hours." Eric said.

Eric had always been the level-headed one of Angel's two childhood best friends. A good thing too, because he was now attached to Alex's little sister Sofia. Not that anyone would ever be good enough for his younger sister. Still, he was glad that between the two friends, Eric was the one Sofia had fallen for. It would've driven Alex crazy had it been crude and outspoken Romero.

Alex's dad stopped by as he made his rounds. Alex clapped him on the shoulder. His dad saw the shot glasses. "One more," he ordered.

Romero smiled. "Help me out here, Mr. Moreno. These two don't want any."

Alex's dad glanced at both Alex and Angel who were now both gazing in the girls' direction again. "Grow a pair!"

Romero and Eric both laughed. Alex and Angel exchanged discomfited glances. They were going to have to take at least one shot. Whatever their old man wanted, he got.

They all held their shot glasses up and toasted to Sarah and Angel. Alex grimaced, sucking on a lime slice and turned just in time to see the girls walking toward them. Valerie looked so unbelievably good to him. It almost felt as if he was watching her move in slow motion. She never once even glanced in his direction. Sofia was the first to address them. "Are you guys having fun?" She hugged her dad, and he kissed her on the forehead.

"Keep your brothers in line, Sofie." Her dad said, walking away and immediately starting a conversation with the group at the table nearest to the bar.

"What? My brothers are not behaving?" Sofia teased.

Alex could hardly concentrate. His eyes again roamed every inch of Valerie.

"Your brothers are being wusses," Romero stated, already setting up more shots.

"I'll take one." Valerie said.

Even her voice sounded more womanly than he remembered, *sultrier*.

"Valerie, no." Isabel warned.

Romero frowned. "Who brought the nark?"

"Pardon me?" Isabel glared at Romero.

Romero stopped pouring, backed up, and did an elaborate bow, bringing his arm over his head and down to his feet. "*Pardon* me?"

Normally Alex would have laughed along with everyone else, but he was too distracted trying to figure out why Valerie was still avoiding his eyes.

Romero brought out another shot glass. "You in, Nark?"

Alex took his eyes off Valerie just long enough to glance at Isabel, who seemed to be as annoyed as only Romero could annoy women. "Easy, Ramon."

Valerie smiled. "Yes, please pour her one."

Alex squeezed the edge of the bar. He had to get a hold of himself. This was the same Valerie he'd known all along: the Valerie he'd carried on with and laughed with such ease for years. The one he'd had earth-shattering sex with many, many times. He gulped hard. *His* Valerie.

Romero looked pleased and pulled out another shot glass. "Coming right up."

Alex was determined to not take his eyes off her until she looked at him, and then the mariachis walked in. Everyone turned to watch the entire ensemble stroll in playing loud and proud.

For a moment, his eyes met with Valerie's, and he thought he saw something in them. Maybe he was searching too hard, but for a split second, he thought he saw alarm in her big dark eyes. Just when he'd not only finally made eye contact but was getting some kind of emotion out of her, she turned away to face the musicians.

~*~

Valerie concentrated hard on not wavering and stared at the mariachi band. She could feel Alex's eyes on her, and her body heated. Her heart hadn't stopped hammering from the moment she walked in and spotted him. She'd expected some excitement when she saw him, but this was a bit much. She'd been happy he was busy with the guys at the bar, because she couldn't bear to even make eye contact. She thought the shot of tequila might help settle her nerves. It hadn't.

How was it that every time she saw him, he seemed even bigger than the last? He was without a doubt the most devastating man she'd ever met. What he did to her without so much as saying a word even after all this time was absurd. She wasn't even facing him now, and she could still feel his incredible presence weighing heavily on her back.

People began clinking their glasses. Valerie clutched her small purse and forced a smile when Sarah and Angel kissed.

She almost jumped when she felt his face at her ear and his hot body against her back. "You gonna say hello, Z?"

The suggestive murmur in such an otherwise ordinary question infuriated her as much as it spiked her senses. He'd only ever referred to her as Z when he was agitated with her for whatever reason. It was a football thing. They all called each other by their last names on the team, and he'd imposed it on her but only when he was mad. He didn't sound mad now. He sounded *amused*?

That was just like him. He was probably enjoying seeing her squirm. She wouldn't let him have the upper hand. Closing her eyes for a moment, she took a deep breath and then turned to face him with a smile. "Hello, Alex."

"So did I pour that for nothing?" Romero pointed at the shot he'd put out for Isabel.

Valerie took advantage to glance away from Alex's penetrating eyes. "Romero, this is my roommate Isabel. Isabel, this is Romero."

Isabel softened her glare. "I thought it was Ramon?"

Valerie felt Alex's big hand slip into hers, and his thumb caressed her knuckles. It took everything in her power not to tremble.

"It's Romero." He said flatly and pushed the shot glass toward Isabel.

Isabel gave her an exasperated look but reached for the shot glass anyway. Valerie would deal with getting scolded later. She had more blaring things to deal with now.

She licked her teeth to make sure no lipstick was on them before she spoke again and felt Alex squeeze her hand. His eyes watched her every move.

Her full attention was back on Alex. He was incredible as usual. His loose dress shirt did nothing to conceal his hard chest and bulging muscles. It was impossible not to take it all in, so she admitted, "You look good."

"Thank you. You look amazing." His dark eyes stroked over her. "I've missed you."

She gulped. Really? Was that all it took? Just hours ago, she was convinced she was over him, and she now felt ready to swoon over three little words. Could she be more pathetic?

His fingers were still playing with her hand, and it completely unnerved her. She thought about what she and Isabel had gone over in the car all the way there. Play it cool. Indifference is the key. You're no longer interested, haven't been in over a year. She'd laughed at Isabel's unnecessary worrying. Now she was irritated at herself for not having taken the preparation more seriously. Before she could recover from his remarks, he threw yet another nerve dagger at her.

"Have you missed me?" The intensity in his eyes was exactly as she remembered. It hadn't lessened at all. If anything, it was even more acute than ever.

He stood so close to her now she could smell the hint of tequila and lime on his breath, feel the tension in his body. Her phone rang. She couldn't have been more grateful for the timing. Alex was still waiting for a response. She reached for her purse and fished her phone out. It was Luke.

"I gotta take this. Luke?"

Alex's eyebrow shot up.

She began to walk away, when Alex's grip on her hand tightened.

"Valerie," Luke sounded a bit anxious. "I'm sorry to be calling. I know you said you'd be at a party today. I won't keep you long. I just need to know if you have a key to the Lemon Ridge property, the warehouse specifically. Trinity took my only spare, and I can't find mine."

Valerie had a hell of a time focusing on what Luke was saying. He'd spoken much too fast, and Alex's eyes had been on her, eyebrows slightly furrowed the entire time. She'd gotten the gist of what Luke had said and cleared her throat. "Yes, I do. You need them now?"

"No, tomorrow." She heard the relief in Luke's voice. "I can pick them up in the morning if you want. You don't have to come into the office."

"No, that's okay. I was planning on going in for a few hours anyway."

Luke thanked her and as promised, didn't keep her on the phone. The moment she hung up, Alex spoke up.

"Luke?"

She smirked and lifted a shoulder, offering no explanation. Alex was never one to hide his possessiveness. Something that she wasn't ashamed to admit at times she'd found exciting. But she wasn't getting pulled back in, not this time. She made her decision long ago when she decided to finally give up on Alex and move on with her life.

Alex didn't push, didn't say anything for a moment. His eyes were so piercing. Her stronger, more self-assured act was beginning to wane.

"I hear you're working on your broker's license now, didn't you just get your real estate license?"

Valerie smiled, glad for the safe subject. "It's been almost a year, Alex. But I have to be an agent for at least two years. I have another year to go. You know me. I'm starting to get my ducks in a row, so as soon as that two year mark hits, I'm on it."

"Yeah, I know you. And I've no doubt you'll get it and run with it."

He flashed that beautiful smile of his. The dimples alone should be illegal. The way his smile enhanced his already incredible features was just so unfair. Valerie stood firmly, not wanting him to see how just one smile from him nearly crushed her resolve. She cleared her throat again.

"So how have you been? I hear the restaurant is doing great."

His eyes had been on her lips the entire time she spoke. She kept her chin up, pretending not to notice. Except her eyes betrayed her, and she couldn't look away when he licked his bottom lip. She gulped hard and glanced back at his eyes. He'd caught her looking, and his lips slowly curved up on one side. The dimples appeared again, taunting her.

"Yeah, it keeps me busy. Not much time for anything else these days."

Valerie almost rolled her eyes and tried hard not to frown. She didn't want him to get the idea that she still cared. No matter how busy he got, she knew he found time for all the female attention.

"So what else have you been up to besides real estate?" His thumb caressed the outside of her hand gently. Valerie nearly lost her train of thought. Somehow, she managed to stay poised. Alex had never even tried to disguise the hunger in his eyes when he gazed at her. She'd always loved that about him, but at the moment, she wished he'd stop. She was trying so hard to remain collected.

She shrugged casually. "I work a lot too. The market's been really hot lately. Writing up offers and showing properties takes up most of my time. It's a good thing I got into it when I did, because I had no choice but to learn fast. It's a piece of cake now, just time-consuming."

Alex seemed to hang on her every word.

"I'm not surprised Val. You've always been so determined." He glanced around "Can we talk somewhere more private?"

Her heart sped up. She'd thought about the possibility of Alex being his usual forward self. He certainly wasn't wasting time, but even with all the preparing she'd done for this moment, she didn't feel ready.

Apparently, it was a rhetorical question. Ready or not, Alex didn't wait for an answer. They were already moving through the crowd, and he held her hand tightly in his. The moment they were around the corner and out of the canopy area where they were keeping all the boxes of soda and water bottles, he pulled her to him and kissed her, at first gently, holding her face in his big hands as his tongue traced her lips slowly.

Valerie's legs almost gave out, but she didn't resist. She couldn't. God, how she'd missed his kisses. She welcomed his tongue and kissed him back—to hell with the strong woman act.

When he felt her eagerness, he moaned and sucked her tongue with a hunger that matched what she'd seen in his eyes earlier. They kissed without restraint for a few lingering moments until Valerie managed to pull away long enough to catch her breath, her thoughts.

He gazed in her eyes, breathing hard. "I'm sorry, sweetheart. It's been too long. I just couldn't wait another moment."

For a fleeting moment, he'd managed to daze her, but Valerie regained her composure, her wits. This was what he always did. She couldn't start this all over again. She owed it to her mangled heart to stay away from Alex for good.

She pulled away from him and stepped back. "I can't do this, Alex."

"Do what?"

"Me and you."

His eyes furrowed again, and he took a step forward. "Is there someone else?"

She stared at him, wondering what he'd think about the fact that she couldn't even bring herself to sleep with someone else since she'd last been with him, let alone start up a relationship. The kiss made her realize just how much he still affected her. One more "sweetheart" out of him and she'd be tangling in his sheets tonight for sure. She had to stop this now.

"Actually, yes."

Alex stopped cold. "There is?"

She nodded, holding her chin up, doing her best to appear convincing. Her only attempt to be with someone else had turned out to be such a disaster. But Alex didn't have to know that.

"How long?" His expression was a mixture of anger and disappointment. He worked his chiseled jaw as he waited for her response.

She knew she'd probably just killed whatever attraction he had for her, even if it was only physical. She'd always known her involvement with another man would be the end for them. He'd never tolerate it. But it was for the best, and she stood her ground. "Not very long, a couple weeks maybe."

Angel walked around the canopy area and stopped when he saw them facing off.

"Sorry, I just need to grab one of these." He pointed at the boxes of bottled water. "I'll get it and leave you two—"

"Nah, we're done here." Alex's grave eyes never looked away from Valerie. "I'm happy for you, Val." She took in his wonderfully masculine scent one last time as he walked by her toward Angel. "Need anything else?"

Angel picked up the box of waters and glanced around. "Yeah, grab one of those crates of champagne, will ya?"

Valerie stood there even after both Alex and Angel had walked back into the party. The hot tears burned in her eyes, but she brushed them away, knowing she'd done the right thing. Letting Alex Moreno and the heartache that inevitably followed back in her life was the last thing she needed right now.

She dreaded walking back in the party and having to see him all night. Turned out her apprehension was for nothing. He'd apparently left and never came back. Valerie tried to enjoy the rest of the shower.

She couldn't believe it was finally over. Valerie had been in love with this man since she was in high school. She'd only admitted it to herself a couple years ago though. It had suddenly made sense why no matter how long he'd disappear for, and how lame his excuses were, she was always so willing to work things out. He always had a way of melting her heart, and she craved him as she'd never craved another man in her life. But seeing him with another woman had done something to her. It broke her in a way she never wanted to be broken again.

Coming here today, she never imagined she'd leave feeling a hollowness in her heart that topped all the heartaches in her past. She was proud of herself for not falling for him all over again, but something had died inside her today. Seeing him again had been the final test, and she'd done it. Finally, she killed that frail but stubborn bit of hope that lingered for years. She just never figured doing so would hurt so damn much.

CHAPTER 2

The next morning, Valerie woke up with a raging fever. She'd been that way as long as she could remember. It went as far back as when she was a little girl. The most memorable time was when a dog had killed her cat and she cried all night. Her dad rushed her to urgent care the next morning because her fever was so high. The doctors attributed it to dehydration, and Valerie knew this time the tequila had added to it. She had more than a few more shots after Alex had left the party last night.

Luke had already come by and picked up the keys to the property he was showing that day. She called early to let him know she wasn't feeling well.

Valerie sat on the sofa, sipping her Gatorade. She put up a front at the party last night after Alex left. Originally, she planned on not admitting to Isabel just what a mess she'd actually been. But Isabel knew all about her crying herself sick from her past heartaches. There was no way to hide the embarrassing fact that she'd cried herself to sleep last night. So she fessed up and let Isabel in on how pitiful she was.

There was very little she kept from Isabel anyway. Isabel wasn't just her roommate; she was her best friend. They met in college their freshman year and were forced to share a dorm. At first they hated each other. They were polar opposites. Valerie was a tiny, messy, blonde, party girl, and Isabel was tall, brunette, as anal as they came, and all about hitting the books.

It wasn't until one of the first times Alex broke Valerie's heart that they bonded. That night, Isabel had been the only one around to console her. After talking almost all night,

Valerie decided to help Isabel come out of her shell and live a little. Isabel wasn't unattractive just a little too simple in her taste in clothes and makeup. Valerie always told her she had the sexiest eyes. Once done up, she was actually pretty hot. Unfortunately, most of the time, Isabel chose to go with simple.

In return, Isabel helped Valerie bring her grades up and stick with school. There were a few times she'd come close to giving up and just taking the state exam, but Isabel convinced her to at least get her Associates Degree before getting her real estate license. In Isabel's family, degrees were everything.

They kept in touch even after Valerie got her AA and ran with it, moving back in with her dad. By the time Isabel graduated with her bachelors in teaching, they were best friends and now shared an apartment. After living in the same dorm room with Isabel for two years, Valerie knew there was no getting around her meticulous ways. She learned long ago to just go with the flow rather than fight it.

"Let's check again." Isabel handed her the thermometer.

Valerie took it and smiled. Isabel was going to be such a great mom someday. She sure knew how to baby you, and boy did she know how to nag.

Valerie had been so busy last night, playing the strong-woman part and secretly wishing Alex would come back to the party. She hadn't really paid attention to Isabel, not that Isabel had been neglected. She got plenty attention from Romero. For someone who seemed as put off by his first impression of Isabel, Romero sure stuck by her the whole night.

"So how'd it go with Romero last night?"

"Don't talk with that thing in your mouth. It won't register correctly." Isabel plopped down on the sofa across from her. "He's … different. And good Lord, he loves to debate."

Valerie smiled but followed her orders and didn't speak. Isabel went on. "I mean he even admits he loves it. You know what he told me?"

Valerie's lifted both eyebrows.

"He said when he goes to a sports bar and his team isn't playing, he figures out who the majority of the crowd is going for, and he goes for the opposing team just so he can cheer when the other team scores."

Valerie laughed and the thermometer beeped. She took it out of her mouth and read it: 102.4.

"It's going down." She grinned, tossing it at Isabel.

Isabel read it and frowned. "Valerie, this is still so high. You sure you don't want to go to the doctor?"

Valerie shook her head and went to the fridge to get more ice for her Gatorade. "I'll be fine."

Although this wasn't the first time she'd woken up feverish because of Alex, it was by far the worst. It ranked right up there with the morning after she'd caught him that awful night. And here she thought because it'd been so long she was going to breeze through this like nothing. She actually expected to leave the party, feeling like a brand new woman, one who'd finally conquered her demons. She frowned, putting the cold Gatorade bottle to her forehead. "I think you and Romero are cute together."

"No way, Valerie. Don't even start."

"Why not?"

Romero wasn't a bad looking guy at all. Like Alex and his brothers, he'd always worked real hard to stay in great shape. He had to. Being a bouncer for years, he needed to be strong and fit.

He wasn't nearly as big as Alex, but his build *was* impressive. He'd just always been the clown. Back in high school, she'd been attracted enough to flirt with him and even let him kiss her once.

"Because he's annoying, and I find his lack of decorum appalling."

"Decorum?" Valerie sat back down on the sofa. "Isabel, you are too much. You always said you have trouble finding taller men than you. Did you notice he's much taller than you?"

Isabel peered at her over her glasses. "Yes, I noticed."

"Well then it's settled."

Isabel let out a sarcastic laugh. "Looks aren't everything, missy. I think you know that better than anyone."

Valerie pouted.

Isabel jumped off the sofa where she sat and sat next to Valerie, putting her arm around her. "I'm sorry, honey. I shouldn't have said that."

Valerie shrugged. "I'll get over him if it's the last thing I do."

Even as she heard her own words, after last night, she knew it would be a long time, if ever, before she got over Alex Moreno.

~*~

It was almost impossible to concentrate on the payroll with Valerie on his mind again. The whole damn week Alex had thought of Valerie and how different it felt to kiss her now. He was still trying to figure out what bothered him more: that she moved on or the fact that he'd been so blown away by seeing her again. He'd figured as much about her moving on. What didn't make sense was why the hell it troubled him so much.

When he first met her his freshman year of college, it was supposed to be just for fun. She was still a senior in high school, and Angel had just started seeing Sarah. When Sarah mentioned her cousin having a crush on him, he was curious. After meeting her, it had been just that, fun. Then his grades started plummeting, and it almost cost him his scholarship.

In the very beginning, Valerie was all for a physical relationship, no strings attached. And though he didn't like the idea of her with anyone else, he pretended to go along. He needed to find the time to get some school work done and still try to get his fill of her on his downtime. But he never seemed to be able to. The more he was with her, the more he wanted her.

Though their relationship had never been classified as a bona fide exclusive one, the time he'd spent with her was the closest he'd ever come to being in one. She seemed content with their off and on rendezvous for a while, some of which had begun to get longer and longer. But then he'd have to leave for road games and cram for tests, and it was off again. Sometimes he disappeared on her for days without answering her calls. He never told her why. He couldn't, even though he knew she was thinking the worst.

Then after showing up and catching him with his tutor, she said it was over. The only time she'd bothered to answer her phone in the entire time since then was a few days after that night. That was only to warn him not to show up unannounced at her place in case *she* had company. She said she didn't want things getting ugly. Things sure as hell would've gotten ugly, and he was furious. But after calming down, he knew it was his own fault.

At first he thought it was just like one of the many other times she'd cut him off. But he soon found out she meant it this time. After the one maddening call she answered, she never once picked up any of his calls or returned any of his texts again. He thought if he gave it time, she'd come around. But after months of not hearing from her, he figured she'd moved on. Strangely, all this time, he thought he was okay with it.

With everything going on in his life, he had little time to dwell on his love life. After breaking his ankle pretty badly during one of his college football games, several surgeries later, the doctors confirmed the worst. His playing days were over, and just like that, his scholarship was gone. Alex had fallen into a major self-pity, damn-it-all-to-hell funk.

His parents insisted they'd pay the rest of the way until he was done. Alex knew how expensive that would be, and as hard a time as he'd been having keeping his grades up, he wasn't going to waste their money. He dropped most of his classes, promising he'd finish up eventually. He was now down to one online class a semester and had taken the restaurant full on.

With the restaurant doing so well, the family decided it was time to expand. His father had talked about it for years. Since his dad had been smart enough to purchase the property years ago rather than continue leasing, the place was theirs to do what they pleased. So in the last year, on top of everything else that was going on in his life, Alex took on the major task of overseeing the renovations.

They weren't just any renovations either. In the past couple of years, it had become harder and harder to accommodate large parties without having to reserve a big part of the restaurant if not the entire thing. Alex suggested adding some kind of banquet room so they could reserve that for private events without having to shut down the restaurant. He meant a small room off to the side that maybe held forty to fifty people.

He should've known better. Like the wedding, his father thought big. A second floor was added with a lavish banquet room that could accommodate up to five hundred people but could also be broken down into smaller rooms for smaller parties. The restaurant was under construction for months.

With everything going on, he hadn't put much effort into reconnecting with Valerie. He had to admit he'd never stopped thinking about her and every now and again still called in vain.

Ironically, as bitter as it was losing his scholarship and having to go to all the therapy to get his ankle back to at least feeling normal, it had served as a distraction.

Then his parents started leaving for weeks at a time to visit his ailing grandfather in Mexico. They left him with the full responsibility of running the restaurant while they were gone. When his grandfather passed, his father took it very hard. He decided it was time to retire and spend more time with the family back in Mexico.

The reins were passed on to Alex who was the only one of his brothers not in school full time. He took his responsibility of keeping the family business running as well as it always had very seriously. His older brother Sal was working on his master's, and his younger brother Angel had just graduated from college—before him. This was his way of making it up to his parents about school, and he'd be damned if he screw it up.

But now he couldn't get Valerie out of his head. It didn't make sense. He'd always known she drove him crazy, but he always told himself it was more physical than anything. What he felt at the party was different. Very different. He couldn't even hang around after she told him about her boyfriend.

Normally, his reaction to any thoughts of her with another man was instinctive carnal rage. This time it was different. Aside from the rage, he'd felt something he never had in the past. He suddenly hadn't been able to bear even looking at her, knowing she belonged to someone else. This time his rage had been accompanied by an unexplained ache. An ache that had settled in his heart and hadn't left since.

He hadn't gotten much sleep and had been in a hell of mood all week. Today he'd worked a full day at the restaurant, staying as busy as he could. It wasn't hard. It was nonstop all day. Sundays were always that way.

They were closed now. As usual, he was still there working late, avoiding going back to his empty home at all costs. He glanced at his cell phone that sat on the desk and picked it up. Knowing the shower was just around the corner, Alex hadn't tried calling her in a while. He wondered if maybe after seeing him at the shower she'd pick up.

He stared at it, thinking about what he'd say to her. All the other times he'd called her since their falling out, he hadn't given it much thought. Now he was a mess. He dialed and held his breath. As usual, the call went to voicemail, and Alex sat frozen at the sound of her voice. It was the damnedest thing. Her voicemail hadn't changed since the last time he called, yet just hearing her voice now made his heart speed up. He hung up without leaving a voicemail, acutely aware of the thud in his chest. *What the hell?*.

CHAPTER 3

This was the second time this week Valerie was running late. It wasn't like her, but her mind had been so muddled lately. Her phone rang. Thankfully she glanced at the caller I.D. before automatically answering. She froze when she read Bruce Nash. She knew he'd been out for weeks but really prayed she wouldn't hear from him.

Bruce was a perfect example of what happens when you go out in hopes of forgetting someone. He was the reason Valerie stopped frequenting nightclubs and going out period.

After weeks of wallowing over Alex last year, she'd finally taken the plunge and went out again. She met Bruce at a nightclub that evening. They exchanged information and with the encouragement of Isabel decided to take him up on his offer of going for coffee.

She mistook his overbearing personality for intensity, something she'd always loved about Alex. But it only took a few weeks of seeing Bruce when it became clear that his overbearing personality might actually be detrimental. Alex may have been hard as nails on the outside, but she was one of the few people who knew how soft and wonderful he was on the inside. Never once had she felt threatened by him.

Bruce was different altogether. Something disturbed her about the way his anger seemed to control him. He became a different person and more than once had to apologize for his outbursts.

They'd only gone out for several weeks. Then after he showed up at her place enraged and under the influence of something that appeared to be more than just alcohol, she called it off. Never in her wildest dreams did she imagine the nightmare that would ensue. When it was over, she'd all but sworn off men.

Valerie waited to see if he'd leave a message. He didn't. Her insides grew heavy. She could only pray that, now that he was out, the nightmare wouldn't start all over again.

She turned into the parking lot of the building she was going to show. The clients were already standing outside.

Valerie smiled at the two men in suits as she pulled her car in next to theirs. Doing her best to snap out of the sudden plunge in her mood, she smiled brightly at her clients. She got out and apologized for her late arrival. Within minutes, she was back to her energetic self, showing them the property.

When she returned to her office, Luke, her office manager was waiting for her at the door. He had a big smile on his face, and she had a feeling she knew why.

"Lemon Ridge just closed."

"You're kidding?"

"No, it's a done deal, baby." He opened the door for her. "I was about to call you."

Valerie had closed a lot of deals since she'd gotten her license, but this was by far the largest. She'd been working on it for months. As soon as she put her things down on her already cluttered desk, she did a little dance and hugged Luke.

"God, I'm so glad that's over. That was such a pain."

Luke smiled. "But totally worth it. And you know what? You'll probably get a lot more clients in that range because of it."

That's exactly what she was banking on. She'd worked so hard on that one, going back and forth with the sellers and then the lenders. This was her ticket to making a name for herself in the commercial world of real estate. It felt so good when her hard work finally paid off.

"So are you done for the day?"

Valerie smiled even bigger. "Actually, my clients wanna make a full price offer on the La Jolla building. I was going to write it up, now."

"Impressive, Val. I knew you'd be good the moment I met you." Luke looked at his watch. "Do it in the morning, though. Let's go get a drink to celebrate."

Luke had been suggesting they go have a drink for months now. Valerie had a feeling by the way he looked at her sometimes that it wasn't just a friendly offer. She'd always made one excuse after another not to go out with him. But it had been weeks since the shower, and she'd been in a funk ever since. She finally had something to smile about. What the heck.

"All right."

Luke seemed surprised but smiled. "You can leave your car here if you want. We'll come back and get it."

Valerie shook her head. "No, that's okay. We can take two cars. That way I can go straight home from there." She wanted to be able to leave if the urge suddenly struck her, and she had a feeling it would.

Luke arrived at the restaurant before her and was waiting in the parking lot, leaning against his car. He was a good-looking man: tall and well built. And she'd always liked his hazel eyes. He'd obviously been well trained in management. His charisma and ease when speaking in front of the whole office was another one of his attractive qualities. The only reason Valerie had never considered taking him up on any of his subtle offers was the same reason she'd put off going out with anyone else until Bruce. *Alex*.

Well that was in the past. She wasn't even sure what exactly Luke had in mind if anything. But Bruce shouldn't set the example of what it would be like to date after Alex. Not only had Bruce paled in comparison to Alex she liked to think that dating a man like Bruce was a once in a lifetime mistake—one she'd never make again.

They walked in together. Even with her big heels, she barely came up to his shoulders. They took seats in the bar and ordered drinks. After a bit of real estate chatter, Luke stopped and gazed at her. Valerie sensed he'd been trying to bring something up from the moment they'd sat down.

"So what do you do when you're not working, Valerie?"

She lifted a shoulder and took a sip of her drink. "I hang out with my roommate, visit my dad, paint."

Luke raised an eyebrow. "Paint? Really?"

Valerie nodded. "Yeah, I've always liked to, but it wasn't until college when I took a few courses that I really started to get into it and discovered my hidden talent."

"What do you paint?"

"Anything really, landscapes, portraits, the ocean. I'm done with sunsets." She giggled. "The walls in my dorm were plastered with so many paintings of sunsets my roommate swore she'd burn the next one I painted."

Luke smiled. "That means you're a romantic."

Valerie glanced at him, and their eyes locked. He'd done that to her before in the office, and it made her uncomfortable then too.

She turned back to her drink and stirred it. "No, it means I was cheesy."

"I don't think sunsets are cheesy."

Valerie looked back at him. "I'm working on a portrait now. Kinda nervous about it. It's a wedding gift."

"Really? Who's getting married?"

"My cousin. I'm her maid of honor." She smiled. "Yeah, it's really sweet. They met and fell in love in high school and have been completely inseparable since. I'm surprised they even waited this long." She glanced at him. "They're the ones I told you about. I'm looking for a place for them to lease for their restaurant. As soon as they get that up and running, I'll be finding them a house."

Luke smiled, "Nice. So why are you nervous about the painting?"

Valerie chewed her lower lip. "I dunno. It's of an older picture of them when they were first dating in high school. They look so young and in love. I just hope I can capture the nuance of true love. I'm not sure that I can."

Luke was staring at her now. "Why not? Haven't you ever been in love?"

She was almost locked in another one of his stares but managed to turn away. The bartender passed by, and she ordered another drink. Luke was still working on his. He stirred his drink and said nothing. He was obviously waiting for her to answer.

"Yeah, I have." That's all she'd offer. She wasn't about to get into a bitter conversation about Alex, not when she was supposed to be here celebrating.

"Has it been long?"

Her drink came, and instead of answering, she took a big swig of the drink. It seemed stronger than the first one.

"I don't mean to pry. I'm just saying maybe if you can remember, you can pour those feelings into your painting."

"That's true." Valerie made sure that was the end of that subject. She asked him about what he did on his time off, and he told her. She wasn't too surprised to hear he was a bit of a workaholic, leaving little time for himself. What time he did get, he played golf and cooked. He loved cooking.

A few drinks later, she was felt more relaxed and began to wonder if driving herself had been such a good idea.

As expected with a few more drinks, her sense of humor picked up, and she started to giggle. If Luke noticed she was getting silly, he didn't say anything. She kept having to break out of his stare.

After a few trips to the ladies' room, she knew she either had to slow down on the alcohol or Luke was going to have to drive her home. She didn't want to leave her car there, so she made her decision on the way back from the ladies' room. Water was her only option. Lots of it. But by the time she got back, Luke had already ordered her another drink. She hadn't even finished the last one.

She noticed a few drinks earlier that Luke had stopped trying to be discreet. He sized her up again as she made her way back to the bar. Her unabashed smile obviously pleased him.

"Damn, you're sexy. Is it okay if I say that?"

Valerie couldn't help but laugh. "I think maybe we should stop drinking."

"If you're suggesting I've developed beer goggles, you couldn't be more mistaken. I've always thought you were sexy as hell."

She smiled but stared at the drink she stirred. She knew if she even glanced at him she'd be locked into another one of his lustful stares.

"So when's the wedding?"

"Just a little over a month."

The thought of having to be at all the upcoming dreaded events and seeing Alex there made her stomach turn. Without thinking, she downed her drink, and that was it. She knew she wouldn't be driving home.

Luke took a sip of his drink, but she noticed he wasn't drinking nearly as fast as she had. When she was done with the drink he'd ordered her, she called it quits.

"I don't think I'm going to be able to drive home."

"I can take you home." He said quickly. "Your car will be okay here overnight. We'll come back and get it in the morning."

Valerie looked at him, and their eyes locked again. She hoped he wasn't getting the wrong idea.

He held her hand on the way out and all the way to the car. It felt good. She was sure it was the alcohol, but she felt a little more attracted to Luke. She leaned against him. He let go of her hand, wrapping his arm around her shoulder. When they reached his car instead of opening the door, he leaned against it and pulled her to him. The desire in his eyes was undeniable.

Valerie didn't say anything. She leaned against him and stared at his lips. He leaned over and kissed her. Damn it, she knew it. The first thing that came to her mind was Alex. His ravenous kiss at the party was instantly all she could think of.

Luke kissed her softly and ran his hands up and down her back. Valerie kissed him back and concentrated on not thinking of Alex. Her tongue stayed in rhythm with his, slowly at first, then she could feel him breathing harder as the kiss intensified. She heard a faint but unmistakable moan.

Valerie pulled away. Luke was breathing heavily. "I'm sorry, Luke." She pulled away from his embrace just a little. She felt him through his pants and was angry with herself. "I don't mean to give you the wrong idea."

She could tell Luke was trying to read her thoughts "And what idea would that be?"

"That I'll be spending the night with you."

He seemed relieved. "That's all right. As long as you're not saying that me getting the idea that there could be something more between us is wrong. I don't have a problem taking things slow. In fact, I'm sorry if I came on too strong."

Valerie forced a smile. That wasn't the idea she wanted him to get either. She hadn't even been ready for the kiss much less any kind of relationship. "Don't be sorry. I was a willing participant."

The ride back to her place was a bit awkward with Luke holding her hand the whole way. All she could think about was how kissing Luke was nothing like kissing Alex. Admittedly, she hadn't tried hard. But there'd been nothing, not so much as a spark.

When they got to her apartment, Valerie dreaded his walking her to the door. She knew he'd be expecting another kiss, and she was already regretting the first one. She turned to him when they reached her door. "Luke, I don't know if us getting involved is such a good idea. Isn't it some kind of conflict of interest at the office?"

She saw that look in his eye again, and he leaned into her. "Don't worry about the office. I never would've kissed you if I thought that might be a problem."

Before she could say anything else, his lips were on hers again. This time she tried to feel something. She actually wanted to. She wanted hope that she could ever get over Alex. But again she felt him become quickly aroused and the instant bulge against her stomach. All Valerie felt was discouraged.

She pulled away gently. He looked at her and smiled then caressed her face one last time. "You have no idea how long I've been waiting for this."

The guilt sunk in, and Valerie could barely smile back. Once he left and she was back in her apartment, the reality of everything that had happened that day came crashing down. She wondered where Isabel was but didn't wait up. The alcohol had really done a number on her. She was out as soon as her head hit the pillow.

***

The next morning Valerie was up early and ready before Isabel was even out of bed. Luke would be over soon to take her to pick up her car. Of course, he insisted they get breakfast together, so she had to get ready for that.

Last night she was sure she'd regret the whole Luke thing enormously in the morning. But now clearheaded, she didn't think it was so bad. She'd definitely tell him they were going to be taking things slowly, but she didn't have to rule it out altogether.

She'd come to realize if she waited until she was over Alex to move on, she never would. It was time she just accepted that Alex was the love of her life and she may never get over him.

That didn't mean she couldn't be happy. She knew she'd never be as happy as she was when she was with him, but maybe if she put a little effort into it, she could come close. At least she knew that meant no one could ever hurt her as much as he could. Pathetic consolation, but she had to find the optimism somewhere.

Isabel walked in the kitchen just as she was finishing her coffee. "You're up early."

Valerie always slept in on Saturdays. She explained to Isabel briefly about Luke. She'd be more thorough later when she had more time. Isabel was thrilled when she mentioned the kiss and assured Valerie she'd feel something soon enough.

To her surprise, Isabel had run into Romero at the mall the night before, and they had dinner together. Valerie was just beginning her inquisition when she had to leave.

Luke was right on time, but that didn't surprise her. Being the office manager, he'd always had a penchant for punctuality.

They picked up her car, then she followed him to one of the more upscale bed and breakfasts in La Jolla. Luke insisted the place had the best breakfast in the area.

Valerie was pleasantly surprised at the ease she felt during breakfast. She completely expected to feel some kind of awkwardness. They talked and laughed as if nothing had happened the night before to change things between them. She even told him about what a big fan she was of George Stone, the well-known real estate guru and motivational speaker. She had several of his books and DVDs but had yet to see him speak in person.

Luke immediately texted someone about getting them tickets to his next event. He said he was sure he could get them. Valerie had to admit she was impressed. She'd tried getting tickets before, and they were always sold out. She knew getting tickets through a third party would be expensive.

That was one of the biggest differences between him and Alex. That would take some time to get used to. While they were both well off financially, Alex never flaunted it. He was low key about it from the clothes he wore right down to the truck he drove. He wasn't cheap just didn't feel the need to drive a flashy car. Luke, on the other hand, drove a Jaguar and wore a different pair of very expensive cufflinks every day. He dressed in designer clothes all the way, even his sunglasses.

After breakfast, they walked back out to her car. Once there, Luke embraced her. "I hope you're not going to feel weird about this at the office. I promise I'll be as discreet as possible."

Valerie smiled. If things felt anything like breakfast had, she could live with it. "I think I'll be all right. But I definitely want to keep it to ourselves. I don't want people talking."

"Deal." He said. "Just one question."

Valerie looked at him curious. "What?"

"You're not seeing anyone else, are you?"

She bit her lip, glancing away but shook her head. "No, I'm not."

"You sure?" He chuckled. "That wasn't very convincing."

She glanced back at him. "No, I would be honest if I was."

"Good," Luke smiled. "Because when I'm seeing someone, it's just the one person. I hope you're the same way. I'd hate to get my hopes up and then find out there's someone else."

Valerie surprised Luke and herself by kissing him. It was a soft one, but she actually felt something.

After the nightmare she'd gone through with Bruce, she knew a guy suggesting they be exclusive after only a couple of dates should set off a few red flags. But she knew Luke well enough to know he wasn't the crazy person Bruce turned out to be. He was a good guy.

The truth was all this time she'd been stuck on someone who would never be satisfied with just her, and now here was Luke. Just one day after kissing her for the first time, he was telling her she was the only one. It felt good. Real good.

CHAPTER 4

Instead of going back to the office to write up the offer from the day before, Valerie decided to work at home for the day. She was dying to talk to Isabel about Romero.

It was funny the way things seemed to work out with her and Isabel's social lives lately. When she'd dated Bruce, Isabel started dating their neighbor from two doors down, Lawrence. They both turned out to be jerks, though Lawrence wasn't nearly as bad as Bruce.

Lawrence was just an arrogant professor who thought he knew it all. Isabel tried to deal with him, but he was too annoying. He liked correcting everyone. He made the mistake of correcting Isabel's mom, who Valerie loved because she was such a spitfire. Valerie was mad she'd missed it but laughed hysterically when Isabel gave her the blow-by-blow. After that, Isabel said she'd had enough of him and told him it'd be better if they simply remained friends.

Now here they were both starting new adventures at the same time again. Though she'd call her experience with Bruce a lot of things before she'd call it an adventure.

Well at least she hoped Isabel and Romero would hit it off. Then the bittersweet reality hit her like a brick. Yet someone else in her life would be closely involved in Alex's circle. He'd never be entirely out of her life.

She shook it off. Isabel deserved to be happy. With her cousin marrying his brother, she was doomed to run into him forever anyway. She'd have to make the best of it. Besides, it was only one dinner Isabel had with Romero. Chances were she was making way too much out of it.

First thing she noticed when she walked in the door was Isabel dancing along to the radio in the kitchen. Then she noticed how nice she looked. Though she was in jeans and a sweater, she'd really done herself up. She'd curled her hair, done her eyes the way Valerie always said made her look so sexy, and she had her contacts on. But most noticeably she wore her high heel sling backs.

Valerie couldn't help smiling. "Are you going out?"

Isabel didn't even try to hold back the silly grin, but she stopped dancing. "Yes."

"With Romero?"

Isabel nodded, and Valerie thought she saw her blush.

Valerie dropped everything and rushed to jump onto the kitchen counter. She put her hands under her thighs.

"Okay tell me, tell me. I wanna know everything." She didn't care if he was Alex's friend anymore. She'd never seen Isabel this giddy, and she was happy for her.

Isabel pulled a water bottle out of the fridge and opened it. "Well I mentioned to him at the shower that I get my nails done at the mall every other Friday." She rolled her eyes. "Don't ask. I was trying to make a point about the parking at the mall. Anyway, so yesterday I walk out of my nail place, and guess who I run into?"

Valerie sniggered. "Gee, what a coincidence."

"Well, I didn't think anything of it at first. He said he was there looking for some tool he needed."

"Oh God, who goes to the mall for tools, Isabel?"

"There's a Sears there." Isabel paused and then giggled. "I totally fell for his story. Then after dinner, he admitted he'd been there the week before and yesterday, hanging around waiting to see if he'd see me."

"Ha!" Valerie covered her mouth when Isabel made a face. "Sorry, go on. Go on."

"At the shower, I also mentioned what a big Padres' fan I am. Of course, he argued with me about them but in the end, admitted he was a fan too. Someone gave him tickets to today's game a few weeks ago, and he thought maybe I'd wanna go."

Isabel shrugged in an attempt to make it out to be less than it really was, but Valerie knew better.

"I knew I saw something that night between you two." Valerie remembered her comments about him the morning after. "You weren't mean were you?"

"No, of course not." Isabel sipped her water. "I thanked him for thinking of me but told him I had a lot of papers to grade today."

"What? You turned him down?" Valerie looked at Isabel up and down. "So why are you all done up?"

"I'm not all done up." Isabel glanced down at her clothes. "It looks like I'm all done up?"

"Of course, but you look great. So you *are* going to the game with him, right?"

Isabel seemed worried now. "Well, after closing the place out, he talked me into going to the game. But that's all it is: two friends going to a game together."

Isabel walked into the front room and stopped at the mirror on the wall. "You think he's going to think I got all done up for him?"

"Well, didn't you?" Valerie giggled, jumping off the counter and followed Isabel.

"No!"

"What's the big deal, Isabel? You're obviously into him."

"No, I'm not."

Valerie rolled her eyes. "Really? So the dancing and all this," she pointed at Isabel's curled tresses. "is something that's the norm for you?"

Isabel's eyes were opened wide. "All right, so he's not usually the type of guy I date."

"Ah ha! You said it. It *is* a date." Isabel's expression was warning enough. Valerie attempted to hide the smirk.

"Valerie. I don't want him to think I'm all into him. I just thought it'd be interesting to try something new." She dabbed at her eyes, trying to remove some of the makeup.

"Stop that. It looks really great."

There was a knock on the door, and Isabel turned to Valerie with a look of sheer panic. Valerie grinned but couldn't help feeling guilty that she'd managed to take Isabel's mood from dancing and smiling and giddy to an anxious mess. "Relax. You wanna get that, or shall I?"

"You get it." Isabel rushed into her bedroom.

Damn. Why did she have to open her big mouth? Valerie hoped Isabel wasn't changing. But she hadn't even finished saying hello to Romero when Isabel was already out of the room. She'd just gone in to grab a jacket and her purse.

Romero's expression was almost comical. He'd never been discreet about anything. If she thought she saw something in the way Romero had looked at Isabel at the party, there was no doubt about it now. Isabel wouldn't be walking away from this one as easily as she thought.

Romero didn't look too shabby himself. He wore a Padres' t-shirt that hugged him pretty well. He was obviously still working out as much as she remembered he used to. There was no way Isabel could not notice that.

After a bit of awkward hellos and goodbyes, they were out the door and Valerie stuck her nose through the curtains. Even with Isabel's heels, Romero was half a head taller than her. They made a really cute couple, and Valerie giggled as she texted Isabel to tell her.

She walked back to her room to get ready for her own date with Luke. Even though things were beginning to look positive, Valerie couldn't help feeling a dull ache in her heart. She was really counting on Luke to help her get rid of it. She needed to remind herself to stop comparing him to Alex. As much as she hated to admit it, no one would ever live up to him. She may as well stop hoping someone would and accept Luke for the man that he was.

~*~

The restaurant was busy as it always was lately. With renovating done and the construction all cleared out, Alex and his older brother Sal had started a campaign on the internet. They even ran a commercial twice a day on the local radio station.

Because Angel and Sarah were already looking for a place to lease to open their own restaurant as soon as they got married, Sal had plans of possibly making the restaurant some kind of chain eventually. But he didn't want it to be too commercial. He wanted to keep the authentic quality his parents had created with the same recipes. Alex had no doubt he could do it.

Sal was by far the most driven of the three brothers. Alex and Angel had gone to college because it was expected of them. Their dad hadn't given them a choice. But Sal loved it. Even though he was the oldest, he was still in school.

He went to school in Los Angeles, so he stayed out there and only came home on the weekends, but lately he'd been coming home less and less. His schedule was heavier. He was really trying to finish up school faster, so he'd taken on a full load the past couple of semesters. That's why Alex had been surprised to see him at the restaurant that morning.

He supervised all day and put in his two cents on everything. Alex didn't mind. Sal knew what he was talking about. He'd helped his dad run the place for years, so Alex welcomed the help. Alex had made the Excel spreadsheets for payroll and scheduling. He'd expected Sal to be pleased but hadn't expected just how impressed he'd been.

Alex was in the back room, showing Sal more of the changes he'd made when Angel walked in.

"Hey, did you hear about next door?" Angel asked.

Both Alex and Sal turned to face him. "What about it?" Alex hadn't noticed much of anything lately.

"Old man Mason is finally gonna retire. I ran into his son this morning. They're putting the place up for sale."

Alex and Sal exchanged knowing glances. They'd been waiting for this for years. If they bought the place, they could expand the restaurant further out to allow for a bigger bar area. Already the place had gained so much popularity. The weekend evening crowd had outgrown it.

"He owns the place right? He's not leasing?" Alex knew what Sal was getting at, because it was exactly what he was thinking. They'd make him an offer before it even went on the market.

"I'm one step ahead of you, Brother." Angel grinned. "They already signed the papers with the listing agent. So it's scheduled to go on the market this week."

Alex sat up. "It's not gonna last. That's prime location." He could kick himself for being so damn distracted. He should've known about this sooner. If he'd just gone over there more as he used to, he might've gotten the inside scoop sooner.

"So call Valerie." Sal said standing up.

"Already did." Angel walked over and opened up one of the cabinets. "Well, Sarah did anyway."

"Whoa, wait." For some unknown reason that made Alex uncomfortable. "Why Valerie?"

Angel turned back to him. "Why not? She's handling finding a place for the new restaurant. Plus she's good." He pulled out a file and waved it at him. "Matter of fact, we're meeting with her tomorrow to walk through a few properties. Dad's coming with us. She'll bring the paperwork for the offer dad needs to sign."

Sal gave Angel a high five. "Way to handle it."

"That fast?" Alex asked. "Doesn't it have to actually be on the market for us to make an offer?"

"Nope, Sarah said Valerie told her it wouldn't be a problem. She'd take care of everything." Angel winked at him. "Told you she's good."

Angel grabbed his keys from the desk. “I’ve gotta go pick up Sarah. We’re going to drive by some of these properties first.” He waved the file at Alex and Sal again. “No sense in having Valerie walk us through the ones we don’t even like the location of.”

After Angel left, Alex made an exit himself. He needed to work off some tension. Just thinking about being around Valerie again tensed his muscles to no end.

After working out, Alex was tempted to go back to the restaurant. He wanted to avoid sitting around his place brooding. But he knew Sal had things covered. The one thing he couldn’t get out of his mind tonight was what Valerie had said. It only been a few weeks that she’d been involved with someone else. Maybe it wasn’t too late to change her mind. Maybe if he’d finally just come clean about why he’d always been so elusive all those years.

He had to really think this through. Is that really what he wanted? A relationship with her? All those years he could have had one with her, but they both chose not to.

He knew one of the main reasons was time. Or was it? Now that he’d cut down on school so drastically and football was out, things could definitely be different between them. If only she’d answer her phone or at least return his calls. He stopped leaving messages long ago. He was pretty sure she didn’t bother listening to them. All the messages he left always came out wrong anyway.

When he got home, he busied himself. He had a ton of laundry he had to catch up on, and he got right on it. He was hardly ever home, so there wasn’t much else to clean in between loads.

He made himself a protein drink and sat down to watch some T.V. After flipping the channels around and finding nothing that interested him, he turned it off and let his head fall back. He stared at the ceiling for a while, trying to put his feelings into prospective.

Was seeing Valerie at the shower really that caustic? Or had he been in denial all this time? This was insane. He was fine with the way things were until that damn shower.

He checked his watch. It was still early. He considered going back to the restaurant again, and then it hit him. He'd hardly been home alone since Valerie stopped coming around. The only time he was ever home was when he had to study or sleep. The rest of the time he kept himself busy elsewhere.

Between all the therapies he had to get for his ankle and trying to prove he could not only run the restaurant he could do it well, the past year had been a blur of going back and forth, spending little to no time at home. Hell, he'd even opted to spend the night at his parents more than a few times rather than come back to his empty house. He could hardly stand to be here now.

Alex sat up. Could that be it? He held off pursuing Valerie because he'd known it was just a matter of time before all the wedding hoopla would come around. She'd have no choice but to show up, and he'd get his chance to win her back in his life. That *would* explain the unreasonable nerves the morning of shower.

In hindsight, what he had with Valerie before *was* a relationship. Just because they'd never called it that didn't mean it wasn't. During the time they were supposedly just hanging out, if he had found out she was seeing someone else, he would've been absolutely livid. Unlike her, he wouldn't have had any qualms about telling her either.

He knew what she thought when he'd avoided her for days. She thought that he was with other women. But she never asked outright, so he never had to actually deny it. Though, he never really confirmed what he *had* been doing either.

If only he could leave her a message that didn't sound so stupid. Every time he tried, it came out all wrong. So he gave up. He stared at the pad of paper and pen on his coffee table for a moment before finally grabbing it. He began jotting some things he could say.

After a while of scribbling a few sentences down and scratching things off, he had something he could live with. He read it back a few times and decided there was no getting around sounding robotic, so he tried memorizing it. That was even worse. Frustrated, he threw the pad back down on his coffee table. He was getting a headache.

Who was he kidding? She probably wouldn't listen to it anyway. With a full-blown headache now, he decided to take an aspirin and call it a night. Maybe with some rest and a little luck, he could come up with something else.

CHAPTER 5

Inspections for commercial buildings typically took a lot longer than for residential ones. This latest sale was another big one. There were offices, multiple restrooms, a kitchen, and even a small gym. Valerie had hoped because it was an afternoon appointment they'd hurry to get out of there early, but no such luck. She had been there for hours while the inspectors meticulously did their thing. She'd spent most the time on her laptop writing up even more offers. Luke had been right about the Lemon Ridge sale. It *had* opened up doors for her. Since things had gone so smoothly for a building that size, she was getting referrals left and right.

By all accounts, everything in Valerie's life was going favorably. She enjoyed the kind of success that Luke said only seasoned agents got to enjoy. Her relationship with Luke moved along. Albeit, she made sure they took things at a cosmically slow pace. Luckily, Luke had turned out to be as patient as he was charismatic.

With the inspectors gone, Valerie walked around, making sure she locked up everything. Her hollowed heart made her feel guilty. She'd never been one to whine about the little stuff and was grateful for all the blessings in her life. Despite all the positive things going on in her life, she still missed Alex terribly.

Almost done locking up, Valerie thought she heard something. It sounded like footsteps. The inspectors left long ago. She watched them drive away. She stood still and listened but heard nothing else. This wasn't the first time she got the creeps in a big empty building. She'd to have to get used to it because, from the looks of it, she'd be dealing with big empty buildings a lot from here on.

After double-checking a few more doors, she headed back to the table she used as her desk for the day. She slowed her pace when she heard something again. She glanced around but saw nothing. With everything packed in her briefcase, a loud buzzing made her jump and clutch her chest. Her phone vibrated against the table.

"Shit." She let out a relieved breath.

She glanced at the caller ID. It was Luke. Deciding she just wanted to get out of there, Valerie ignored the call. She grabbed the phone and rushed toward the entrance of the building. She could call him once safely in her car.

The heels she wore caused her footsteps to echo noisily. That only rattled her nerves even more. When she turned the corner, rushing into the small entrance lobby of the building, she stopped cold, feeling the icy chill to the very marrow of her bones.

"Hello, darling." Bruce sat on the counter of the receptionist station, smiling. "You really should lock the door when you're here alone, you know. You never know who might stroll in."

Valerie stood frozen, her heart pounding at her throat. She thought of the pepper spray in her purse, and Isabel's words echoed in her head. "*What good is that thing going to be for you buried at the bottom of your purse? You need to carry it on your keychain.*"

She cleared her throat and tried to conceal the alarm she felt. "I was just leaving."

Bruce jumped off the counter, forcing Valerie to move. She started for the door. Bruce's hand touched her elbow, and she flung her arm away. He raised his hands in front of him to show he meant no harm and smirked. "Take it easy."

"Why are you here?" She demanded.

"I saw your car parked outside and thought I'd drop in so we could talk."

Valerie hurried out the door. "I've nothing to talk to you about."

"What's the rush, Valerie? Meeting up with the manager again?"

Valerie continued to walk toward her car determined to not let him see that not only had he stunned her, which he obviously meant to do, but that he'd managed to add to her already growing anxiety. Had he been following her around again? She and Luke had gone out of their way to be discreet. And the parking lot of this building was too far away from the main street for him to have spotted it as he claimed.

He caught up to her, and they walked out side by side. "Did you think I wouldn't find out?"

Valerie forced a laugh. "I've no reason to keep anything from you."

After making sure she locked the door securely, she headed back to her car, but Bruce stepped in front of her. She took an irritated, but cautious step back and glared at him.

"Can you give me a sec, please?"

It would be dark soon, the parking lot was empty, and she knew she was no match for him. At this point, she didn't know what to expect, so she decided to play along. That always worked in the past.

"Okay, you have a sec."

He exhaled and frowned. "First of all, I want to apologize." He reached for her hand, and she flinched, taking another step back.

"Apology accepted." She tried to walk around him.

"I'm not done." He said firmly. The craze in his eyes brought back memories of her past with him. "Tell me something. This guy's different than Alex, isn't he? Is that the attraction?"

Valerie took a deep breath in an attempt to calm herself. Before things blew up between her and Bruce, she shared with him about Alex. Of course, that was before she uncovered the truth about him and only after he opened up to her about what she now knew was a fake past. "I don't know what you mean."

"Sure you do." He took a step forward. "Alex never appreciated what he had. Luke does, and you're falling for him, right?"

He couldn't be further from the truth, but maybe if he thought so, he'd leave her alone.

"Maybe."

The glimmer in his eyes went from smug back to crazed in a moment. "I see it, Valerie. See it in the way you look at him. It's what you've always wanted, isn't it? A man who would want you and only you?"

She nodded this time without another word. Her mind raced, trying to think of a way to get away from him.

"You'll be in love soon. But before that, you owe me first."

"Owe you for what?" Her voice almost trembled.

"For ruining my life. You know I can't even get a job now? Can't see my kids." His feral eyes took her in up and down. He cupped his hand to her chin as the corners of his lips rose slowly. "Oh, yeah, you owe me."

His tone made her think of how easily he could go from calm to crazy in a matter of seconds. Valerie held her breath. She didn't even know he had kids. She felt even stupider now for having gotten involved with a man she knew so little about.

It was dark now, and the headlights of a car coming toward them made them both turn to it. Valerie took advantage of the distraction and started toward her car. The car was still moving in their direction. Bruce didn't follow her.

He didn't say anything until she was almost at her car. There was no hiding the disdain in his voice. "You ruined my life, Valerie." His voice rose with every word. "You decide how you're going to make it up to me, the easy way or the hard way. Just remember, darling, it *will* happen."

Valerie glanced at him as she got in the car but didn't bother with a response. The car that had distracted him apparently was just passing through. She threw her car in reverse and skidded out of there. Once around the corner, it sunk in, and she clutched her pounding chest. That could've been so much worse.

It wasn't until she adjusted the rearview mirror that she realized her hands were shaking. She squeezed her hand into a fist and placed it on her lap.

Her phone vibrating in the cup holder made her jump again. One look at the caller ID confirmed what she had been dreading: her nightmare was starting up all over again. She hit ignore and held her breath as she waited to see if Bruce would leave a message, but again he didn't.

She called Luke on the way and told him how the inspection went. After giving it some thought, she kept Bruce's appearance to herself. Luke didn't know anything about him. She hadn't told him. Not yet. If things got any worse or if Bruce did even one more thing to spook her, she might. For now, it was best to not make a big deal out of it. She'd give it a few days and pray that he only wanted to scare her but wouldn't be stupid enough to actually do something to get thrown back in jail.

By the time she got home, her nerves had calmed considerably. Isabel wasn't there when she got home, as was the case ever since she'd started seeing Romero. She still insisted they were just going out as friends. Valerie laughed at that. She saw the way Romero gazed at her. She'd never seen him that way before. Sure, she hadn't been around him in a while, and it made sense that he'd matured some. In his days as a bouncer, he was quite the ladies' man. He met a different girl at every gig he worked.

She stood in the kitchen, struggling to get the pepper spray bottle onto her keychain when Isabel walked in the door followed closely by Romero. When they made it all the way in, Valerie could see they were holding hands, and she smiled.

Isabel was done up again, but Valerie had stopped mentioning it since the Padres game. It was about time Isabel started showing off the goods. She wasn't about to spoil it by making her feel self-conscious about it.

"Hey," Valerie still struggled with the pepper spray bottle. "Where've you guys been?"

"The show," Isabel headed toward the bedroom, leaving Romero behind. "but I'm only here to pick up something. We're going to go eat now. You wanna come?"

The expression of horror that flashed over Romero's face and almost made Valerie laughed. "No, that's okay, I already ate."

The look of horror was replaced with curiosity the moment Valerie passed on the invitation, and Romero asked. "Whatcha got there?"

"Pepper spray."

Isabel halted just before she walked in the room. "Why? Did something happen?"

Isabel lived the Bruce nightmare alongside Valerie, and she knew he was out now. Valerie glanced at her and shook her head. She wasn't about to get into it in front of Romero. The last thing she wanted was for it to get back to Alex that she'd been stupid enough to get herself in such a predicament. "No, I just thought it'd be best to have it handy. I almost forgot I had it until today."

Isabel stared at her but seemed to pick up that Valerie wasn't going to talk about this in front of Romero.

"Lemme see," Romero offered after watching Valerie continue to struggle.

She handed it to him, frowning. "I don't know why they make it so difficult."

"It's not." Romero chuckled.

Within seconds, he had it on, making Valerie feel totally incompetent.

"So what made you remember you had it today?" He handed it back with a knowing look.

Valerie glanced at him but shrugged and said nothing.

Romero leaned over the counter and whispered. "I won't tell Izzy. I know how she worries."

Valerie examined the keychain ring that was much too tight now with the pepper spray on it. She didn't look up at him. "I just got a little spooked today on my way to my car. It made me wonder if I still had this in my purse."

"Someone spook you?" She looked at him just long enough to see his eyebrow arch then back at the keychain and shook her head. "No, it was nothing. I thought I heard something. That's all."

Isabel walked out of the bedroom, and Valerie could not have been more thankful for the interruption. They said their goodbyes and headed out. Valerie had been so into rearranging the keys on her key chain she hardly noticed what Isabel had gone into her room to get. She was almost out the door, and Valerie's jaw almost hit the ground.

She couldn't say anything, of course, not in front of Romero. As soon as the door closed behind Isabel, Valerie ran to her phone and texted her.

Was that an overnight bag you were carrying?

A couple of seconds later, Isabel texted back.

Maybe.

Valerie laughed out loud in delight. She'd teased Isabel she would get cobwebs down there if she didn't get any soon, not that she was one to talk. Valerie had actually named her hand held companion *Mr. Perfect*. He did the job and was reliable without any of the heartache.

Isabel, you whore!

Valerie stared at her phone with her hand over her mouth, still giggling.

Friends with benefits ;)

What a joke. Isabel had never had a friend with benefits in her life. There was no such thing as far as Valerie was concerned. For years she'd tried to refer to Alex as that, and he'd turned out to be the never ending anguish of her broken heart, exactly why Mr. Perfect had taken over that part of her life.

Valerie glanced at the clock: only nine. Technically it had been early enough to catch a movie with Luke when he asked her on the way home. But she wasn't feeling up to it. She didn't want him to get used to seeing her every night. She wasn't feeling that got-too-see-you feeling for him yet. Spending a quiet evening by herself would be fine. Besides, they already had plans for Wednesday night. That was good enough.

She took advantage of the time alone to work on Sarah and Angel's painting. Every time she looked at the picture, she remembered the simpler times. She'd taken the photo herself. In the photo, Sarah and Angel are at the beach. Sarah is sitting between his legs leaning her back into him. Angel's chin is on her shoulder showing off that famous Moreno smile with the deep dimples—dimples, just like the ones that tormented her.

An image of her and Alex just like this came to her. It was the summer after her freshman year in college. They'd been going back and forth, but this was just after his first ankle injury, so he'd had no choice but to take time off from everything.

She remembered that particular day, especially because it was the day he said something that stuck with her until this day. He'd told her he didn't think he'd ever get enough of her. He said it was almost embarrassing how often he thought about her. It bordered on creepy. She remembered laughing and accusing him of embellishing. But he'd been adamant and *had* sounded so genuine. No one could look you in the eyes and lie that well, could they?

Then a few weeks later, he disappeared on her again for almost a week, and she'd wondered who else he was feeding the same lines to.

Valerie sighed, shook her thoughts off, and went back to painting—the one thing that helped her relax and get away from her endless thoughts of Alex. The last thing she wanted was to start associating it with him and start avoiding it. Before long, she fell back into her rhythm. Her thoughts submerged deep into her painting. She kept at it for about another hour before going to bed.

~*~

When you run your own restaurant with a full bar, it's kind of hard to justify going out to someone else's restaurant and paying for alcohol. But lately, Alex was there *all* the time. He needed to get out. With Angel and Sarah closing tonight, he knew the place was covered.

Eric was there waiting for Sofia to finish her shift and had already invited him once to the new sports bar they were going to. Alex had already said no but was beginning to rethink it.

"You sure you don't want to go?" Eric asked as Alex walked out of the office. "Romero said it's pretty awesome. He and some of his guys have worked the security a few times already. He said it was crazy packed. They're having open mic later in the evening. Stand-up comedy. It's supposed to be pretty good."

"Is he gonna be there tonight?" Alex didn't want to be there with just Eric and Sofia. The last thing he needed in his agitated mood was to have to deal with watching Eric's hands and lips all over his sister all night.

"Yeah, this'll be the first time he gets to actually have a drink and enjoy the place. You should come."

Sofia walked out of the back, pulling her purse over her shoulder. She'd obviously heard Eric because she added, "Yeah, Alex, you really need to take a break from this place. Come with us. It'll be fun."

Alex mulled it over. He supposed a few laughs would do him some good. He finally agreed but insisted on driving himself in case he decided to duck out early.

The place was huge with televisions in all sizes everywhere. They'd definitely be getting more televisions at the restaurant when they expanded the bar. More and more people were starting to come in to watch games and just hang.

Alex scanned the place as they walked in. Certain areas looked as if they could be reserved with their own pool table and several pub tables. Romero was in one of them, racking up the balls on the pool table. A girl sat at one of the tables, watching him.

It more than surprised Alex when he got close enough to recognize Isabel. She looked really different too. It made sense when Valerie had first told him about Isabel being a middle school teacher because she dressed every bit the part. But tonight, she wore jeans and big heels and looked rather alluring.

"No way! They actually got you out of the restaurant?" Romero grinned at him from the other side of the pool table. As pleased as Romero seemed to see him, Isabel, on the other hand, appeared troubled by his presence and sat up straight. Maybe she was embarrassed about her less-than-modest new look.

Alex nodded then smiled at Isabel. The waitress, a brunette with a very healthy cleavage, walked in right behind them.

"Are you guys okay in here?"

Romero ordered everyone a round then turned to Isabel. "You think Valerie's ready for another one?"

Alex's eyes darted to the two beer bottles in front of Isabel. Romero held his in his hand, so the other was obviously Valerie's.

"Just bring her another one," Romero told the waitress.

Isabel glanced at Alex, and now he knew what she'd been troubled by. She turned away quickly to talk to Sofia, who made herself comfortable in the seat next to her. The anxiety made its way to his stomach. He hated that damn feeling. He turned casually back to the rest of the restaurant, hoping to get the first glimpse of her out of the way before she was too close.

"So how'd they get you out of your cave, big guy?"

Alex shrugged, sitting on the edge of one of the bar stools around the pool table.

"It was time for a break."

"You think?" Eric asked. "Sofie says you practically live there now."

Romero leaned over the pool table and took a shot. "What's wrong with you, man? When's the last time you went out?"

Alex didn't even remember. He'd been so caught up this past year he couldn't even remember the last time he'd had sex. That fact alone spoke volumes about the meaningfulness of the experience.

The waitress walked in with their beers. She handed him a bottle with the kind of smile he always got from women. He reciprocated out of habit but went back to looking for Valerie. Romero got busy paying the waitress. Alex took advantage and continued to search for Valerie. His anxiety spiked when he spotted her near the entrance, not just because she looked even more amazing than when he'd seen her at the shower but because she wasn't alone.

The sight of her with a guy who stood close enough to kiss her made him squeeze his beer bottle. Alex took a deep breath and a bitter swig of the beer. This wasn't his idea of taking a break. He felt more angst at that moment than he had in all the weeks since the shower.

No way could he spend the evening around Valerie and her new man. He took a longer drink of his beer. He'd be out as soon as he finished. Still gripping the bottle tightly, he had to concentrate on not breaking it. As much as he hated the sight, he couldn't move his eyes away from her and the guy.

The guy held her wrist but not in the way a boyfriend holds his girl's hand. The moment Alex saw Valerie pull her hand away, he stood up. He welcomed the new tension that seeped through him. Unlike the tension he felt from seeing her with another guy, he knew exactly how to deal with this one.

They weren't talking. They were arguing, and Alex should be happy. Instead, he went on an instant state of alert. Her boyfriend's aggressive expression and the fact that he tried to grab her hand again was all Alex needed. He put his beer down and started toward them.

CHAPTER 6

"Where you going?" Romero asked.

Alex didn't answer. He hurried his step when he saw the menacing way her boyfriend stood over her. As he approached, he could hear the guy. He was pretty loud, and their argument began to turn heads.

"You think I'm playing? I said I need to talk to you outside *now*."

Was she really involved with this guy? Boyfriend or not he'd be damned if he'd stand there and let him speak to her that way. He didn't hear her response. Unlike the idiot, she tried to keep her voice down.

"Is there a problem?" He asked as soon as he reached them.

They both turned, the guy's expression enraged, hers startled.

"This doesn't concern you." The guy sneered.

Alex turned to Valerie, ignoring her boyfriend. "Are you okay?"

She nodded, but before she could answer, the guy continued even louder than before.

"Of course she's okay. This is none of your damn business."

Alex stepped closer to the guy, speaking inches from his face. "I'm making it my business."

Valerie grabbed Alex's hand. "No, Alex, he's not worth it."

Alex glanced back at Valerie, somewhat relieved she hadn't defended the asshole. "Is this—"

"No!" She shook her head adamantly.

He felt the guy's hand on his shoulder. Alex turned slowly, trying not to lose it. The guy had made a huge mistake touching Alex. The idiot knew it too. The moment their eyes met, he immediately pulled his hand back.

"Bruce," Valerie stepped in front of Alex in an attempt to make him step back. Alex didn't budge, not even when he felt her behind press against his thigh. "I've nothing to speak to you about. I've made that perfectly clear already."

Making an even worse mistake, Bruce reached for Valerie's arm. Alex caught his wrist just in time. With one step, he stood in front of Valerie, and Bruce's wrist was one squeeze away from being broken. Though he felt like tearing him apart, he managed to keep his voice level and spoke in his face again.

"Touch her again and you're dead."

Valerie tugged at his arm. Bruce cracked a very forced smile and pulled his wrist away from Alex. Alex let go, but he wasn't backing down now. Bruce backed away from him a couple of steps.

"Wow, Valerie, you must really have them lining up." He cackled and glared at Alex. "Your turn to tap that loose little ass tonight?"

The cannon in Alex went off and with it his fist. Bruce didn't even see it coming. Nothing could explain the satisfaction he felt landing that right hook on Bruce's eye. His body hit the floor with a flop.

"Whoa!" Romero jumped in front of him. In seconds he was surrounded by Romero, Eric, and the bar's security staff. Romero waved them off. "I got this, guys. We're cool."

Eric who'd gone down on his knee immediately tapped Bruce's cheek with his fingers. He looked up at Romero and Alex. "He's out."

Romero frowned but assured the security staff again everything was under control. He addressed the main guy personally. "Randy, let me handle this one, okay? Don't worry."

Randy nodded. He spoke into his radio, saying things were under control but gave Alex a stern look. Security worked to disperse the crowd that had cheered and laughed when Alex knocked out Bruce.

Alex worked hard to calm the rage he was still feeling over Bruce's comment. The thought of Valerie sleeping with this guy made him squeeze his fist so hard it shook. He turned to Valerie, who stood there staring down at Bruce. Instinctively, his fist opened, and he slid his hand in hers. She looked up at him. Those dark anxious eyes did things to him he couldn't even begin to understand.

"You think he's going to be okay?"

"Do you really care?" Alex clenched his jaw.

"About him? No, but I'd hate for you to be in any kind of trouble."

Alex forced his eyes away from Valerie long enough to watch Romero and Eric bring a very groggy Bruce to his feet. The guy was so out of it he struggled to focus his eyes. Romero laughed. "You okay, buddy? Need some water?"

Romero glanced at Alex, holding back a laugh. "You should get back to our pool table, dude, before they ask you to leave."

Valerie slipped her hand out of his gently. Alex didn't persist. She'd had enough male forcefulness for one night.

"Who was that?"

"A mistake I made a while back."

Alex squeezed his hand into a fist again, wondering what kind of mistake but didn't ask. "Well, what's he want now?"

"To talk about us going out again." She sighed. "I guess some guys just can't take no for an answer."

Alex wondered if there was anything in that last sentence meant for him. "So why isn't your boyfriend here?"

"Oh." She paused and glanced away. "He's coming, got caught up with a client. But he'll be here."

Alex worked his jaw some more. He'd actually gotten his hopes up, thinking he might be able to talk to her tonight.

They made their way through the crowd until they reached the area with the pool table. Isabel and Sofia stood by the entrance.

"Alex, what did you do?" Sofia frowned.

"Took some guys lights *out!*" Romero laughed behind him.

Sofia's eyes opened wide. "You did?"

Alex attempted to smirk, but he still reeled with thoughts of Valerie and the other men in her life now. He glanced at Romero. "So what happened with him?"

Romero walked around the pool table. The girls sat down at the table, but Alex stayed at the entrance of the room.

"The bartender is going through that guy's phone. If they can't get someone to pick him up, they're gonna call him a cab. He almost went out again at the bar. That guy's gonna have a shiner of all shiners for weeks."

Eric laughed. "What happened? Why'd you clock 'im?"

Alex shrugged. "He pissed me off."

"Obviously, but why?"

Alex and Valerie exchanged glances. "Valerie can tell you about it. I gotta get going."

"What!" Both Romero and Eric asked in unison.

"Yeah, I forgot about some paperwork that needs to be turned in by tonight."

Romero was looking at him, disgusted. Eric had a more understanding, almost sympathetic, expression. Alex finished his goodbyes and waved at the girls, taking one last look at Valerie. Her expression was blank. Probably embarrassed about what Bruce had said.

"You're leaving?" Sofia asked.

He nodded and walked away without explaining. He was just outside the door, his heart feeling heavier than ever when he heard someone call out his name.

He turned to see Valerie walking towards him. She stopped in front of him. "I wanted to thank you."

Alex detected a bit of anguish in her eyes. "Don't worry about it. You sure you're okay?"

She nodded, putting her hands together in front of her. Alex couldn't stand it. He had to tell her how he felt. Even if she was with someone else, she had to know. It was killing him.

"Valerie, I…"

Valerie's eyes looked past him, and she smiled. "Hey, Luke."

Alex turned around. A guy in a suit with a huge smile walked toward them. He nodded at Alex as he reached for Valerie's hand.

Valerie introduced them, and Alex instantly excused himself. He knew it was rude, and Luke looked at him funny, but there was no way he could take another moment of her with someone else.

He was fuming by the time he reached his car. The one night he decides to get out and relax a little and it turned into this. The need to have Valerie back in his life was even more implacable now than it had ever been. *Great. Fucking great.*

***

Alex drove at an uncharacteristically slow speed. He was still trying to shake yesterday's blow. He tossed and turned the entire night with images of Luke holding Valerie. It was torture. Even now, he couldn't help wondering how she'd be spending her day. He remembered spending, what Valerie called "lazy Sundays," the entire day making love, stopping only to eat and nap in between. He hated to even think it, but she may very well be doing that today.

He banged his steering wheel hard and gnashed his teeth. The visual alone turned his stomach.

Eric called first thing in the morning to ask if he wanted to go work out. He was so exhausted from the lack of sleep and the emotional turmoil he said no at first. But after slamming a few doors and nearly punching a hole in the wall, he decided a hard work out to let out some steam would do him some good.

Eric was spotting Romero when he got there. “You didn’t tell me this crumb was gonna be here. I wouldn’t have come.”

Romero looked up from the bench. “Two days in row you make it out of the restaurant? What’s the world coming to?” Then Romero frowned. “But I guess last night doesn’t count since you went back.”

Alex rolled his neck around getting the cracks out. “I took care of what I had to.”

He really had gone to the restaurant in hopes of staying busy. After snapping at a couple of employees for no good reason, he decided he was in no mood to be around anyone and headed back to his place. He’d be doing some apologizing later.

“Well you missed out.” Eric said.

“I did?”

Romero suddenly laughed. “First, let me tell him about that guy’s eye!”

Eric brought his fist to his mouth and started laughing himself. “Dude, you should’ve seen that guy you cracked.”

Alex smiled, feeling a tiny bit of satisfaction drown out a little of his turmoil. “What about him?”

“The cab they called him took a while to get there.” Romero continued chuckling. “I saw him still sittin’ at the bar a half hour later. His eye was black and swelled shut. It was too fucking funny!”

Alex laughed, wiggling the fingers on his right hand. With all that had happened last night, he hadn’t even really felt it until he went to bed, and even now his hand was a little sore. A lot of the frustration he’d been feeling for weeks had gone into that punch. Besides seeing Valerie again, which was bittersweet, knocking out Bruce had been the only good thing about last night.

"Yeah, well that prick had it coming."

Romero and Eric continued chuckling. Alex dropped his keys and his towel on the floor. He took a seat on the bench next to Romero but waited before starting to work out. He had a few questions first.

"So why were you there with Valerie and Isabel?"

"Yeah, I didn't know you were seeing Isabel." Eric added.

"You're seeing her?" Alex was even more surprised than when he saw her last night. He had a feeling Romero was there with her, but he thought maybe it was a one night thing or they were just hanging out. As far as he knew, Romero had never been in any kind of serious relationship.

"I told you." Romero said.

"No, you didn't."

Romero thought about it. "Oh yeah, that was Angel. Well, dude, maybe if you'd come out of your cave more often. Yeah, it's been a couple weeks."

"Seeing her. Like seeing her?" Alex still couldn't believe it.

"Yeah, why not?" Romero frowned.

"I thought you said she wasn't your type?" Eric stood over him ready to spot him.

"I didn't know anything about her then. Turns out she's pretty cool."

"Whatcha do to her?" Alex pinched his eyebrows curiously. "She looked different last night."

Romero sat up. "What do you mean?"

"She looked hot." Eric added.

Romero turned and glared at Eric. "You were checking her out?"

"Kind of hard not to notice, Romero." Alex smirked.

Romero turned back to Alex. "You too?"

Alex laughed. "I'm not the one that said she was hot. I said different." He threw a towel at Romero. "I just remember her being so damn conservative. That's all. Don't get your panties all in a bunch."

"Well, I didn't do anything to her, and I don't remember her looking any different." Romero scowled at him then at Eric. "I didn't realize you two were paying so much attention."

Alex laughed. "Shut up. So what else did I miss?"

"Valerie's new man's a high roller." Romero seemed to dig that one in. "At least he was acting like it last night."

Just like that, Alex jolted out of his laughing mood. He pretended not to be bothered but squeezed the bar on the bench. "Yeah, how?"

"He was buying rounds all night." Romero continued. "He must think we're real tight with Val, 'cause it seemed like he was trying to impress us, even invited us to his place sometime. Probably has some big pad he wants to show off. But he's too …" Romero tried to find the word.

"Too what?"

Romero had spiked his interest.

"He tries too hard." Eric said.

"There you go." Romero nodded. "Even his jokes felt forced."

"He had jokes?" Alex rolled his eyes.

"A couple." Romero said. "He got some pity laughs, and even Valerie seemed put off by them. I don't know if she's just not that into him or if she was still worked up about that guy you knocked out, but she didn't really seem to have a good time last night."

"So what was up with that?" Eric asked. "Valerie didn't say much, especially after lover boy showed up. He seemed interested when he heard you'd knocked someone out because of her, but she cut the conversation short."

Alex shrugged, trying to act as indifferent about the use of lover boy to describe her boyfriend as any. "She dumped his ass a while back, and the asshole is still harassing her."

Even as he snarled the words out, the reality of Valerie having really moved on dug into him like a razor sharp blade.

"I wonder if he's the reason she put a pepper spray bottle on her keychain."

Alex stared at him. "Last night?"

"No, Friday. We stopped by the apartment to pick something up, and Valerie was there, trying to get the pepper spray on her keychain. She didn't really wanna say why but admitted to being spooked."

That didn't sit well with Alex. He'd thought maybe she'd just run into Bruce at the bar. The idea of that asshole stalking her was a whole other story.

"Has Isabel said anything about it?"

"She seemed worried about it, but then Izzy worries about everything."

It surprised Alex that Romero already had a pet name for Isabel, but he didn't comment. Instead, his mind went back to Valerie and her possible stalker.

Romero didn't say much more. After working out for about an hour, Alex went back to his house and showered up.

The thought of heading to Valerie's place crossed his mind as he got in his car. He remembered her warning about him showing up unannounced. Enraged, he gripped the steering wheel and took a deep breath. This was only going to get worse with every passing day. He skidded out of his parking spot and headed back out to the restaurant.

CHAPTER 7

Sal sat at the bar in the restaurant talking to Julie, one of the waitresses, when Alex walked in, adding guilt to Alex's growing list of unwelcome emotions. She'd been one of the ones he snapped at the night before.

"Hey, man." Alex clapped Sal on the back of his shoulder.

"Heard you finally took a night off and then didn't." Sal smirked.

Alex frowned. "I'll tell you about it later."

Julie gave him a timid smile and turned to walk away, but Alex stopped her.

"C'mere." He put his arms around her and hugged her hard, rubbing her back. Then pulled away. "I'm sorry about yesterday. I shouldn't have said what I said."

She smiled, then giggled "That's okay. I should've known better than to ask why you were back."

Damn, he felt like a jerk. She walked away with a smile. Alex felt a little bit better, until he turned his attention back to Sal, who looked disgusted. "What the hell was that about?"

"I snapped at her yesterday. I felt bad."

Sal stared at him with that hardened expression Alex so rarely saw on him.

"Well you know, she's so soft-spoken and sweet, and there I was, raising my voice at her just 'cause I was in a hell of a mood."

Sal glanced in Julie's direction then back at Alex. "Yeah, well I hope you don't make it a habit of hugging your employees that way. Ever heard of sexual harassment?"

Alex lifted a shoulder and walked behind the bar. "Why you here, anyway? I thought you'd be with mom and pop."

"I hadn't been here in a while. Pop said you've made some changes. I just wanted to check it out."

Alex brought out a glass and made himself a drink. Sal already had one in front of him. Alex peered at him, feeling a smirk tug at the corner of his lips. "Weren't you just here not too long ago?"

Sal scanned the restaurant. "That was weeks ago. So you wanna tell me what happened last night that made you come back and yell at poor little Julie?"

Alex shook his head. He knew what Sal would think if he told him the whole truth. But he hadn't told anyone about it, and at this point the situation was so desperate, he could use some sound advice.

Sal knew he'd hung out with Valerie in the past, but had no idea how bad Alex had it for her. Hell, Alex hadn't figured that out until just recently.

"Valerie was there last night."

Sal stared at him blankly. "And?"

"With her boyfriend."

Sal nodded knowingly. "Ah, what happened?"

"Nothing, I left."

"What? You didn't blow up?"

Alex frowned as if Sal was being ridiculous, but he knew damn well Sal hit it on the nose. Only reason he hadn't was because he'd already let some steam out on the first guy. If he'd hung around for even a while longer, who knows what might've happened?

"I thought you two stopped going out a long time ago?"

"We did."

"So what's the problem?"

Alex leaned his fists against the counter. "I don't know. I guess this past year with everything that happened and the restaurant keeping me so busy, I was too preoccupied to notice I missed her. Then I saw her at the shower and … I just can't stop thinking about her now."

That was an understatement. The woman invaded his every thought. Alex stared at Sal, who looked at him weird. He wasn't use to this kind of guy talk, but it felt good to finally talk to someone about this.

"So did you tell her?"

Alex shook his head, pulling a glass down from the overhead cupboard. "She didn't give me a chance. Worst thing is it's too late."

Sal pinched his brows. "What do you mean too late?"

"She's with someone else now." Saying it aloud was just another blow to his gut.

"That doesn't mean anything. If she still has feelings for you, you can change that."

"That's the thing, Sal. I really screwed things up with her. I don't think she wants anything to do with me anymore."

Sal gave him that look he'd always given him when they were growing up. The same look he got when Alex had blown up and beat someone's ass. The "*What did you do now?*" look.

"I never told you this because it was embarrassing. I'm not like you when it comes to school. I had a hell of time keeping up with all the classes, and that scholarship meant everything to mom and pop. There was no way I was gonna blow it over my grades."

He hesitated to continue. Even now, he wasn't sure he wanted Sal to know.

"So?"

Alex stared at the drink he'd poured himself not wanting to look at Sal. "So I hired a tutor. Not just one, several."

"So what?"

Alex rolled his eyes and took a hard swallow of his drink. "It was humiliating. No way did I want Valerie to know about that. She breezed through school, finished before everyone else."

"She's a real estate agent, Alex."

Alex glared at his brother. "What the hell does that mean?"

"Relax, I'm just saying it's not law school. She didn't even need to go to school to become an agent. All she had to do is pass the state exam. Besides, what does that have anything to do with you screwing things up?"

"Well, whenever I had the tutor over, I made sure Valerie wasn't coming around that week. I'd have to ignore her calls or text her I was too busy to talk her. I couldn't even risk calling her before the tutor would show up because she'd know something was up if I didn't ask to see her. She assumed I was with other girls." Alex glanced at Sal embarrassed to admit it. "And I let her."

Sal stared at him, revolted. "God, you're stupid. So why not just tell her now."

"I actually did tell her."

"What did she say?"

Alex took another swig of his drink, eyeballing Sal. "I wasn't planning on it, but she came over one night, and my tutor was there."

Humor brightened Sal's eyes. "Don't tell me your tutor was a chick?"

Alex didn't see the humor. Here he was, pouring out his heart, and Sal was getting a kick out of it. "Yeah, and of course she thought the worst. I tried explaining, but she was hysterical. I thought she was gonna spit in my face when I told her the girl was a tutor."

Sal really laughed now. Alex felt like flattening him. If he wanted this kind of reaction, he may as well have told Romero and Eric. Angel was the only one that knew. He'd heard about it from Sarah, and they both believed the same thing Valerie did: that she'd caught him with another girl and he'd try to pass her off as his tutor.

He never told them the truth, of course. As upset as Sarah had been with him, he'd preferred they all believed he'd used the lame excuse rather than the humiliating truth.

Alex scowled at Sal. "Are you done laughing?"

Sal nodded but couldn't quite wipe the smile. Alex poured himself another drink.

"Take it easy on that." Sal warned. "That's not going to solve anything."

"Yeah, well it'll help me sleep."

"But you still have to drive home." Sal watched Alex pour the liquor. "That's enough, dude."

Alex stopped and poured in some soda. "Hell, I'll sleep in the back if I have to. That bed's still back there."

"Is that why you're here on your day off? To get drunk and pass out in the back?"

Alex stared at his drink. "No, I'm here because if I were home, all I'd be doing is thinking about her."

"And you're not now?" Sal straightened out and took a sip of his drink. "Listen. If it were me, I'd talk to her."

Alex shook his head. "Ever since the tutor thing, she's made it impossible for me to get a hold of her. She won't take my calls or return any messages."

"So go see her at her place."

Alex stared, not even attempting to hide his annoyance. "What do you think will happen, Sal, if I get there and that guy is there?"

Sal seemed to reflect on that for a moment before saying "All right, not a good idea. Hmm." He brought his fist to his mouth. "Let's think. When's the next wedding shindig? She's gotta be there, right?"

"Yeah, but that's not for another few weeks at the rehearsal dinner."

They threw a few ideas back and forth for a few minutes about what they could plan that would get him and Valerie in the same place but came up with nothing. The biggest issue with whatever they came up with was what if she brought her new man?

Sal pulled his ringing cell phone out from his holster and answered. "Yeah, he's here." He mouthed *Angel* at Alex. "He wants to know why you're not answering your damn phone, ass." he chuckled.

Alex patted his own holster and realized he'd left it in his truck. Sal figured it out. "He doesn't have it on him. Why? You wanna talk to him?" Sal paused then looked up at Alex again. "Yeah we're gonna be here. Sure we'll wait."

Sal hung up with a smug grin. "Looks like you're gonna get your chance to talk to Valerie."

"When?" Alex squeezed the glass in his hand.

"Right now. Dad wanted us to look over the offer for the property next door. She wrote it up already, but before she sends it, dad wants to make sure we're okay with it. She was going to fax it, but Angel thought it'd be best if she went over it with us instead. He's been trying to get a hold of you."

Right now? With a frown, Alex patted his holster again out of habit. If he hadn't left it in his truck he might've had more time to prepare. He had no idea what he was going to say to her, but he damn sure wasn't going to let her leave without telling her how he felt.

~*~

As if last night hadn't been hard enough, Valerie had been a wreck all morning. She'd written up the offer for the property next door to Alex's family's restaurant. All she had to do was fax it. They had a fax machine at the restaurant—simple enough. But no, nothing was ever that simple. Sarah had called her to tell her Mr. Moreno was requesting she go over it with him.

She'd planned a peaceful Sunday: rest all day, maybe get some painting done to get her mind off seeing Alex again.

Last night had been even harder than seeing him at the shower. She did her best to appear impassive about their chance meeting. She thought Alex had bought it, but she had a feeling Luke hadn't. Alex's rank departure had been anything but tactful. Her trivial explanation of him just being an old friend was squashed when the guys kept going on and on about Bruce's eye.

Luke hadn't asked a lot of questions. She knew he wouldn't, not in front of them, that is. On the way home was a different story. Still, she kept the explanation of her relationship of Alex to a mere sentence: someone she'd gone out with a long time ago. As to the explanation of Bruce, someone she'd gone out with more recently and who got rude tonight. Alex, of course, handled it as he always handled things.

She hadn't even gotten over fixating about why Alex had such a strong hold on her still when Sarah called. She assured her Alex wouldn't be at the Moreno family residence. Even so, her heart had raced the whole way there. What if, just what if he showed up?

For a moment, she actually thought she was home free. She'd gone over all the specifics, explained the offer in detail, and Alex hadn't shown up. Then her worst nightmare happened. Mr. Moreno said he'd feel better if she could go over it with his son. She turned to Angel who'd been in and out of the kitchen the entire time and prayed somehow he meant him. In the next moment Angel was on the phone, trying to get a hold of Alex.

Sarah walked over and squeezed her shoulder, which only unnerved her even more. There'd been a tiny glimmer of relief when Angel hadn't been able to get a hold of him. Although she did wonder what, but mostly *who,* could be keeping him so busy he couldn't answer his phone. He always kept it handy.

So when Angel set the phone down after speaking with Sal to ask if she was okay driving to the restaurant her voice nearly squeaked, "Today?" She quickly cleared her voice and tried again. "Um well, I wasn't planning on—"

"They're both there, Sal *and* Alex. But they both can't leave."

When she didn't respond and just bit her lip, Angel picked up the phone again. "Or I can call him back and tell him to just send Alex over if that's more convenient."

"No!" *God no.* Angel stared at her confused. She glanced back at Mr. Moreno and forced a smile. "I mean, it's easier if we go there. It's on my way home."

She'd never survive being in such a private setting with Alex. It would be hard enough seeing him again, but at least in public, it was safer. She still didn't trust herself around him.

On the torturous ride to the restaurant, she called Isabel who tried in vain to calm her. "I can't do this." Valerie's voice almost trembled. She squeezed the steering wheel with both hands.

Isabel's voice came into her earpiece loud and clear. "Listen to me, hon. You can and you will. Remember what your dad always says. Everything happens for a reason. This is going to make you stronger. Every time you see him, you'll gain a little more control over your emotions around him. He's just another guy. Remember that."

Oh, but he was so much more. This guy owned her heart and soul. Seeing him last night only confirmed that further. She drove into the parking lot of the restaurant, amazed at how different it looked. Sarah told her about the renovations, but she hadn't expected this much of a change. The place was huge, and they were going to expand even further?

She took a deep breath, hoping for some more words of comfort from Isabel. "All right, I'm here."

"Be strong, Valerie. You're a professional. Go in there and do your thing as if he were any other client."

Sarah and Angel had driven there also. They parked and got out of the car, giving Valerie little time to prepare herself.

She stepped out of the car, upset that her legs felt so damn weak. Even though Sarah had insisted she didn't have to dress up, she was glad now she decided to wear a pant suit and do her hair anyway.

Her stomach roiled wild with anxiety. The three of them walked in the front door. The renovations were amazing. Valerie stopped just inside the doorway, taking in the beauty of the restaurant. The family had never spared any expense on decorations, making it into one of La Jolla's most breathtaking establishments. Elaborate archways like the ones you only saw in old Mexican movies or paintings separated the rooms. Multi-colored clay pots overflowing with bright flowers and shrubs adorned every corner and crevice.

Painted murals of scenery from the old country covered the brick walls. As an artist, she could appreciate the amazing talent of whoever painted them. It must've taken months. One of them took up an entire wall. It was a portrait of an old Mexican town. The detail was astounding from the mules that stood tied outside the quaint brick buildings to the children that played in the dirt road.

They walked through one of the archways and into the bigger dining room she remembered so fondly. The place was packed. Sunday brunch was always like this. The delectable smell of food brought back bittersweet memories. She shook them off and continued walking.

Her eyes gazed all around, taking in all the changes they made. All this in one year? It was unbelievable. Valerie was transfixed on another mural. This one was a close up of an old Mexican woman making corn tortillas by hand. Every detail, even of the wrinkles around her smiling eyes, was remarkable.

Feminine giggling finally pulled her attention away from the mural. She turned to see Alex and one of the waitresses carrying on. His back was to her, but it was plain as day he was flirting and the girl ate it up.

Immediately she felt immersed in a heat of jealousy. It infuriated her that after all this time, she cared so much it hurt. But she needed this: a reminder of why she could not, *would* not, allow him back in her life.

"Alex, you ready?"

Alex spun around at the sound of Angel's voice. Valerie stood tall. Alex turned back and said something to the waitress. The waitress quickly walked away into the kitchen. He brought his attention back to them, and his eyes met Valerie's. Even from a distance, they were so piercing her determination almost faltered. Almost.

CHAPTER 8

As usual, Alex was nearly incapable of keeping his eyes off Valerie. Even as she pulled her reading glasses on and was all business, he couldn't stop the thoughts that invaded his mind. She helped herself to a plate of food from the buffet and tortured him with every bite she took. He always loved watching her eat. To Valerie, eating was like an aphrodisiac. She loved eating and practically made love to every bite.

He hardly heard a word she said. They were sitting at one of the booths in the back dining room that wasn't opened up anymore, now that brunch was nearly over. It was just her, Sal, and himself. No part of her was exposed except her face and her hands, but he had a throbbing hard on the entire time. It was madness. Her perfectly manicured fingers drove him crazy now. All he could think of as she flayed them around haphazardly, pointing from her laptop to the paperwork, was the many times those very fingers had dug into his back.

Then like a brick shattering through the window of his thoughts, the image of her and Luke broke through, and he almost growled. Both Valerie and Sal stopped and looked at him.

"What the hell's your problem?" Sal asked.

"We can change the numbers." Valerie started typing on her laptop. "I told your dad that. I'm just saying with property like this in this area—"

"It's fine." Alex strained to speak. "The offer's fine, Val." Maybe if she didn't drive him so completely insane, he'd actually know what the offer was.

"I think so too." Sal added standing up. "Sounds good to me, Valerie. If Alex is good with it also, go ahead and send it over."

Sal patted Alex on the shoulder in an entirely obvious gesture that this was his chance to talk to her. He thanked Valerie for going over the offer and excused himself, explaining it was Angel's day off and he had to relieve him now.

Valerie stood up and started packing up her things in what seemed too much of a rush.

"You got somewhere to be?" *Someone to see?* His fingers fisted involuntarily.

Concentrating on her briefcase, she didn't look up. "As a matter of fact I do."

His nostrils flared, and he stood with her, not missing her flinch as he moved toward her. "I was hoping we could talk."

"No." She worked even faster to finish stuffing her briefcase.

"Why not?"

"I gotta go."

Unable to stay away from her anymore, he moved in from behind her close enough to smell her, but what he really wanted to do was taste her. She stiffened when she felt his breath against her temple. He could barely restrain himself from rubbing her back. "You can't give me a few minutes?"

"No." Her tone had lost a bit of its conviction.

"I miss you so much, Valerie." He whispered in her ear. Unable to hold back any longer, he ran a finger up her hand.

"Stop it, Alex." Her voice was a near whisper, but she didn't pull her hand away.

"Stop what?" He grazed at her temple with his lips, his insides on fire.

As much as he could tell she struggled to hide it, Valerie trembled. She wanted it as much as he did. Why the hell was she fighting it? He stepped closer behind her, letting her feel just how badly he wanted her. Needed her. She stiffened immediately, and he heard her breathing hitch. For a moment, she dropped her head allowing access to her neck. Without hesitation, Alex kissed it, feeling her tremble even more.

"I can't …" She jerked her head up and stood tall again, pulling her hand and entire body away from him. "I won't do this anymore, Alex."

In an instant, her briefcase was in her hand. Alex reached for her arm. "Valerie please, I just need you to know—"

"I know, Alex." She pulled her keys out of the side pocket.

"That's just it, Z. You *don't* know. Hell, I didn't even know."

She shook her head and began to walk away, but Alex held her arm.

"Alex," her protest was forced. She turned back to him. To his surprise, her eyes glistened, reminding him of that night a year ago she fell apart before his eyes because of his stupid ass. "I asked you to stay away from me for a reason. I just can't do this anymore. While I appreciate the business, if this is how things are going to be, I can find someone else to write up this offer."

"No. Valerie, I just—"

"I'm seeing someone else now, Alex. Please respect that."

With that, he backed up. She'd rubbed the rawest of nerves. The thought of her with Luke was the cause of his sleepless nights, and now she threw it in his face again. With his breathing now labored and feeling as if he was about to explode, he nodded but asked, "Are you in love with him?"

Valerie's eyes widened. Sarah walked into the dining room, and Valerie turned to face her. "Just so you know, they're putting all the food away from brunch, but I can grab you some more if you want me to."

Valerie shook her head and headed toward Sarah. "No, thank you. But you can walk me to my car." She turned back to Alex. "I'll have that offer in tonight. I'll keep you guys updated. Say bye to Sal for me."

Just like that, he'd blown his only opportunity to tell her how he felt. He watched as she walked away, looking as elegant as only Valerie could. Damn, but she drove him nuts.

Sal walked into the dining room with a smile that dissolved as soon as he saw Alex's expression. If his expression matched his black mood, Sal knew already things hadn't gone well.

"What happened?"

"Her fucking boyfriend happened." Alex stalked toward the back office. "She threw that shit in my face, and I clammed up. I never even got a chance to tell her anything."

Sal followed him. "Well maybe you can—"

"No, I'm done." She hadn't answered him about being in love with Luke, and it nearly sucked the life out of him. He didn't want to know, didn't even want to think about her anymore.

He charged in the back room and grabbed his keys from the desk. "I'm outta here."

Sal moved out of his way. "Where you going?"

Alex didn't answer. He felt ready to kill. He needed to get out of there—get the scent and image of Valerie out of his mind. He stormed past Angel on his way down the hall to the back exit of the restaurant.

"Don't do anything stupid." Sal warned.

"What's his problem?" He heard Angel ask.

"Valerie." Sal said.

Julie was on her way in when he bolted past her. "You okay?"

A grunt was his only response. He walked out into the bright sunlight. When the door slammed behind him, he let out a carnal roar so loud the birds flew off the roof, scattering in different directions.

He drove in no direction for hours. The more he thought about it, the more he realized he couldn't just give up. It finally dawned on him. No girl had ever come close to making him feel what he was feeling. His entire life was on hold now because of Valerie. There was no moving on. He needed to do something about it.

When he finally made it home that night, he reread the message that still sat on his coffee table. What the hell was his problem anyway? Why couldn't he just leave a damn message like a normal person? He ripped the page out of the notebook and did some more tweaking

He picked up his phone and dialed before he could change his mind. His heart raced at the chance that she might actually answer. She didn't. He cleared his throat during her voicemail greeting and took a deep breath. It beeped and he stared at the paper in his hand. "Valerie. I'm sorry. I've been an ass all this time …" He sounded like a robot to his own ears, so he crumpled the paper and sat down, running his hand through his hair. "Look Valerie, I didn't even realize how much I missed you until I saw you again. I am *so* sorry about everything. I know I screwed up bad. And I know you have lots of questions, but I have answers. I promise. If you'd just give me the chance, I can explain it all. All I do …" He paused and took a deep breath. "All I do is think about you, baby. Today was torture. You have no idea what you do to me. Val," his voice dropped almost to a whisper, "please tell me you haven't given up on us. I'm going crazy here. Call me."

He clicked the phone and hung up, surprised at himself. He hadn't even realized he felt all that until the words just came out. He threw the phone down on the sofa and sat back. Frustration now clouded all the other emotions he'd felt for weeks.

~*~

Despite the fact that days passed since Valerie saw Alex, she still felt the effects of being so close to him again. Luke was her only hope now. But every time she saw Alex again, that hope slowly lost ground.

In some ways, she was very surprised that the whole relationship thing with Luke was still working out. Luke promised he'd be discreet at the office, and so far he'd kept his promise. That really helped, because she had to admit she had been worried about things changing. They would go out on the weekend, but she always claimed to be too tired during the week, her way of keeping things from getting too heavy. The night at the sports bar had been the first weeknight she spent with him. Even that had been on the insistence of Isabel.

She tried not to spend too much time at the office, and that was easy. Her clients kept her busy outside, showing properties and doing open houses. Like today, she showed so many properties she didn't even bother going back to the office. She called Luke and told him she was done. All she could think of was getting home to take a shower and relax. Luke made a comment about her coming back to shower at his place, but she politely passed on the offer.

Valerie made a point of reiterating to Luke that she wanted to take things *reall*y slow. After having a few more heated moments with him, she could tell Luke was getting anxious to do more. She just wasn't ready for it. She wondered if she ever would be. How was it so damn easy for Alex to be with someone else? It hurt that he actually enjoyed being with other women while she was still waiting to feel that special something when Luke kissed her.

Alex hadn't stopped calling, and seeing his name on her caller ID still made her heart speed up. She didn't dare answer. She knew it would take so little to fall for his lies again, and she'd be right back where she'd been for years, waiting for the next heartache. Just hearing his voice had such an effect on her.

He'd stopped leaving her messages until Sunday night. She couldn't bring herself to listen though she hadn't erased it. It was still sitting in her voicemail box unheard, and she thought about it all week.

She threw her briefcase down and kicked off her three inch heels as soon as she walked in the door.

Isabel was in the kitchen, making something. Valerie was famished. "Smells yummy."

Isabel glanced up from her cutting. "The shoes, Missy."

Valerie walked toward the kitchen. "I'll get them after I eat. I'm starving."

Isabel shot her a stern look. Valerie slumped her shoulders and went back for the shoes.

While she was in her room putting her shoes away, she decided to change into shorts and an old t-shirt. Her phone rang. It was Luke.

"Hey." She held the phone against her shoulder while she pulled on her shorts.

"Valerie, I know you're tired. I won't keep you. I was just wondering if instead of going out to dinner tomorrow night, you wouldn't rather come over to my place. I'll make you dinner."

Valerie didn't answer immediately, and he added, "I make a kick-ass lasagna. I'm at the supermarket now, so I thought I'd call before I pick up all the stuff."

Valerie winced. Talk about no pressure. "Yeah, that sounds good."

"You sure? We don't have to. I just thought since I've bragged so much about my cooking, I should make something for you already.

Valerie smiled. "No, it really sounds good. Do you need me to bring anything?"

"No, just your appetite."

After hanging up with him, she walked back into the kitchen where Isabel was still cutting up stuff at the counter. Isabel looked up at her.

"I hope you're hungry. It's clean-out-the-fridge day."

"Again?" Valerie walked over to the stove. "What smells so good?"

"Those party weenies we had left over from the bridal shower."

Valerie took one out of the barbecue sauce they were simmering in with a fork and bit it. "Mmm, I thought we'd left all the leftovers at my dad's house."

Valerie had thrown Sarah an all-girl bridal shower at her dad's house a few weeks ago. She'd hoped it would it would be enough and maybe they wouldn't throw any other showers where she'd inevitably have to see Alex. But Angel's family was party crazy and went ahead with their enormous co-ed shower anyway.

"Your stepmom dropped this off today and said your dad isn't supposed to be eating this stuff anymore."

Valerie grabbed a water out of the fridge and sat down on one of the bar stools in front of the counter, facing Isabel.

Isabel had all kinds of goodies out. Once a week, she cleaned out the fridge, throwing out all the bad stuff. She then cooked and cut up anything about to go bad. Between her and Valerie, mostly Valerie, they got rid of it all.

"I'm surprised you're not with Romero tonight."

"He wanted me to come over but … I dunno. I just don't want to overdo it with him."

"Isabel, I thought you liked him?"

"I do. That's what scares me."

"Why?" Valerie frowned. "It's a good thing he wants to be around you so much. He's a good guy."

"I know. I know." Isabel continued cutting cucumbers. "I've just never been with anyone like him. He's so different from all the overly polished guys I usually go out with. He's raw, and he doesn't care about being politically correct. He says things like he sees them, all bullshit aside. For someone who's so up front and open, he hasn't mentioned anything about a relationship yet. What if this is just a fun thing for him? I'm having fun, but I'm afraid to put my heart out there like that until I know for sure he's serious."

"Oh, he seems serious to me." Valerie popped a couple of cheese cubes in her mouth.

"I'm just slowing it down a little before I get too far gone." Isabel shrugged and gave Valerie a weak smile.

Valerie didn't push it. She knew Isabel was being her usual self, over thinking everything. Instead, she changed the subject. "Luke's making me dinner tomorrow."

Isabel glanced up from her cutting. "Really? So things are getting serious? I'm glad, Valerie."

Valerie had filled her in about the nightmare at the restaurant. She'd been so close to giving in to him again. She knew Isabel was rooting for things to take off with her and Luke.

"It's just dinner, Isabel. What's so serious about that?"

"A man doesn't cook dinner for just anyone." Isabel said and continued her cutting. "Heck, most men don't cook, period. Plus it's what happens after dinner that makes it so serious."

Isabel put the plate of cucumbers she just finished cutting in front of Valerie. Valerie grabbed one and shook her head. "Nothing's happening."

"You don't know that."

"Yes, I do." Valerie insisted.

"Why? It's been a few weeks now. And you know him well enough to know it's not going to be a one-nighter. I thought you liked this guy?"

"I do but …" Valerie jumped off the bar stool and put the water back in the fridge. She'd had a long day and deserved a glass of wine. Plus Isabel made her nervous. Maybe Luke did expect something to happen tomorrow.

Isabel stopped cutting and turned around to watch Valerie pour herself a glass of wine. "But Alex, right?"

Valerie didn't look at her. "No."

"Pour me a glass too. And you're lying."

"I'm not lying." Valerie pulled out another glass from the cabinet.

"You always avoid eye contact when you lie, Val. You're doing it now."

Valerie turned to look at her and handed her the glass with a smirk. "I hate you."

Isabel took the glass but frowned. "Valerie, you were doing so well. You can't let a couple of run ins with him pull you all the way back. These are all tests. You have to get through them."

Valerie sipped her wine and frowned. "I had no idea being near him would be so hard. I really thought I was over him, but …"

Isabel shook her head. "Honey, I won't speak badly of Alex. I know how much he means to you, but he's done you wrong so many times. I really think you should give Luke a shot. You finally kissed another man. Maybe finally sleeping with someone else will help you move on. What's the worst that can happen?"

"I've slept with other guys since I met Alex."

"Doesn't count. That was back in your early party college days. And you were still in denial about actually being in love with Alex."

Valerie sat back down and thought about it. It was true. It'd been so long since she even considered sleeping with someone else. What was the worst thing that could happen? She really had to move on. She couldn't go on putting it off forever. Because she knew that's how long it would be before she got over Alex.

"You really think it would help?" She sipped her wine again.

"I really do. I hate to say this, Val, but I'm sure Alex has been moving on again and again since you two have been apart."

That hurt, but Valerie knew it was true. "What if Luke isn't even thinking like that?"

Isabel sipped her wine and gave her a look. "Are you kidding?"

Valerie giggled. "You think I should wear anything special?"

Isabel smiled big, thrilled that Valerie was actually considering it. "I'm sure you have plenty to choose from. You can't go wrong with black satin though."

Valerie felt her insides churning.

"To moving on." Isabel held out her wine glass.

Valerie clinked it with her glass. "To moving on."

She was really moving on. Somehow, she thought she'd feel more excited or at the very least relieved. Something heavy settled in her stomach as she took a sip of her wine. But it wasn't relief and most certainly not excitement.

CHAPTER 9

The next day Valerie didn't even make it to the office until after noon. She had clients she had to meet in the morning. Luke was already there and motioned for her to come in his office. The moment he closed the door behind her, he greeted her with one of the most sensual kisses he'd given her to date. It took her by surprise, and left her a bit breathless. But as usual, she didn't feel much else.

"What's that about?" She turned to make sure the blinds on his office windows were closed all the way. They were, but if someone really wanted to, they could easily see through the small opening between the blinds.

"I just missed you." He smiled and kissed her neck. "I hardly saw you yesterday."

Valerie pulled away a little. "Luke, I don't think this a good idea, not here."

He pecked her then backed off. "All right, I'm sorry. I'll have to control myself."

He walked back around to his desk and picked up a file. "I have a few things here for you."

"What?"

He pointed at some files on his desk. "A couple of cash buyers, looking to buy something fast."

Valerie stared at him. "Aren't those supposed to get passed around the office?"

Luke shrugged. "It's just a couple. You're the fastest and most efficient. I need this done yesterday. I don't want to waste my time with those slackers. It's no big deal."

Valerie took the files and read them. They were both looking to buy commercial buildings and had big budgets.

She didn't feel comfortable. If anyone in the office found out, they might accuse Luke of playing favorites.

"You think you can get a list together and set up something by next week?"

"Yeah, sure." She started to walk toward the door.

"Hey," Luke said, "is sevenish okay for tonight? I'm gonna try to get out of here earlier than normal. I'm a good cook, just not very fast."

"Yeah, that's fine." Valerie still wasn't one-hundred-percent sure about tonight. She'd just play it by ear.

She walked to her cubicle and pulled out her laptop. The envelope on the screen of her phone when she set it down reminded her of the unheard message from Alex.

She stared at it for a second before picking up the phone and dialing her voicemail. Her heart fluttered when she heard his deep voice. Every word he said made her heart race faster. Then she felt the knot at her throat when she heard the words, "*Please tell me you haven't given up on us.*"

Taking a deep breath, she saved the message. She knew she should just delete it, but there was no way. God, how did he do that? One message and she was close to tears. She missed being with him so much, and hearing his voice made her miss him even more. He sounded so sincere. He always did. There was no way she could concentrate now. Valerie glanced at the time. She hurried outside with her phone and immediately dialed Isabel.

This was Isabel's hour between classes. She paced outside until Isabel answered.

"What's up?" Isabel chirped.

"He left a message."

"Who?"

"Alex."

She heard Isabel exhale. "And?"

"Isabel, it sounded so sincere." Valerie pulled her hair behind her ear and moved the phone to her other ear. "He said he hopes I haven't given up on us."

"Val, hon, he always sounds sincere. We've been over this a million times. He has a huge ego. Always has. He can't stand the thought of you with someone else, but he'll never be a one-woman guy."

Valerie's heart was still pounding with excitement from his words. "I don't know, Isabel. I've never heard him like this. You think … You really think it's just wishful thinking on my part?"

"I know it is. This is the longest you've been away from him. He must be feeling the weight of it too. Seeing you with someone else I'm sure is contributing to this sudden urge to be with you. But you know what'll happen if you go back again."

Valerie nodded. "Yeah, I know. I want you to hear it though when I get home tonight."

Isabel took a deep breath. "Okay, but you're not backing out on tonight."

"No, I won't." Not the dinner anyway. She was still on the fence about the rest of the evening.

She finished the list of properties to show in a matter of minutes. Then she called Sarah to let her know the offer had been accepted on the property next door to the restaurant. She begged her to please let Alex know and she'd update them on the escrow. As unprofessional as she knew that was, there was no way she was calling him directly.

After hanging up, she left early without even saying goodbye to Luke. She'd see him tonight. There'd been plenty of times she rushed out of the office without saying goodbye to him. She didn't want to start any new habits now. But mostly, she was avoiding any possible embraces. It was happening already. Just hearing Alex's message had begun to affect the way she felt about her relationship with Luke.

Back home, she did everything she could to keep her mind off the message. But she couldn't fight the urge to listen to it just one more time. She hated to admit it, but it made her feel good. Too good. That damn lingering hope was back. As much as she told herself he would never change, something about the way he sounded in the message stood out to her. He'd always been good about pleading his case in the past, but this time he sounded almost desperate.

Damn it, Valerie. Stop it.

As soon as Isabel got home, Valerie rushed to her with her phone in hand.

"Okay, just listen to the message, and tell me what you think. But be open-minded."

Isabel put her things down on the counter and peered at Valerie. "Really? One message and you're acting like this?"

"C'mon, Isabel." Valerie dangled the phone in front of her. "Just listen to it."

Valerie dialed the voicemail and hit the prompts until Alex's message was about to start. She put it against Isabel's ear and watched Isabel's unreadable expression closely. But when it was over, she frowned.

"Valerie, I don't doubt for a second that he misses you. But what exactly is it that you're supposed to not give up on? The possibility that he may one day be able to be with just one woman? That's pretty selfish, don't you think?"

Valerie listened and watched as Isabel gathered her things from the counter. She followed her into her room and sat on the bed while Isabel put every little thing back in its place. She even had a holder on her dresser for her sunglasses.

"So you really don't think it's any different than all the other times?"

"Honey, the only difference is that you've stuck to your guns longer this time than all the others and most importantly, that he knows you're seeing someone else now. He's probably missing you more than he ever has before, and you can hear it in his voice. But I wouldn't get my hopes up."

Isabel was right, and Valerie knew it. After chatting for a while longer, she forced herself to get ready for her dinner with Luke. She remembered the way he kissed her today. She hadn't felt much, but he definitely knew what he was doing. Maybe tonight wouldn't be so bad.

~*~

Friday nights weren't as busy as the weekend. But Alex was helping out in the kitchen, because two of his cooks had called in. This wasn't the first time these two had called in on a Friday night. He'd find replacements for those two bums soon enough.

He walked out of the kitchen and into the office. Angel was in there, working on the computer. Alex looked around to make sure Sarah wasn't within earshot. He'd been dying to ask all week, and he couldn't hold back anymore. "Sarah here?"

Angel looked up at him. "No, why?"

"Has she said anything about Valerie?"

"Yeah, I thought Sal told you. They accepted the offer. Escrow opened up today."

Sal had told him, but that's not what Alex wanted to know. "Yeah he did. I already made an appointment for the contractor to come out when it closes to give us an estimate on the work and how long it's going to take."

"Cool," Angel turned back to the computer. "Valerie found us this place over by the marina for the restaurant. Sarah fell in love with the location. Check this out."

Angel moved over so Alex could see the pictures on the screen. Angel scrolled through shots of an abandoned old seafood restaurant, but it was right on the marina. That's usually all that was out there, seafood. Top quality too. Alex wasn't sure how well their Mexican cuisine would hold up on the marina, although they did have quite a bit of seafood on their menu.

"The Marina? Isn't that going to be pricey?"

Angel glanced back at him. "Valerie says we could get a good deal because it needs so much work. We'll get a good price, but we'll have our hands full getting it up to code. Best part about it is it's for sale. So we wouldn't be leasing. We'd be buying."

Just hearing her name did things to Alex. He stared at the pictures a little longer, trying to focus on that instead. The place was going to need a major overhaul. "What did pops say?"

"He hasn't seen it. We're taking him out there tomorrow."

Alex shrugged. "You should have Sal go with you guys too."

"I'll let him know we're going."

Angel clicked on a few more pictures on the screen, and Alex made small talk about the place. Then he finally walked away. He stopped just before walking out.

"Did Valerie say anything else to Sarah?"

Angel glanced back at him. "About what?"

"You know, about that guy she's seeing."

Angel turned his attention back to the computer. "No, not really."

Alex frowned. He wasn't one of those guys, so he wasn't about to keep asking. If Angel knew anything, he'd tell him. He'd just have to wait until the rehearsal dinner.

He started back out when Angel spoke up. "I'm not sure because she didn't actually tell me, but I overheard Sarah on the phone last night. It sounded like Valerie was telling her about him."

"Yeah, what did you hear?"

Angel looked up, trying to remember. Something seemed to come to him, but he hesitated. "I don't think you wanna hear it, Alex. I know I wouldn't."

Alex squeezed the doorway with his hand. What the hell could he have heard? "Tell me."

Angel shook his head and looked back at the monitor. "Only reason it caught my attention was because I overheard Sarah ask her something about wearing lingerie."

Alex felt the hair on the back of his neck rise, and his gut tightened. He banged his fist against the doorway. He didn't need to hear any more. Angel had been right: that's the last thing he needed right now. He charged back out of the office, infuriated with himself. Why the fuck had he asked?

"I told you." He heard Angel yell from the office.

Yeah, he did. Alex should have listened. Angel was just like him when it came to his Sarah.

~*~

Dinner had actually been better than Valerie expected. Maybe it was just because hearing Alex's message distracted her so much, but she actually skipped lunch, and she'd been starving. Whatever the reason, she wolfed her food down in minutes. Luke laughed as usual, impressed by how much she could take in for such a dainty woman.

"Oh, I almost forgot." Luke said as Valerie worked on her cheesecake dessert.

He got up and took an envelope from the top of the refrigerator. He handed it to Valerie.

"What's this?"

"Open it."

She did. It was a brochure to a weekend-long George Stone real estate seminar held at one of La Jolla's most upscale resorts. She opened the brochure, and there were two tickets in it. Valerie couldn't help but smile. She leaned over and kissed him.

"Thank you."

Purposely, she kept the kiss to a soft peck, but he leaned over and kissed her again. Only his kiss was much longer, and he licked her bottom lip when he was done.

"Since it's two days, I got us a suite there. We can make a weekend out of it."

Valerie gulped, hoping he didn't notice and forced a smile. "I heard that place is really nice."

"Oh, it's awesome. I've had meetings there a few times but never actually stayed there."

Later in the evening after a few glasses of wine, they danced on the romantic terrace that overlooked his backyard. This was the first time she'd been to his place, and as expected, it was lavish. The backyard resembled a resort with a huge pool and outdoor kitchen. He said it was all about the investment. A single man obviously didn't need such a big home. Resale value is what he was looking at when he'd bought it.

She thought of Alex's simple, more unassuming house. Alex said the more house he had, the more there was to clean, and he was hardly ever home, so what was the point? Valerie knew as modest as his place was, it was still expensive because of the area he lived in.

Luke promised her the grand tour later, and she had a feeling what room the tour would end in. He was already being more passionate than usual, and he'd started to call her "honey." But it didn't sound like when Isabel or her dad called her that. With Isabel it was like having your older sister say it, even though they were the same age. The way Luke said it felt intimate.

Luke kissed her neck as they danced slowly, and squeezed her a little tighter. Then he kissed her lips. Valerie focused more than usual on trying to enjoy it. She felt him start to breathe heavier as their tongues intertwined faster. His hand lowered on her back and caressed her behind softly.

"Do you know how long you've been driving me crazy?" He gasped between kisses.

Valerie shook her head. She didn't want to know. It was hard enough trying to enjoy the moment without thinking about Alex. Now he was going to add guilt to the mix?

He stopped dancing and kissed her with more aggression. Thrusting his tongue deep in her mouth, his hand slid up her blouse and caressed her breast. Surprised that she was beginning to feel a little aroused, Valerie closed her eyes and let herself go with it. She welcomed his tongue and kissed him back with just as much passion, even biting his lip softly.

In a flash, he picked her up. She instantly wrapped her legs around his waist, causing her skirt to lift. His hands squeezed her behind as she continued to kiss him, even as he walked into the house. She held his face in her hands, kissing him with the kind of yearning she only ever felt with Alex. Her heart raced. She closed her eyes tightly, excited by the unexpected enjoyment of it.

By the time they reached his bed, she was fully ready to go to the next step, and it thrilled her. They fumbled, undressing each other partially while still trying to keep their mouths together. She fell back on the bed, and he fell on her. He took her naked breast in his mouth while she ran her frantic fingers through his hair.

"I want you so bad." His strained voice was barely understandable.

She was so incredibly aroused at this point she could barely muster up the words herself. "I want you too, Alex."

Luke froze then jerked his face away from her breast. Valerie's eyes flew open, and her hand flew to her mouth, covering it as if that would take back what she'd just said. Mortified, she tried desperately to understand what just happened. Alex's words rang in her head. *Please tell me you haven't given up on us.*

CHAPTER 10

Luke stared at her. "Alex?"

Valerie moved away from him slowly. "I'm sorry ... I don't ..."

He moved off her, and she sat up pulling the sheet over herself. "I'm so sorry, Luke. I didn't mean—"

"The guy I met outside the club?"

Valerie nodded and climbed off the bed with the sheet around her, feeling like a complete idiot. She didn't even want to look at him. Her hand instinctively flew to her face for a second.

"Is there something you want to tell me?" His demeanor was unusually calm. She could only imagine the reaction she'd get if she ever called Alex by another name in bed.

"I was seeing him for a long time. I haven't been with anyone else since." She looked away, still trying to grasp what had just happened.

She finally turned back to him again. His expression had turned to stone. "You were real quiet that whole night. You still have feelings for him?"

Her eyes went from the bed to the door. Maybe she could make a run for it.

"Talk to me, Valerie. You said you'd be honest."

"I *was* honest." She maintained. "I didn't lie when I said I wasn't seeing anyone else."

Luke motioned for her to take a seat on the bed.

She shook her head.

"C'mon Valerie. This is dumb. I'm not going to stand here, talking to you with the bed between us. At least sit down."

She sat down slowly, clutching the sheet in front of her. She'd never regretted being somewhere so much in her life. The absurd thought of flying out the window crossed her mind.

"So are you going to answer the question?" Luke sat on the edge of his side of the bed. "You still have feelings for him?"

For a second, she thought about lying and then thought better of it. She may as well come clean. Worst that could happen is he'd want to stop seeing her, and she actually hoped he would.

"I thought I was over him." She whispered.

He was quiet for a moment. "I see."

"But it's not like I've done anything with him recently. It's just taking me a lot longer than I thought to get over it." That was putting it lightly.

"How long has it been?"

"Over a year." She chewed her lip.

Luke grabbed a pillow and put it between him and the backboard. He made himself comfortable. "Well looks like we have time to talk now. So tell me about it."

Valerie couldn't believe he actually wanted to hear about it. She shrugged, making herself a little more comfortable and leaned against the backboard too. "I've known him since high school. We'd been on and off ever since. But it's been off for good now for over a year."

"Can I ask who broke it off the last time?"

"That's the thing." Valerie felt ridiculous. "We've never actually been an official couple. He's never been able to commit to a relationship. He always has a million things going on: school, his business. He played college football for a while there, until he got hurt. Then he had a ton of therapy he had to go through. But mostly …" She frowned unable to believe she felt like crying. "Mostly he just can't commit. I finally accepted it and moved on. I'm just not over him yet."

"What kind of business does he have?"

Of course that would be the only thing Luke would get hung up on.

"A restaurant. It's his family's, but he's taking over now, and he's been real busy with it." She paused, still feeling guilty. She didn't want to say too much, but she felt he at least deserved an explanation. "My cousin, Sarah, is marrying his brother. I hadn't seen him in over a year, but when I had to go the wedding shower a few weeks ago, I saw him there. I just hadn't realized until then that …"

"Listen." He reached across the bed and put his hand over hers. "I know what it's like to have feelings for someone who's not exactly reciprocating."

He gave her a half smile. Here Valerie hadn't thought it wasn't possible to feel any guiltier than she did already.

"Give it time. I'll be patient. I've had a taste of what may happen someday, and let me tell you, it's worth the wait."

Valerie yawned then smiled. No way would she continue this act with Luke. She owed it to him to be honest, but not tonight.

"Why don't you stay here tonight? I promise I won't try anything." He squeezed her hand. "I know where your heart is now, and I'll respect that. But it's too late, and we've both been drinking."

Valerie did feel tired. The effects of the wine had really kicked in. "But I didn't bring anything to sleep in." She had. But that piece of lingerie would definitely not make an appearance tonight.

Luke stood up and walked over to his dresser. Valerie felt funny, seeing him in his boxer briefs. At least he wasn't naked. He held a white t-shirt in one hand and a pair of shorts in the other. "Will this do?"

She nodded. He tossed them on the bed. "I'll give you some privacy. Be back in a few."

Valerie didn't have to wait too long to find out if they'd be sleeping in the same bed. He climbed in less than fifteen minutes later. He asked if he could hold her and nothing more. Valerie let him. She fell asleep with him spooning her. It was actually nice and just like earlier, she'd imagined he was Alex. This time it was a conscious choice. Alex's arms were much bigger, but it brought back memories of his holding her nonetheless.

***

Isabel was busy vacuuming when Valerie walked in with her shoes in her hands. She stopped the second she saw Valerie. The huge smile on her face was very telling of what she must've been thinking.

"No, nothing happened."

Isabel's smile dissolved. "But you spent the night."

"It was a nightmare." Valerie plopped on the sofa.

"What happened?"

"We were in his bed. Things were getting pretty hot and …" Valerie put her face in her hands.

"And what?" Isabel sat across from her.

Valerie looked up at her and winced. "I called him Alex."

Isabel's eyes opened wide. "Valerie, you didn't!"

Valerie fell back into the sofa. She stared at the ceiling. "I did. Isabel what the hell is the matter with me?"

"What did he say?"

"He was actually very understanding, which only made me feel worse. I think I would've felt a little better if he'd told me off."

Isabel started laughing. "Wow. So why'd you spend the night?"

Valerie told her the whole thing, as usual not leaving a single detail out and then added, "I'm breaking things off on Monday."

"What? Why?"

Isabel had started making coffee halfway through Valerie's story. They were both in the kitchen now, and Isabel poured two cups. She handed one to Valerie and leaned against the counter. Valerie sat on the barstool at the counter.

"I can't keep stringing him along. Last night was just further proof that I'm in no way ready for a relationship. I'm a mess. It's not fair to him."

"What are you going to tell him?"

Valerie shrugged and drank some of her coffee. She wasn't sure what she'd say. Whatever she did say, she knew Luke would try to convince her otherwise. But she was done faking it. Every kiss was so forced, and she knew it would get even worse now.

"The truth, I guess." She said. "I'll be gentle though and not mention that the only time he managed to turn me on was when I was imagining he was Alex."

Isabel smiled, tilting her head. "Maybe after the wedding, when you don't have to think about seeing Alex anymore, it'll get easier."

Valerie got up and started toward her room. "I hope so, Isabel, 'cause this sucks."

She decided she was going to have a lazy weekend: take a shower, read, then maybe work on the painting some more—anything to keep her mind off Alex. God, she felt pathetic.

She thought of perhaps making a date with her handy Mr. Perfect later that night then thought better of it. That, if anything, would probably bring the most vivid thoughts of Alex. Well hell, Alex was going to be the cause of yet another break up.

***

Monday came fast enough, and Valerie had only one thing on her mind. She was breaking things off with Luke, no stalling.

She needed a clean break before things got any heavier. She didn't want to ruin their work relationship, although she knew it would be damaged.

Valerie had uptime, meaning she answered the office phone and any leads that came in were hers. The whole office rotated. Monday mornings were hers. She liked having Monday morning uptime. Anyone that had been out during the weekend looking at homes would be calling. The phones were busy, and she was glad for the distraction.

She would take a couple more calls before she took a break and went to talk to Luke. The next call she took, she was sitting back in her chair, but it straightened her right up from the moment she answered.

"So you're really doing the boss now huh, Val?"

Unbelievable, even after being knocked out, Bruce was still following her?

"Are you going to need your other eye swollen shut too?"

"That was a sucker punch, and you know it. That asshole better watch his back or—"

Valerie hung up on him. She wouldn't give him the pleasure. The phone rang again. Either she picked it up, or someone else would. She took a deep breath and answered again.

"Do you want me telling everyone in that office about you and the boss?"

"Whatever floats your boat." Valerie did her best to sound unconcerned. "You're not bullying me into giving in to you."

"All I want is a little time alone with you so we can talk. I have a lot to tell you. It's all I wanted that night."

The skin on her arms immediately prickled with goose bumps. What could he possibly say that he hadn't already said? There was no way Valerie would be alone with this psycho. No way would she give him any more of her time.

But what if he did start calling the office telling everyone about her and Luke?

"I'm listening."

"In person."

"No."

"Valerie, it's going to happen. Why not do this the easy way?"

"Are you threatening me?"

Bruce chuckled. "Take it however you want, just consider yourself warned. I tried being nice."

"I'm agreeing to talk to you on the phone. Take it or leave it."

Bruce lowered his voice. "Was making love to a man who wanted you and only you exciting?"

Valerie squeezed her eyes shut. She wasn't bringing Bruce into her private life. Obviously, he knew she'd spent the night but didn't know what really happened. Still maybe this would work to her advantage. "Yes, Bruce it was. I'm in love and finally happy. Can you respect that?"

The line went dead. Valerie took a deep breath and ran her hands over her arms. She gave it a few minutes in case the phone rang again. When it didn't ring for a while, she stood up, and leaned into the cubicle next to her as she walked by. "I'm taking a break, so go ahead and answer the main line if it rings."

Andrew, the agent in the cubicle, nodded and gave her the thumbs up as he sipped his coffee.

She was still thinking about what Bruce had said when she walked into Luke's office. Her expression must have looked as anxious as she was feeling because Luke immediately asked if something was wrong.

"I don't think it's going to work out." She stood awkwardly in the middle of his office.

"What's not going to work out?"

"Me and you. I have too much going on in my head right now. I don't think it's fair to you."

Luke leaned back in his chair and fiddled with his pen. "Don't use me as an excuse, Valerie. I told you I'm willing to be patient."

Valerie shifted her weight from one leg to the other, beginning to wonder why she'd gotten out of bed that morning. "Okay, I'm just not ready for a relationship right now. And to be honest, I really don't think this is a good idea." She gestured toward the door. "If anyone out there gets wind of us, it's not gonna to be pretty. I think it's best we just remain friends."

Valerie wished he would just agree so she could get out of there already. But the expression on his face said otherwise.

"I disagree. I think you *are* ready for a relationship, obviously not a sexual one … yet. But as I said, I'm willing to wait." He tossed his pen on the desk. "As far as anyone finding out, how would they?"

Only because Bruce calling the office again was a definite possibility, she decided to fill him in on it. She explained briefly the latest incidents she had with Bruce and the phone call she just received. Luke wasn't happy.

"I could care less about him calling here and saying anything, but maybe you should think about getting a restraining order on the guy. He sounds dangerous."

Valerie nodded, hoping that was the end of it. "I still think you're making a mistake about us, Valerie. I really wish you'd reconsider."

No way was she having this conversation again. "No, I'm sure, Luke. I'm sorry. I really think it's best this way. I hope this doesn't affect our business relationship. I'll get the tickets to the seminar back to you tomorrow."

She started toward the door, angry she forgot them. He had her hold on to them for safekeeping. She planned to avoid any private conversations with him from here on. Giving him the tickets back would inevitably incite one. Maybe she could mail them to him.

"Keep your ticket, Val. I know how much you want to see him. It was a gift. I don't want it back. You can have the suite too if you want."

Valerie turned around, his wounded tone adding to her guilt. "Thanks. I'll get your ticket back to you, but I'll pass on the suite. You probably still have time to cancel it."

She packed up and headed out. From here on, she'd be spending a lot of her time outside of the office, at least for a while.

***

More than week passed since Valerie broke things off with Luke. She managed to stay busy out of the office the whole time. After another busy day of showing properties, she was on her way home when Sarah called her.

"Hey, Sarah."

"Valerie, please tell me you don't have plans for this weekend."

The only plans Valerie had were to sit and veg in front of the television, and as usual work on the painting.

"Why?"

"Answer the question."

Valerie was cautious. "Not anything solid."

"Good, since Romero and Eric didn't get to do their stupid bachelor party," Sarah giggled, "the guys came up with something else."

Valerie couldn't help sniggering herself. She remembered Sarah calling her, worried about the guys planning a bachelor party in Vegas. With Angel not really being a drinker, she wasn't sure how he would handle himself drunk around strippers.

Valerie had come to the rescue. She had a plan that would have Angel canceling his own party. The thought of Alex around a bunch of money hungry whores didn't sit well with her either. Knowing Sofia couldn't be too thrilled about

Eric taking off to Vegas and partying with a bunch of strippers, she gave her a call. Valerie made sure to clue her in and asked her to lay it on thick about Sarah's bachelorette party when she mentioned it around Angel.

Well lay it on she did. The next day, Sarah called Valerie. She laughed so hard Valerie could barely understand her. She told her about Angel overhearing her and Sofia talking about the party and the hot "cop" that would be making an appearance to frisk the bride-to-be. Angel had immediately taken her aside to propose canceling both parties. Sarah and Valerie still got a good laugh about it. This should be interesting. "What did they come up with?"

"Well, since everything has been so formal up until now, they want just friends, no older folks, no distant family members. Just a younger crowd of singles getting together casually to enjoy one of our lasts weekends being single."

Valerie had to smile. Sarah had been far from single ever since Angel had staked his claim on her in high school. But she didn't say anything.

"That actually sounds kind of nice." Then it hit her. Alex would be there. "Wait."

"No, no wait. I know what you're going to say."

"Sarah, you don't understand. It's so hard to be around him."

"I know, sweetie, but he's Angel's brother. We can't *not* invite him. And you're my maid of honor, Val. It just wouldn't be the same without you. We're not even going to be in an enclosed space. It's going to be a bonfire at the beach for old times' sake."

Valerie sighed. "Okay, I guess."

"Yay! Are you bringing Luke?"

"No." She hesitated. "He'll be out of town this weekend."

As much as she trusted Sarah not to tell Alex she wasn't seeing Luke anymore, she had a feeling she told Angel everything. She still needed to arm herself with at least a fake boyfriend if she had to be around Alex. The restaurant incident had proved just how weak her resistance to him still was. She still didn't trust that she wouldn't give in if he tried to talk her into even one night with him.

CHAPTER 11

When she got home, Isabel was in the kitchen, cooking. It smelled delicious. Valerie's eyes grew wide, and she smiled excitedly. "Are you making *albondigas*?" It was one of Isabel's specialties and Valerie's favorite Mexican meatball soup. She hadn't made it in a while.

Isabel smiled at her. "I kind of made Romero mad. So when it was all said and done and he was over it, he said I owed him *albondigas*. I'd bragged once that my *albondigas* were to die for." She smiled at Valerie. "He's coming over for dinner."

"But you made enough for me too, right?" Valerie rushed over to peek into the soup Isabel was stirring.

Isabel laughed. "Of course. I told him they were your favorite. He said he's seen you eat and I better make enough for an army."

"Ha, ha." Valerie leaned against the counter. "So how'd you make him mad?"

Isabel made a face. "Well you know how I was telling you I've been trying to slow things down because I wasn't sure exactly how serious he was?"

"Yeah?"

"A few nights ago, he asked me about my family. I told him a little about them. He was really impressed." Isabel stopped to taste the soup.

Valerie wasn't surprised Romero was impressed. She sure had been when Isabel first told her about her insanely accomplished siblings. Isabel was the only one that didn't have a master's degree, but then she was the youngest and was still working on it. Her oldest sister Patricia was always on her about it.

"So yesterday," Isabel continued, "I was on the phone with my sister, Pat, at Romero's place. I didn't think he was listening to my conversation. I told her I was home, getting ready to take a shower. When I hung up, he called me on it. Asked why I lied about where I was." Isabel shrugged. "I didn't really have an answer. So then he asked if I'd even told her about him."

Valerie watched Isabel sprinkle some more cumin into the soup and waited. Isabel turned to her and bit her lip. "I haven't."

"Why?"

"I don't need to hear what I know she's going to say."

"What's that?" Valerie had a feeling she knew. Patricia hadn't even liked Lawrence, the professor. It wasn't just because he was an idiot. It was because she felt he wasn't ambitious enough. She thought that at his age he should own his own place by now, not still be living in an apartment.

Isabel rolled her eyes. "You know what she's like. Romero doesn't have a degree. He works security at events and bars."

Valerie frowned. "But he's not just a security guard he owns the company."

Isabel shook her head. "It won't matter. I promise. She'll say he's beneath me regardless. I can already hear her."

That made Valerie mad. Romero was a hard-working honest guy and now proving that the word commitment was actually in his vocabulary, unlike some people she knew. "You didn't tell him all that, right?"

Isabel shook her head. "No. I just admitted I hadn't told her about him yet."

"What did he say?"

"At first not a lot, but I could tell he was hurt. Then he asked who I *have* told in my family. He hears me on the phone with them all the time, so he knows how close I am to all of them. So when I said I hadn't told any of them, that's when things got heated." Isabel sighed. "I told him he hadn't been real clear about what *we* were exactly. I didn't want to tell them anything until I was sure. Then he really blew up. He couldn't believe that all this time I didn't consider us to be in a relationship. He started asking if I was still going out with other people. He made a really huge deal out of that and kept asking if I was sure about this or not."

Valerie couldn't help laughing. "I hope you said you were."

Isabel stirred the soup some more. "Of course I am." She turned to Valerie. For the first time, Valerie saw the worry in Isabel's eyes. "I really am, but this is going to be tough. My family is so nit picky about this kind of stuff, and Romero holds nothing back. They're going to butt heads. I'm not looking forward to it."

Valerie rubbed Isabel's back. "Well if they really care about you, they'll just have to accept it." It hadn't hit Valerie until this conversation. "I think you've really fallen for him, Isabel."

Isabel's expression said it all. She definitely had. Before the shower, she would've never imagined Isabel with Romero. This proved the theory even further. Opposites did attract. Isabel had told her sleeping with Romero was different than with any other guy she'd been with. Valerie got the feeling she was holding back the juicy details because Isabel felt bad for Valerie. She knew the struggle Valerie had, just trying to get so much as a flicker out of Luke's kisses. Judging from Isabel's past experiences with all the uptight guys she usually dated, she was probably enjoying the best sex of her life.

"Did you hear about this weekend?"

Valerie groaned. "Yes."

"You'll be okay. Romero just told me about it today." Now Isabel's eyes were the sympathetic ones. "I'll be there with you."

Valerie pulled a bowl out of the cabinet. "Is that almost ready? I need comfort food."

"Yeah, it's done."

Valerie served herself a big helping just as the doorbell rang. She took her bowl to her room to give Romero and Isabel some privacy. Isabel insisted she didn't have to, but Valerie wanted to be alone. This week would to be hell, having to prepare herself mentally all over again to see Alex. She'd be back for more soup that was for sure.

~*~

Feeling like a damn nervous teenage kid, Alex approached Sarah as she filled salt and pepper shakers. The restaurant hadn't opened yet, and Angel wasn't due to arrive for a couple of hours. This wasn't a conversation he wanted to have in front of him. He almost stopped and turned around but forced himself to keep walking. She looked up. Her big green eyes sparkled when she smiled. Angel was a lucky guy. He resisted telling her for the millionth time how beautiful her eyes were only because Angel wasn't around; otherwise, riling Angel by flirting with his soon to be sister-in-law was one of his most entertaining pastimes.

"Hey." She picked up a few shakers. "Need some?"

"No, actually, I just wanted to talk to you if you have a minute."

He had no intentions about confessing the truth to Sarah about the tutor … for now. All he wanted now was to find out more about Valerie and Luke. He needed a little insight before this weekend. Maybe if he knew a little more, he'd know at least if he even had a chance of winning her back.

"Sure." Sarah stopped what she was doing and searched his eyes. "Something wrong?"

"Not really. I was just wondering …" Annoyed as hell, he brushed his sweaty palm on his pants. "How serious is Valerie about this guy she's seeing?"

Sarah's expression changed, and her eyebrow went up. "Why, Alex?"

Alex lifted a shoulder. "I'm curious."

"I hope you're not planning on toying with her again." She went back to filling a saltshaker.

"Toying? I never toyed with her."

Sarah stopped and looked at him. "Are you kidding me?"

"Look I know what it looked like, but believe it or not, I cared about Valerie. I still do." Saying he cared about her didn't even begin to cover all the emotions he felt for her now.

Sarah's expression softened. "I've always known you did. That's why I could never figure out the things you did. Why would you hurt her like that?"

"It was never my intention." He glanced away. "I just … It was complicated."

He turned back to her and just like that, Sarah's expression was rigid again.

"It's a long story, Sarah. But you have to believe me when I say I do care about her. I need to know if there's even a chance of us working things out." He reached over and placed his hand on hers. "Can you help me out here?"

Sarah pressed her lips together. "I'm not sure she'd be okay with me divulging that kind of information, especially to you."

Alex frowned "Well, I'm not asking for any secrets, just your opinion. Do you think she's really into him?"

With a sigh, Sarah gave in. "It's only been a few weeks that I know of. But she's known him for quite some time. She works with him, so I can only assume she got to know him pretty well before getting *involved*."

The emphasis on that final word was like sandpaper to an open wound. Alex stared at her hard, not wanting to speak for his words would surely boom. As much as he had wanted details earlier, he didn't want to hear another word. Never in his life had he felt so damn tormented.

Luke wasn't someone Valerie had just met a few weeks ago. She'd known the guy for *quite some time*. They had an established relationship and were now i*nvolved.* This was so much worst than he thought.

"Thanks, sweetheart." He began to walk away. As much as it hurt to admit it, he was probably too late.

"Alex."

Alex stopped but didn't want to turn around. He couldn't stomach the sympathy in her eyes any longer.

"Look at me."

Grudgingly, he turned to face her. The sympathy replaced by a determined glare.

"You promise you're not just looking to play with her?"

"What do you mean? I never—."

"Promise." Sarah raised her voice. If he hadn't been so enraged still about the thought of Valerie and Luke's *involvement,* he might've been amused by sweet Sarah's sudden hardnosed demeanor. "Of course, I promise."

She said nothing for a moment, just stared at him as if she still wasn't completely persuaded. "Don't you dare tell her I told you this, Alex Moreno."

He nodded but said nothing, wondering where this was going.

"She puts up a good act sometimes like she's really moving on with this guy." She paused, giving Alex time to grind his teeth. Hearing about Valerie moving on wasn't exactly what he was expecting when she made him promise. "I can tell she's trying really hard to get over you. But I think if you try hard enough, she'd be more than willing to give it another shot." She took one resolute foot forward. "But I swear, Alex, if you hurt her again, I will never forgive you."

The tiniest sliver of light, escaped through the storm cloud that had loomed over his head for weeks. He walked back toward Sarah and hugged her nice and tight. “Don’t worry. I don’t break my promises. Ask anyone.”

That’s all the encouragement he needed. He’d get Valerie to hear him out one way or another.

~*~

That week, the office received a couple of calls from someone saying that Valerie was getting special treatment because she was *doing* the manager. Two different people had taken the calls and brought it to Luke’s attention.

There was no doubt about who made the calls. Valerie wanted to kill him. She was definitely going to look into getting a restraining order on Bruce, possibly even sue for defamation. She started getting a definite feeling she was being followed, but she was more angry about it than creeped out.

Of course, Luke denied the accusations made on the calls, but some people in the office were beginning to look at her differently. Valerie wanted to believe she imagined it. She was so mad at herself for getting involved with either Bruce or Luke in the first place. She’d worked too hard to have people believe she was sleeping her way to success.

Twice this week, she got into it with Luke for things she thought he was doing to save face. He sided with another agent in the morning meeting about something she knew she was right about, then later he claimed he misunderstood.

“Why are you here so late?” Luke startled Valerie. She was deep in thought when he stuck his head in her cubicle.

She looked up at him. “I was just finishing up writing up a counter offer.”

“Another one? That’s great.”

She smiled but wasn’t feeling it. She hadn’t talked to Luke in a couple of days and thought maybe he was still angry about her calling him out about the meeting incident. She hadn’t been very nice about it.

"So you're done?"

Valerie glanced up at him again and then around at her messy station. "Yeah, just about."

"Listen, Val. What do you say we go grab a drink—kind of a peace offering?"

Valerie shook her head but smiled. "No, I don't think so."

She stood up and began gathering things to stuff in her briefcase.

"Why not?"

"Because I don't think us going out in the first place was ever a good idea. We both knew it would be frowned upon, and now look what's happening."

"C'mon Val, since when can't two colleagues get together for a drink after work? I know a place that serves the best peach Mojitos. Ever been to Moreno's?"

Valerie's face shot up from her briefcase, expecting to see a smirk on his face, but he was serious. It took a moment, but then she couldn't help laughing. "You wanna take me to Moreno's?"

"Yeah, why's that so funny?"

Valerie pictured herself walking in there with Luke while maybe Angel or possibly even Alex waited on them and laughed even harder.

"What?" Luke obviously didn't get it, but he seemed pleased with her sudden change in mood.

She hadn't laughed so hard in a very long time. When she was finally composed enough, she wiped the sides of her eyes. She'd been so uptight lately she actually felt some of the tension release. "You know what? I think I will have that drink with you after all, only not at Moreno's."

Valerie was starving as usual, so they went to an all-you-can-eat sushi bar. She began to give him a vague explanation about Moreno's and then decided just to tell him the truth. They weren't seeing each other anymore, so what did it matter?

Luke took it in stride and didn't ask any more questions. He teased her about the amount of food she could put away as usual. They talked about the seminar that Valerie had no intention of canceling. She was counting on George Stone to pull her out of this mood.

Luke wasn't the wittiest. He was a bit too on the uptight side for that. Maybe it was that she was already in a giggly mood from his invitation to Moreno's, but she laughed a lot throughout dinner.

In the end, she was glad she went. It was nice not to think about Bruce or Alex for at least a few hours.

***

First thing Friday morning Valerie got a call on her private extension from Bruce. "You must not care too much about your reputation in that office. Do you?"

Valerie stood up. "Your calls are doing nothing to change what anyone here thinks about me. Everyone thinks you're a psycho idiot. You're not taken seriously, Bruce."

"You better watch what you say to me, Valerie. I swear to God I'll make you regret it." His tone was much harsher than she heard before, and it sent a chill up her spine.

"You don't scare me, Bruce." She lied. "I saw what you were made of at the club. Why don't you just do us both a favor and get a damn life? I want *nothing* to do with you and never will."

"I *had* a life, darling, a good one, until you ruined it. Remember that!"

Valerie squeezed her eyes shut. He was going to blame her forever. "You ruined your own—"

"Tell me something, darling. Is Luke the first man you've been in love with?"

Jesus, for someone who thought he knew so much, he had no idea how far from the truth he was. Apparently, he fell for her story. Hadn't he noticed she wasn't seeing him anymore?

"Yes." She kept her eyes closed, concentrating hard on sounding as sincere as she could. Not wanting anyone in the office to hear her, her voice was barely a whisper. "I've never felt for anyone the way I feel about him."

"But you broke up with him. Why?"

Her eyes bolted open. How could he know? She heard his maniacal laughter low at first then louder with more conviction. The line suddenly went dead. Squeezing the receiver, she stood there even after the dial tone started blaring in her ear. With a deep breath, she hung it up. She had enough on her mind than to add this to her plate.

Valerie was out of the office most of the day, showing properties and meeting with potential clients. Managing to keep her mind off Bruce, she went back to the office and worked for a while before finally calling it a night.

It was already getting dark, and she walked quickly through the empty parking lot. Her briefcase weighed heavily on her shoulder, and the stack of files she carried rendered her completely vulnerable if anyone approached her. She thought she heard footsteps behind her but decided she was just being paranoid. Still, she picked up her step, feeling her heart beat a little faster. She'd almost reached her car when she heard the footsteps again.

"Hey, Valerie."

Valerie jumped and half the files she held dropped to the floor.

CHAPTER 12

"I'm sorry, Val. I didn't mean to startle you." Alex felt terrible. He was down immediately on one knee, retrieving the papers she'd dropped.

"Oh my God." She put down the stuff she managed to hold on to on the trunk of her car and then leaned against it. Her hand clenched her chest. "My heart almost stopped, Alex."

"I can see that," Alex glanced up at her from where he finished gathering her things. "I'm sorry. Why you working so late anyway? I was beginning to think maybe you got a ride home and just left your car overnight." Among many other infuriating things he'd been imagining she could be engaged in at this late hour in an empty office. He'd been this close to barging in there to find out for himself.

"I've been swamped all week." She was still catching her breath.

Alex stood up, holding the files in his hands. He glanced at them and hoped her getting them in order wasn't what had kept her at work so late. They were a mess.

His eyes roamed as they always did when he saw her. She looked fantastic. The gray skirt suit she wore made her blond highlights seem brighter, and it brought out the sparkle in her big dark eyes—eyes that were entirely too frightened still. He frowned, knowing he'd been the cause.

He held on to the files while she opened her trunk and noticed her hands trembled when he handed them to her. "You all right?"

She nodded but didn't say a word. He handed her the rest of the files. When she closed the trunk, she finally glanced at him. Alex noticed her eyes glimmered. Had he really scared her that bad?

"Are you crying?"

She shook her head and let out a laugh. "You just scared the hell out of me. That's all."

Alex looked around at the empty parking lot and pressed his lips together. "Well, it is pretty dangerous you being out here so late and all alone. You really—"

"No, it's not that. I work late all the time. It's just that, well, nothing. I've just been a mess lately." She leaned against her car and tilted her head slightly. "So why are you here?"

Alex stared at her, wondering why she was so jumpy. Was that idiot still harassing her? Then he thought about her question. "I wanted to talk to you."

He hadn't been able to wait until tomorrow. There was always the possibility she'd show up with Luke and ruin the whole bonfire idea. He knew it was a risk. But the last few weeks had been the most agonizing weeks of his life. So he decided he'd take his chances.

Her expression was unreadable, and she didn't say anything for few moments. "About what, Alex?" She finally asked.

"I know you're with someone now." His own words were hurt. "But I thought maybe you could hear me out." For once, she didn't avoid his eyes. She stared right at him. "Can we go somewhere and talk? I can buy you a drink. It's the least I can do after scaring the hell outta you." He smiled and thought he saw the corner of her lip lift a little. "Might help calm the nerves?"

To his surprise, she agreed and rather quickly. "But just one. And we'll have to take two cars. I can't leave mine here."

"I can bring you back, and we'll pick it up later."

Valerie shook her head. "There's nothing around here. We'd have to drive all the way back."

"Or we can drop off your car at your place."

The expression she made at that was a strange one. She seemed almost alarmed. "No," she said firmly and walked around to get in her car. "Just follow me. I know a good place we can talk."

Alex followed her and thought about the uncompromising attitude she had when it came to dropping off her car. Was there someone there that wouldn't be pleased, seeing her get in his car? He rolled his neck and tried cracking it. Something that always helped calm him even if only a little. He didn't want to blow it tonight with his temper, so he took a deep breath before getting out of his truck.

The place Valerie picked was a trendy pizza and brewery place. Alex smiled as they walked in. He knew she would pick a place with food.

They picked a booth in the corner. It was Friday night, so it was already packed, and there was a Padres game on the big screen. Some of the people watching the game were pretty loud. Not exactly the atmosphere he'd hoped for, but it would have to do.

"As much as I scared you, I thought you'd want a place where you can get a shot."

"Oh, they serve shots here." She grinned.

The waitress came over and looked at Alex, but he gave Valerie the go ahead with a gesture. She never disappointed when it came to ordering food.

"We'll have the large meat lovers, deep dish, a large order of wings, extra ranch, and I'll have schooner of Amber Bach and shot of Patron."

The server turned to Alex and took his order of drink. He ordered the same minus the shot. He needed a clear head tonight.

When the waitress was gone, Valerie pulled her phone out of her purse, looked through it for a moment, then put it back in her purse. That alone made Alex edgy. Was she checking for calls from her boyfriend?

"So let's have it." She said and again looked him straight in the eye. "What made you show up at my work and wait 'til I got out? You've never done that before. I'm curious now."

Alex drew a blank on all the stuff he rehearsed in the car while he waited for her. But he was glad he had her full attention. He was about to start when the waitress brought over their drinks. They thanked her, and she quickly walked away.

Valerie took the shot. His train of thought went off course again when she sucked the lime wedge and licked her lips. "I needed that." Her hoarse voice didn't help either.

Alex shifted in his seat, trying to accommodate his expanding crotch. It annoyed him how effortlessly anything she did could impinge on him. No other woman had ever done that to him.

"Valerie," he finally managed. "I don't know how serious you are about this guy you're seeing, but I want you to know I can't stop thinking about you."

Her expression changed. She seemed *irritated*? That definitely wasn't what he was going for here. "What?"

"That's so typical of you, Alex" She took a sip of her beer. "Why do you think that is?"

"Think what is?"

"That you can't stop thinking about me?"

Why else? "Because I'm crazy about you."

She seemed stunned but only for a second. "You've done this the entire time I've known you."

"Done what?"

"Turn it off and on. I'll give you that you enjoy … *being* with me. You can't be that good of an actor, but I can't be like you, Alex. I can't just be with you then turn around and go out with others as if you're just another number in my contact list."

"Well, that's good to know, but I'm not like that either."

Valerie's sarcastic laugh was so loud the couple in the booth across from them glanced at them. Alex frowned and leaned in a bit, lowering his voice. "I'm not."

"Is this really what you brought me here to discuss? Because I'm sorry, but I've heard enough of your bullshit to last me a lifetime."

Alex reached across the table and took her hand in his. "Listen to me. The girl at my place *was* a tutor. I can get you proof of that. It wasn't the only time I needed to be tutored. I didn't want you to know what a hard time I was having in school. It was humiliating, okay?" He took a deep breath.

Valerie glared at him, "She had an overnight bag, Alex."

Alex's brain scrambled to remember. Then it came to him. No wonder she'd been so hysterical. "That was her book bag, Val. She did her school work too while she helped me with mine."

Valerie's eyes didn't waiver, but her expression softened a bit.

He continued quickly. "All those times I'd disappear on you was because I had some damn paper to finish or I was cramming for a test. I was having a hell of time keeping up. I couldn't afford to lose my scholarship. I had to keep the grades up. You've always been such a huge distraction. Half the time you were all I could think of."

The food arrived, and Alex had to take his hand back. Damn, he wished they had gone somewhere else. This was going to be one interruption after another. The waitress put out the plates and napkins. Valerie still stared at him.

"Anything else?" The waitress asked.

Valerie never took her eyes off him. Alex glanced at her then back at the waitress and smiled. "We're good, hon. Thanks."

He told her all about the past year: the restaurant renovations, the wedding planning, all the time his parents spent in Mexico, making his presence at the restaurant more demanding, and then about his grandpa's passing. She listened and ate, asking few questions while he explained his heart out.

"I heard about your grandpa. I'm sorry. I was going to call you but …"

"It's better that you didn't."

She stared at him, the lament deep in her eyes. "Why?"

"That wasn't a good time in my life. It was right after they told me I wouldn't play football anymore and I lost my scholarship. I wasn't the most pleasant person to be talking to those days."

He glanced away from Valerie's compassionate eyes. "I'm over it now but not over you."

Alex didn't eat very much. He'd done so much talking, yet the food was just about gone. He watched as Valerie drank the last of her beer and stared out into space.

"What are you thinking?"

Her eyes were back on him, devoid of any expression. "I don't know what to think."

"You want another beer?

She shook her head. "I want to go home."

This wasn't the mood he hoped she'd be in after spilling his guts. Maybe she *was* really into her new boyfriend. Maybe Sarah was wrong. Maybe he *was* too late. He swallowed hard.

Alex didn't want to add any more to his already sinking heart. But he had to know, now. Had to know if all hope was lost. "Are you in love with him, Val?"

Valerie glanced away quickly. He pressed his lips, wishing to hell he knew what that meant.

He reached for her hand. "Are you?" The panic in his voice surprised him. He wondered if she noticed. He didn't care anymore: to hell with his pride.

"No."

Relief drained through him. Alex hadn't even noticed he'd held his breath until he let it out slowly. He squeezed her hand. "Good."

He paid and they left, without saying much as they walked out. They ambled silently to her car. Alex wanted nothing more than to take her in his arms, but he would have to be patient.

"You're going tomorrow, right?"

She nodded, opening her car door. He held the door as she got in. She seemed lost in thought. "You bringing …"

Valerie finally smiled. "No, I won't be bringing anyone but Isabel to all the wedding events."

With the weight lifted, Alex smiled. "With Romero attached to her hip, I'm sure."

That made her laugh. She thanked him for dinner and drove off without so much as a hug. Well, damn. Even after all the thought he put into tonight, he still didn't know where they stood. One thing was for sure. Tonight sealed it. There was no way he was giving up on her.

~*~

The drive home was longer than normal. Valerie purposely drove slowly, thinking of everything Alex told her tonight. Could it really all be true? She didn't even care about the earlier stuff years ago. They were both younger and immature. Was it possible that he had really been studying and she just jumped to conclusions? She had to admit that before she and Isabel got close, she was having a hell of a time keeping up with her own schoolwork.

Ironically, the times Alex disappeared on her did help because she would throw herself into the books to keep her mind off him. Had he been around, she would not have worked so hard at it, opting for sure to hang out with him instead.

It did make a little sense as stupid as it seemed. He should have just told her. She frowned, knowing that if it was all true, he chose his pride over her feelings the whole time.

She got her hopes up so many times in the past. Just like now, she wanted so badly to believe him, and then each time Alex trampled her heart.

The thoughts of seeing him with that other girl at his place came flooding back, twisting her insides. She vowed never to let him hurt her again.

What if all this simply stemmed from the fact that he really believed there was another man in her life? She always knew that was something that would drive him crazy. He had always been that way from the very beginning: jealous, almost to a fault. He even admitted it but seemed to think it was okay because he claimed no one else brought it out of him except her.

So what if she gave into him yet again? What if she got rid of her make-believe boyfriend, opened up herself up to him, and he did something stupid again? She didn't know if her heart could take any more.

Valerie was glad she insisted on taking her own car. It wouldn't have been a problem if she left her car overnight, but she didn't trust herself around Alex. Even with the fear of getting hurt, he still had a way of getting her to melt in his arms and end up in his bed. It happened so many times in the past it was almost embarrassing.

Isabel was getting ready to go out when she got home. Valerie smiled. Before Romero, most of Isabel's social life consisted of tagging along with Valerie, usually at Valerie's insistence like at the shower.

"Where are you going?" Valerie plopped onto Isabel's bed.

Isabel stood in front of her mirror applying lipstick. She looked really nice. Her outfits were definitely sexier now that she was dating Romero.

"My sister set me up on a stupid blind date."

Valerie's mouth flew open. "And you're going? Does Romero know?"

"Are you crazy? No way. I told him I'm having dinner with my sister. She set this up before I met Romero. I forgot all about it, and I haven't told her yet about Romero. This guy's a friend of her husband from the service. He's only in town for a few days."

"Whoa, Isabel. You sure Romero's not gonna find out?"

Isabel looked at her through the mirror. "He shouldn't. He's working some concert tonight in the marina, so it kind of worked out. I wouldn't have seen him tonight anyway."

Valerie knew Isabel was used to well-mannered, easy tempered guys like Lawrence, the professor. Romero was anything but. If his reaction to her not taking the relationship as seriously as he did was any indication of how he might react to this, Isabel could be in for it.

"Well you better hope he doesn't, Isabel." Valerie made herself more comfortable on Isabel's bed, using the pillow to rest her chin on.

Isabel turned around and gave her a look. "I actually considered telling him the truth, you know. It's not that big a deal. I don't even know the guy. I'm basically just doing her husband a favor."

"So why didn't you?" Valerie smirked.

Isabel turned back to the mirror. "I chickened out. When he asked if I had any plans for tonight and I said yes, he wasn't happy about even that. So I said it was just dinner with my sis."

Valerie nodded. "I don't think you realize how big a deal this really is, *Izzy*. But I'll keep my fingers crossed for ya."

She saw Isabel stop applying mascara for a second then took a deep breath. "So why are you home so late?"

Valerie knew Isabel couldn't have too much time, so she filled her in quickly on her day's happenings, including Bruce's call then Alex showing up at her work. Isabel was far more interested in the call than Alex. Like Valerie, she'd become pretty jaded on the whole subject of Alex.

"Maybe you should contact the police about this now, Valerie. That's really scary."

Valerie chewed her lip. "I get the feeling he's all talk. He hasn't showed up again since Alex knocked him out."

"But that was a flat out threat. 'I'll make you regret it?'"

"I know, and I'm gonna get a restraining order just as soon as I find the time."

They mulled it over for a bit then went back to the subject of Alex.

"I wouldn't kill the boyfriend off just yet. Alex has never gone very long without screwing up. Let him keep thinking someone else is giving you the undivided attention he never has." Isabel turned away from the mirror to face Valerie, who was really taking in everything she was saying. "Besides, if what he is saying is true, that was still pretty shitty of him to let you hurt all that time just because he was a dumb ass."

"Hey!" Valerie sat up. "That's mean. He's not a dumb ass, Isabel. He runs a highly successful restaurant. Sarah says it's been incredibly busy lately. They have more employees now than ever, they're expanding it even more, and he's pretty much running it all on his own!"

Isabel laughed, walked over to the bed, and hugged her. "I meant he was a dumb ass for thinking that having to be tutored would matter to you."

Valerie tried to keep the glare going but couldn't help smirk then shrugged. "Dumb pride."

"Pride or not, I still think it was shitty of him. So if it's really true and you're going to consider giving him another chance, maybe he does deserve to suffer a little longer like he made you."

Valerie didn't like the idea of playing games, but it did make sense to be cautious. She'd been burned too many times, even if some of those burns weren't necessarily what she had initially thought they were. It still hurt, and Alex had known it all along.

CHAPTER 13

The next morning Valerie met her dad for breakfast. She usually met both her dad and Norma, but Norma had her final dress fitting for the wedding that morning, so she passed. Valerie was glad. She had nothing against Norma. She'd actually been glad when her dad met her and fell in love.

It had always been just the two of them since her mom died of cancer when Valerie was only six. She'd hardly known her mom, but her dad did his best to keep her memory alive. The pictures of her stayed up for years.

She remembered staring at the pictures of her mom when the memory of what she looked like began to fade.

As she got older and began to attend sleepovers with friends and summer camp, she worried about her dad being lonely. She encouraged him to go out, but he was a hopeless homebody.

Then when she was eleven, there was an accident. Her dad had left to run some errands, and Valerie insisted on staying home. She hated the Home Depot. She made herself a grilled cheese and accidentally set a dishrag on fire. She tried to put it out, but it only got bigger.

Panicked, she ran to the neighbors who, upon hearing the word *fire,* called 911. By the time it was all over, the kitchen was a flooded mess, and she was at the police station. They fined her dad for child endangerment, and she was doomed to spend every visit to the Home Depot with her dad for the next few years.

The following week they sent a social worker to the house to interview her and her father and to inspect the living conditions. That social worker was Norma. Even as nervous as her dad had been before she got there, she saw the twinkle in his eye when he spoke with her. She was thrilled when he told her weeks later that he had a date with the social worker.

"Everything happens for a reason, pumpkin," she remembered him saying even back then.

After so many incidents in her life that proved his theory right, she believed it. For some reason, she couldn't talk to him about Alex in front of Norma. She didn't think Norma judged him or anything. Certain things she felt better about talking to her daddy alone, and this was one of them.

In the beginning, her dad hadn't liked Alex. Of course, Valerie was in high school then and still his baby girl. Here was this big "muscle head" picking her up and then making her cry. Her dad said Alex was one of those guys that was just full of himself and would never get his fill of women since there were probably so many throwing themselves at him.

Although, a few times he'd surprised her, saying he'd seen something in Alex's eyes when he looked at her. He said it was something so genuine only another man could understand. Then there would be heartache, and he'd be pissed as ever that Alex had broken his little girl's heart again.

They met at the Pancake House by the mall. Her dad was already having coffee and reading the paper when she got there. It didn't surprise her that he'd already ordered for them. More than anyone else, he knew her appetite well. She did make sure he hadn't ordered anything bad for himself. After grudgingly filling her in on what he had ordered, she was satisfied.

As usual, her mood hadn't gone unnoticed by her dad. She'd barely taken her first sip of juice when he asked, "You wanna talk about it?"

Valerie smiled weakly. "Alex is back."

He nodded and set the paper aside. "I figured as much, what with the wedding and all."

"No, it's not just that, daddy. Remember all those times I thought he was out with other women?"

Her dad frowned, taking a sip of his coffee. "Yeah, I remember."

Valerie eyed his cup. "That's decaf, right?"

He responded with an annoyed nod.

"Well," she continued, "he showed up at my work last night. He's never done that. He said he wanted to talk to me, so I agreed."

Her dad was already up to date about the tutor and all the other occurrences, so she filled him in on everything else—from Alex kissing her at the shower to her lying about being involved with someone else. She even told him about her nightmare evening with Luke. Then she told him what Alex had admitted to the night before. Her dad listened, sniggering and at times shaking his head as he ate.

"So what do you think? Isabel says I should keep up with the boyfriend thing for at least a while longer until I know for sure he's not just saying all this because of my make-believe boyfriend."

Her dad stopped and seemed to ponder for a few moments. "That's a tough one, pumpkin. We men are idiots when it comes to women. But I believe wholeheartedly that that boy did all he did because of his foolish pride. It all makes sense to me now. I never understood how a guy who could look at you the way he did could turn around and do half the crap he did to break your heart."

Valerie's heart swelled. She hated getting her hopes up as she had so many times in the past, but her dad always saw things she didn't catch.

"I'll tell you what." He said pointing his fork at her. "There's one thing I've always liked about that boy. As much as I hate his body language screaming he owns you, with him next to you, ain't no one gonna mess with my little girl. It may as well be written on his chest in neon lights." He shrugged, sprinkling some raisins into his oatmeal. "I like knowing you're in good hands."

Valerie had a visual of Alex's hands all over her and giggled.

"Stop that. You know what I mean, brat."

Valerie laughed. "So you really think he's telling the truth?"

Her dad dabbed his mouth with a napkin. "It makes sense now, honey. I always knew he was crazy about you."

When they finished eating, Valerie praised him again for his choice of healthy meal. He waved her praise away with a grunt. He left, but she strolled around the mall, shopping, lost in thought for a couple of hours. She stopped at a market on the way home to pick up drinks for the ice chest.

Isabel wasn't home yet. Valerie began to worry she wouldn't make it home in time to go with her to the bonfire. No way was she showing up alone.

Isabel stormed in just before five. "Sorry Val, got caught up with my sister and mom. I won't be too long to get ready. What time does this thing start again?"

"In about an hour."

Isabel was ready in no time. They rushed out and talked about their mornings all the way to the beach.

There was a nice size crowd when they got there, mostly people Valerie knew but a few new faces. Alex wasn't there yet, so she was somewhat relaxed. They sat around the unlit fire pit. Valerie poured herself a beer in a cup and poured Isabel a wine cooler. Angel and Eric were busy putting wood into the fire pit.

"So how'd the date go last night?" Valerie asked, once she was comfortable in her chair, drink in her hand.

Isabel gave her a look. "Not here, I'll tell you about it later."

"Oh right," Valerie whispered.

"Not much to tell anyway."

"Not much to tell about what?" Romero startled both of them from behind.

Valerie saw Isabel try to hide a horrified expression. She glanced back, taking in Romero's deadpan expression and wondered how much he had heard.

Eric was working on getting the fire started. Thinking quick, Valerie glanced toward Eric. "Girl talk, Romero. Go help out." She gestured toward Eric. "I've heard legendary stories of your fires."

"All lies." He hesitated then leaned over and kissed Isabel sweetly before walking toward the guys.

Isabel took a big drink of her cooler. She leaned toward Valerie and whispered. "Oh my God."

Valerie giggled. "Holy crap, that was close. You don't think he heard the first part, do you?"

"No, he would've definitely had something to say about it."

Valerie sipped her beer more than grateful she hadn't been louder. She sat up a little straighter when she saw Alex's truck pull up. He was with Sal. It didn't surprise her that Sal was able to make all these functions even if he was attending school in Los Angeles. One thing she always knew even back when they were all kids in school is how close all the three brothers were.

They got an ice chest out the back of the truck. Alex was in a tank top and khaki shorts, most of his hard muscles exposed for the entire world to see. Though Sal was older and had an impressive build himself, it was clear which of the two spent more time in the gym.

She tried not to stare as they walked toward the crowd. He smiled at someone, and Valerie followed his gaze. Her stomach dropped when she saw he was smiling at one of the girls she hadn't recognized earlier. She was standing with the crowd around a radio, smiling back, her eyes all lit up.

The girl hurried over to them and gave Alex a big hearty hug and then Sal one. Alex smiled a bit too much, and

Valerie was immediately glad she hadn't fessed up about her fake boyfriend. Alex would never change.

She forced her eyes away from him and glared instead at the guys getting the fire going. Romero was pouring lighter fluid on the wood.

"That's enough, Ramon." Angel warned.

"You don't know about this." Romero protested.

"That's what you always say." Eric said. "Remember that one time?"

Romero looked up at him exasperated. "We were in high school!" He touched his brow. "My eyebrow grew back."

She finally glanced back at Alex, and he smiled at her: that same beautiful smile that usually melted her heart, but she was furious. She hated being so damn insecure. What was even more infuriating was that he'd made her this way. She took a deep breath and a swig of her beer.

The girl didn't linger around him too long before going back to the crowd she'd originally been with. It bothered Valerie that she didn't recognize her, yet Alex apparently knew her well enough to brighten up her smile and warrant a big hug.

Sarah took a seat next to her and leaned in. "So I heard you and Alex went out last night?"

"Really, he told you?" That was a first, Valerie thought.

"No, I overheard him telling Sal at the restaurant today. He'd get all hushed when he saw me in the room, so I only caught bits. But he said you guys talked, and Sal told him to keep at it, whatever that means."

Keep at it? Keep up the games? Geez, she had to stop thinking so negative. Sal was a nice guy with a good head on his shoulders. The whole world couldn't possibly be plotting against her.

"We talked." Valerie said. Eric walked toward them. "I'll tell you about it another time."

Sarah understood immediately and sat back in her seat.

Valerie glanced over at the crowd with the girl who Alex hugged. Sal was over there talking to them now. Maybe the girl's bright smile was directed toward Sal. It would make sense since all three brothers were so damn good-looking it was maddening.

The fire was roaring now, and Angel glared at Romero. "You had to get stupid about it, didn't you?"

"What? That's a damn good fire." Romero said.

Isabel laughed, and Romero turned to her. "Tell me that's not a fire."

"That's a fire." She agreed.

Sofia walked over to them. "Anyone need to go to the ladies' room?"

Sarah lifted her hand. "I do." She turned to Valerie. "Do you?"

Valerie shook her head. She watched as they trotted off then turned her direction back to the fire. Romero took a seat on the ice chest next to Isabel.

"You guys done with the girl talk?"

"Over before it started." Isabel said, taking a sip of her cooler.

Romero smiled. "You can take this off now." He pulled her sunhat off.

The sun had gone down about twenty minutes earlier. He leaned over and kissed Isabel again, this time longer and deeper than the first time.

"I missed you last night." He whispered, staring deep in her eyes.

Valerie smiled almost jealous. She missed being kissed that way and actually enjoying it as Isabel seemed to be, not like when Luke kissed her.

"Hey." A hand on Valerie's shoulder made her jump.

"I'm sorry, babe … I mean Val. I keep doing that to you." Alex sat down next to her, holding a bottle of water in his hand. "How long you been here?"

"Not long, half hour maybe." She decided not to give in to her insecurities and ruin the night. So she smiled, forgetting about the girl with the big smile for the moment.

Alex looked up at the sky. "Beautiful night."

"Yeah, it is."

She gazed at the enormous fluorescent moon against a nearly black sky. It was almost full. It brought back memories of lying on the beach with him holding her when they used to just look out into the endless sky and talk freely about everything and anything. She loved their talks. The good times with him were always so wonderful. Too bad they never seemed to last very long.

Loud music and more voices and laughter brought her attention back to the bonfire. Sofia and Sarah were back. Sarah was snuggled next to Angel on the sand, and Sofia stood near the fire. Eric was next to her, holding her hand and sneaking a few kisses. Alex straightened out in his chair and frowned. It surprised her that even after all this time; Alex could still get uptight when he saw them getting too friendly.

Sal walked over to say hello to Valerie and hugged her a little tighter than usual. For some reason, Sal still made Valerie nervous. Maybe it was because he was hardly around and was so much more serious than his younger brothers.

He was always incredibly nice to her. She just thought of him as so much older, even though he was only a couple years her senior. Alex had always told her how smart Sal was. She was always afraid she would say something stupid and embarrass herself.

Isabel leaned over and asked if she was ready to make a run to the ladies' room. She was. After checking with Sarah to see if she needed to go, Isabel and Valerie excused themselves.

When they were far enough away, Valerie clutched Isabel's arm. "So did Romero bring up what we were talking about again?"

"Actually, he did. I had a feeling he would. But he just asked if we were talking about him."

"He didn't hear the first part, did he?"

Isabel shook her head.

"Thank goodness." She would've felt so bad if she had gotten Isabel in a snag because of her big mouth.

"So the guy was a dud?"

Isabel frowned. "Not really, but obviously I'm not interested. When he asked for my number, I felt bad. I gave him the landline number, just so I wouldn't have to totally reject him."

Valerie tsked disapprovingly. "Isabel you should've just told him the truth."

"I know, I know, but I figured he's going back to Germany tomorrow and won't be back for months, so what did it matter? I didn't want to chance him telling my brother-in-law and then having to explain to Pat."

They reached the restrooms and waited in line. Isabel gave Valerie a look. "So you telling him you're done with Luke or not?"

Valerie bit the corner of her lip. "I don't know. If it comes up, maybe."

She still wasn't entirely sure, but after talking to her dad today, she was leaning towards being honest. There was a time when she was younger that she engaged in head games like nobody's business, especially when Alex made her so confused. She wanted to confuse him right back. It was childish and sent mixed messages.

No more head games, she finally decided. If it came up, she'd just tell him the truth. On their way back, Valerie saw Alex eyeing them. When she reached her seat, he approached her. "They're gonna start passing the bottle of the tequila around. I'm not really in the drinking mood tonight. You wanna go for a walk?"

Isabel had already sat down, and Romero was quick to sit down next to her. Romero was really throwing a wrench in the plans she made for all these events. She couldn't use the, 'I don't want to leave Isabel alone,' excuse she'd rehearsed so much. So she nodded and grabbed her sweatshirt.

CHAPTER 14

They walked toward the water, and Valerie's heart sped up with every step. She felt her phone buzz in her pocket, and she pulled it out to check it. She had a weird text. The kind that was sent from a computer and you can't tell who it's from.

It's just a matter of time, darling.

She felt her stomach do a flip and everything went mute until she heard Alex's voice.

"Your boyfriend?"

She shook her head but couldn't hide the dread fast enough. Her eyes searched around. Was he watching her now?

"Something wrong?"

She glanced back at Alex. His brows pinched, and he seemed startled. "Valerie you're as white as ghost. What is it?"

Valerie was surprised he could tell. It was dark already. But the moon was pretty bright. She tried to compose herself. This was really freaking her out now. Still she shook her head. "Nothing."

Alex stood in front of her. "No, Val. It is something." He looked down at her phone. "You're trembling." It was more of an accusation than a statement.

There was no hiding the concern in his eyes. "Last night you were almost in tears when I startled you. Is that guy still bothering you?"

She shrugged in an attempt to play it down. "It's just a text."

With a razor sharp stare, he asked, "A text that drained the blood from your face and has you shaking?"

Alex wasn't going to drop this. She'd have to get creative without lying. But he didn't need to know *everything*. She hated getting tangled in lies. She'd never been good at it. Alex was still searching her eyes for answers.

"Yeah, well it's the first I've gotten on my phone, so it freaked me out a little."

Alex's stare seemed unyielding for a moment, then he glanced back down at her phone. "What did it say?"

Even with all the fear and apprehension she felt about sharing this with Alex, she couldn't help be distracted by his incredible arms and shoulders. Instead of telling him, she showed him the text.

~*~

Every muscle in Alex's body tensed as he read the text in Valerie's small trembling hand. "Is this the same guy from the club?"

She shrugged. "It's not his number, but I'm sure it's him."

"A matter of time for what?" Alex remembered how adamant that guy had been about taking Valerie outside that night. What could he tell her outside that he couldn't in the club? Or worse, what was he planning on doing to her?

He could tell Valerie was contemplating whether she was going to tell him or not, but he sure as shit wasn't dropping this. This guy was threatening *Valerie*. He wanted to know everything.

"C'mere, sit down." They sat on the sand. Her dainty leg brushed against him alerting all his senses. "Tell me, Val. What's going on?"

She stared straight ahead into the ocean and took a deep breath. “It’s just like I told you. I got involved with this guy a while back, and he’s still not over it.”

Valerie wasn’t fooling anyone, least of all Alex. There was more to this. “What about the matter of time part? What’s that about?”

“A matter of time before he gets what he wants.”

“And that would be?”

Valerie put her hand on his leg, “Can we not talk about this now? It’s such a beautiful night. I don’t want to ruin it because of this jerk.”

Alex exhaled sharply. He held back all questions he still had. But he didn’t hold back the urge to put his fingers through hers. He held her hand tightly, and she let him. His half-baked bonfire idea was turning out okay after all. He did have other things he wanted to talk to her about, but he would definitely get back to this later.

“Did you give any thought to what I said last night?”

She nodded and glanced back out into the ocean. “A lot actually.”

Her expression was vacant. He wasn’t sure if that was a good thing or not. He squeezed her hand gently, and she turned to him.

“I’m not with Luke anymore.”

Alex let that simmer for a moment. There was a hint of apprehension in her eyes, like there was more. She turned away again “I didn’t even start dating him until after the shower. I lied about seeing someone that day.”

He waited until her cautious eyes were on his again. “Why?”

“Because I was afraid of getting sucked back in, Alex. The pain of walking in on you and your tutor was still so raw. I didn’t even realize it until I saw you at the shower. It was safer to just lie and keep you away. I never want to feel that kind of pain again.”

"You won't. I promise." Alex could feel his heart speeding up. If he patched things up with her now, he'd make sure he never screwed up again. He was never going to be away from her now. Ever. "When did you break up with him?"

"It's been almost two weeks. We tried to keep it discreet, and as far as I know, nobody in the office knew. That is until Bruce, the jerk from the club, started calling the office and told anyone that answered."

"That's why you stopped seeing Luke?" This wasn't what he wanted to hear. Did she still have feelings for the Luke?

Valerie shook her head and put her hand on his thigh. "No, I was going to break it off anyway. It was going nowhere. I felt nothing for him. Only reason I even went out with him was to try and get over you."

Despite the elation he felt, he needed to ask something that might kill the evening—something that had burned in him ever since Angel mentioned the lingerie conversation with Sarah. He *had* to know. "Did you two ever …?"

Her eyes searched his, and then they opened wide. She immediately shook her head.

"No," she said softly, "never."

That's all he needed. The relief was immeasurable. He'd been tossing and turning for weeks about it. She was his, and the thought of any other man with her, especially one she saw on a daily basis still, absolutely *killed* him.

He stared in her big eyes, and he couldn't hold back anymore. He leaned over and kissed her gently. She let him, even parted her lips inviting his tongue in. He pushed her back softly until they were both lying down. It had been so long since she'd been underneath him. "Valerie," he whispered in between kisses.

"Hmm?"

"Come home with me tonight."

He felt her stiffen, and he stopped to look at her uneasy eyes. “What’s wrong?”

“I’m afraid.”

Alex felt his jaw tighten. “About Bruce? Don’t worry, I’ll—”

“No, Alex,” she sat up, “about getting hurt again.”

Alex was up, caressing her back in an instant.

“I need more than just a sexual relationship.” Her eyes glistened. “I can’t do that anymore.”

Anger and shame crept up Alex’s spine. She was close to tears because of him. He couldn’t even bear to think of how much he’d made her cry in the past. “Baby, you got it. I was going to wait until later, but I’ll put it out there now. I want you to move in with me.” Then he stunned himself by adding. “I love you, Val. Always have.”

Valerie stared at him, her lips slightly parted but said nothing. Alex wasn’t done. He was going for it all. With a sudden urge to make up for all the hurt he’d caused her or die trying, he declared, “Or marry me. Either way, I don’t want to be apart from you ever again.”

She finally blinked, but her stunned expression didn’t waiver. “Alex, you can’t be serious.”

“I’ve never been more serious in my life.” He could hardly believe he’d just asked her to marry him, but he meant it. He wanted nothing more than to have her in his life forever, so why not? “What do you say?”

Valerie seemed thrown. “Alex, you’re all I’ve thought about since the shower. I’ve dreamed of nothing more than being back with you. But moving in? Marriage? That’s a big leap. We’ve never even been able to work out a steady relationship, how do we know—”

“Trust me, sweetheart. I know.” He brought her hand to his lips and kissed it. “I don’t want to go another day without you. I can’t, Val.”

Up until the moment the words had flown out of his mouth, Alex hadn’t even given marriage a thought. But he’d never been surer of anything in his life than now. He wanted Valerie to be his in every way. He understood now why his brother Angel had been so anxious to make Sarah his wife. If that's what made him feel whole, made him the happiest man alive, why not make it official?

Valerie stared at him and then down at her small hand that Alex still held firmly. She bit her lip. "Alex, can't we just start off slow?" She paused when Alex pressed his lips together. "You have to understand. Just allowing myself to open up my heart to you again is terrifying enough."

Alex hid the incredible disappointment. But he had to admit she had a point. He'd have to prove himself first, and he would do whatever it took. At least she was willing to give him a chance. That was far more than he expected coming here tonight.

He pulled her to him and hugged her. Feeling her in his arms again was overwhelming. He squeezed her tightly and whispered in her ear. "Whatever it takes."

His hands caressed her back, and he leaned in to kiss her. She let him. When he felt her tongue slip in his mouth, it was all he could do to control himself. Every inch of his body yearned for her, his muscles taut with anticipation. He'd felt lust for her before, but this was entirely different.

Alex would just have to be patient. The last thing he wanted to do was push and have her think he was only anxious for one reason. Although, that part of his anxiety had reached the frantic stages. He buried his face in her hair.

The urgency had changed. Strangely, the thought of consummating the relationship as it never had been before, in an exclusive, no qualms, everything out on the table relationship, was more overwhelming than anything. It occurred to him he'd never actually had one of those relationships. She'd been the closest he'd ever gotten. All those years he'd managed to screw things up every time things were beginning to really get serious, all because of his stupid pride. He was determined now to show her that all he wanted was her and her alone. It's all he'd thought about since the shower, and he wasn't going to blow it now.

"We'll take it as slow as you want, Val. I just hope you believe me when I say that nothing would make me happier than to know you'll be mine forever. I'm just sorry it took me this long to figure that out." The thought of making her his wife and sealing his future with her for good was beginning to sound better and better. It amazed him now that he hadn't thought about it sooner than tonight. But then his hopes for getting her back in his life were frail at best. He pecked her lips. "If I can make you half as crazy as I am about you, I'd be the happiest man in the world."

She stared at him in disbelief. "Alex, I can't believe all those years you didn't see that I was. Ever since we first started seeing each other back in high school, you pretty much ruined it for every guy I went out with after that."

Alex frowned. The last thing he wanted to think about now was her with anyone else. "I doubt that."

It was her turn to frown. Any trace of tears was gone. Humor now danced in her eyes. She leaned in and spoke right in his face. "Alex Moreno, you knew I had a crush on you before I even met you. Sarah told you. From the moment we met, you always had the upper hand, and you knew it."

"No I didn't." He put his forehead against hers. "Remember from the very beginning, you're the one that made it clear you just wanted a physical relationship, no strings attached." He clenched his jaw. "I went along with it because I was so busy with school, and what guy in his right mind would pass that up? Then you went and let Romero kiss you." He gnashed his teeth before going on. "Really? Romero? He was so scrawny and stupid back then. You have no idea what a blow to my ego that was. I thought for sure I'd made no impression on you at all. Sure, you may have been into me, that is, until you got to know me. From then on, I never knew what to think."

Valerie seemed more stunned now than when he'd asked her to marry him. "You still remember that?"

"Of course I do." How could he forget? It was the first time in his life he'd ever felt jealousy. For the longest time, he thought it was just an emotion Valerie brought out in him because he'd never felt it for anyone else. Now he knew better. Good or bad, he'd never even come close to feeling *any* of the emotions Valerie brought out in him for anyone else.

A smile finally broke on Valerie's face. Alex stared at her plump lips as she licked them. "You're unbelievable. You wasted all that time, not knowing how hopelessly insane I was about you."

Alex kissed her then stood up. "Too much time. Let's go."

He pulled her up and immediately picked her up in his arms, squeezing and kissing her, wanting to eat her up.

She laughed when he finally put her down. "Let's blow this party, Valerie."

They started back toward the bonfire. "We can't. Sarah might be hurt."

Alex frowned then looked at her hopefully. "So we hang out for a little bit, then we go back to my place and catch up?"

"If that's what you want to call it." She giggled.

Alex hugged her again, squeezing her with a groan. He still couldn't believe what an enormous weight had been taken off his chest tonight. Valerie was coming home with him, and she was never leaving. There was still the issue of Bruce. He'd get back to that soon enough, but at the moment, he just wanted to enjoy his long awaited reunion with his future wife. Normally he'd be filled with raw anticipation, but now an overwhelming tenderness consumed him.

When they got back to the bonfire, the first to make eye contact with him was Sal, and he smiled. He saw Alex holding Valerie's hand firmly in his. The second they stopped walking, Alex waited only for her to slip on her shoes before wrapping himself around her from behind. He loved that she always wore the biggest shoes she could find even for the beach. Her sandals must've been at least three inches tall. She looked so damn sexy in them.

Valerie undid his hands around her waist and pulled him toward their chairs. Leaning over, she said something to Isabel after sitting down. Alex took the seat next to her, never once letting go of her hand. When Valerie finished chatting with Isabel, she leaned over and whispered. "Of course she's okay with Romero taking her home."

Alex glanced over at Isabel and Romero. Romero pulled Isabel to him and whispered something that cracked her up. He hadn't seen Romero so well-behaved at a gathering with alcohol in, well, ever. He'd always been the *fun,* loud, and loaded guy at these kinds of gatherings. He was so distracted with Isabel now that he wasn't even drinking.

He would've never put those two together. They were completely different. But there was no denying they were enjoying each other. Alex just hoped Romero wasn't toying with Valerie's roommate. He knew how much she meant to Valerie.

They hung out for what seemed like an eternity before making their exit. As discreet as he thought they'd be, there was no hiding the looks he got from all the idiots, including his own two brothers. Even Sal got in on it by bouncing his eyebrows at him when Alex tossed him his keys.

He drove back to his place, and even though Valerie's car was stick, he wasn't able to keep his hands off her the whole way.

CHAPTER 15

They barely made it through the door when clothes started flying off. Alex picked Valerie up in his arms, kicked the door shut with his foot, and took her into his room.

He slowed the pace once he had her in his bed. He'd always done that. It drove her insane, but he always said he wanted to enjoy every minute. He took his shirt off, revealing his massive chest and biceps and crawled on top of her. She kissed him deeply, running her hands along his hard back. She couldn't get enough of his lips, his tongue, his taste.

She kissed him as savagely as he kissed her. Then his mouth moved all over her: her ear, her chin, her neck, and he made his way down slowly, causing her to arch her back. He sucked one of her nipples just hard enough to make her cry out with pleasure.

"God, I've missed you, baby."

"I missed you too." She promised breathlessly.

There would never be another man that made her feel as Alex did, no question about it now. She pressed her body against him and moaned with anticipation. From this, his breathing grew faster and heavier. While his hands caressed and teased, Valerie ran her hands over his rock solid arms.

He continued to run his thumb against her nipple while sucking on the other one. As long as the wait had been, Valerie couldn't believe he was taking his time. She wanted him in her *now*. She was so ready. All she could do was gasp with pleasure as his tongue tugged at her nipple.

His hand moved slowly down her stomach, making her tremble. When he reached down into her panties, she felt his breathing get rougher. "Alex, please." She could barely get the desperate plea out.

He pulled at her panties, ripping them in the process, and she moaned, spreading her legs for him, willing him on to her already. His big hand cupped her, and he groaned. His finger moved slowly in between her legs. Valerie licked her lips and kissed his beautiful hard shoulder. His finger found the most pleasurable of places, and he toyed with it. "You're so warm and wet, sweetheart."

He lifted his face to hers. Even his breath against her lips was a torment. But he didn't kiss her. His piercing eyes watched her as his finger played with her slowly. She wriggled and gasped, squeezing her eyes shut. She was going to climax much sooner than she'd expected. She bit her lip and spread her legs wider as her arousal heightened to a place only Alex could take her.

The expression on his face was pure awe. He was enjoying making her go wild.

"Alex." She gasped.

"Go with it, Valerie. I wanna feel you on my fingers."

His finger moved faster now but rhythmically. He did it so perfectly she wouldn't last much longer. She could feel the buildup. Her body tingled in delight. Then just as she felt her arousal peak, he leaned over, licked her bottom lip, and whispered, "You're mine, Valerie. Always have been."

She cried out as the lightning bolt of sensation overwhelmed her entire body. The finger that devastated her senses slid in her and moved around making her orgasm that much stronger. She closed her eyes tightly. His finger never stopped as she moaned unashamed.

Catching her breath was a struggle. When she opened her eyes, he was still staring at her, "Beautiful, baby." Then he donned that perfect smile. "My turn."

Valerie lay there still breathing hard and enjoying the aftershocks. All her senses were still at their peak.

She didn't even realize, but Alex had stripped down to nothing, had slipped a condom on, and was now on her. His chiseled body was beautiful. She'd only seen sculptures that even came close to his. Everything was perfect, and then she saw *it* as big and ready as she remembered and fantasized about all this time away from him.

Immediately, she was aroused again. She spread her legs in raw anticipation, and he lowered himself onto her. She arched her back, letting out another moan when she felt the hot wet tip touch her. Her hips lifted upward eagerly.

She was still throbbing down there, and yet she felt so ready for more. Alex put his hand behind her waist, lifting her to him and entered her. He slid in, thrusting slowly at first.

"I'm sorry, baby. I can't hold back anymore." He strained to speak.

"Don't" She wrapped her legs around his big hard waist, wanting him in her deeper and harder.

Alex groaned louder, and she felt another climax building. Valerie lifted her hips, wanting him as deep as possible. Each time she got closer and closer, and when she finally cried out in pleasure, Alex groaned loudly. He buried himself in her and held on tight. She usually loved watching him come, but she was busy enjoying her own immense pleasure. It was stronger than the first time. She continued to moan softly with every throb.

Alex laid his body on her gently. She felt his heart pounding against her own heaving chest.

"Never again." He gasped.

That confused her. "What do you mean?"

"Never again will we be apart."

Valerie smiled. "I love you, Alex."

"I don't think I'll ever get tired of hearing you say that, sweetheart." He lifted himself on his elbow and kissed her. "I love you, too. Forever."

Valerie still couldn't believe the impossibility of this night. If she woke up in her bed and this all had been a dream, she was going to kill someone.

~*~

The next morning Alex was up early, annoyed that he hadn't anticipated last night going so well and didn't schedule enough people to cover him today. He wanted nothing more than to stay home and enjoy Valerie all day. Instead, he'd be at the restaurant all day.

He just poured himself a cup of coffee when Valerie walked in the kitchen. She wore one of his t-shirts and nothing else. Remembering he'd torn her panties off last night, the thought of nothing on underneath gave him an immediate erection. "I'm sorry, Val. I didn't mean to wake you."

Valerie smiled, walking to him. "After the night we had, I thought we'd sleep for days."

She wrapped her arms around his waist. He kissed her head and frowned. "I have to go into the restaurant today. But I'm gonna try to duck out of there early."

Valerie looked up at him. "That's okay. Do what you have to do. Just don't disappear on me."

"Never again." Alex leaned down and kissed her.

She looked so beautiful even in the morning. All her makeup was gone. Not that she wore that much, but after several sweaty rounds last night, they'd taken a shower together. Her face was breathtakingly fresh.

Thoughts of everything they did last night flooded his mind, and he was ready to take her again. But it would have to wait. Time wasn't on his side this morning, but there were a few things Alex wanted to get straight with her immediately.

"You want coffee."

"Mmm, yes, please."

Valerie walked over to his breakfast nook and sat down at the table. After pouring her a cup, he brought it over to her and sat down next to her. “So tell me about this asshole who’s harassing you?”

Her expression changed at once. This obviously was not something she’d been expecting to talk about this morning. But if she was in any kind of danger, he needed to know now.

Valerie avoided his eyes and sipped on her coffee. “He’s angry.”

“About what?”

Alex watched as she did everything to avoid looking at him straight in the face. She gripped her mug. “He blames me for getting thrown in jail.”

Alex stood very still and breathed in deeply. If she told him this guy had done anything to hurt Valerie, he didn’t want to lose it. “Why?”

Valerie glanced at him then looked back at her mug. He hated seeing her so tense. He leaned over and put his hand on her knee. “Baby, just tell me.”

Valerie finally looked him in the eye. “We went out for a few weeks, and he started getting really weird on me. Then I found out he was married. I broke it off immediately, but he became obsessed. He followed me around and called nonstop. I warned him I would tell his wife if he didn’t stop.” She stopped and glanced up at the ceiling and took a deep breath. “When he didn’t stop, I called his wife and told her. She was hysterical. Apparently, it got so ugly when she confronted him about it, he pulled a knife on her. She pressed charges, and they locked him up. He was supposed to do three years. Instead, he got out after only nine months. Now he blames me for everything wrong in his life: his divorce, the loss of his job, the fact that he can’t see his kids—everything. He says I did this to him.”

“That’s bullshit.”

"I know, but he's not all there. He thinks I need to make it up to him one way or another."

Alex stared at her big frightened eyes. Why hadn't he hit the asshole harder? He'd knocked him out, but now he wanted to kill him.

"How come no one ever told me about this?"

Did Angel know? He must have. Sarah would've told him. He concentrated on remaining calm.

"I begged Sarah not to tell Angel. I didn't want you to know. It was so mortifying."

"Valerie, the guy's a maniac. That's not your fault."

Valerie shook her head. "But it is. I should've never gotten involved with him in the first place. I should've known from the moment I started to get to know him how disturbed he was."

"No." Inundated by a gentleness he'd never felt, he caressed her face. "This isn't your fault, babe."

He couldn't help thinking that if he himself hadn't been such a stubborn ass for so long, she may have never met this guy. "So has he been specific about what he wants, or is he just taunting you?"

She stared at the floor. "We never did anything more than kiss. He says since he lost everything for me, it should've at least been worth it. He wants us to …"

Never. Not in Alex's lifetime. The animal wouldn't get within miles of her. He'd make sure of that.

"And …" Valerie stopped.

Good God, there was more. "What?"

"He said it's going to happen no matter what. He's already showed up at one of the properties I was at for an inspection and tried to corner me."

"What happened?" Alex realized he spoke through his teeth now, but it was all he could do from completely losing it and going out to look for Bruce right then.

Valerie stopped clutching the mug and put her hands together on her lap. "He's determined to ruin me if I don't give in to him. He's starting with my reputation at the office, my sanity." She looked up at Alex. "I'm pretty sure he's following me again. I can feel it. He knew every time I was with Luke. Just the other morning …"

Alex studied her expression. Something seemed to have come to her. "Just the other morning, what?"

"He called the morning after I had dinner with Luke."

It took Alex a second, but he figured out why she'd stopped. "Just the other day? I thought you said you'd broken up with him weeks ago?"

When Valerie's eyes met his, she seemed nervous, and Alex felt a new tension in his muscles. Whatever it was, he was getting it out of her today. All of it.

"Well, we're still friends. We have to be. We work together."

The deep breathing wasn't working quite as well anymore. He didn't like where this was going.

"We had dinner the other night after work."

Alex remained cool. He did not intend to blow up the first morning after they'd gotten back together. He spoke calm but firmly. "First of all, all the dinner or lunches or anything with Luke are going to stop, right?"

Valerie nodded.

He stared at her for a moment. Her agreeing so easily should've been more satisfying. Knowing she'd be seeing the guy everyday took from the satisfaction, still he continued. "But you're telling me the text yesterday is not the first time Bruce has threatened you? There've been more times?"

"Just that one other time." She said quickly. "The morning after we had dinner."

"Which was?"

Valerie avoided his eyes again. "Friday."

Alex was glad she wasn't looking at him, or she might see how incredibly annoyed that made him. He was determined to get through this without blowing up. "Anything else I need to know, Z?"

"That's it. Other than he calls my cell all the time, but I don't answer."

Alex got up and walked to the sink. He poured his coffee out; his appetite for anything right now was shot.

Valerie stood up and walked toward him. She put her arms around his waist. He was completely tense, but her touch soothed him. "Alex, I hate to burden you with all this. You have so much on your mind already. Let me handle it. I don't want you worrying."

Was she insane? The guy was threatening her. "Valerie, I want you to tell me everything when it comes to this idiot, right down to every call you don't answer."

She looked up at him and frowned. "Everything? Really?"

"Yeah, really."

She nodded and put her head against his chest. "Okay."

Alex rubbed her back and kissed the top of her head. He'd been a fool to keep her out of his life for so long. She looked up at him. "Are we good?"

He smiled. It amazed him that minutes ago he felt ready to tear down a wall with his bare hands, and now just having her in his arms soothed him so deeply. What peaked now was his curiosity, and he reached down under her shirt. He'd been right; she wasn't wearing any panties. His hand caressed her naked behind. Feeling a rush of heat, he picked her up. Instinctively she wrapped her legs around his waist, and her arms around his neck.

He'd always loved that about her. She was always so ready for him. He devoured her mouth, walking over to the pool table in his den. He set her down and pulled the shirt off. Seeing her completely naked in the daylight on his pool table like this had him so hard it hurt.

But he had something else in mind first. Part of that conversation had left him wanting to make sure she knew no other man could love her as much as he did. He wanted to drive her insane with pleasure. "Lie down for me, baby."

She did as he asked, and he pulled her legs up, kissing her inner thighs. Her trembling aroused him to no end. All his muscles clenched at once. He worked his way inward, kissing and sucking her soft inner thighs. He spread her legs wide. She was so petite. It was easy to pull her behind off the pool table and closer to his face, his mouth, his tongue.

Alex licked his lips, taking in what his dumb ass had missed for too long. This was just the beginning of making up for lost time.

CHAPTER 16

The front door had all three locks on including the inside chain. That was odd. Maybe Isabel got the creeps being alone. Valerie sure did when Isabel was gone overnight. But Isabel normally didn't. That suddenly worried Valerie. Had Bruce come by and spooked Isabel? She knocked softly and waited. When Isabel didn't open, Valerie began to fish for her phone in her purse.

Thankfully, she heard the chain unlatch. Her phone was hopelessly buried somewhere in the pit of her purse. Isabel opened the door. She appeared to have just gotten out of bed. "Were you still asleep?"

It was only nine, but Isabel was usually out of bed by eight on the weekend. It drove Valerie crazy because she'd always liked to sleep in. Isabel just nodded and hurried back to her room. "I'll be right out."

She was wearing a robe. She never wore a robe. Valerie dumped everything down on the sofa then rummaged through her purse again for her phone. The phone in the kitchen started ringing.

"I got it." She yelled, still digging through the messy purse.

The phone was on its third ring when Valerie finally found her cell and started toward the kitchen. She was halfway there when a bare-chested Romero walked out of the restroom into the kitchen. They both froze at the sight of one another. He wore last night's jeans and nothing else. Valerie glanced away from his very impressive chest. She knew he had a good build, but seeing him shirtless was something else.

He cocked a crooked smile and gestured toward the kitchen. "You gonna get that?"

She shook her head quickly. No way was she taking another step closer to her roommate's half-naked boyfriend. "It's probably just a fax."

That's really the only reason they even had a landline. Her dad called her on it occasionally when he couldn't get her on her cell. She'd let the answering machine handle it if that was the case.

Her own voice came on the machine, apologizing for not being able to answer just as Isabel walked out of the bedroom. She donned a pair of denim shorts and a t-shirt now. She attempted to calm her wildly tousled hair with her hands. Valerie pressed her lips, holding back a smirk. Isabel's night had obviously been as pleasurable as her own. The machine beeped, and someone cleared their voice then spoke.

"Isabel, this is Michael. I just wanted to tell you I had a fantastic time with you Friday night."

Valerie's eyes grew wide. Isabel started toward the machine, but Romero stepped in front of her, blocking her way. To both Isabel and Valerie's horror, the message went on. "I'll be here a little longer than I thought, so I was hoping I could see you again before I leave."

Romero stared at Isabel the whole time. Valerie's feet were stuck to the floor. She had visions of leaping over the counter and kicking the machine to its death, but it was way too late for that.

"I hope we can make this happen."

He rattled off his number before the agonizing message was finally over. Valerie didn't know whether to leave the room or stay there for moral support.

The room was deathly silent until Isabel spoke up. "Funny story."

"Yeah, Isabel? Tell me about it."

Uh, oh. What happened to Izzy? Romero looked anything but amused. He backed a step away from Isabel. Valerie still stood there, clutching her cell trying to think of something to blurt out that might save the day. But her mind had gone blank.

"My sister set this up before I even met you—"

"You were on a date with this guy Friday night?" Romero's voice rose slightly, but his tone was definitely on the verge of erupting.

As if anyone had asked her anything or was even looking in her direction, Valerie shook her head violently.

"No, we just had dinner."

"That's a date." Romero snapped. "What else did you *just* do with him, huh?"

His hands flew up in the air before she could answer. "You know what? I don't wanna know." He charged toward the bedroom. "Whatever you did, it was fucking fantastic."

Isabel's panicked eyes met Valerie's as he fumed past her. Valerie gestured for Isabel to follow him. "Go! Explain!" She whispered loudly.

The bedroom door closed behind Isabel, and she could hear Isabel's muffled voice plead her case. Romero's voice boomed, but she couldn't make out all he said. One sentence came through very clear though because it was the loudest. "You lied to me!"

Valerie had inched her way into the kitchen. She chewed the nail on her thumb wishing she could think of a way to help Isabel. The bedroom door flew open, and Romero stormed out, wearing shoes now but holding his shirt in his hand. He glanced at Valerie. The anger in his eyes didn't hide the hurt, and she felt for him, but not a word came to mind that she could say to fix this. Isabel came after him, her eyes welled with tears.

"Romero, I'm sorry."

"Yeah, I am too." He grabbed his keys and wallet off the counter. "Go call him back, Isabel. Make it happen."

The door slammed shut behind him, and Valerie rushed to Isabel. Not sure what else to do, she hugged her tightly. Isabel cried softly on her shoulder, then Valerie heard her chuckle sarcastically. Valerie pulled back to look at her. Was she *that* hysterical?

"God, I'm stupid." Isabel wiped her eyes. "This is all because I let my sister get to me about the kind of guys I should date. If I'd had the backbone to tell her truth, that I was already dating someone, someone she wouldn't approve of, this would've never happened."

Valerie bit her lip. "Well maybe when he calms down …"

Isabel looked at her exasperated. "It's not even about the date, Valerie. I think he's madder about the fact that I haven't told my family about him. He asked me in there why my sister hadn't just cancelled the date since I was seeing someone already. When I didn't answer, he stormed out the door before he could even get his shirt on. He couldn't stand to be in there with me another minute. He thinks I'm ashamed of him."

Valerie felt so bad for both Isabel and Romero. "So what are you gonna do?"

Isabel grabbed a napkin from the counter and wiped her face clean. She took a deep breath. "I'm gonna call my sister, then I'm going over to Romero's. He has the whole day off. We were supposed to spend it together." She scrunched her face. "Maybe if he's not too mad, we can have lunch with my mom and my sister."

Valerie patted her on the back. "Good, Isabel. The sooner you clear this up, the better." She tried to sound as optimistic as she could. "Everything will work out. You'll see."

She really hoped things would. Somehow, she got the feeling it wasn't going to be so simple.

This was definitely not the time to fill Isabel in on her wonderful night with Alex. Isabel obviously knew she'd spent the night with him, so she had to know things had changed. Valerie could give her the details later.

Isabel rushed to take a shower, and Valerie went to call her dad. She could hardly wait to tell him the news.

~*~

Even after the night they'd had, Alex couldn't wait to get home to be with Valerie again. He talked to her several times during the day. She mentioned her lease again and not being able to move in with him right away, but he'd figure something out. He wasted too much time already, being away from her.

She also said she had something she wanted to talk to him about. He wondered how long it would be before he'd be all caught up with her life. He wanted to know everything.

Alex smiled when he saw her car was already in his driveway. He gave her a key that morning and asked if she could please be there when he got home. He could certainly get used to this. They still had a lot to talk about, but mostly he just wanted to be with her as much as possible.

She was in the kitchen, preparing something when he walked in.

"Hey." She said over her shoulder. "I hope you're in the mood for tuna salad. You know me. I'm no cook."

Alex wrapped his arms around her small waist from behind and kissed the side of her face. He murmured in her ear. "That's not what I'm in the mood for eating."

Valerie giggled and turned around and kissed him. He kissed her with the hunger he'd felt all the way home. She pulled away.

"Alex," she was breathless already, "let's eat first. We have a lot to talk about."

She turned around and grabbed the bowls of tuna salad off the counter, and he followed right behind her. He had to control himself at least until after they settled this whole thing about her moving in.

"You said you had something you wanted to talk to me about?"

Valerie nodded her head and put bowls down on the table. "Isabel and Romero broke up this morning."

"Really?" Alex thought about the way Romero gazed at Isabel yesterday. "Why?"

Valerie crinkled her nose as they both sat down. "She went on a date Friday night, and he found out about it."

Alex stared at her for a moment before his face soured. "Why'd she do that?"

He did more watching than listening as she explained the sordid story of Isabel, her family, and the blind date. He took in every detail about her: her face, her hair, and the subtle movements she made when she spoke. Her big dark eyes shined when she said something that really moved her. She was amazing. He had to stop thinking about what he'd do to her later and pay attention.

When she was done, Alex lifted an eyebrow and finally ate some of his food. After chewing it he said, "Well, that's what happens when you lie. Sucks for Romero, but I would've walked out too."

She looked at him funny. "You think maybe you can talk to him?"

"And say what?"

"That she really is sorry. She tried going over to his place, but he wasn't there, and he won't answer her calls. She was so miserable. I hated to leave her today."

Alex didn't like the sound of that. "Baby, he's probably gonna be mad for a while. As well he should be. But if he does get over it, I doubt it'll be overnight. I seriously doubt anything I say will change that."

She made the most adorable pouty face, and Alex laughed. "He probably won't even answer my call, sweetheart. Knowing Romero, he's been at the gym all day and by now has had a few drinks."

Valerie stood up and walked to the counter to get the rest of the tuna salad. Alex's eyes followed her very nice behind. "You know," she said, reaching over to the end of the counter for Alex's phone, "if they get back together, maybe Romero can take over my part of the lease. Otherwise, I have to stay there 'til next year."

"Next year?" Alex frowned as she sat back down next to him.

"Yep, just signed a one-year lease earlier this year." She placed his cell next to his bowl and gave him the most beautiful puppy dog eyes. With eyes like hers, he was toast. She *did* have a point about the lease. No way was he waiting until next year. He'd already taken half the day off tomorrow to get her stuff moved in.

He picked up his cell grudgingly. "So, what? I just tell him she's sorry? Didn't she already say that?"

Valerie gave him a look. "Tell him to answer his phone, that she really wants to explain, and that she's really upset."

Alex went through his contacts. He couldn't believe he was doing this only for Valerie. He couldn't even remember the last time he talked to Romero on the phone. He rarely chatted with any of his friends on the phone, especially not about women. This was going to be awkward.

The phone was on its third ring. Valerie watched him anxiously. Alex began to get his hopes up that Romero wouldn't answer when he picked up.

"Hello?"

"Hey, Romero."

Valerie stood up and hugged him then tried to lean in for a listen. Alex backed off and put his finger to his lips.

"Sup?"

"You, uh, talk to Isabel today?"

Romero was quiet for a moment then spoke up. "Yeah, I'm with her now."

"Oh, you are? All right then. I'll let you go."

"What? Wait, why?"

Great, now he'd have to explain he was calling to talk to him about his love life. "I heard about what happened today. I just wanted to see how you were doin'."

Another pause from Romero, "What are you? Dr. Phil now?"

Alex smiled, standing up to put his bowl in the sink. "Hey I'm a sensitive guy, what do you want from me?"

"Dude, get out. Seriously, that's really what you called for?"

Alex leaned against the counter and put his arm across his chest. "Yeah, Ramon. I called 'cause I wanted us to talk about your feelings. Who do you think made me call?"

Romero laughed. "Ah, okay that makes more sense. For a moment, I thought you were getting soft on me."

Alex laughed. After hanging up, he told Valerie what Romero had said. She was more than appeased.

"So that settles it. Romero can take over your part of the lease."

Valerie laughed, putting her arms around his waist. "We still don't know if moving in together is something they've even talked about."

He'd never get over the pleasure of having her in his arms, his life. "Well next year ain't happening, Z. You won't have to pay anything here. So just keep giving her your half of everything until the lease is up."

Valerie peered at him.

"Why not? It'll be kind of like before when you would spend several nights a week here, but you were technically still living at your place. Only now you'd be here every night."

"I won't live here rent free, Alex. Besides, I thought we agreed we were going to take it slow?"

Alex leaned over and ran his hand over her perfectly round behind, "We are. First you move in for a while, then we get married." He kissed her nose and grinned. "And there are other ways you can pay me that don't involve money."

Valerie giggled and kissed him but then pulled back before he could get too crazed. "I'll have to talk to her. I have a feeling she won't want to take money from me if I'm not actually living there."

Alex hid his frustration. "So don't tell her you're moving out then. Just call her every night to tell her you're staying over *again*. You're staying tonight, right?"

"Yeah."

He smiled and couldn't resist kissing her. "I rearranged the schedule at the restaurant, so I'll get out of there early tomorrow. You think you can take half the day off?"

"Yeah, as long as I go in for a few hours in the morning, I can spare an afternoon off."

Alex frowned, remembering she'd be in the same office with Luke. He'd have to think of a way to change that. He wasn't going to be able to deal with that for very long. That one would require more thought. In the meantime, he'd settle on thing at a time. "Good, so I'll drop you off tomorrow, and when I pick you up, we can go see about getting a restraining order against that guy then pick up your things in my truck."

Valerie unwrapped her arms from his waist and went back to the table. She grabbed her empty bowl and walked it back to the sink "Alex, I told you I have to talk to Isabel first, and I'm not going anywhere near a courthouse on a Monday."

Alex pulled her to him as soon as she was close enough. "We can still pick up some of your stuff like more clothes and all your shoes. You can model them all for me tomorrow night."

She tried to resist, "Let me wash these dishes."

"I'll get that later." He picked her up, and she screeched.

The visual of her prancing around in her high heels for him and nothing else had done it.

"I'm done talking." Instantly her legs wrapped around him, her breathing already labored by the time he reached the bedroom door.

***

The next morning Alex dropped her off at her office bright and early. He made sure he got out of the truck and gave her a very public goodbye kiss: a kiss no one would mistake for a friendly goodbye.

He was just loosening his hold on her when the black Jaguar drove in the parking lot. Valerie went tense the second she saw it.

Luke glanced at them as he drove by.

Alex couldn't leave now. He had to check the guy out. The night at the club he'd barely glanced at him before taking off. He watched as Luke opened up the backdoor of his car and pulled out his suit jacket. He was a good sized guy, but he had nothing on Alex. The irritation of Valerie having to be in the same office with him all day rubbed Alex like a cheese grater.

Valerie finished gathering the things Alex hadn't given her a chance to grab earlier. He'd been around to her side as soon as he stopped the truck.

"All right, Alex. I'll see you around one?"

Alex looked away from Luke long enough to address her. "Yeah, maybe earlier. I'll call you."

He kissed her one last time just as Luke walked by. He got in his truck and watched as Luke waited and held the door open for her then walked in after her. Oh, this would definitely have to change.

CHAPTER 17

Valerie sat at her desk, still trying to shake the incredible discomfort she'd felt when she walked in the office with Luke. He immediately asked if Alex was back in her life, and she had no choice but to say yes. She knew Alex would lay it on thick, but she hadn't anticipated Luke driving in at such an inopportune moment. The way Alex stared him down didn't help either.

She gathered her things and walked to the conference room with everyone else. She tried to concentrate on what Luke was talking about during the meeting. It seemed Luke was avoiding looking her way at all. But she didn't mind. The last thing she wanted was to get locked into one of his stares. He began wrapping it up.

"I made a few changes to the uptime schedules. Check your emails."

That caught Valerie's attention; she was supposed to have uptime that afternoon. It was odd. Luke had always made her uncomfortable from the moment she met him with his excessive eye contact then later with his locked stares. Today it seemed he'd gone out of his way to avoid looking her way during the meeting.

She checked her email first thing when she logged onto her computer. She typically had a ton of email to sift through Monday mornings, especially if she hadn't looked at it over the weekend, and this weekend she hadn't touched her laptop. His email was the very first one. That meant he'd sent it that morning.

There were only a couple of changes, but he'd changed her uptime to Wednesday afternoon. Valerie felt her face heat. Was he kidding? It was bad enough he'd changed it already from Monday mornings to Monday afternoon. Wednesday was their slowest day, especially for calls.

Valerie marched straight to his office. He looked up when she walked in without knocking. "I've had uptime on Mondays for as long as I can remember."

"Yeah," Luke didn't miss a beat, "and it's time someone else got a chance at a Monday."

"And when did you decide this, Luke? This morning?"

Luke sat back in his seat. "You really think I'd be that petty?"

"I don't know. You tell me. Why today?"

"Because others have requested to have Mondays, so I changed it. It's not permanent, Val. I'm going to rotate it."

She glared at him still unable to believe he'd be this way.

"So is Mr. Wonderful back for good this time, or is it a temp thing again?"

Valerie ignored his question. "When are you rotating it again? Wednesday's pure shit. I'd rather not have uptime."

"Whoa, Val. A little harsh there." He chuckled and sat up, looking at his computer. "What day would you prefer?"

"Monday."

"Can't do it. How 'bout Thursday mornings?"

Valerie could almost feel the steam rising out of her ears. He was enjoying this. Thursdays were just as slow.

He looked up from his screen. "C'mon, Val. I'm trying to work with you here. You would think you'd be in a better mood."

"What is that supposed to mean?"

He turned back to the screen in front of him. "Am I wrong to assume that kiss he gave you is any indication of what else you two have been doing?"

"Assume whatever you want."

"What's with the hostility?" His smirk irritated her even further. "You're still doing the wine tasting this Thursday, right?"

Valerie did her best to remain unruffled. "Of course, why wouldn't I?" She knew what he was getting at, but she'd never let on.

He sat back in his seat, his elbows on the armrests and put his fingers together in front of him. Something he did often when speaking to her from behind his desk, but for some reason today, it annoyed her. *He* annoyed her. Maybe it was the obvious sarcasm in his smirk.

"Oh, I don't know. I just thought maybe you'd feel uncomfortable bringing the new boyfriend to an event where your ex-boyfriend slash manager is going to be. And something tells me by his friendly glare out there, not to mention our gracious introduction, he's not going to be too keen on you attending alone."

"Don't flatter yourself, Luke. Alex knows he has nothing to worry about. I'll be there." Valerie started to the door. "If you're not changing my uptime back to Monday, I'm done here."

"Valerie?"

Annoyed she turned to look at him before walking out. "What?"

"Did you tell him *everything*?"

"There wasn't much to tell, Luke." She rolled her eyes and walked out before he noticed that he'd hit a nerve. She'd been as honest as she was going to be with Alex about Luke. They'd gone out, and they'd never had sex. He didn't need to know anything else.

She didn't think Thursday would be such a big deal until she saw Alex's reaction to just seeing Luke that morning. Luke hit it right on the nose. No way would Alex be okay with her going wine tasting with Luke, and it would be awkward at best if Alex went with her.

She had to go, though. The California Association of Realtors threw this annual event bursting with investors. She didn't get to go last year, and she knew the only reason she was going this year was because Luke had pulled some strings. Tickets were limited. Luckily, when he'd gotten her tickets, it was before they started dating. He gave her two. She planned to take Isabel at the time.

The event would have an entirely different feel now that things had changed. But as long as she worked with Luke, Alex would have to start getting used to things like this. They had been through enough. They could get through this.

~*~

They'd been at Valerie's all afternoon. Alex was determined to get as many of her things as possible. The only big things Alex had to carry out to his truck from Valerie's apartment were her two-drawer file cabinets. The girls looked at him funny when he asked if they had a dolly, so he'd been more than grateful they lived on the bottom floor. Valerie still insisted, especially in front of Isabel, that she wasn't moving out.

Alex stood outside, tying down her things in the back of his truck when a car pulled into the apartment parking lot. It parked a few doors down from Valerie and Isabel's open apartment door. A guy who looked to be in his thirties got out. Alex noticed he peeked in their door as he walked by then stopped. Alex stopped tying and watched. Valerie came to the door then went back in. Moments later, Isabel came out and stood there talking to him.

Alex wondered if the guy was the one Isabel had gone out with Friday. She couldn't be that dense, could she? Valerie had already filled him in on Isabel and Romero. Apparently, Romero got over it a lot sooner than Alex would've, but then she did say they pulled an all-nighter, talking things out. They were having dinner with her family tonight.

Valerie came out and walked to Alex's truck.

"Who's that?" He asked as soon as she was close enough.

"Our neighbor, Lawrence."

"Isabel's neighbor."

Valerie laughed. "I still live here, Alex."

"Not for long."

Isabel went inside, and Lawrence followed her. Alex gestured toward her apartment door. "You guys invite all your neighbors in like that?"

Valerie glanced back to the apartment then turned back at him. "Well, don't say anything to Romero, but Isabel used to go out with Lawrence."

Alex gave her an annoyed look.

"I can't stand him." She said quickly as if that made up for the fact that Isabel had just invited an old flame into their apartment.

"Why?"

"He thinks he's so damn smart. He's a professor at the UCSD."

"A professor, huh?" Alex finished up with the load in the back of his truck. That sounded more like someone Isabel would date than a meathead like Romero.

"Yeah," Valerie said, slipping her hand in his, "and he's the type that makes sure you know it too."

They walked back to her apartment. Alex didn't like the guy already, and once in the apartment with a closer look, the guy did look like a prick. Only morons wore turtlenecks as far as Alex was concerned.

Lawrence had two books in his hands and was busy telling Isabel about a book he was writing when they walked in. Isabel looked up at them from the cheese she was slicing in the kitchen.

"All done?"

"Yeah, I think so." Valerie replied. "That's all for now anyway."

Lawrence sized up Alex. Valerie introduced them. Annoyed that she didn't refer to him as her boyfriend, Alex smiled anyway. Lawrence held out his hand, and Alex shook it.

"So you moving out, Val?" Lawrence's eyes made their way down Valerie's body.

Alex definitely didn't like the guy.

"No, not yet, but soon." Valerie glanced back at Alex and smiled. "Just let me grab one more thing."

She walked into her room, leaving Alex alone with Isabel and the prick. Lawrence immediately turned back to Isabel. "I'm telling you, Isabel," he tapped the book in his hand, "the classics are not to be taken lightly. You have to take your time, digest them. Read them as many times as you can before you can really appreciate what the author is trying to elucidate."

Alex rolled his eyes and walked over to a table with pictures on it. There was a knock on the door, and then he heard Romero's voice.

"Hey, Alex." Alex turned just as Romero walked in. He wore a black polo with his security firm's name on it.

Alex acknowledged him, and Romero turned to Isabel and Lawrence.

"Izzy? You cooking? I thought we were going out for dinner?"

Lawrence seemed taken aback. He scrutinized Romero the way a man would scrutinize a busboy at a restaurant who was flirting with his wife.

"No, just making snacks." She introduced Lawrence to Romero. Romero barely cracked a smile. Alex could only imagine what Romero thought: the same thing he'd be thinking if he walked in and Valerie was standing there with him. *Who is this crumb and why is my girl making him snacks?*

Romero walked into the kitchen and planted one on Isabel. Alex smirked. Romero didn't do subtle.

Lawrence was obviously bothered but tried to keep his composure. When Romero took it a step further and rubbed his hand over Isabel's behind, Lawrence cleared his throat and excused himself.

"Let me know, Isabel, when you're ready for some Tolstoy. I have them all." He started to the door.

"Tolstoy?" Romero asked.

Lawrence shook his head with what could construed as a sneer. "Nothing you'd be familiar with, I'm sure."

Romero peered at him. But before he could say anything, Isabel spoke up, "I'll walk you out, Lawrence."

Romero gave Alex a look when Isabel hurried around the counter and walked out the door with Lawrence. "Who is that guy?"

"Their neighbor." Alex shrugged. He wasn't about to open up that can of worms.

Valerie finally came out of her room, holding a small duffle. "Okay, I'm good. Oh, hey, Romero." She glanced around. "Where'd Isabel go?"

"Outside with that dude. Does he come over here a lot?"

Valerie glanced at Alex then back at Romero. "Lawrence? No, not really. He was just here to pick up some books Isabel borrowed."

She started to the door, and Alex followed. They were just out the door when Alex heard Lawrence talking to Isabel. Lawrence's back was turned to them.

"I mean really, Isabel. I can see Valerie with someone like that, all brawn and undignified. But you? I gotta say not only am I stunned but a bit disappointed."

Alex clenched his fist. Before he could say or do anything, Romero jumped out from behind them. "What the fuck does that mean?"

Lawrence backed up, startled when Romero got in his face. He regained his poise quickly and held his hands up. "I was just making an observation. There's no law against that."

"You don't know shit about me, asshole."

Lawrence made the mistake of pointing his finger at Romero's chest about to say something. Romero pushed him in the chest with both hands. That's all it took, and Lawrence was in the bushes in front of Valerie's apartment.

"Oh my God," Valerie gasped.

Alex jumped in front of Romero who was ready to charge at Lawrence and stopped him. "Easy. "

Romero was furious, and he didn't blame him. But Lawrence looked the type to make a big thing out of something like this, so Alex held Romero back. Isabel tried helping Lawrence up.

"You see." Lawrence barked at Isabel. He stood up red-faced, swatting her hands away. "This is exactly what I'm talking about."

"Did you just push her?" Romero almost broke free from Alex, and Alex had to bear hug him.

"Get him out of here, babe." Alex warned Valerie.

Surprised by Romero's strength, Alex wasn't sure how much longer he could hold him back. Valerie hurried over to Isabel's side while Alex struggled with Romero. "Relax, dude, if he'd pushed her, I'd let you at him."

"You should leave, Lawrence." Valerie urged.

Once they were all back inside, Alex could laugh about it. But Romero wasn't laughing. "Why does that asshole even care who you're with?"

Valerie gestured to Alex that they should leave.

"We're out." Alex said as they walked out.

Isabel glanced at them and waved, but Romero didn't take his eyes off her.

"She's gonna have to tell him the truth." Valerie said as they walked to Alex's truck.

"Yeah, she better."

Alex thought about what Lawrence had said as he fastened Valerie's duffle in the back of his truck. If Romero hadn't jumped him first, he might've hurt the guy himself. He didn't even mind the assumption the idiot made about him and Romero, but he wouldn't stand there and let him insult Valerie.

Valerie was already in the passenger side when he got in his truck. "It wasn't that big a deal." She said as she fastened her seatbelt. "She only dated him a few times. She doesn't have to tell him everything."

Alex looked at her. "What more is there to tell?"

Valerie glanced at him and then out the window. "I just mean she could leave the details out. No need to get into anything explicit. It'll just make him mad."

Alex gripped the steering wheel and stared at Valerie. "Are we still talking about Isabel?"

Something resembling panic flashed in her eyes when she glanced at him again.

"Of course."

He tried shaking off the unease her last statement gave him as he drove. She must've sensed his tension, because she reached over and squeezed his thigh.

"I packed a lot of shoes."

That straightened him out real quick. Now here was something he'd prefer to think about. He looked at his dash. It was still early. He had her all to himself for the rest of the evening. There was already movement in his pants.

~*~

Days later Valerie was still trying to grasp the enormous change her life had taken. Since it felt almost too good to be true, she cautioned herself about becoming too optimistic. Anything could happen.

She told Isabel that she would be staying with Alex a few days out of the week for now. But she did mention that he wanted her to move in. Isabel told her not to worry about it, that she'd figure something out but never once mentioned the possibility of Romero moving in. Valerie didn't mention it either. She didn't want Isabel thinking she was just trying to push the issue so that he could take over the lease. With Lawrence two doors down, she wasn't sure Romero moving in would be such a good idea now anyway. One thing was for sure. She planned to pay Isabel her share of the bills every month until the lease was up.

Isabel had called her the day after the Lawrence incident. She'd told Romero the whole truth about Lawrence, which only made him madder. He said he couldn't tell her who she could and couldn't have over to her place, but made it clear he wouldn't be responsible for his reaction if he ever showed up and Lawrence was there again. Valerie told her she didn't think he'd have to worry too much about that. She highly doubted, after his embarrassing roll in the bushes, Lawrence would *ever* come over to their place again.

They both got a good laugh about that. Then Isabel told her about the dinner with her family. It hadn't gone as well as she hoped, especially since Romero knew Pat had set her up Friday night. He was in no mood to play nice, and the dinner had been a bit tense. Nevertheless, she was glad it was over. Her family knew about him now, and whether they approved or not, Isabel had no intention of breaking things off with Romero. Valerie assured her she'd done the right thing.

CHAPTER 18

Valerie had shown properties all morning. As usual, she was running late again. The wine tasting was that night. Alex would be attending with her and was probably already home, getting ready.

On her way back to Alex's, she got a call from a restricted number. Valerie hesitated to answer. She hadn't heard from Bruce in days and had hoped he finally just gave up. There were two important phone calls she was waiting for from clients, and she didn't want to chance missing them. She clicked the button and paused before saying hello.

"So I see you switched from doing the boss to the steroid freak this week." Bruce's words were slurred. "You got me penciled in for next week?"

Valerie gripped the wheel. "Not if my life depended on it."

"Well it just might!" He went from calm and teasing to loud and wild in an instant. "I'm watching you, Val. It's just a matter of time—"

She hung up before he got any more obnoxious. Her heart was pounding already; she didn't need to hear anymore. She glanced in her rearview mirror. The car behind her was too close. She sped up, and so did the car. There was no making out if it was him, but it was definitely a guy.

With her heart at her throat now, she panicked and grabbed her phone. She wasn't even sure who to call. She didn't want to alarm Alex. The police were out of the question. What would she say? The car behind me is tailgating? The light turned yellow, and she sped up to catch it. No way was she stopping. The car behind her sped up as well and took the yellow as it turned red.

Valerie hit the speed dial and called Isabel's cell. Just as Isabel answered, the car made a right on the street behind her. Valerie sighed in relief.

"Jesus!"

"What's wrong?"

"Nothing, Bruce just called, sounding all crazy. Then I got freaked out and thought someone was following me, but I was being paranoid."

"Are you sure he wasn't?"

"Yeah," she gulped, "I'm sure. They turned the other way."

"What did Bruce want?"

"Same as always and to make sure I know he's watching me."

"Maybe you should get a restraining order, Valerie. We already know what he's capable of. I still can't believe they let him out so early."

Valerie couldn't believe it either. She'd never forget the day she found out about his release. Isabel reminded her constantly to check at least twice a month. He'd taken a plea bargain of three years. If the case had gone to trial and he lost, he would've been slammed with five to fifteen years for attempted murder.

He didn't even do the whole year. She was in tears the entire day. Her dad insisted she stay at his place the first few nights. She thought Bruce would have the common sense to stay away from her and any trouble that might get him thrown back in jail, but he seemed determined now to make her life hell.

She squeezed the wheel. If only he'd had the balls to go to trial. Having him locked up for that many years would've been so wonderful. She still couldn't get over how he'd been offered the plea bargain to begin with.

Maybe pepper spray wasn't enough. She'd look into getting a gun if she ever found the time. She already put off getting a restraining order this whole week. "I'll I just have to make the time."

She hung up and thought of the night ahead of her. As if thinking and worrying about how this evening was going to turn out wasn't enough, she now had to tell Alex about the call.

He'd just stepped out of the shower when she walked in. He wore nothing but a towel around his waist when she walked in the room. No matter how many times Valerie saw his chiseled body, she'd never get enough. He walked over to her and planted a breathtaking kiss on her. Immediately, his towel tented, and he groaned, kissing her neck.

As much as she could go for a quick one right now and it would definitely calm her nerves, she knew it was late. "Alex, honey we're already running late." She pulled away gently but couldn't resist kissing his hard chest before taking a step away.

"I know. I'm surprised I beat you home. What happened?"

Valerie rushed to the closet. She didn't have time to change. She'd just have to dress up the skirt suit she was already wearing with a different pair of shoes and silkier top. Taking her hair down would help too.

"I put more on my plate than I should've this morning."

She glanced over at Alex who was already in his silk boxers and slipping into slacks.

"I, uh, got a call from Bruce today."

Alex's eyes were on her at once. "What did he want?"

"Same thing." She didn't want to lie, but she was telling him about the call as he'd asked. She didn't have report it to him verbatim. "Asking when he gets to see me again."

"What were his exact words?"

Okay, apparently he was expecting it to the letter. "I don't even remember, Alex. I hung up on him mid-sentence.

Only reason I even answered is because he used a restricted number to call me. I was expecting a few calls from clients. I didn't want to miss them."

"When did he call?"

"On my way home."

"And you don't remember?" His eyebrows furrowed.

Valerie pretended to have to think about it. "He knows I'm with you now. He wanted to make sure I knew."

Alex walked toward her. Valerie slipped a shoe on. Why did she bother trying? She knew Alex wouldn't just drop this. She bent over to slip on the other. Already he stood over her as she stood up straight.

"Why are you being vague, babe?" He sought it out in her eyes. "What did he say exactly?"

~*~

Valerie would have to understand that when it came to this guy or anyone that might be out to hurt her, Alex needed to know everything. Hell, he wanted to be in on everything about her life, no matter what it was. The comment she'd made on the subject of Isabel not having to tell Romero all the details of her past still didn't sit well with him It was almost as if she was trying to tell him something.

He wouldn't push on that, but this was different. He stood there waiting for a response. They weren't going anywhere until he got one.

She took an exaggerated deep breath. "He said he knew that I had moved on from Luke to you and asked if I'd penciled him in for next week. I said not if my life depended on it, then," she bit her lip and glanced away, "he said it just might. He started to say he was watching me and it was just a matter of time, but I didn't let him finish. I hung up."

Alex went rigid, feeling a slow boil start up inside him. He stared at her for a moment, taking in how fragile she seemed to him all of a sudden. *A matter of time?* Before they got back together, hearing something like this would've simply enraged him. Now, rage wasn't the only thing that bolted through him. Now there was an unfamiliar sensation coursing through him. A sensation he'd never felt before: ice-cold fear.

Protecting Valerie was his priority now, but he couldn't be around her twenty-four seven. He knew there were a lot of sick people out there; one of them was after the woman he loved. The thought of something happening to her ripped at him like scorching bullets.

"We're going downtown tomorrow and getting that restraining order. I want this guy locked up the second he tries to contact you."

Valerie nodded and stepped forward, putting her arms around him. Alex hugged her tightly, wishing he could have her in his arms every moment of the day. He'd know, then, for sure, she'd be safe.

"Don't worry, Alex. I'll be fine."

Alex kissed her head. "Yeah you will. I'll make sure of it."

***

The ride to the winery was a bit tense. Alex wanted to know more about Bruce and her relationship with him. Valerie wanted to just drop it. She said she didn't want to think about it anymore. Alex let it go for now. But he wanted to know more about this guy. Knowledge was power, and he wanted to arm himself with as much of it as he could if he was going to go up against this guy.

Wine tasting wasn't new to Alex. He'd had plenty of invitations from wineries that were hoping to add their wine to the restaurant's shelf. These events were always the same: a bunch of arrogant idiots who knew a lot about wine and a bunch who were pretending to. Wine wasn't his first choice of alcoholic beverage, but it was up there, and he knew his way around it.

Unlike most of the wine tasting events Alex had attended at the actual wineries, they held this one at a wine club. The entire place was reserved exclusively for this event. Valerie gasped as they walked up the entrance stairs.

Alex glanced at her then around at the people entering the club. "What's wrong?"

"He didn't tell me it was a black-tie event."

Alex let out a breath of relief. Most of the men were in tuxedos and the women in lavish evening gowns. He shrugged. None of them held a candle to Valerie. "You look beautiful regardless."

The place was already crowded as they walked in. Alex scanned the parking lot and now scanned the people at the event. He could care less about what he wore. The only thing on his mind was keeping Valerie safe.

His comment didn't seem to change Valerie's concern about being underdressed, though she didn't let it slow her down. They'd only been there a few minutes, and she'd already worked her way through a good part of the crowd. After several instances of Valerie introducing Alex as "a friend of mine," Alex leaned over, touching her arm and asked, "Why do you keep introducing me as your friend?"

She turned to look at him a bit surprised. "How would you like me to introduce you?"

Alex smiled. "Your fiancé?"

"But we're not engaged." She whispered.

"Minor detail." He frowned, "And why are you whispering?"

Just as the corner of her lips began to rise, an older woman in a black velvet gown interrupted them. "Valerie, I thought it was you. How've you been little lady?"

Valerie's eyes shot open and immediately went to hug the woman. "Bernadette! Oh, my gosh. It's been forever."

They caught up quickly, then Valerie turned back to Alex. "Alex I'd like you to meet, Bernadette. She used to babysit me when I was a little girl."

Alex smiled, leaning over to shake Bernadette's hand.

"Bernadette, this is Alex," Valerie glanced at Alex, "my boyfriend."

Only then did Alex realize he'd never been introduced as anybody's boyfriend in his life. It was a little weird, but he liked it, especially hearing Valerie say it.

After the introduction, Bernadette turned to Valerie again. "How's your father doing? I heard he was in the hospital not too long ago."

"He's better," Valerie smiled. "It's been over six months now since he got out of the hospital. We had quite a scare. He just has to watch his diet real close. His blood pressure is really touch and go."

Bernadette shook her head. "Oh, yeah, Valerie. He really needs to watch that. Hypertension is no joke."

Valerie talked to Bernadette for a few more minutes before Bernadette excused herself to get back to her sister who'd she'd come with. Alex hadn't taken his eyes off Valerie the entire time she'd spoken with Bernadette. He saw the usual tenderness in her eyes as she spoke of her dad. There was no doubt how close she was to her father. It bothered him now that he hadn't been there for her.

"I didn't know your dad had been in the hospital."

Valerie tilted her head. "A lot happens in a year, Alex. It'll probably be a while before we get all caught up."

Alex thought about that for a moment. He wanted to tell her how sorry he was that he wasn't there for her, but they were interrupted again. The interruption this time wasn't as welcome as Bernadette's.

"I'm glad you made it." Luke wore a tuxedo and sloppy grin.

Alex refrained from frowning. Valerie stood her ground, appearing as unfazed as ever. "Thanks for telling me it was black tie."

Luke glanced down at her clothes. "I'm sorry, hon. I thought you'd know." His eyes averted to Alex who took a sip of his wine. "Sorry there's no beer, champ. But then we wouldn't want you punching holes through walls anyway, right?"

Luke laughed a bit too loud. The walls were the last thing he'd have to worry about if Alex started doing any punching. But Alex held back what he really wanted to say and smiled instead.

Alex's eyes met Valerie's. For the first time that evening, she appeared troubled. Alex winked to let her know she had nothing to worry about. He wasn't about to let this drunk ass get to him.

Luke downed the rest of his wine. "Oh hey," he addressed Valerie with another sloppy grin, "guess what I was able to get us."

Valerie didn't ask. She waited for him to continue.

"Me and you are invited to George Stone's meet-and-greet before the seminar."

Valerie's reaction confused Alex. Who the hell was George Stone, and why did Valerie seem excited about it?

"You're kidding?"

"No," Luke grinned, opening up his arms as if that warranted a hug.

Valerie glanced at Alex but leaned in and hugged Luke anyway.

"Are you serious? A meet-and-greet with him?"

Luke rubbed his hands against Valerie's back. "Absolutely. You know me. I had a feeling that would make your day, so I pulled a few strings."

Normally it would take everything in his power to stay composed, but Alex had a feeling what Luke was up to. He didn't flinch. As much as he wanted to stare the fucker down, he resisted and glanced around the room casually, taking another sip of his wine instead.

Valerie's eyes stayed fixed on Alex even as she pulled away from Luke. Before she could say anything, Luke spoke up again. "Did she tell you about George Stone?"

"Can't say that she has." Alex exchanged glances with Valerie.

"Ever heard of him, Alex?" Luke peered at Alex smugly but didn't wait for an answer. "Oh, what am I thinking? What would a guy like you know about real estate motivational speakers?"

Luke laughed, placing his hand on Alex's shoulder and leaned into him. "Even I didn't know much about the guy. But since I got us tickets to his event, I've read up on him a bit, and I gotta say the guy is impressive. I'm actually looking forward to meeting the man." He turned to Valerie. "Good choice, Valerie."

Alex noticed Valerie chew her lip the way she did when she was nervous. Her eyes were on Luke's hand, the one that still sat on Alex's shoulder.

"Yeah," Alex smiled, reaching his hand out to Valerie. "I have to agree with you there, Luke. Valerie's always been good about making the right choices."

Valerie's eyes widened, but she took his hand anyway. Alex squeezed her hand. She took a drink of her wine and glanced away. "I've never actually been to one of these events." Valerie said.

Alex noticed Valerie avoided looking back at Luke. She took a sip of her wine and continued, "Aren't we supposed to be wine tasting?"

"Nah, that's optional." Luke finally moved his hand off Alex's shoulder. His mood seemed to have staled. "We're here to schmooze, remember?"

Valerie still looked around. "Oh gawd, is that who I think it is?"

Both Alex and Luke turned to see a heavyset man who looked to be about in his sixties, making his way through the crowd. He walked in their direction.

"Well, what do you know?" Luke grinned as he took another glass of wine from the passing waiter.

"Pretend you don't see him." Valerie took a step behind Alex.

Alex peered at the man and stood firmly in front of Valerie. She was too late. The man had spotted them and was already on his way toward them with a fat grin. Alex squeezed her hand, suddenly feeling on edge. "Who is he?"

"Relax, champ." Luke raised his glass at the man and smiled. "He's just an investor with lots of capital."

"And lots of corny jokes," Valerie muttered.

Having no choice, Valerie came around and stood next to Alex.

The man was almost close enough to hear them, and Luke spoke through his big fake smile. "Oh, you handle his jokes pretty well. That's why we got Lemon Ridge, remember? Work your magic, Valerie. He likes you."

The idea of Valerie working her magic on any other man, even one old enough to be her dad, made Alex grind his teeth. This night was getting more irritating by the minute.

"Hey!" The heavy man said loudly as he reached them. He held his glass out at Luke. "How merlot can you go?"

His explosive laugh was so loud it turned heads, but Luke followed his lead, laughing right along and shook his hand. Alex smiled politely. He was used to dealing with all kinds of characters at the restaurant. The man then turned to Valerie. "How are you, beautiful?" He leaned in, giving Valerie a big hug.

"Is that a corkscrew in your pocket, or are you just happy to see me?" Valerie's impression of Mae West was spot on. Alex was impressed and surprised he'd never heard it. He saw a side of Valerie tonight he'd never seen.

The man put his hand over his mouth and feigned embarrassment. "Forgive me for I have *zinned*."

He wheezed long and hard before breaking into cackles. Valerie laughed genuinely, and even Alex had to chuckle. The jokes were awful, but the jolly man's laughter was contagious.

Once done with his fit of laughter, the man pulled out a handkerchief from his pocket and wiped his forehead.

"Alex, this is Joe Newman, a client of ours." Valerie said, smiling big. Alex reached out and shook Joe's hand. "Joe this is my friend, Alex."

Alex glanced at Valerie. She looked at him and quickly turned back to Joe. Alex wondered if the reason he'd gone back to being just her *friend* had anything to do with Luke standing there.

As the evening went on, Alex was continually surprised with the side of Valerie he'd never had a pleasure of witnessing. She was in her element. He now knew why she'd become so successful so quickly. She was definitely a people person. As if she'd done this a million times, she worked the room like a pro. Everyone they spoke with seemed genuinely taken by her. No one would've ever guessed this was her first time at one of these events.

He also noticed how the men ogled her and almost all seemed to turn into gushing idiots around her. It was as if she'd put a spell on them. He had to wonder if he ever acted that way with her and didn't even realize it. These men sure didn't seem to. It was hard to believe she managed to stay single for an entire year. Well, except for the two short-lived incidents she told him about.

Even with Alex standing next to her making it glaringly obvious she was with him, they still had no qualms about being overly friendly. This was especially true as the night persisted and the wine continued to flow.

By the time it was all over, Alex was as ruffled as a wet rooster. By the same token, he was equally impressed with

Valerie. He didn't think he could be anymore fascinated with her than he'd already been before this event.

After making their exit, Alex stopped just as they turned the corner of the club and pulled her to him, looking her in the eyes. "So how come I've never heard your impression of Mae West before?"

The corner of her lips went up. "It's something I only picked up a few months ago."

Alex wasn't sure what to think about that. Before he could say anything, she smiled the sexiest of smiles and stroked his chest with her small hand, making him suck in a breath. "A hard man is good to find."

The impression of Mae West was again perfect. Alex squeezed her then kissed her softly as he'd wanted to all night. He'd never forgive himself for having wasted an entire year being an idiot.

They walked back to the car, slowly kissing every few feet. A few feet away from his truck, she stopped him just Alex was about to kiss her "Alex, you have a flat."

He turned to his truck. Sure thing, as flat as they got.

"Damn. How did that happen?" He let go of Valerie's hand and went over to get a better look.

"Maybe you ran over a nail?" Valerie offered.

Alex crouched down and saw the damage. "No nail, babe."

Valerie stood, trembling, hugging herself, and rubbing her arms. "What was it then?"

"Someone slashed it." Alex stood up and looked around. As far as he could see, the other three tires were fine. Whoever did this might not have had time to do the rest. That meant only one thing, they hadn't gotten far. His eyes searched the parking lot, but there was no one suspicious anywhere.

When his eyes finally met Valerie's, he could see she'd been unnerved. He knew what she was thinking because it was exactly what he was thinking: Bruce.

Great, he'd been all set for a night of digging further into all that he'd missed out of in her life this past year, especially finding out more on her relationship with Luke and the ridiculous notion that she'd be attending a seminar with him—one she seemed too damn excited about. All that would have to wait now. There was a bigger issue to talk about first.

CHAPTER 19

Valerie sat in Alex's truck feeling terrible. Alex replaced the tire. He'd also called the police and was now outside as they finished taking the report. Alex was convinced this was Bruce's doing, and he wanted everything from here on documented. He said when, not *if,* Bruce went down, he wanted him put away for a very long time if not for good.

According to *prosecutor* Moreno, each one of these incidents would add to the severity of the penalty. Alex wouldn't let her deal with this on her own, not by a long shot. He was beyond concerned, and Valerie knew he wouldn't let up, especially now.

His eyebrow had been up and stayed up at attention the entire time he spoke with the police. Valerie held her breath as he climbed in the truck. They'd already had a pretty long night, and it was about to get longer.

Valerie knew Alex would go into full-blown warden mode now. But she wasn't about to let him take over every aspect of her life. She had her pepper spray, and though she hadn't had time to tell Alex, she'd already started looking into purchasing a gun. It was a trivial detail she knew she should've mentioned sooner, but her gut told her he'd overreact.

"I already talked to Sal." Alex turned the ignition on and began pulling out of the parking space. "He was coming down anyway for the rehearsal dinner this weekend, so he's cool with coming in a day early. He'll cover for me at the restaurant all day. We'll go see about that restraining order first thing in the morning."

"Alex, I can go by myself. You don't have to take the day off just for that. The rehearsal dinner is on Saturday. Don't you have a million things to do at the restaurant for that?"

This was exactly what she didn't want. Alex had enough on his plate already. The last thing he needed was to add to it.

Alex didn't even flinch. "Sal can handle the restaurant. Listen, I was thinking maybe you can start going to your apartment after work, especially when I'm working late. Then when I get off, I can swing by and follow you back to my place."

"What?" Valerie shook her head. "Alex, no. There's no need for all that. You can't—"

"You said this guy showed up at one of the properties you were showing, right?" Alex stared straight ahead, his brows furrowed in deep thought. "When and where is the next property you'll be showing?"

"I'm not sure. I was supposed to tomorrow, but …"

He turned to look at her. "What time?"

"In the afternoon." Valerie felt the frustration building. He was doing exactly what she'd thought he'd do: taking over her life and forgetting about his own.

Alex's eyes were back on the road again. "We should be done by the afternoon. I can go with you."

"Wait, Alex, you're not listening to me. I show properties all the time. You can't be there every time. It's not even necessary."

"I'll think of something."

"No you won't."

Alex turned to look at her. His forehead fully pinched. "This guy's dangerous, Val. I'll be damned if—"

"You can't possibly think that you are going to guard me twenty-four seven. You have your own life. I won't have you putting it aside for me. Besides," she glanced out the window, not wanting to see his expression when she made her next statement, "I'm getting a gun."

They were only blocks away from his place, but Alex pulled over abruptly anyway. “What?”

Valerie turned back to him. Alarm and intensity clearly filled his eyes.

Determined to not let him intimidate her, she lifted her chin a bit. “I’m getting a gun.”

“Do you even know how to use one?”

Valerie shrugged. “What’s there to know? Point and shoot, right?”

She didn’t think the intensity in his eyes could get anymore piercing, but it did.

“Are you crazy? A gun in the hands of someone completely inexperienced is more dangerous than a gun in the hands of some psycho.”

Valerie wasn’t sure what irritated her more: the tone he was taking or his complete lack of faith in her. “I can learn, Alex. Isabel said Romero is taking her to a shooting range soon. I’ll ask to tag along.”

Alex shook his head. “You don’t know the first thing about guns, babe. Do you even have a permit to carry one?”

Valerie bit her lip. He had her there. “No, but I can get one.”

He pulled back on the road and continued to shake his head. To her surprise, she heard him chuckle. “Point and shoot, geez.”

Valerie resented his thinking she was so helpless. “Well it’s not like I’m looking to become some gun-slinging badass. All I need to know are the basics.”

“Yeah and how to make sure it doesn’t go off in your purse or that you don’t accidentally shoot someone or yourself when you’re *just pointing*.” He glanced at her then back on the road. “But you will need some kind of protection. I’ll take care of it.”

Valerie glared at him as they pulled into his driveway. For the first time since she’d been staying with Alex, she actually wished she could be back in her own apartment at least for the night. She was in no mood for anymore of his alpha-male tirades.

She got out of the truck and closed the door a little harder than she had intended. "I'm going back to my place tonight."

Alex came around the truck. "What? Why?"

"Because I want to. I just need to get my briefcase."

He caught up to her just as she made it to his porch and tugged at her hand.

"Hey, what do you mean you want to?"

She tried to look away then to her surprise felt the hot tears overwhelm her eyes. Alex searched her eyes. The stern expression now softened. "What's wrong?"

Valerie stared at him for a moment then leaned against his chest. He hugged her, rubbing her back and kissed her head. He lifted her chin and wiped her tears with his fingers. "Talk to me, baby. What is it?"

"I didn't want you involved in this, Alex. I'd never forgive myself if something happened to you because of me. I already feel terrible about your tire."

She'd felt the anxiety building from the moment Bruce had brought up Alex on the phone earlier. She hated Alex being involved in this at all. When she realized his tire had been slashed, her stomach had nearly bottomed out. Then listening to him talk about wanting to be there when she showed property and knowing this was already going to begin affecting his time at the restaurant really did it.

His comments about her not being able to handle a gun had only sharpened her already ragged emotions.

Alex hugged her tightly. "Silly girl. Nothing's going to happen to me. And don't worry about the tire. I planned on getting new ones anyway."

Valerie looked up again. Alex started to open the door. "But you said it yourself." She sniffed. "He's dangerous. Now he's included you in this madness."

"But that's good, Val." They walked into the house. Alex took her by the hand to the sofa. "He's stupid. The more he does, the deeper he digs himself. Once we get the restraining order, he'll be hanging himself the second he decides to do anything else."

He sat down and sat Valerie on his lap. Valerie couldn't help feeling safe in his arms. But she didn't want him feeling obligated to look after her every minute of the day, especially if it meant putting himself in harm's way. She had no doubt he wouldn't think twice about doing that, and that scared her the most.

Alex could more than hold his own in a fair fight. She wasn't worried about that. But Bruce didn't fight fair. She wouldn't allow it. Couldn't. "Alex, I was serious when I said you're not going to be babysitting me. I don't want you tying up all your time, trying to watch me. I'll be fine."

She watched his expression grow hard again. It took some effort, but she could see he took a moment before responding. "We'll talk more about that tomorrow. Right now what I want to know is what's this nonsense about going back to your … Isabel's apartment."

Valerie lifted a shoulder then leaned her forehead against his. "I knew I was getting upset, and I didn't want you to see me break."

Alex smiled, deepening his dimples further. She still couldn't completely wrap her brain around the idea that this amazing man was actually in love with her.

"Do me a favor." He said.

She pulled her face back to look at him.

"Don't do that again."

Valerie tilted her head, not fully understanding.

He pulled a strand of her hair behind her ear, his expression suddenly going serious again. "Don't think just because you're upset, no matter what the reason is, that the answer is to bail. That's not how I want things to be with us."

He leaned over and kissed her softly before speaking again. "We can work anything out. You're here with me now to stay." He kissed her again. "I don't know about you, but I have no plans on spending another night of my life away from you, not if it can be helped."

Valerie smiled. From the moment she first met Alex, he'd always had a way of making her melt. She understood now more than ever that she never got over him. Nothing felt as perfect as being right there in his arms. "All right. Never again. I'm sorry."

Alex scooted her off his lap and onto the sofa, lying over her gently. "I don't want you to be sorry. I want you to be happy," he ran his hand up the side of her leg, making her tremble as only he could, "and safe." His hand made its way up the inside of her skirt. Valerie felt how hard he was already as he pressed against her thigh, "And mine, always mine, Val."

His hand continued up the inside of her legs, and she spread for him. "Always," she whispered.

"I love you, baby."

His finger suddenly in her, Valerie barely managed a breathless, "I love you too, Alex."

~*~

Things didn't go exactly as planned the next day. Alex was under the assumption that you just walked in and asked for the restraining order, but there was a lot more to it. They'd be filing paperwork, lots of it. After that, there would be a hearing the next available day. That wasn't until the following Wednesday.

Being that Alex's patience was as short as his fuse, he was not too happy about it. Valerie wanted to just take the paperwork home and bring it back next week, but Alex wasn't having it. It was bad enough they already had to wait. The sooner they filed the paperwork, the sooner they'd get the hearing. Even then, it wasn't a for sure thing. The judge could rule that it wasn't necessary. Although, Alex couldn't see that happening, not given the man's history.

They were out by noon, and Valerie insisted he go back to the restaurant while she prepared herself for the properties she would show later. Alex just didn't feel comfortable about leaving her side, knowing the maniac was out there somewhere watching her. But Valerie was so damn stubborn. She forced him to give in.

"I'll drop you off at the office, Val then pick you up in a few hours." Alex gripped the steering wheel, still not believing how mulish Valerie was about this. She knew it was dangerous. "But I'm going with you to show the property. I'll stay out of your way, just keep an eye out."

Valerie stared out the passenger window, frowning. "Only because I don't want you wasting any more time driving all the way back to your place to pick up my car. But you're not going to do this every day. It's ridiculous. You have a restaurant to run." She reached over and put her hand in his hand. "Can you please give me a little credit? I am capable of looking out for myself, you know."

Why the hell were women always like this? There was no reasoning with them. "Our place," he said through his teeth.

"What?"

"You said your place. It's ours now, remember?"

He glanced at her and saw her smirk. "We're taking things slow, don't *you* remember?"

"You have your reservations, not me. I don't do slow." He squeezed her hand, and she squeezed back.

They reached her office, and Alex watched her until she was safely inside. He glanced around the parking lot. There was no way he'd be comfortable having her drive around alone. The psycho was following her. He'd told her that, damn it.

For a moment, he considered staying put, being a look out until she was ready to go. Then he had a thought. He picked up his phone and dialed.

"Hey, Romero, you busy?"

"No, what's up?"

"I need a favor."

***

Showing properties that afternoon had gone smoothly. As usual, Alex was thoroughly impressed with Valerie's wit and elegance when interacting with her clients. He kept his distance as promised, but even from afar, she was amazing. There was no way Luke wasn't still feeling for her. He saw it in his eyes the night before—the reason why he planned to talk to her a bit more about him. Then the whole tire thing happened.

Tonight was different. There were new things he needed to get straight with Valerie. Alex wasn't wasting any time either. He'd get right to the point. But there was one thing he needed to do first. He was waiting on a phone call, and he didn't want to be in the middle of the conversation with Valerie and get interrupted.

She was busy finishing some work on her laptop in the kitchen. Alex stepped outside with the excuse of checking some things on the truck. He really had planned to get new tires for his truck. He was having it lifted as well, so he was outside rounding the truck pretending to examine his tires when his phone rang.

It was the call he was waiting on.

"What happened?"

"Well, it's gonna take a few days to run a background check on this guy. As extensive as you want it anyway." Romero said. "But I did get someone that can keep an eye on Valerie. It's not gonna be cheap. I mean I'll cut my share out, but I'm paying this guy by the hour, so if you want him on her at all times, it's gonna get pricey."

"I don't care. I just need your word he's good. The guy following Valerie has a history of violence. I can't take any chances." He glanced back to make sure Valerie was still inside. "Whatever you do, do NOT mention a word about this to Isabel. Valerie will flip."

Romero assured him the guy was reliable and that his lips were sealed. They discussed it for a few more minutes until he heard his back door open and cut the call.

Valerie was still in her work suit and high heels. She looked good enough to eat. She leaned against the doorway. "You hungry?"

"Funny you should ask."

She seemed puzzled. Alex chuckled. He'd explain later. "Yeah, actually I'm starving. You wanna order a pizza?"

Her excited expression made him laugh. He couldn't help kissing her as soon as he reached her. "Go ahead. Just make sure you order enough. You eat as much as I do."

***

They ate in his front room on the floor in front of the television. Valerie had changed into shorts and one of his T-shirts. Alex loved seeing her in his shirts. He especially loved the smell of her in his shirts later.

After a few slices and going over their plans for the next day, Alex was ready to get down to the business of Luke. The box of pizza sat on the coffee table, and Valerie reached for another slice then sat back down facing Alex, legs crossed in front of her.

"Tell me about this seminar you're going to."

Valerie glanced at him and took a swig of her beer. "It's the weekend after the wedding at that fancy resort on the marina."

Alex always noticed Valerie would avoid eye contact whenever the conversation made her nervous. She was doing it now. Though she did her best to try to hide her unease, he could see it, and it bothered him.

"And you're going together? You and Luke?" Alex braced himself. He didn't want to turn this into an argument, but this was her ex-boyfriend they were talking about: One she worked with on a daily basis. Based solely on the way he'd looked at Valerie at the wine tasting, the guy was far from over her.

"No." Again with the glancing at anything but his eyes. "Well, originally that was the plan. But once I broke things off with him, I offered to give him the ticket back. He said he wanted me to have it." She looked at him for a second then took another swig of her beer. "He did buy two tickets, and they weren't cheap. So we're both still going, just not together."

"What about the meet and greet? Luke said you're both invited. Are you sure he doesn't still think you guys are going together?"

Valerie shook her head. "No, I'm sure he means once there, we'll meet up."

Alex didn't like the sound of that either. "Is this an all-day thing?"

"All weekend."

"*What?* You're staying overnight?" That was definitely out of the question.

Valerie stood up and grabbed their empty beer bottles from the coffee table. Alex sensed she was getting irritated. That made two of them.

"Nope. He is. I'm not."

"He told you he was staying the night?" Alex kept his eyes on her as she walked into the kitchen. He wouldn't put it past Luke to casually mention something like that.

Valerie dropped the bottles in the trash. They crashed loudly as they hit the bottom. She opened the refrigerator. "He reserved a room when he bought the tickets."

Alex straightened out, literally feeling the rise in his temper. "I thought you said you never slept with him?"

"I didn't." There was no hiding her irritation now, but Alex didn't care.

He stood up, no longer comfortable sitting. "Then why the room, Z?"

Valerie stared into the refrigerator without saying a word. Alex stalked toward her, his temper pushing with every step. "Why would he get a room if you two weren't sleeping together?"

Rationally, he knew it shouldn't matter. This was in her past. But he wanted it straight. What was the point in lying about it, unless she had reason to.

She finally turned and glared at him. "I don't ask you about the girls you slept with while we were apart."

He knew it. *He fucking knew it*. "So you did sleep with him?"

"No. I didn't."

"Then why the room?" He wanted to believe her more than ever. It was hard enough to accept how much time she spent around Luke now. If she'd slept with him, it changed everything.

She finally closed the refrigerator doors and turned to him. "I don't know, Alex. I guess he assumed we might be sleeping together by then. But I knew things were over between us the same night he gave those tickets to me. I broke things off the very next time I saw him."

She didn't avoid his eyes this time instead looked straight at him. Every muscle in his body tensed up now.

"Sweetheart," she reached for his hand, "I'd tell you the truth if I had. But things were never that serious between us. I never felt anything for him." She took his other hand and kissed his knuckles then stared in his eyes again. “I wanted to feel something for him. I really did.”

Alex didn’t want to hear that.

“But I couldn’t. Isabel kept assuring me I would eventually. It just never happened.” She slipped her arms around his waist and leaned her cheek against his chest. Alex couldn’t hold back hugging her as much as he was still feeling on edge. “All I could think about was you, Alex, the entire time I was with him: every embrace, every kiss.”

Alex pulled back. She’d killed it. “Stop, Z. I can barely handle the thought of you going out with that asshole, much less the visual of him touching you.”

Valerie smiled at him lopsided. “How ’bout we never talk about this again?”

Alex wasn’t sure about that, but for now, he’d had about as much talk of Luke as he could stand. He hugged Valerie, thinking of everything she just told him. He still wasn’t too sure she was telling him everything. There was one thing he was sure of: he definitely had to come up with a way to get her out of that office.

CHAPTER 20

The morning went without a hitch. Valerie had a couple of more properties to show the same clients from the night before. To her pleasant surprise, Alex didn't put up much of a fight when she'd told him she was doing it alone.

A few cautionary warnings were all he gave her, and he reminded her to keep her pepper spray handy. He even left before she did that morning. Valerie felt guilty, knowing that he'd probably been in a hurry to catch up since he was busy babysitting her the day before.

She'd gone back to his place to change. She was supposed to meet Alex at the restaurant, and they would drive out to the church together for the wedding rehearsal. But Valerie was running late. After changing, she called him and told him it would be faster if she met him at the church.

Just a few blocks from the church, her phone rang.

"Hey, where are you?" Luke sounded a little irritated.

"On my way to church, why?"

"Church? You have clients waiting for you at La Jolla Mesa. Did you forget?"

Valerie's jaw dropped. "Oh my God. I completely forgot!"

She scheduled it over a week ago. With everything that had happened this past week, it had slipped her mind.

"How do you forget something like that?"

"This week's been crazy, Luke. I was going to reschedule, but I totally forgot about it. I'm on my way to my cousin's wedding rehearsal. I can't miss it because I'm the maid of honor. Is there any way you can …"

She heard him grunt then what sounded like papers rustling. “Shit, Val. Is it just a combo, or do I need keys?”

Valerie put her hand on her face and made a U-turn. “You’ll need keys for the warehouse in the back. I have them on me. I can meet you halfway.”

“Call the clients and let them know I’ll be late. Don’t tell them you forgot.”

Ten minutes later, she was at the gas station they agreed to meet at. She dug through the box in her trunk where she kept all her property keys. She still couldn’t believe she forgot. Luke drove up just a few minutes later. He had a stern expression as he drove in next to her car but smirked once out of the car.

Valerie smiled, relieved that he wasn’t too upset with her. She handed him the keys then gave him a quick hug. “Thank you so much for doing this. I owe you big time.”

He caught her hand as she pulled away, and without warning, she locked into one of Luke’s stares. “Don’t worry about it. I’ve been meaning to ask you, did you ever finish your painting?”

Feeling a bit uncomfortable but at the same time surprised he remembered, Valerie smiled. “Almost. I didn’t have any time to work on it this week. But it just needs some final touches, then I gotta get it framed.”

“I know where you can get a good deal. Remind me when we’re back at the office. I’ll give you their card.”

Valerie remembered all the expensive artwork in Luke’s house. She hadn’t unveiled her painting to anyone yet, not even Isabel. It was still sitting back in the closet at her apartment. She planned to make some time next week to work on it then take it in to get it framed. The wedding was next week. It was crunch time, but she hoped to get someone’s opinion on it first. She was still so nervous about it. Maybe she could show it to her dad once she framed it.

"Thanks, I will." Luke still held her hand, and Valerie tugged it away. "I really appreciate you saving me like this. I gotta go. I was already running late before you called."

She rushed to the church, making a few unnecessary sharp turns along the way. Fortunately, it seemed they were running late at the church as well. Things had just started when she got there. Alex's eyes questioned her late arrival, but she told him she'd explain later.

After the rehearsal, they headed to the restaurant for the dinner. Her visit to the restaurant to explain the offer had been so nerve-racking she hadn't even noticed the pictures on the walls near the bar area. She slowed to examine them.

"Wow, so many." Valerie remembered a few pictures of local little league teams hanging on the wall back in the days. Now, two entire walls displayed not only pictures of teams thanking the restaurant for their sponsorship, but awards as well.

"They've accumulated over the years." Alex made light of it, but Valerie was impressed. Many of the photos appeared to be team parties in the new banquet rooms Alex had told her about. He was in most of the photos, surrounded by adoring mini football players wearing their jerseys. Their smiles were big, and they seemed to be relishing the moment next to Alex as if he were some kind of celebrity.

Valerie noted the majority of the dates on the pictures were in the last year. Then she saw the pictures of him with a team on the field and the inscription, *To Coach Moreno, the best coach ever!* There were scribbled names all over it.

She turned to him in surprise. "You coached?"

"Coach." He pulled her by the hand away from the wall and toward the dining room where the dinner awaited. "I'm only taking a break right now from coaching because this damn wedding has tied up just about every weekend of mine. But the season doesn't start for a couple months, so I'll be good by then."

Valerie tugged his hand, and he turned to face her. “When do you find the time?”

Alex shrugged. “It doesn’t take too much time. Practice a couple hours a week then a game or two on the weekend.” He pulled her to him, wrapping his big arm around her waist. “Don’t worry. I’ll still have plenty of time for—”

She shook her head. “That’s not why I was asking. I’m just surprised you had the time. I know this past year was so hectic for you.”

Alex kissed her nose. “Yeah, well, I may’ve done things to keep myself as preoccupied as possible, besides, the kids are great. I only volunteer seasonally now, but I’m thinking of picking up a year-round team.”

She didn’t think it was possible, but her heart swelled even more now. Even with everything he’d gone through, he still found time to volunteer. “Could you be anymore wonderful?” she whispered.

Alex rolled his eyes. “It’s just football, Z. I’m not saving lives or anything. I’m coaching a sport I’ve lived and breathed my whole life. I’d hardly say doing something I love on my downtime is noteworthy.”

It was to Valerie. She leaned in for a long heartfelt kiss.

“Hey, break it up.” Romero said.

Valerie turned to see Romero and Isabel stroll in hand in hand. She pulled away from Alex.

Alex frowned. “Your timing sucks, Ramon.”

Valerie smiled at the sight of Isabel. She’d missed her. Once seated inside, Alex got caught up with coordinating things in the kitchen. He came over and sat with her and Isabel a few times, but each time, he’d been pulled away.

Valerie hadn’t realized how much she missed chatting with Isabel in person. All week, she’d only had short conversations with her on the phone. It was hard to believe it had only been a week, and yet she and Isabel had so much to catch up on. Romero was at the bar at the moment, hanging with Angel and Eric.

Valerie told Isabel about everything, including her conversation with Alex the night before about Luke.

"Why do they need to know everything?" Isabel frowned. "I haven't asked Romero a thing about any of his exes, yet he continues to ask about mine. Don't get me started on the whole 'fantastic date' I had with Michael. He's still hung up on that, though the last time he brought it up again, I told him I was done discussing it."

Valerie giggled. With the exception of Eric and maybe Sal who were a bit more laid back, all these guys were so much alike. She remembered poor Sofia referring to them as cavemen on more than one occasion back in high school. They had made her life miserable, *protecting* her even when she insisted she didn't need it.

Nothing had changed, at least not with Alex. He was still overdoing the protecting. He already ordered her a Taser gun, and Romero would be coming over as soon as they got it to show her how to use it. Valerie didn't mind so much that Alex was taking such precautions, but she couldn't help resenting that he was taking liberties in her life without even checking with her. She knew he meant well, but she worried it might become a habit that extended into other parts of their relationship.

~*~

Even though Alex felt a little deceptive about having someone tailing Valerie, he was glad he'd done it. If he didn't know someone was looking out for her today, he might've gone a little crazy, wondering where she was earlier. It still made him nervous that she showed up so late. But Romero assured him that if she was in *any* kind of danger, his guy would not only protect her he'd call Alex immediately.

Angel and Eric went back to their tables, and Alex was finally going to get a chance to talk to Romero about what he knew so far.

"You got anything on this guy yet?"

Romero glanced around to make sure no one was listening. "I was gonna call you back last night. But I figured you wouldn't be able to talk, and I've been with Isabel all morning. This guy's bad news, Alex."

Alex braced himself, even more convinced now that having Valerie watched was the right thing to do.

"I'm still not done with the whole background check, but the guy's rap sheet goes way back. This last stint he did in jail isn't his first. He was in and out when he was younger. And Valerie's not the first chick he's stalked. His first wife had a restraining order on him until, get this, she disappeared."

Alex went numb. "You're shitting me?"

"Nope, I don't know all the details yet. The guy I have running the background won't be done for a while, but he called me yesterday to give me that tidbit. Thought it might be something I'd wanna know ASAP."

That unfamiliar emotion consumed Alex again. He turned to where Valerie sat laughing with Isabel, so unaware of the amount of danger she was in.

"When will you know more?"

"Probably not until sometime this coming week."

Alex grimaced. He had no patience for all this waiting around, especially not when it came to this. "This guy you have watching Valerie—he knows not to let her out of his sight until she's with me even when she's home, right?"

Romero nodded. "Yep, he followed her even after the church rehearsal because you two were in separate cars."

"Good."

"By the way," Romero glanced at Valerie then back at Alex, "was she supposed to meet up with Luke earlier?"

Something about Romero's tone bothered him. "I don't know. She was showing property all morning. Maybe. Why?"

"Well, this guy knows he's looking out for my friend's girl. So he thought it was kind of weird that she had a quick meet with this dude. He saw you leave your house this morning, so he knew it wasn't you."

Alex frowned. He hadn't planted this guy on Valerie to spy on her. He was supposed to be watching her, not reporting anything he thought might be suspicious on her part. But he had to admit Romero had his attention. "What do you mean quick meet? Like at one of the properties she showed?"

"No," Romero picked up the beer the bartender placed on the bar for him. "She was on her way to the church then suddenly made a U-turn. He thought maybe she'd caught on to him, so he backed off a little. He followed her to a gas station where she met with some dude. It didn't sit well with me. He said they hugged, and he even held her hand for a minute there, so I had him run the plates. Car's registered to Luke Faust. That's him right?"

Held her hand? *What the fuck?* "Yeah, that's him."

"Yeah, so I, uh," Romero took a drink of his beer, "just thought I'd mention."

Alex eyed him, knowing exactly what he was thinking, his mood deteriorating with every word Romero said. From the very beginning, his gut told him there was more to Valerie's relationship with Luke. He wouldn't have such an issue with it if she didn't have to see him every day. Incidents like this one were exactly the reason.

He turned to look at Valerie. Sarah, Sofia, Angel and Eric now joined her and Isabel. He took a long deep breath. This was neither the time nor the place. He'd just have to fight the urge to go ask her why she was late until after the dinner.

Alex turned back to Romero. "Is that it?"

"About Valerie and Luke?"

The sound of that had Alex clenching his teeth. "About everything."

"Yeah, for now. I'll know more soon."

Alex's thoughts went back to Bruce and his missing first wife. His only consolation was with a rap sheet like his, it would be easier to throw him in jail longer if he tried anything. He clenched his fists. The fear of anything happening to Valerie wrenched his insides.

"Listen, if you get any more big news like last night's and you can't talk, text me. I wanna know as soon as possible."

"Hey." Romero pointed at his own chest. "I got this."

Alex grabbed a peppermint candy from a bowl on the bar. He popped it in his mouth, needing a moment to digest everything Romero had just dumped on him. Getting through the rest of this dinner without being able to ask Valerie about her morning would be a challenge.

~*~

Valerie would be so be glad when this whole wedding thing was over. As happy as she was for Sarah and Angel, she really needed a weekend off. It seemed when she wasn't working, she was busy doing something wedding related.

Tomorrow would be the first Sunday in a while she got to just relax. She was so looking forward to it: no appointments with clients, no dress fittings, nothing but pure self-indulging relaxation with Alex.

She drove slowly with Alex following closely behind. He seemed a bit quiet at the rehearsal dinner earlier. She even caught him spacing out a few times during dinner. Valerie hoped he wasn't still worrying about Bruce.

Valerie waited outside the back door for Alex. He'd warned her not to go in the house until he was there with her.

She watched as he looked around the yard, making sure Bruce didn't lurk in the bushes no doubt.

They entered the house, Alex up front and cautious. She saw his eyes search the room. Did he really think the situation was that bad?

"Honey, you need to relax. You're so tense." Valerie kicked off her shoes and flung her purse on the sofa.

After checking the bedroom, Alex made his way back to the front room. Valerie plopped down on the sofa. "Seriously, Alex, would you please bring it down a notch?"

Alex began unbuttoning his shirt. "So what happened today? Why'd you get there so late?"

Valerie's eyes fixated on his fingers. They were making their way down the row of buttons on front of his shirt. "I'm always running late, Alex. I'm sorry. I'll have to work on that."

"Nothing happened though? You just got caught up at work?"

He was now working on the cuff buttons. In a second, he'd be out of his shirt completely. Valerie watched, anticipating. If she were with him forever, she'd never get enough of watching him remove his shirt.

"Are you listening to me?"

Valerie finally brought her eyes away from his chest and rested them on his face. The coy smirk, a hint that he was easing up finally.

"Not really." She smiled and went back to shamelessly enjoying the view.

"I asked if anything happened to make you late today."

Thoughts of Luke interrupted Valerie's happy ogling. *Gawd*, she didn't want to bring him up now. But Alex was staring at her, so she figured she may as well get it over with it.

"I was almost at the church when I had to turn back to meet Luke."

"For what?"

She explained what happened. The smirk was long gone replaced now by an unmistakable glower. Although, she could tell he did his best to conceal it.

"Did you have to get out of the car?"

Valerie thought about the odd question for a moment. "Well, yeah, the box with all the keys I carry around is in my trunk. I had to get them for him."

Alex continued to stare at her as if he were waiting for her to say more. When she didn't, he pulled off his shirt one delectable arm after the other. Valerie sized up his strong arms, his shoulders, and that beautiful chest. He wore just a white snug tank now that traced his muscled chest nicely.

She glanced back at his face. His hardened look hadn't softened at all. She patted the cushion next to her on the sofa. "Come here."

He didn't move at first, then he dropped the shirt on the arm of the sofa. He sat next to her, exhaling as if he'd been holding something in.

"Baby, you need to relax." She massaged the shoulder closest to her. He was even tenser than she'd expected. "Look at this. What's the matter with you?"

He didn't respond, instead he let his head fall back on the sofa and closed his eyes. Valerie leaned over and kissed his cheek. "I know what you need," she whispered.

His eyes flew open immediately, making her giggle. She slid off the sofa and positioned herself between his legs. She massaged his hard thighs as she eyed him wickedly.

Alex was ready, and she could see the push against his slacks. She loved how easily she could change his mood even if it was just for the evening. She undid the button on his slacks and slid the zipper down slowly.

He was immediately out through the slit in his silk boxers. She touched the wet tip with her finger then brought the finger to her mouth and licked it, all the while staring at Alex. His big Adam's apple moved as he gulped, his eyes gleaming with eagerness.

Bringing her hand back down, she wrapped it around his length. Alex flinched at her touch. "Relax," she ordered, smiling at him before bringing her head down.

She licked the rim slowly as she began to work him softly with her hand. Alex inhaled deeply just as she took him completely. She'd never told him, but he was the only man she'd ever done this to. Sure, she'd performed a few hand jobs back in high school and in her college days, but this she couldn't even imagine doing to anyone else.

There was no mistaking the quiver in Alex's legs. He groaned, beginning to squirm in his seat, the taste of salty sweetness becoming stronger in her mouth by the second. He moved his back away from the sofa, making her look up.

"Let's go," he grunted through his teeth.

She pulled away, and he helped her up. He was immediately on his feet. He picked her up, cradling her in his arms. "I need you right *now*."

The very thought moistened her panties immediately, and she kissed him profoundly. How she went an entire year without him was beyond any comprehension. They'd made love every day since they'd gotten back together, each time feeling more urgent than the last. Tonight was no exception.

CHAPTER 21

After working out for an hour, Alex headed back to his house to shower. The day before had been the first since he and Valerie had gotten back together without any drama or unsettling revelations. They'd spent their entire day doing one of Valerie's "Lazy Sundays." It was heaven.

It helped Alex rest his rigid nerves for at least a day. But he was back to reality now, and with reality came stress. He'd checked and double-checked his phone all morning to make sure he hadn't missed a call from the guy watching Valerie.

Valerie still hadn't mentioned anything more about her meeting with Luke. *They held hands for a minute.* Romero's comment still gnawed at him. There was no way he could ask her about it. He'd just have to wait and see if she ever brought it up on her own.

He saw the note as soon as he walked in the door. It was on the dining table. He smiled the moment he was close enough to see what was on it. Valerie had drawn a picture of them: There were two stick figures, one with circles for muscles on the arms and the other half the size with curls and giant heels. Three hearts floated above them. Just beneath the stick figures she wrote.

I could never go even a day away from you now. I miss you already.

Love you madly.

~Z~

Alex felt like a grade school kid, reading it over several times. He'd die before admitting he'd actually felt flutters inside as he read it. He put the note down and picked up his phone. He texted Valerie exactly what he was feeling that moment.

Just read your note. You never will. I promise. Miss you too and I love you more than you'll ever know.

He *did* miss her. He hated to leave her that morning, but Romero had called, asking if he wanted to meet him at the gym to work out. Alex thought that might be code for something if Isabel was anywhere near him. So he left in a hurry. Turned out Romero really wanted to just work out. He still didn't know anything new.

Alex folded the note into a very small square and took out his wallet, slipping it under his license, smiling.

After showering, he headed to the restaurant, again double-checking if he'd missed any calls. He hadn't.

~*~

The painting turned out better than Valerie envisioned. There was just one small thing she wasn't completely sure of. Though they both looked just as happy as they did in the picture, there was something so special in their eyes. She didn't quite see it in the painting. Maybe she was just looking too hard. She gazed at it some more. She should've asked Isabel for her opinion. It was just so nerve-racking unveiling her work to anyone. She hadn't even told Alex about it yet.

That morning she found the card to the framing place Luke told her about on her desk. She'd already called for a quote. The place was only minutes away from her apartment. Since she didn't have any appointments that morning, she figured she may as well get this out of the way.

Her phone rang. Valerie answered it, still staring at the painting.

"Hey, did you get the business card I left on your desk?" Luke sounded cheerier than normal. Valerie was glad he'd stopped being such an jerk and went back to acting as he had before they'd ever dated. Though he still looked at her in ways that made her feel uncomfortable.

"Yeah, thanks. As a matter fact, I'm going over there now."

"So you're done with the painting? Were you able to capture that nuance of true love that you were so worried about?"

That made Valerie smile. She wondered if it was part of his management training to somehow remember even the smallest details of long ago conversations. "I think so, but—"

"But what?"

"I don't know. I'm staring at it now. Maybe it's just me."

"Has anyone else seen it?"

Valerie chuckled. "No."

"Well that's your problem. Artists are always their own worst critics." He paused. "Where are you at?"

"My apartment." She chewed the corner of her pinky nail.

"I'm only five minutes away. I can swing by if you want. I'd love to see it. I promise I'll be completely honest."

Valerie stepped back, as if looking at it from a distance would somehow change her outlook on it. She considered Luke's offer. What could it hurt? "You're really only five minutes away?"

"Closer now."

"Okay, I'll wait for you."

Valerie set the phone down and continued to scrutinize the painting. She was being obsessive. She knew it, but this was important. Sarah's relationship with Angel was what bonded her to Sarah in the first place. Valerie had been there for her through their whole roller-coaster beginning. If it hadn't been for those two falling in love, Valerie may have never met Alex.

Alex Valerie winced. He wouldn't be thrilled about her having Luke over to her apartment. She shook it off. There was no way he'd ever know. Luke would be in and out in five minutes. She'd been alone with him plenty of times at the office. What difference did it make?

The doorbell rang. Valerie hurried to get it. Luke was suited up as usual. She let him in and walked him to her bedroom, growing a bit unsure with every step. Maybe she should've thought this out a little more.

Luke stopped in front of the painting. He didn't say anything for a moment just stared. Valerie bit her lip, her eyes bouncing from the painting back to Luke impatiently. Luke turned to her, his expression blank. "Valerie, this is amazing."

She couldn't help but grin. "You really think so?" She grabbed the picture from her dresser and handed it to him. "This is the actual picture."

Luke held it, his eyes lifting from it to the painting and back again a few times. He turned to her with a big smile. "I say you nailed it. Your cousin is gonna love it."

He handed her back the picture. "He looks exactly like Alex by the way. In a younger, smaller kind of way, but, yeah, the resemblance is uncanny."

The mention of Alex reminded her she shouldn't be there too long with Luke. Valerie set the picture back on her dresser. "Well, I feel better now, Luke." She glanced at her watch. "Thanks for stopping by. I hate to rush you out, but I do have an appointment in a couple of hours, and I still need to drop this off first."

Luke left quickly, again praising her painting before walking out. Valerie grabbed a slice of cold pizza from the fridge and groaned after taking a bite. Isabel's homemade pizza—just another one of the things she'd miss about living with Isabel.

She walked in the bedroom to get the painting when the doorbell rang again. Luke must've forgot something. She hurried to the door and opened it without looking to see who it was. Her heart nearly stopped at the sight of Bruce standing at her door.

"I see you're letting them take turns, Val. Do I get my turn now?"

It took her a moment to regain her thoughts. Instinctively she tried closing the door, but he pushed at it. Valerie leaned her entire weight at the door with a grunt. She was no match for him.

"Stop right there!" An unfamiliar man's voice yelled outside.

The door slammed shut, and she heard running footsteps. Her hands trembled uncontrollably as she fumbled with all the locks. She brought her trembling hands to her face and covered her mouth, peeking out the window. He was gone, and she didn't see anyone else. Her cell phone rang in the bedroom.

She started toward the bedroom, feeling more alarmed as the reality sunk in. What if whoever yelled hadn't yelled in time? What would Bruce be doing to her this very moment?

She picked up her phone, barely able to hold it in her still trembling hands. Two missed calls from Alex. It rang again, causing her to almost drop it. It only rang once and then stopped—a good thing because she needed to calm down before speaking to him.

Something turned in her stomach. She was going to be sick. Dropping the phone on her bed, she ran to the restroom. The phone rang again as she heaved into the toilet. Nothing came out but her stomach roiled again and again forcing her to continue to heave loudly. When it finally passed, she sat on the cold bathroom floor, back against the tub, too afraid to try to get up. She feared if she stood it would start up again.

This nightmare was never going to end. It was only getting worse. She brought her knees up slowly, not wanting to fluster her stomach. Hugging her legs, she leaned her head against her knees. Finally, she had no choice but to accept what Alex had been trying to tell her all this time. She was in very serious danger. Bruce wouldn't stop until he got what he wanted.

Something rattled in the front room. Valerie was on her feet at once. Her heart wouldn't be able to take much more. She looked around for any kind of weapon barely able to breath. The only thing even close to resembling a weapon was a plunger, and she grabbed it. The front door opened, and she braced herself, plunger in the air, ready to swing.

"Valerie, you here?" She never thought she'd be so happy to hear Romero's voice.

She dropped the plunger and hurried into the front room. He gaped at her. "What happened to you?"

Valerie knew she looked a mess. The dry heaves had made the tears come in mass. "I came by to pick something up, and Bruce," she stopped suddenly, overwhelmed with the need to cry, "the guy that's been stalking me, tried to force himself in."

Romero walked over to comfort her, hugging her softly. "It's okay." He pulled away. "Are you hurt? Did he touch you?"

Valerie shook her head. There was a knock at the open front door. They both turned to see two uniformed officers. "Someone called about an attempted forced entry?"

Apparently, one of the neighbors had heard the commotion and called the cops. By the time Valerie finished answering all their questions, she had about eight missed calls from Alex.

Romero stayed there the whole time then went outside when they were done interviewing Valerie. He stood outside chatting with them.

She called Luke first to ask if he could call to cancel her appointments for her. There was no way she'd make them the way she was feeling. This incident had thrown a wrench in her entire day's plans. Not only that, she knew she'd be on the phone with Alex for a while. He'd want to know every last detail.

She dialed Alex, sat on the sofa, and held her breath.

~*~

The morning started out well enough. Busy as usual up to his eyeballs getting things ready for wedding, he'd hardly had time to worry about Valerie. Now he stood out back in the alley behind the restaurant struggling to remain as calm as he could. It was a relatively cool day for summer, but Alex was burning up. He gripped the phone as he listened to Valerie. He'd spoken to her for nearly an hour. Not once had she mentioned Luke at her apartment.

When Hank, the guy watching Valerie had called to inform him that he'd just chased a man who tried to force his way into Valerie's apartment, Alex dropped everything. He was already in his truck when Romero called to tell him. Romero had just pulled into the parking lot of her apartment. Alex was halfway there before Romero could convince him it was best he didn't blow Hank's cover just yet. Bruce was still loose after all. Valerie needed someone watching her more than ever now. Reluctantly, Alex had to agree it was better if he didn't tell her yet, not before making Romero promise he'd call the cops and have a report taken.

Romero promised then told him about Luke. Like Alex, Romero thought there had to be some kind of reasonable explanation. It couldn't be what it looked like. Besides Hank said Luke was there less than five minutes. What bothered him most was that Valerie didn't mention it. Even if she wasn't doing anything wrong, that still broke some kind of relationship rule in his book.

The worst thing about the entire situation was that because Valerie had actually opened the door, they couldn't go after him for attempted forced entry. It was bullshit. Even though he was still on probation, assuming they ever tracked him down, he probably wouldn't get more than a slap on the hand.

Thoughts of Bruce and Luke slammed back and forth in Alex's head. He dropped the phone in his apron pocket and pulled out his wallet. Leaning his shoulder against the wall, he pulled out the note Valerie had left him that morning. There was no way Valerie could be doing anything. He felt it in his heart. The note went back in to its safe place. There was just no way. He knew this.

So why was he still pacing outside, trying to calm himself before going back in the restaurant? With his nerves stretched raw, the adrenaline still hammered through him. It hadn't stopped since the moment he'd seen Hank's number on his caller ID. He grabbed his keys before he'd even answered.

Hank was an expensive commodity but worth every penny. Alex didn't even want to think how grave the circumstances might be right now if Hank hadn't been there.

He'd almost gone nuts not being able to get a hold of Valerie. When he finally heard her voice, even with the questions he had regarding Luke, he was still extremely relieved.

Finally feeling calm enough to walk through the restaurant without biting anyone's head off, Alex stepped in the back door. Sergio, one of the busboys appeared concerned as he passed him. "Everything okay, chief?"

They'd all seen how he ripped through the restaurant to get out of there. And he'd been in and out taking phone call after phone call ever since. He demanded Romero call and update with every little bit of info he gathered.

Alex clapped Sergio on the shoulder. "Yeah, I'm good. Thanks."

To his surprise, Sal sat at the computer in the back room. "What are you doing here?"

Sal spun his chair around. "Dad didn't tell you?"

"Tell me what?"

"I talked to him this weekend. He said you guys were going to be real busy all week. I'm done for the summer, so I told him I'd help out. I'll be here the whole week. I just gotta go back for one test on Friday, then I'm here until I start up again in the fall."

"Well, that's a relief. Where were you this morning when we were swamped?" Alex pushed the door to the office closed.

"I just got here. I didn't even go home. Came straight here." Sal raised an eyebrow. "What's going on with you? I heard you bolted out of here like a maniac."

Alex frowned. He didn't even want to think about it anymore. "Someone tried to force their way into Valerie's apartment. I'll tell you about it another time. That shit's giving me a headache."

"She okay?"

"Yeah, she's fine. Shaken up but fine."

Sal studied him for a moment then spun his chair around to face the computer again. "Is this really the guest list for the wedding? Good Lord!"

Alex sat down on a chair near the door and leaned his head against the wall. "Yep, that's it. Mom and Pop are nuts. Sarah only has her mom and one aunt. Angel said there's a couple of her friends coming down from Arizona and a few local ones. The rest are all our side."

"You sure you ordered enough food?"

"Yeah, the list is on that same file. Everything for the wedding is." He watched as Sal clicked open some of the other files.

"Damn, Alex. When did you do all this?"

Alex leaned his head back again, rubbed his temples, and closed his eyes. "I started when pop said he wanted the wedding here. You know how he can be. I had a feeling this thing was going to turn into a circus."

"Dude, you have graphs for the seating arrangements?"

Without opening his eyes, Alex chuckled before responding. "Mom and her sisters? C'mon, we all know who's gonna snap and who's not. I had to keep things under control."

"Seriously, Alex, I'm impressed. I've hated every computer class I've taken so far. I just don't have the patience. This is something else."

Alex took a deep breath, still keeping his eyes closed. Deep inside, though he'd never admit it, there was a part of him that still delighted in impressing his older much more anal brother. "The software does it all, Sal. It's not rocket science."

Sal didn't respond. Alex opened one eye and saw Sal still clicking through all the hours of work he'd put into organizing this wedding.

"Has Angel seen this?"

Alex sat up, remembering all the work he still had to do. Valerie's incident had thrown his whole day off. "I dunno. He's been busy, trying to find a place for his restaurant." He stood up, checking his phone just in case. "Oh, I meant to ask you. You bringing anyone to the wedding?"

Sal turned to look at him. "Probably not."

"What happened to that Melissa chick?"

Sal shook his head and turned back to the computer. "She's too damn … everything."

"What does that mean?"

"Too swank. Too in your face sexy. Too outspoken." He turned back to Alex. "I might've been able to live with all that. It's when she got too pushy that really did it."

Alex smiled, curiosity getting the best of him. "How so?"

Sal shrugged. "She knew we weren't exclusive. I made it clear from the beginning, and she said she was okay with that." He shook his head. "Somehow she got into my place one night, made dinner and was waiting for me in her birthday suit when I walked in."

Alex lifted an eyebrow. "Sounds good to me."

Sal spun around and faced the computer again. "Yeah, it would've been if my date hadn't been with me."

It took a second, then Alex burst out laughing.

"Yeah, laugh it up." Sal said without turning around. "It still doesn't top your tutor story."

The remark didn't lessen Alex's laughter. He walked out the office, still laughing. Knowing how proper Sal always strived to be only made the visual of him walking into that with a date even funnier. Sal muttered something under his breath, but Alex heard him chuckle as well. Today of all days, he needed the laugh. Thankful for the break in his mood, he threw himself back into his work.

CHAPTER 22

The restaurant was a madhouse on the eve of the wedding. Food and supplies rolled in all day. Angel opened the place, helping with the setup of the banquet room. Certain things like the dance floor and the stage setup he wanted done just so. It was his wedding, so Alex watched and let him have at it. In a way, he a was a little surprised Angel didn't seem nervous at all. Then again, Angel had been sure since he'd met Sarah back in high school that she was the one. The only reason they'd waited this long was because they both wanted to finish school first.

As if the wedding preparations alone weren't enough to make things hectic, Sal arranged for the pay-per-view heavyweight champion fight to be watched at the bar that very evening. He mentioned doing a little promoting on the internet. Alex now knew what was behind the sly grin when Sal had told him. The place was already packed. The main fight wouldn't even start for another hour.

Alex should've known when Sal mentioned he'd hired a couple of Romero's guys to make sure things stayed under control. They'd never needed security before, but the bar area was already nearing capacity, and customers were still arriving. Romero was there, throwing a few back. He said he was off duty, but Alex could see he was doing more looking out than drinking.

Valerie, Isabel, and Sofia had taken Sarah out for dinner and some drinks. They assured Angel it wasn't a bachelorette party, more of a dinner and girl talk the last night before the big day. Alex told Valerie it sounded an awful lot like a bachelorette party to him. She just laughed and promised it wasn't.

With the exception of Monday's incident, the week went without episode. Wednesday, Alex accompanied Valerie to the hearing. There was no doubt the judge would rule in favor of granting Valerie the restraining order, especially after what just happened.

He did, but the problem was the restraining order was only good for three weeks. Bruce had to be served first for it to be permanent. Anybody but Valerie could serve him. Alex wouldn't have had it any other way.

Unfortunately, when Romero went to serve him at the homeless shelter listed as his primary residence, they hadn't seen him in weeks. His probation officer was no help either. He'd finally returned their calls today simply to say Bruce was only required to check in every ten days. The last he'd heard from Bruce, he'd said he was staying at the shelter at night and looking for work during the day. Bruce wouldn't be required to check in for another week. There was no way of getting a hold of him either since Bruce supposedly didn't have a cell phone. The whole system was a damn joke.

Bruce was more frightening than Alex expected. He'd been in the armed forces until he was dishonorably discharged for computer fraud. Most of that information was classified, so Romero was having a hard time getting the details of it. But apparently this guy was some kind of computer whiz. Great. This just kept getting better and better.

All his priors were violent ones. His stalking wasn't just limited to following his victims around. In all the cases, he'd done extensive snooping, and of course, hacking into their computers to gain more info. He'd even served a couple of weeks in a mental facility. Why they ever let this nut out was beyond anything that made sense to Alex.

Most of his crimes included attacks against women. The only one that included an attack on a man was when he tried to run an ex-girlfriend's new boyfriend off the road. Alex more than welcomed the animal's coming after him. He'd make sure the guy got what he deserved, but most importantly, they'd have him locked up.

The only positive thing that came from the background check was that it appeared his ex-wife's disappearance was more of a self-initiated disappearance. There was evidence she'd already changed her name once. Her family never even attempted to file charges against Bruce. Basically they accepted she'd disappeared and went on their merry way. Not likely, a family wouldn't do that unless they knew where she really was and were wittingly keeping quiet about it.

A very small consolation, but at least as far as Alex knew, Bruce didn't have blood on his hands … yet. With that thought lingering, Alex decided to check on Valerie. He walked toward the back room. The restaurant was just too damn loud for him to make a phone call out there.

Once in the back room, he was quickly distracted, going over some more of the wedding details on the computer. When he was done, he decided it was better to leave Valerie alone. Hank would call and update him if anything happened. He went back to the bar. The place overflowed with loud patrons now. Alex leaned over to Sal. "You sure we're not over capacity?"

"We're good now, but we had to turn some people away. They weren't too happy about it either. It's a good thing we had Romero's people here. They started getting rowdy."

Alex frowned, taking it all in. The tables were crammed, and every booth at the bar was taken with people crowding around each booth. He sure hoped Romero's guys knew what they were doing.

He took a stroll to check everything else out. Workers diligently transformed the banquet room upstairs into wedding paradise. The flowers would arrive in the morning. His parents would be pleased. They were both home working on the trinkets they'd pass out at the wedding. Alex told them he could just order them already made, but they insisted they had to be personal and handmade.

By the time he'd made it back to the bar, the fight was in full swing and everyone cheered loudly. Alex watched along with the crowd. It was a good fight with both fighters going at it.

One of the waiters nudged him on the arm. "You have a call on line one."

Alarmed, Alex reached for the cell phone on his hip. Maybe he hadn't heard it with all the noise. He had no missed calls, but he still felt the need to rush to the office to take the call. He picked up the phone as soon as he got to it, forgetting to close the door behind him.

"This is Alex."

"Whose ass do I have to kick to get a beer around here?"

Alex pressed the phone against his ear, not sure if he'd heard correctly. "What was that?" He reached for the open door with his foot and kicked it shut.

The caller raised his voice. "I said whose ass do I have to kick to get a beer around here? The service sucks! I've been waiting for over twenty minutes."

Alex felt his adrenaline jump-start. Almost certain he knew, he asked anyway, "Who's this?"

"Who do you think it is, asshole?"

Alex smiled, gripping the phone. "You here, Bruce? I can get you a beer. Where you sitting?"

Bruce cackled. "No, I'm not at *Moreno's* anymore. No, no … I'm at Tres Italiano. You know where that is, *Alex*?"

Alex squeezed his fist shut. It was where the girls were having dinner. He gulped hard in a failed attempt to remain calm. He texted Romero to come to the office ASAP. "Yeah, I know where that is."

Bruce cackled until he was coughing, then he started up again. "Is that your pretty little sister with Valerie? And your brother's lovely wife-to-be? Her name escapes me. Oh that's right, Sarah."

Alex's heart thudded a little harder. He listened for background noise. It didn't sound like he was in the restaurant. It was too quiet. Romero swung the door open. Alex brought a finger to his lips.

"You must have a death wish, Bruce 'cause I swear to God if you so much as—"

"Does Valerie know you're having her tailed? I'm getting pretty good at timing his piss breaks."

Romero stood next to Alex, hanging on every word. Alex motioned for him to get Hank on the phone. "What do you want, Bruce?"

"Oh, I think you know what I want."

Angel walked into the office.

"You're fucking crazy." Though his words were harsh, his voice remained calm. He'd die before letting this idiot know his mind games were working. "That'll never happen, Bruce."

Alex had both Romero and Angel's full attention now. He covered the receiver, "Ask Hank where the girls are exactly. This fucker is watching them."

Angel's eyes narrowed. "Who's Hank? What girls—"

Both Romero and Alex shushed him.

"Valerie," Alex mouthed.

Alex could almost pinpoint the moment it hit his brother. His eyes opened wide. "She's with Sarah and Sof." He whispered.

"And Izzy," Romero added with a frown.

Alex had missed most of Bruce's crazy rant. None of it made sense anyway.

"…mine! She was meant for me you ungrateful, stupid bastard!"

The blood scorched through Alex's veins like fire. Bruce sounded like a raving madman. "That's where you're wrong Bruce." He said calmly. "Valerie's always been mine."

Bruce cackled even louder this time. "Is that so? So even when Luke was fucking her, she was yours?"

No way would Alex let this guy rile him. He took a long deep breath, glancing at Angel who was standing, arms crossed, waiting anxiously to hear the next words out of Alex's mouth. "Listen here, Bruce—

"No you listen!" He was screaming now. "If you think you can stop me, you're stupider than I thought. You keep trying, and I'll make you sorry!" He stopped screaming and started laughing. This time in a low droll. "I didn't realize you had such a pretty sister, Alex. And wouldn't your brother be sorry if he had to cancel his wedding?" He paused for a moment then added, "Valerie looks beautiful tonight. I'll be sure to tell her."

Alex's calm vanished. He spoke through his gritted teeth, careful not to let out the rage that built so quickly. "I'll kill you."

The line clicked and went dead. "He hung up." Alex slammed the receiver down.

"What the hell is going on, Alex? Who's watching them?" Angel looked as alarmed as Alex felt.

He didn't have time for long explanations. "Valerie has a stalker."

"What? Why didn't you tell me?" Angel's eyes were ablaze. Alex couldn't say he blamed him. Up until now, he felt pretty safe with Hank watching them.

He tried sounding confident. "Relax, I have someone on them. They're being watched, but you can't tell Sarah."

"Why not?"

"Because Valerie doesn't know."

Romero still spoke to Hank, filling him in on the phone call.

"Tell him Bruce knows he's watching Valerie."

The door flung open. Alex heard glass crash. The waitress' frightened eyes met his. "They're fighting!"

Alex cursed under his breath and charged out of the office with Angel and Romero close behind. He turned to Romero who still held his phone to his ear. "Tell him not to take his eyes off them for a second. I don't care if he pisses his pants!" He'd reached his boiling point now. He turned back to Romero again. "Make sure you tell him I said that."

The fight was under control when they got there, but it left the entire bar area a mess. Romero's guys escorted two big guys out. Sal held back a smaller guy with a bloody nose and a fat lip. Apparently, he wasn't the trouble maker but still yelled obscenities at the guys being escorted out.

Alex had seen this a million times. The guy was obviously putting up a Mr. Tough Guy act for his startled girlfriend to make up for the fact he'd gotten his ass kicked. Well, he was in no mood for it. He had other customers to think of.

Alex got right in little man's face, still reeling from his conversation with Bruce. He spoke just loud enough for the guy to hear him. "Calm the fuck down, or I'll throw you out there with those two and let you settle things on your own."

The guy stared at him but didn't say a word. Alex took in the sight around him. It would be hours before they could get the place back in order. *I'm getting real good at timing his piss breaks*. Damn it, the wheels spun in his head.

Sarah and Sofie met Isabel and Valerie at Isabel's apartment earlier that evening. They'd all driven in one car to the restaurant and were supposed to head back to the apartment after dinner for drinks. Valerie told him they'd play it by ear. Depending on how the night went, they'd either drive home tonight or spend the night if they didn't feel well enough to drive. Alex's money was on the latter. The wedding wasn't until three in the afternoon tomorrow, so they'd have plenty of time to get home and get ready the next morning.

Of course, Alex had offered to pick Valerie up, but she said if the girls all stayed, she would too. If that was the case, Romero would have to put someone else on the nightshift, someone unfamiliar with the case. That didn't sit well with Alex. He could only hope Valerie decided to go home tonight. The notion of not having her in his bed all night wasn't a welcome one either. He'd made it a point several times to tell her that would never happen again. Here just two weeks into it, the possibility of it happening was already upon him.

~*~

Valerie got the text on the way home from the restaurant. Alex explained briefly about the call from Bruce. He said he didn't want to call her because he didn't want the girls overhearing and becoming alarmed. But he warned in all capital letters to stay in the apartment and lock all the doors and windows. Valerie understood completely about not wanting to alarm the girls, most specifically Sarah. This was way too heavy to dump on her the night before her wedding.

He didn't tell her everything Bruce said but mentioned a lot of ranting and crazy talk. Valerie was surprised he didn't tell her to just cut the night short and insist on picking her up that minute. But she supposed not wanting to alarm the girls had a lot to do with it.

They all kicked off their shoes as soon as they walked in. Valerie held in a laugh as she watched Isabel cringe at the sight of shoes flying in all directions. Isabel was a good sport about it and said nothing. Instead, for the first time Valerie had ever seen, she kicked off her shoes and left them where they landed. Valerie knew Romero had a lot to do with Isabel's newfound liberation from her obsessively anal personality.

Valerie broke out Sarah's special wine, the kind that came in a jug rather than a bottle.

"My Precious!" Sarah clapped her fingers together in front of her.

Valerie laughed, pouring her a glass. Sarah always called it that even back in high school. They'd all made fun of her for bringing a cooler with a small jug to the backyard parties rather than just a six pack of beer like everyone else.

A cell phone rang in the front room where they'd all dropped their purses. "That's me." Sarah rushed to her purse.

"If that's my brother again, Sarah, tell him to take a chill pill." Sofia shook her head. "Geez what's that? The third time in less than an hour?"

Sarah pulled the phone out of her purse and smiled when she read the caller ID. She looked at Sofia and nodded. "It's him again."

Sarah took the call in the front room. After everyone poured their drinks, Valerie jumped on the kitchen counter and took a long swig of her beer. Still a little shaken by Alex's texts, she was determined to enjoy the rest of the evening. "If Sarah could ever pull herself away from her phone," she said loudly, leaning her head in the direction of the front room, "we should play a game." She turned back Sofia and Isabel, "One of those girlie games like back when we were teens."

"Ooh fun." Sofia grinned, taking a sip of her wine. "I don't think ever played any, but I remember hearing about them."

"Don't worry," Isabel clinked Sofia's wine glass with her own and took a drink. "I never played any back then either."

That didn't surprise Valerie. By the time she'd met Isabel, they were well past the girlie teen years. But even in college she rarely joined her in their drinking games. Once or twice Valerie had managed to twist her arm.

Sofia was a whole other story. That poor girl was lucky to do anything with those three brothers of hers watching over her like the secret service, especially Alex.

Sarah hurried in the kitchen. "Okay, I'm sorry. I think it's because he hasn't seen me all week that he keeps calling to check on me."

Sofia rolled her eyes but smiled. "You'd think it's been a month with the mood he's been in all week."

Valerie couldn't believe it. Those two had literally been inseparable since high school. "You haven't seen him all week?"

Sarah seemed pleased with herself, picking up her glass of wine from the counter. "I always said I would do this the week before we got married. I don't think he ever believed I'd actually go through with it even after I asked Alex for the week before the wedding off. I'm sure he thought he'd weasel his way somehow and see me." Sarah giggled and drank some of her wine. "He tried to act like it was no big deal, but by Tuesday, he was already trying to talk me out of it. Ever since then, he's been making excuse after excuse why we *have* to get together."

Valerie laughed. She was surprised Sarah had stuck to her guns. She wasn't sure she could do it. Even now, she was beginning to consider taking Alex up on his offer of picking her up. "Okay, so we're playing girlie games, Sarah. Remember those?"

"But we have to have a theme." Isabel added. "In this case, I say all games have to do with *love*."

Sofia squealed. "I've never even had a sleepover."

Valerie jumped off the counter and patted Sofia on the shoulder. Poor girl, not only had she dealt with her brothers, she'd also been claimed by Eric the moment she turned seventeen. Sarah told her all about Sofia falling for Angel's other best friend.

"Follow me ladies," Valerie walked into her front room and turned on the iPod sitting on Isabel's neat media center. She set the music to a slow and easy station.

They all took a seat on the sofas, except for Valerie who sat on the floor. "Let's play Truth."

"Isn't it Truth or Dare?" Sarah asked.

Valerie crunched up her nose, "I don't feel like doing any dares. Do you? But I'd love to hear some juicy truths."

Isabel grinned and lifted her hand, almost spilling her wine. "I'll start. Mine is for Sarah. Where was the first place you and Angel did it?"

Sarah turned to Valerie, completely scandalized. "Wait, aren't there rules?"

"Yes," Valerie laughed, "the rules are, 'the hostess makes the rules.' So answer."

Valerie already knew the answer, but she was having fun watching Sarah squirm. Sarah glanced at Sofia. She turned back to Isabel then took a sip of her wine. Just when she was about to answer, she decided to take another sip.

"Quit stalling, Sarah. What's the big deal?" Valerie tossed the napkin she'd held her beer with at Sarah.

"It was at the restaurant." Sarah put her hand over her face, peeking through her fingers at Sofia.

"Oh, Gawd, Sarah. You really think I didn't know?" Sofia curled her legs under her.

"Is that bed in the back room still there?" Valerie spent quite a few glorious hours in that bed, back before Alex got his own place.

"It sure is." Sofia winked, smiling wickedly.

Valerie's jaw dropped. They all burst into laughter. Sarah always told Valerie how brazen Sofia could be. She'd gotten a taste of Sofia's gutsy behavior over the years. But to have sex in the back of the restaurant with the possibility of any of her three brothers walking in was pure insanity.

After about another hour, not only had Alex, Angel, and Romero interrupted them several more times but Eric had now gotten in on the check-in calls. Sofia stood up. "All right, hand them over."

Sarah handed hers over, looking very remorseful. Isabel laughed, tossing hers at Sofia without argument. Any other night, Valerie would have gladly handed it over, but tonight Alex would hit the roof if she didn't answer her calls or return his texts. "But my dad hasn't been doing well. I can't turn my phone off." She felt terrible using her dad. But it was true. Her dad hadn't looked very well when they'd gone to see him that week. Her stepmom let her in on the dizzy spells he'd been having for days. Sofia almost gave in.

"Don't fall for it, Sofia. He can call her on the house phone. He's the only one that ever does."

Valerie glared at Isabel. Sofia held out her hand. She handed the phone to her grudgingly. "I won't turn them off just set them on vibrate. You'll be allowed to check if your dad called periodically. But the guys aren't going to die if we ignore their calls for the rest of the night."

Valerie wasn't so sure about that. Sofia placed all the phones on the coffee table. "I need a refill. Anyone else?"

Sarah stood up. "I do."

Sarah helped Valerie off the floor. They moved the party into the kitchen. Isabel threw some appetizers in the oven and poured a few bowls of chips. The girls dug in and continued to play Truth, laughing hysterically at times.

Even through all the laughter, Valerie couldn't stop thinking of what the guys must be thinking with none of them answering their phones. Alex was probably having a fit.

CHAPTER 23

"Ooh, I love this song," Valerie hurried into the front room to put the volume up. She didn't really love the song, but she was dying to check her phone. She leaned over sneaking in a quick look at the girls who were very much into the snacks and still laughing.

She turned to the coffee table. All four phones had blinking indicators of missed calls and texts. Pretending to dance, she inched her way closer to the coffee table. It didn't matter that the song was a slow soulful song. She still shook her thing, bending over as part of the choreography.

Grabbing the phone with one slick move, she continued to dance with her hands swinging behind her to hide the phone. She turned around sensually so her back faced the girls and continued to dance as she read her texts. She had several. She read the most recent.

Angel's going nuts, Val. Why aren't any of you answering?

There was no way she'd have time to respond to all or even read the rest. She hit the keys quickly to respond at least to this one. All the while, she continued to dance.

"Are you texting?" Sofia sounded appalled.

"Get her!" Sarah yelled.

Valerie jumped on the sofa, giggling and trying desperately to hit send, but the phone was knocked out of her hand when Sarah jumped on her followed by Sofia. Isabel grabbed the phone off the floor and read the first part of her text aloud.

"Sorry, babe, my phone was off …" She looked up at Valerie. "Seriously? You're apologizing for ignoring his calls for what? An hour?"

Valerie smiled sheepishly. "He worries."

Sarah stared at her own blinking phone. Isabel took one look at her then at the blinking phones. "Not you too? All right, we're going to have to hide these, Sof."

Sofia took all the phones and dumped them in her purse. "There. This is my first girl's night and Sarah's last as a single girl. We're not gonna let the guys keep interrupting us."

Isabel high fived her, "Amen, sister!"

Valerie's stomach roiled. She was going to have to find a way to let the guys know what was going on before they all came pounding down her door. She'd never forgive herself if she were forced to let Sarah know what was going on and have her worry unnecessarily. Tomorrow was supposed to be one of the best days of her life. Valerie knew this would definitely throw a damper on it.

Time ticked away as the girls continued to eat, drink, and be merry.

"I should stop," Sarah said, staring at the mozzarella stick in her hand. "My dress is kind of tight around the middle. I'd hate to look bloated."

"Oh, please," Isabel huffed. "You don't have an ounce of fat on you. Don't you run like twenty miles a day?"

Sarah giggled, taking a bite of the appetizer. "Well, not twenty but, yeah, every day."

Sofia reached for an appetizer, "I read somewhere online that …"

That was it. Online. If Valerie could get to her laptop, she could shoot Alex a quick email. This was perfect. She'd left it in the car. She could send it from there, and the girls would never know otherwise. She hopped off the counter where she'd been sitting and rushed into her room.

"What are you doing, Val?" Isabel called from the kitchen.

Valerie slipped on her fuzzy Tweety Bird slippers. She'd have to remember to take these back to Alex's place. "I gotta get something out of my car."

"Now?"

Valerie pressed her lips together. Isabel was being absolutely no help.

"I wanna show Sarah something." She walked out of her room and past the girls who were all looking at her funny.

Sofia's smiled. "I like your slippers."

"Thanks, my daddy gave them to me. I'll be back."

She'd barely stepped out the door when she got the distinct feeling she was being watched. Dread crept through her with every breath she took. It could very well be her nerves, but she could swear she heard something move in the bushes. She opened the trunk as soon as she reached her car.

Staying aware of her surroundings as Alex reminded her to do a million times, she walked around the car and climbed in the driver's side. She locked the doors as soon as she was inside. Of course, the laptop took forever to boot up.

After finally logging in, she sent a very quick but to-the-point email. She only hoped Alex wasn't too wrapped up in trying to get a hold of her to not bother to check the emails on his phone.

The laptop went back in her trunk. Isabel was too slick. If she saw her walk in with it, she'd know immediately what she'd been up to. It was crazy how naked she felt without her phone.

As she made her way back to her apartment, she squeezed the pepper spray bottle, holding her thumb on the button ready to use it. She hadn't even thought of bringing the Taser Alex made her promise she'd carry at all times.

A car raced into the parking lot, and Valerie froze. It stopped just inches in front of her, the headlights flooding her vision. She shielded her hands over her eyes. Her slippers firmly glued to the ground.

Her mouth opened, but no sound came out. The passenger door opened slowly. With the headlights still on her, she could only make out a figure. Even with the pepper spray in her hand, she felt completely vulnerable and useless. She couldn't even move, let alone try to fight.

"Are you kidding me?" The voice boomed.

It took her only a second to realize it was Alex. Though relieved didn't even begin to explain how she felt at that moment, she knew she was in for it.

~*~

Valerie's startled eyes had never looked so beautiful. As irritated as he'd been with her for not answering her phone, knowing she was okay more than made up for it.

"What are you doing out here by yourself?" He closed the door to Angel's car. The tension in his muscles was still there. It had been ever since Bruce's call and only got worse with every call Valerie hadn't answered.

"I had to go to my car." Valerie walked toward him.

"Didn't I tell you to stay inside? This guy was watching you tonight." Alex glanced around. He probably watched them now.

"I had to. They're holding my phone hostage. I went to the car to send you an email from my laptop." Valerie leaned her head against his chest.

Alex hugged her, feeling the tension he'd felt all night drain from his body. The other doors opened, and Romero and Angel got out. They started toward the apartment.

"No!" Valerie pulled away from Alex. "Don't go in there. Angel you can't see Sarah."

"I just wanna make sure she's okay."

"I can see Izzy." Romero protested. "I'm not the one getting married tomorrow."

"She's fine." Valerie assured Angel. "Sofia hid all our phones so we'd stop being interrupted."

Eric was the last out of the car and came to stand next to Alex. "Sofia did?"

"Yes, none of them know about the phone call Alex got. I'd like to keep it that way. No sense in upsetting Sarah for nothing."

"It's not *nothing,* Valerie. The guy is a real psycho." Alex frowned. Valerie didn't even know the half of it.

"You know what I mean, Alex. I'll tell her all about it after the wedding."

"So this is what you're up to?" Isabel stood at the door of the apartment arms crossed.

Angel and Romero started toward her. "Oh, no you don't," Isabel said firmly. "You can't see Sarah, Angel."

Alex, Valerie, and Eric followed behind Romero and Angel. "I just wanna ask her something."

"You have the rest of your life to do that," Valerie interjected, "starting tomorrow."

Sarah peeked through the window curtain. Valerie shot her a warning look. The slit in the curtain closed immediately. Sofia stuck her head out the door behind Isabel and waved. "I'm spending the night, Angel. I just read your text. So no, I don't need you to pick me up." She laughed a little too loud.

"Have you been drinking, Sof?" Alex peered at her. He'd seen her drink, but she was only twenty. He'd never seen her drunk though, and he didn't like it.

"Yes, lots." She put her hand over her grin and ducked back in the apartment.

"Are we done here?" Isabel put her hand on her hip.

Alex could almost picture her handling her middle school students. Romero took advantage and jumped up the couple stairs to give her a quick peck on the lips. "I'll call you later. Answer your damn phone."

Romero and Eric started back toward the car, followed by a very dejected looking Angel. Alex couldn't help smiling. It was amazing how just seeing Valerie, even for just a moment, could change his mood so dramatically. He turned back to Valerie and placed his hand on her shoulders. Back to business.

"Hostess with the mostest, we're waiting on you." Isabel wasn't letting anyone off the hook. No wonder Valerie had to sneak out to email him.

"Give us a minute, sweetheart." Alex spoke up before Valerie could. He really needed to talk to her. He didn't care what Dean Isabel had to say about it, but he smiled sweetly anyway. "Please?"

"Okay, but I'm counting."

Alex resented having to rush but did his best not to lose the smile. She walked in the apartment finally. He wanted to ask Valerie so much about Bruce, mainly what the hell she'd seen in him in the first place. She'd gone out with him for a few weeks, didn't she once notice what a psychopath he was?

All that would have to wait. He knew he had very little time, but he had a few very important things he needed to get out.

"Valerie, I cannot stress the importance of you being careful. I still can't believe you were out here alone."

"I did it for you."

"I know, baby, but you still took a huge risk." He brought his hands up and cradled her face. "I need you to promise me you won't do that again."

"But—"

"Promise."

Valerie finally conceded. "All right."

After making her promise a few more things and Isabel sticking her head out the door to tell them time was up, he forced himself to pull away and let her go. He waited until he was satisfied she'd locked the door. She peeked out the window and blew a kiss.

When he got to the car, he sat down next to Angel in the front seat. His mood hadn't changed. Before getting back with Valerie, Alex would've ribbed Angel about being so damn whipped he couldn't go a week without seeing Sarah. He might've even been a little annoyed by it, but now he understood completely. Hell, he was considering staying at his parents or even the restaurant tonight just so he wouldn't have to go home to an empty bed.

"After tomorrow, dude," Alex nudged his sulking younger brother, "you'll not only be spending every day with her, you'll have her every night too."

Angel glanced at him then back at the road. A second later as if the thought set in, he smiled.

Alex smiled, looking out the passenger window, his thoughts immediately back on Valerie's safety again. He was more determined now than ever to catch this guy. If the law wasn't going to help, he'd have to do it himself. He'd already told Romero tonight that he wanted more than just a background check on Bruce. He wanted everything on the guy. He'd gone too far tonight. It was personal now.

~*~

Maybe it was liquid courage, but Valerie had originally planned on wrapping the painting and taking it to wedding. She knew she wouldn't be there when Sarah unwrapped it, and she kind of wanted it that way. Now she was feeling a little brave. The painting still sat in her closet.

Without giving it another thought, Valerie jumped off the kitchen counter and rushed toward her room.

"Where you going?" Sarah asked.

"I have something for you."

She was going to bring it out into the kitchen, but the girls were all in her room within seconds. The nerves hit her all of sudden.

"What is it?" Isabel looked around her room curiously.

Valerie glanced at Sarah, unbelievably beginning to feel choked up. *Damn beer*. “Okay, I don’t want you to think this is something I’m expecting you to hang up or anything. You don’t need to feel obligated, Sarah.”

Sarah smiled. She knew Valerie painted, but Valerie rarely shared any of her paintings with anyone besides her dad and Isabel. Even Alex had only seen a few.

“So if you don’t—”

“Oh, just show it to me already!” Sarah giggled.

Valerie took a deep breath and slid the closet door open. She pulled out the sheet-covered painting but hesitated to remove the sheet.

Isabel crossed one arm over her chest and held her wine with the other. “Valerie, hon, if you don’t take the sheet off already, I’m going to.”

“Yeah, Val. I’m dying!” Sarah added.

Valerie pulled the sheet up slowly. When it was all the way off, the girls all gasped. She turned to Sarah whose eyes had welled up.

Valerie bit her lip. “You like it?”

Sarah hadn’t taken her eyes off it. “I love it.” She glanced at Valerie. “I haven’t seen that picture in years.”

“Valerie, it’s beautiful.” Sofia stepped forward to get a closer look. “You did this?”

Valerie nodded, almost losing her balance when Sarah suddenly hugged her.

Sara cried, probably a mixture of emotion and the wine. “This must’ve taken you forever to paint.”

Sniffing away her own emotion, Valerie wiped her eyes. “Well, not forever, but I did spend some time on it.”

“This is amazing, Valerie.” Isabel stood in front of it, admiring it.

Sarah pulled away to look at it again. “I want it at the wedding tomorrow. It’s perfect. This brings back all the memories of when we first fell in love. Angel’s gonna love it, Val. Thank you so much.”

Valerie couldn't help feel warmed by her sincere gratitude. But she hadn't expected this. Here she'd been so nervous about showing anyone, and now the painting would be on display in front of hundreds of people. Her insides turned as the reality of it hit her. Everyone she knew would see her work now. She tried to think of a way out of it, but Sarah looked so excited she didn't have the heart. *Damn.*

CHAPTER 24

The Wedding

Alex watched Valerie get dressed after getting back from the salon where she'd gotten her hair done, and still couldn't get over how amazing she looked in her bridesmaid's gown.

The color scheme Sarah had picked was chocolate brown and beige. With the exception of Valerie, the bridesmaids' and even the mothers' gowns were dark brown accentuated with some beige. Valerie's long gown was a solid brown. Her big beautiful dark eyes looked even bigger and brighter.

The entire wedding party now stood just outside the back entrance of the church, waiting for the signal to start entering. Alex glanced at the limousine parked just out front. Sarah had yet to make an appearance. She hid well behind darkly tinted windows. Alex wondered if Valerie would want all this someday. She never mentioned what kind of wedding she'd want even hypothetically. Maybe because he'd come across as so damn commitment phobic for so long, she was afraid any talk of weddings would completely scare him off.

The organ began to play inside the church. That was the signal. Alex took a quick inventory of his surroundings. The thought of that animal doing anything to disrupt the wedding made him clench his teeth.

Luna, Sarah's mom, tapped his arm. "Are you nervous?"

Alex smiled down at her. "Not at all." He held his arm for her, and she wrapped her arm around it. He'd be escorting her in since she was single. Sarah had never met her father. Her childhood best friend's dad, and only father figure Sarah had ever had, would be giving her away. They'd driven in from Arizona just for the occasion.

The wedding party began walking in one couple at a time. Alex hadn't really expected everyone on the guest list to show up. There were just too many, but from the looks of the packed church, they'd all made it.

By the time he made it to the front of the church, he could see the nerves finally got to Angel. He stood with Romero and Eric on either side, stone-faced. Alex was sure it had nothing to do with the fact that his brother was about to take the biggest plunge of his life. The amount of people packed in the church and the possibility of him screwing something up during the ceremony were likely the reasons.

His parents, the last to enter before Sarah would make her entrance, reached the front. The organist started the intro to "Here Comes the Bride" quite dramatically. Everybody in the church stood, and all eyes were on the back door.

And then there she was. His mother mentioned that every bride looked beautiful on her wedding day. She'd hit the nail on the head. Sarah was breathtaking. Alex glanced at his brother. Angel stood there with his eyes glued to her in complete awe. If Alex didn't know any better, he'd think Angel might cry.

Alex brought his fist to his mouth, smiling. That sap never had a chance. From the moment he'd met Sarah way back in high school, he was a goner. If things had been any different, Alex might've talked him into waiting a little longer—live a little before getting married. But it was obvious that, to Angel, his life couldn't get any better than when he was with Sarah.

That made Alex wince. It wouldn't be fun, but he had to eventually give Angel the heads up about Bruce mentioning Sarah by name. No matter how unpleasant that would be, he needed to make sure Angel was on alert.

When it came time for Sarah and Angel to read their vows, Alex glanced at Valerie. She watched them intently, obviously moved by their words. Someday, and the sooner the better, they'd be exchanging the same vows. It didn't matter if it was in a packed church or a courtroom in front of a judge. All that mattered was that it be official. Maybe it was all this wedding business, but for some reason, making Valerie his wife had suddenly neared the top of his priority list, second only to getting the psycho locked up.

After the ceremony, the entire wedding party, minus the newly married couple, all climbed into a limo and headed to the local state park, Mount Soledad. Hours and a million photos taken by the annoyingly energetic photographers later, they were finally free to get back in the limo and start the party.

They toasted with champagne and blasted the music. Sofia and Valerie even stuck their heads out the sunroof. They were back in within seconds, immediately realizing the damage the wind had caused their very expensive hairdos. They seemed upset at first, then burst into laughter. Alex was glad since there was no way he was going to hold it in. He and the other guys were already laughing.

Back at the restaurant, it was another waiting game like the one outside the church. The host lined them up again just outside the upstairs banquet room. They would queue up the music and introduce the wedding party as they walked in. This was way too much formality for his taste. He'd give Valerie whatever she wanted, but he was keeping his fingers crossed this wasn't it.

Abba' s "I do, I do, I do" started up, and they began filing in as the host introduced them. Once the entire wedding party was at the head table, the lights dimmed and the music changed to Barry White's, "My First, My Last, My Everything."

The spotlight brightened the empty doorway.

"Ladies and gentleman," the host announced, "please stand with me and welcome the newly married couple, Mr. and Mrs. Moreno."

Everyone was on his or her feet as Sarah and Angel walked through the door. Applause and cheers greeted them. They hadn't even reached the table when glasses began clinking, not that Alex hadn't seen enough of these two kissing already. He still turned to see a smiling Angel and his blushing bride kiss each other tenderly. Again, everyone clapped and the party was on.

Alex sat at the head table as Valerie walked over to speak with her dad and stepmom. They sat at the same table with his parents and Sarah's mom.

"I got someone good for you." Romero said as he took the seat meant for Valerie next to Alex.

"Who?" Alex glanced over to make sure Valerie still sat with her dad.

"It's a little shady. This guy does intelligence work for the government. I asked around; he's the best out there for this kind of stuff. These jobs he does strictly on the down low. But there's a reason why he's willing to take the risk." Romero's eyebrows lifted in warning.

Alex waited for the catch.

"He's not cheap. We're talking big bucks, Alex, and there's no guarantee that—"

"Do it. I don't care what it costs." Alex's eyes were still on Valerie, now on her way back to the table. "I need the best. Do whatever you have to do."

Romero stood up when he saw her coming. He put his hand on Alex's shoulder. "Consider it done."

Alex smiled as Valerie reached her chair.

She leaned in, putting her hand on his thigh. "What's that big smile about?

Alex put his hand over hers and squeezed. "Have I told you today how beautiful I think you are?"

Valerie brought his hand to her face and leaned her cheek against it. "Yeah, a few times, actually." She smiled, putting his hand back down on her thigh. "But you can say it all you want. I don't mind."

Alex pulled her chair closer to him with his free hand and kissed her. "You are so beautiful."

The glasses started clinking again. Valerie's attention went to Angel and Sarah. "They look so happy."

"They are." Alex took advantage of the moment. "So is this what you want?"

Valerie tilted her head. "What do you mean?"

"A wedding like this with all the bells and whistles?"

She seemed to think it through for a moment. "I dunno. I've never given it much thought."

Probably because he'd never given her much hope. He squeezed her hand, suddenly annoyed with himself. "Well, start thinking about it."

Their salads arrived, halting their conversation for the moment. Alex scanned the room for the fifth time since they arrived. He still wondered if Bruce had actually been in the restaurant last night. As crammed as the place had been, he could've easily managed to blend in the crowd.

Romero's firm had swelled into twelve employees now, and Alex hired them all for tonight. For the sake of anyone wondering why so much security but mostly so Valerie wouldn't get suspicious, he had them all dress the part. Some looked like waiters. Others dressed up like guests. He had Valerie by his side all night, and Hank was on foot patrol downstairs. As the only one of Romero's guys that knew what Bruce looked like, that's exactly where Alex wanted him.

His scanning stopped at the painting that sat on an easel near the entrance. He leaned over to Valerie. "Did you see that painting of Angel and Sarah? I just got a glimpse as we walked in, but it's a damn good painting of them."

Valerie turned to him with a strange expression then smiled. "I painted that."

Alex stared at her for a moment, unsure if she was serious. She smiled, her face turning a bit crimson. "You did?"

She nodded. Yeah, she was definitely blushing. Alex stood up.

"Where you going?"

Alex looked back at her, still not sure what to think. "Seriously, you painted that?"

"Yes." Her flushed face brightened even more.

"Why does that embarrass you?"

"I dunno. Sit down. You're making me nervous."

"No, I gotta get a better look now. Come with me." He took her hand. She hesitated for a second but then stood up. They walked over to the entrance, stopping a few times to greet some guests and family.

When they reached the painting, Alex couldn't take his eyes off it. It was amazing, the detail extraordinary. She'd even caught the twinkle in his lovesick brother's eyes. He'd seen some of Valerie's paintings in the past, but none of them came even close to this. "Valerie, this is incredible. Why didn't you tell me about this?"

She tilted her head, gazing at the painting. "I was going to bring it back to your place this morning to wrap it up. I would've showed you then, but I couldn't wait for Sarah to see it. So I showed it to her last night, and well, she flipped when she saw it and said she wanted it displayed at the wedding."

Alex let the *your place* comment go but did say, "How come you hadn't brought it home? You've been going back to the apartment to work on it all this time?"

For the first time since they'd been standing there, she looked away from the painting and turned to him. "No, it's been finished for weeks." She shrugged. "I was nervous I guess about showing it to anyone. Isabel hadn't even seen it."

"Is that right? You hadn't shown anyone until last night?" Alex turned back to the painting. It really was a work of art. He had no idea Valerie had all this in her.

"Well …"

Alex brought his attention back to her when she didn't finish. She glanced around suddenly visibly nervous. Bruce immediately came to mind. Alex followed her gaze, but she didn't seem to be looking at anything in particular.

He squeezed her hand. "What is it?"

Her eyes met his for a second, then they were on the painting again. "Luke saw it."

Alex let that sink in and tried desperately to not let the discomfort those three little words gave him manifest. "Did he now?" An older couple moved in close to take a look at the painting. Alex and Valerie moved out of the way. "When was this?"

They started making their way back to the table, and Valerie spoke as she glanced around the room. "The day Bruce tried to force his way in my apartment. Remember I told you I was picking up a painting I wanted to get framed?" She glanced at him.

Alex nodded but said nothing.

"Well, Luke had called, and when he said he was in the area, I asked if he could stop by and take a look at it. He was there for all of ten minutes. With everything going on, I thought maybe it would upset you further even though it was nothing, so I didn't mention it."

They reached their table, and Alex pulled out her chair for her. Once they were sitting, he took her hand and kissed it. "Well, don't make it a habit of keeping things from me just because you think it might upset me. I'm glad you told me." He kissed her lips. "The painting is beautiful."

He was glad she'd finally come clean about it. But Alex's unease about her still working with Luke just reached a new height. The fact that Luke had been privy to something that apparently was so important to her spoke volumes about her relationship with the guy. He squeezed her hand and tried not to let this change his mood. As much work as he'd put into this wedding, he wanted to be able to enjoy it.

With the first dance over and all the other traditional dances out of the way, it was time for tossing of the bouquet. Because Valerie was the maid of honor, she got to be front row center. They played the drumroll, counting down starting from five. All the single ladies readied themselves. When they got down to two, Sarah turned around. Rather than tossing it over her head, she threw it at Valerie.

Valerie was startled but still managed to hold on to it. Some jeered; others laughed.

"Hey, she's the queen tonight. She's allowed to do whatever she wants." The wedding host teased into the microphone.

Sarah winked at Alex, and he smiled at Valerie. It paid to know people in high places. Alex put in the request when it was his turn to do the dollar dance with Sarah. Knowing what that meant, Sarah had been thrilled at the suggestion.

Valerie shoved the bouquet at him with a smirk when she reached him. "I don't suppose you had anything to do with this?"

Alex feigned shock at the mere suggestion. Valerie laughed. "You guys are so bad."

The formalities were nearly over. Sarah and Angel stood by the wedding cake, the photographers snapping away as they cut the first slice. Alex would be glad when the photographers were finally relieved of their duties. He'd never posed so much in his life.

All in all, the wedding had been a success, and the service, even for a wedding of this magnitude, had gone smoothly. He put his arm around Valerie next to him and brought her closer. With the wedding out of the way now, he could focus on what he really needed to get taken care of: Bruce.

CHAPTER 25

Since the night before the wedding, they hadn't heard a word from Bruce. Alex wasn't taking any chances. After hearing about Hank's piss breaks, he had Romero add another guy to watch Valerie. Steve was an ex-cop and supposed to be one of the best.

With Angel and Sarah honeymooning in Cabo San Lucas, Alex felt it was safe to wait until they got back to talk to Angel about it. He only hoped by then he'd know enough about this guy to nail him.

In the meantime, he'd let Sofia in on Valerie's stalker, leaving a few of the more alarming details out. He made her promise to tell him if she noticed anything unusual, no matter how insignificant she might think it is. At the moment, he didn't feel it necessary to have anyone watch her, but if he had to, he would. The idea of Bruce coming after his family infuriated him.

He stalked out of the back room and into the restaurant. Sal sat on one of the booths with a couple of young guys. He'd been interviewing potential employees all morning. With Sarah and Angel gone for the week and a couple of employees out sick, the restaurant was really feeling the pinch. Now that Angel and Sarah's restaurant was projected to be up and running before the end of the year, Alex was not only losing them, they'd be taking a few of the seasoned cooks, waitresses, and bartenders with them. His dad said they would need all the help they could get until they got things running smoothly.

Alex hoped to pick up a minimum of ten new employees before then. He was just glad Sal was there to help with the interviewing.

Romero walked in the front door. Alex expected him. He grinned when he saw Alex. He had news, finally.

"This guy's a writer," he said with a king-sized grin.

"A writer?"

"He likes documenting everything."

"Bruce?"

"Yeah," Romero took a seat at the bar and tapped the bar for service.

Alex walked behind the bar. "You wanna beer?"

"Nah, I'm still working. Just give me a soda." Romero drummed his fingers on the bar. "So this guy keeps journals. Online journals. Some of the entries are public, but most of the ones about Valerie are not."

Alex stopped what he was doing. "He's writing about Valerie?"

"Oh yeah, dude, the guy's obsessed."

Alex knew that, but hearing that the guy was writing stuff about Valerie on the internet was still unsettling to say the least.

"If it's not public, how do you know what he's writing?" Alex handed Romero the soda.

Romero gave him a look before taking the glass. "Alex, I told you this guy could get into Bruce's bank account if he wanted. An online journal is nothing."

"So what's he writing about?"

"Most of it is nonsense. But Mr. X assures me that we hit a goldmine."

"Who the hell is Mr. X?"

"The guy doing all the digging. I don't know his real name, so that's what I call him."

"Wait. I'm paying this guy big bucks, and you don't even know his name? What if he's just feeding us a bunch of crap?"

Romero stared at Alex annoyed. "He comes highly recommended from a very reliable source. I'd never steer you wrong. What, do you think I'm an idiot or something?"

Alex attempted a smirk, but he was too wound up. "You couldn't come up with anything better than Mr. X?"

Romero frowned. "You wanna hear the rest of this or not?"

Alex nodded, leaning against the back counter of the bar, crossing his arms in front of him.

"Anyway, Mr. X says any type of documentation is the best way to get into this guy's head. That's why he went looking for it to begin with. Stalkers and serial killers are notorious for being compulsive planners. This will definitely help if he's stupid enough to write down what he's planning next. So far he has been. The problem is he's not *that* stupid."

Romero took a long drink of his soda. Alex waited impatiently. There always had to be a damn catch.

After nearly finishing the entire glass of soda, Romero put the glass down, burped then continued. "These journals, in some cases blogs, haven't been easy to find. They're not in his name, of course. He uses various different emails to set them up. If he were writing out of one computer only, it would be easy. He'd just hack the computer and get everything he done through it. But he doesn't. He goes from one computer to another mostly in public places like libraries and computer cafés."

"So how do we know it's even him writing them?"

"Trust me, Alex. Mr. X knows. He changes the password on the journal's blogs often enough, but not the email he uses to get in them. Mr. X says that's pretty cocky of him since the password's a no brainer to hack. With the same email address, Mr. X can stay on his trail."

"Can you please stop calling him that? It sounds so stupid."

Romero downed the rest of the soda left in the glass. "What's stupid about Mr. X?"

Alex rolled his eyes. "Never mind, what else did he find out?"

"So far that's the main thing. But he seems to think it's pretty significant. He's gonna go back all the way to when Valerie first met the guy. You said this was about a year ago, right?"

The same irritation he'd felt with himself when he first heard that Valerie had met the guy weeks after breaking things off with him sunk in. He felt completely responsible now for her ever meeting this psycho.

"So he's digging into that. He says it helps to find out what motivated this guy to come after her the way he has in the first place. Also, he's mentions friends and acquaintances in the entries. That could lead us to where he might be staying."

Alex chewed on everything Romero just laid on him, his arms still tightly crossed in front of him. "How long is it going to take before we know anymore?"

"He's real close. I tell you he's good. But there's a lot he says he has to sift through. For every clue he finds there's a ton of useless garbage he has to read through." Romero stood up. "As soon as I know more, I'll let you know."

Romero tapped the top of the bar. "I gotta go."

He started to walk away. Alex nodded, lost in thought. Romero stopped and turned around. "Did you ever find out what was up with Valerie meeting Luke the morning of the rehearsal dinner?"

Alex came out of his stupor. "Yeah, she had to give him keys to some properties he was showing, but that's all she said."

"Did she mention anything about him being at her apartment?"

He'd tried pushing both incidents to the back of his mind, but the truth was it still gnawed at him. "He dropped by to take a look at a painting. Why?"

Romero studied him for a moment. "Hank wasn't sure if it was worth mentioning, so he said he'd leave it up to me. Did you know she had breakfast with Luke yesterday and this morning?"

His arms still crossed in front of him, Alex squeezed them even tighter. Valerie had rushed out of the house both mornings, claiming she didn't have time for breakfast. "No. I didn't."

Romero didn't say anything for a moment then shrugged. "I dunno. Maybe it's just me. If Izzy was having breakfast with an ex two days in row and didn't tell me about it, I'd have a problem with it. But Valerie works with the guy, so … whatever. Just thought I'd mention it."

He started for the door. Alex could feel the drumming of his pulse in his ears as he watched Romero walk out. The image of Valerie and Luke hugging and holding hands the morning of the rehearsal assaulted him. Add that to the fact that she'd chosen him of all people to show the painting. This really brought a serious question to mind. Was it possible she'd played down her relationship with Luke, and her feelings for him ran deeper than she was admitting?

~*~

When Luke called Valerie earlier in the week to tell her he wanted to talk to her about something very important, Valerie almost turned him down. He wanted to do it away from the office to avoid anyone overhearing or start to speculate. She had no idea what he wanted to talk to her about. He only said it was completely work-related. She knew how Alex felt about Luke. He'd most certainly have an issue with her getting together with him outside of the office, but if it was really work-related, he'd just have to understand.

After having breakfast with him the first time, she was glad she had. Corporate was looking into opening another office in the La Jolla area. They asked Luke if there was anyone he could recommend to manage it, and he said the only one he'd even consider was Valerie. While there were quite a few with more experience than Valerie in the office, he said none had the drive, dedication, but most importantly, the stamina she did. There was no one else he could recommend that he truly believed could handle an entire office, nor did he think any of them would want to.

This didn't mean she would get it for sure. Luke wasn't the only one being asked for recommendations. But she had to let him know ASAP because they'd be starting the interview process soon. There would be others considered as well. Valerie told him she'd sleep on it and get back to him. By the next morning and after mulling it over with her dad and Isabel, she was convinced it would definitely be a good career move. She'd met him again, certain that when she told Alex that she might not be working with Luke anymore, he'd be willing to overlook her meeting up with him outside of the office.

She wouldn't bring it up just yet. They'd be interviewing all the recommended candidates soon. Luke mentioned he could coach her. That would definitely mean more time alone with him, and she didn't need Alex obsessing about that.

Just the night before, Alex brought up Luke out of nowhere. Obviously, the fact that she saw Luke everyday still bothered him. As she always did when Alex brought up Luke, she tried to change the subject. But last night Alex probed a little more than usual. She'd make sure any coaching would be done in the office. She didn't need to add any more fuel to the fire.

Valerie sat at her desk, feeling exhausted. Deciding to call it in early today and head home, she began to pack things up. Luke leaned into her cubicle as she pushed her laptop into her briefcase.

"You out already?"

"Yeah." She leaned back in her chair. "It's been a pretty productive, but boring contract writing day. I'm done."

Luke was about to say something when her phone rang. She read the caller ID and lifted her finger to gesture Luke to hold on. Her stepmom didn't call her very often, and when she did, it was usually about her father. "Hi, Norma."

"Valerie, your father collapsed." She was frantic. "The paramedics are on their way."

Valerie's heart nearly gave out, and her hand immediately shot to her mouth. "Oh my God, is he breathing?"

"Yes, but barely." Valerie heard voices, and then heard Norma yell out. "In here! Come quickly!"

A devastating weight pushed against Valerie's chest. It was happening all over again. Her dad would be in the hospital again. She could barely catch her own breath. Her hand shook now. She stood up, fumbling around her desk for her keys. "What hospital are they taking him to?" She cried.

She threw her phone on the desk as soon as she hung up and continued to search for her keys.

"What is it, Valerie?" Luke demanded. "Who's going to the hospital?"

"My dad." She sobbed, trying desperately to hold it together. "Where are my damn keys?"

"Probably in your purse, but you can't drive like this, Val."

"I have to!" Valerie grabbed her purse and fished for her keys.

After a few of the other people in the office who had heard Valerie insisted she not drive, Luke rushed to grab his own keys. "Let's go. I'll take you."

They both rushed out into the parking lot. It wasn't until they were halfway there that she realized she'd left her phone on her desk. "Damn it."

"What?" Luke drove fast, swerving at times.

"I left my phone at the office."

Luke pulled his off his from his belt holster. "Here, use mine."

She took it and called her stepmom. "How is he?"

"They just took him in." Norma sounded as emotional as Valerie felt. "Oh honey," her voice broke and she sobbed, "they think he may have suffered a stroke."

"No!" Valerie gasped, feeling as if her heart had stopped.

"Get here fast, honey. I'm so scared." Valerie had never heard her like this.

When she hung up, she buried her face in her hands.

"It's gonna be okay, Val."

"No," she didn't care that she was crying like a baby now, "they think he had a stroke."

Luke said nothing just pressed down on the accelerator. Valerie dropped the phone on her lap and cried helplessly into her hands. "Please God, let him be okay." She repeated over and over.

Luke dropped her off right at the entrance of the emergency room. She'd already pulled off her shoes in the car so that she could run as soon as she was out the door. Sprinting through the doors, she searched for Norma and immediately spotted the red-eyed woman.

They rushed to each other and hugged. "His breathing is stable, and they're putting him in the ICU."

"Oh, thank God." She cried even more now, squeezing Norma tightly.

"But he's not out of the dark yet. They're watching him really close. He's still unconscious."

Valerie's entire body shook. That's when she felt it. Her stomach churned. She looked around. "Where's the restroom?"

"Why what's wrong?" Norma asked concerned.

"I'm gonna be sick."

Expecting the dry heaves again, Valerie was surprised to throw up her entire lunch and breakfast. She stood breathlessly against the bathroom stall. She hated how her body reacted to her emotions. After washing up, she went back to the waiting room. Luke was there now. She caught him up on her father's condition. "When can we see him?"

Norma shook her head but explained, "They said as soon as they settle him into his room, but that may be a while."

Valerie checked her watch. It was almost six. Alex would be home early tonight. He'd told her that this morning.

"Did you want to go back and get your things from the office?" Luke checked his watch also.

"No, I'm not leaving until I see him." She thought about calling Alex from Norma's phone, but she knew he'd rush down, and she didn't want Luke to be here. She'd been under enough stress being in the same room with them the night of the wine tasting. The last thing she needed was to go through that again, especially right now. "You can go if you want, Luke. I may be here all night."

"No, I'll stay for a while. I want to make sure he's okay too. You're okay ..." Their eyes locked for a moment. Valerie glanced away, annoyed. Was he ever going to stop doing that?

Norma took a seat in the waiting room. There was no way Valerie could sit when she was worried. So she paced. Luke paced with her, at times rubbing her back for comfort.

~*~

Finally done with the payroll, Alex texted Valerie.

Can you talk?

He was feeling a little guilty about the night before. He'd been a little short with her after trying to get her to talk about Luke when she still didn't mention anything about having breakfast with him. They'd almost gone to sleep without making love. Almost.

Romero rushed in the office, closing the door behind him and pulling up a chair. He had a small pad of paper in his hand. "This is way worse than we were thinking."

Alex tensed up at once. He hadn't been expecting Romero today. This had to be bad.

"I haven't had a chance to go through everything he sent me, but there are a few key things I think you should know right away." He opened up the pad in his hand. "First of all, Valerie thinks she met this guy, and then he got all obsessed with her, right?"

Alex nodded, not understanding. "Bruce set it up. He's been following her way before that. He worked in the computer lab at her college. That's where he first saw her. He was there, Alex, the night she caught you with the tutor. Saw the whole thing. Then he waited to approach her and woo her. He knew she was vulnerable and used it to his advantage."

Every hair on Alex's body went on alert. Bruce had been stalking Valerie for years? Romero looked down at his pad again, "His entries are especially vicious when he writes about you guys doing it. Like the night you left the bonfire with Valerie, that was your first night you were back with her, right? He was furious."

"He watched us?"

Romero lifted his eyes from his pad. "I guess. He doesn't actually write what he saw, but he definitely knew you had done it. This one might piss you off a little, but it's important. The only time he actually wrote and I quote 'I almost killed her today.' was the morning after the first time she slept with Luke. He stayed the whole night outside of Luke's house and followed her home the next morning. He was so pissed that he dated her for almost a month and never slept with her, then she starts going out with Luke and week two, he nails her."

Romero may as well have given him a flying kick to the gut because that's what it felt like. He felt the air literally sucked out of him. He wasn't sure what was worse: that Bruce had actually considered killing her, or the visual of her sleeping with Luke.

He gulped hard. The pulse in his ears throbbed. He blinked, thankful he was sitting because he thought he might actually be lightheaded. Romero had never been one to pussyfoot around. He sure hadn't this time. Alex's mind was still stuck on those last five words. *Week two, he nails her*.

"Did you hear what I said?"

"No." Alex barked.

"He's more hung up on Luke than he is you."

"And why would that be?" Alex almost didn't want to know, but he had to now.

"Because you cheated on her, and Valerie told him she was in love with Luke. This was just before you two got back together. She may have told him that just to get him to back off. He keeps trying to figure out why she's with you now. But he's noticed Valerie's inconspicuous meetings with Luke, and he's getting frantic about it."

Alex clenched his teeth. That made two of them. His phone rang. It was Hank. The only time Hank ever called was if …

Alex grabbed it and stood up. "What's up, Hank?"

Romero was on his feet next to Alex the second he heard Hank's name.

"Have you talked to Valerie?"

"No why?"

"Well, I don't think anything's happened to her, but I just thought you might want to know she's in the emergency room."

His murderous mood quickly replaced with dread then annoyance. "What do you mean you don't think? Weren't you watching her?"

"Yeah, I was. I was right outside her office. So was Steve. She walked out with that Luke guy, and they got in his car. So we followed them. He dropped her off at the emergency room, and she ran in."

Ran in? "This happened right now?"

"About fifteen minutes ago."

"And you're just now calling me?" Alex's voice thundered.

"Well, Luke parked and didn't seem too worried when he strolled in. So I didn't know what to think."

Alex squeezed his eyes shut and took a deep breath. "What hospital, Hank?"

After getting off the phone with Hank, Alex filled Romero in on what was going on. He called Valerie a few times. Each time it went to her voicemail. Feeling even more annoyed, he grabbed his keys and headed out.

"Are you telling her about Hank and Steve?" Romero knew Alex well enough to know where he was headed.

"If I have to."

"You sure that's a good idea?"

Alex wasn't, but he was done with the guessing games. He'd get to the bottom of this today. Why was Valerie in the emergency room, not answering her phone? And more importantly, why the fuck was Luke with her?

"I better go with you." Romero hurried alongside of him.

Alex passed Sal on his way out. Sal followed him out the back door as Alex explained he was gone for the day and got in his truck. Romero jumped in the passenger side.

The more he thought about Valerie and Luke, the more he felt like punching something or someone. Maybe it was a good thing Luke was in an emergency room. It might come in handy.

CHAPTER 26

Alex tried Valerie's phone again. With a grunt, he hung it up when it went to voicemail again. Why the hell wasn't she answering? Maybe she *was* hurt. The dread crept through him, overpowering any other emotion. He sped up. Suddenly nothing else mattered. He just had to make sure she was okay.

They pulled into the parking lot and jumped out as soon as they parked. Both of them hurried through the parking lot, Alex's heart pounding in his chest. He saw them before he entered the emergency room through the sliding glass doors. They were facing the other way, but from behind she appeared to be fine. Then it happened. It was subtle or inconspicuous as Bruce so nicely put it. Luke's hand touched her neck. Valerie let her head fall back, and he massaged it.

Just like that Alex felt ready kill again. The sliding doors opened. Romero must've sensed the need to interrupt Valerie's neck massage. He cleared his throat excessively loud. Both Luke and Valerie turned at the same time.

There was no hiding the bewilderment in Valerie's expression but most notably the unease in Luke's.

"What is this, Val?" The jealously finally manifested, taking over any kind self-control or common sense Alex might've normally had. He wasn't thinking straight anymore, but he didn't care. "Why the hell are his hands on you?"

Romero took a cautious step in between Alex and Luke. Valerie glanced around. Alex knew people were watching. It didn't matter. All that mattered was that he got the truth. She'd slept with this guy and lied about it. Did she really expect him to just deal with her being around him all day, touching her whenever he felt like it? *Like hell.*

"What are you talking about, Alex?"

"You don't think I know about you rushing out to meet up with him for breakfast twice this week? I asked you last night about your day. You told me everything but that. Why?"

Valerie stormed past him out the sliding room door. Alex followed her. "I can't believe you came here *now* to make a scene about that. How did you know I was here anyway?"

"Just answer the question, Val. Why are you keeping things from me? Why does he think it's okay to put his hands on you?" The more he thought about it, the angrier it made him.

Luke had stayed inside, a good thing too because at this point, Alex might've slammed him against the wall and asked him instead.

Valerie seemed completely puzzled. She shook her head. "You knew, and you didn't say anything?"

"Because I've been waiting for you to tell me, Z! I know everything. I know you slept with him too. You spent the night at his house. Were you ever gonna tell me about that?"

"What!"

He was done with the bullshit. She'd gone crazy on him when she thought he was cheating on her. Now he had every right. There were too many unanswered questions. He was beyond livid. He was ready to explode. "When you met him the morning of the rehearsal, he held your hand. What the fuck was that about?"

Valerie stared at him, her brows pinched. Alex could almost see her mind working. "How do you know that?"

"They told me!" Alex punched his finger toward the parking lot. "They saw everything, Val."

Valerie tilted her head slightly and glanced out into the parking lot. "Who are *they*?"

"The guys I have watching you! Can you just answer the damn questions? Why are you keeping things from me?"

Valerie's eyes opened wide. "You're spying on me?"

"No—"

"You have people watching me?"

"I had to, Val. Bruce is dangerous. If they hadn't been watching the day he showed up at your apartment, he could've—"

"I don't believe this! How long?"

"A couple of weeks." She walked away from him her hand over her mouth. Alex followed right behind. "Can you start answering some of my questions?"

She spun around. "Then how do you know about me spending the night with Luke?"

Alex froze. Up until that second, he'd held out hope that was some kind of misunderstanding, just the made up ramblings of a madman. He swallowed hard. "You told me you didn't sleep with him." His voice was finally down to a whisper.

"I didn't!"

"Yo, Alex!"

Alex turned to see Romero standing with Valerie's stepmom, Norma. "He's awake now, hon." Norma's teary eyes addressed Valerie. "We can go in and see him."

He turned back in time so see Valerie's face crumble, and she rushed to Norma's side. Alex stood there, feeling as if he'd just run a marathon breathing hard, not sure what was happening. Romero came to him. Valerie disappeared into the emergency room with Norma.

Romero filled him in on Valerie's father. Luke told him about her getting the call at the office and her losing it. She'd been in no shape to drive, so he drove her. Alex felt his stomach bottom out. He hadn't been there again when she had to deal with her dad's health. Worse yet, he'd gone off on her at the worst time imaginable.

CHAPTER 27

Overwhelmed with a plethora of emotion, Valerie stepped quietly into her father's hospital room. The doctors explained that the stroke wasn't nearly as bad as they first thought. In fact, they weren't even convinced it was a stroke.

Valerie took a deep breath. She'd completely expected to see her father looking as pathetic as he had months ago when he'd been in the hospital. Except for the IV drip in his arm, he wasn't hooked up to all the machines she was so sure he'd be. He did look very pale and weaker than normal. The enormous fear of losing him was still there, but she refused to break down in front of him.

"Daddy." Her voice squeaked as she picked up his hand and held it to her cheek.

Her dad's sunken eyes followed hers, but he didn't speak. His fingers squeezed back weakly. She kissed his hand then fussed over his hair. All the while, she struggled not to break down. "I love you. Be strong for me … please."

His hand squeezed hers again. Norma stood on the other side of the bed, holding his other hand. "You're gonna be just fine, my love. You have to be. Who else is going to rile up all my friends at bingo every week?"

Valerie smiled. Her dad always hated going to bingo with Norma. The only reason he did was because he'd questioned them several times and spoke out about them quite belligerently according to Norma. All it took was for Norma to mention one time some of her bingo friends had requested she leave him home. He hadn't missed a day since.

After her dad fell asleep, Valerie sat at his bedside, still holding his hand. Thoughts of Alex having her followed and actually looking into her relationship with Luke came crashing back. She'd known all along that he'd been plagued with the need to know more about her and Luke. But she'd never imagined he'd take things this far. It was a complete lack of respect to her privacy. What else had he tapped into? She never would've believed it if he hadn't told her himself.

She'd truly begun to believe she could be with him forever. That he was perfect in almost every way. Having gotten past her false belief that he was a womanizer who could never commit, she could deal with all his other imperfections. Some people might consider his overbearing personality a flaw, but she embraced it. It was part of his charm, and she was used to it. Most importantly, she knew how to deal with it … with him. Or at least, she thought she could. She never thought it would happen, but he'd crossed the line from shielding and protective to controlling.

***

Valerie didn't even remember falling asleep, but she woke up a little after one in the morning, her back feeling the effects of the chair she'd slept in. Her dad was sound asleep, so was Norma on the ottoman they'd provided her. She leaned over and kissed her dad on the forehead.

She walked out of the room a bit disoriented, but she still remembered from the last time her dad had been here the general direction to the cafeteria. She needed coffee. When she reached the ground floor, she couldn't believe it. Alex was there in one of the seats along the hallway, asleep. She almost walked past him, not wanting to wake him then decided she may as well tell him to go home.

Walking up to him, she couldn't help but admire him. Even as he slept in that chair he barely fit in, he was so magnificently beautiful. As mad and hurt as she was with him still, she couldn't help caressing his face before waking him. His eyes opened slowly. Then they were wide, and he sat up straight. "What happened?"

"Nothing," she whispered.

He was on his feet in an instant. Sloppy as he was, he was alert. "How's your dad?"

"He's better."

Alex's arms were around her in an instant. "Baby, I'm so sorry. I didn't know."

As wonderful as it felt to have his arms around her, the thought of their exchange earlier was still too raw. She pushed away. "I don't want to talk about that now, Alex."

She started back toward the elevator, her appetite suddenly shot. Alex walked right alongside her.

"We don't have to. I'm just … Valerie if I had known—"

"Forget about it." She picked up her pace. The reality of what she'd found out earlier slammed back at her. She still couldn't believe it. As if *she'd* ever given *him* any reason to not trust her. Even if she had, that still gave him no right. She'd always known Alex to be over the top and temperamental. She'd felt someone following her all along. The whole time she thought it'd been Bruce.

Alex's main concern when he showed up at the hospital was Luke. He had far too many details about her and Luke. Like hell he was *just* looking out for her. How dare he.

"I will for now, Valerie, but we really have to talk."

She stopped just before they reached the elevator and faced him. "Talk about what, Alex? Don't you already know everything? Didn't you get *them* to dig up everything you just *had* to know about *my* private life?"

A nurse walked by, and Alex glanced at her then back at Valerie but said nothing. She didn't want to make another scene, so she pressed the button for the elevator. "Go home, Alex. I'm gonna be here all night."

"I wanna be here for you, Valerie."

"They only allow family in the ICU. I can't be around you right now anyway." The elevator door opened, and she stepped in. Alex stared at her. "Go home."

"I love you, baby. I'm sorry."

The doors closed, and Valerie felt her emotions switch gears again. She still couldn't believe he'd do such a thing. How much did he know about her night with Luke? Did he honestly expect her to talk about it? The tears rolled down her cheeks as she walked slowly down the empty hallway. Still stinging from the betrayal, she took a deep breath, wiped away the tears, and entered her father's room again.

~*~

Alarmed and not completely sure where he was, Alex sat up. The muffled ringing continued. It took him a moment to realize he'd knocked out on the sofa. Bright sunlight streamed in from the window. He stood still and waited for the phone to ring again. It came from under him. He reached in between the sofa cushion and pulled it out. It was Romero. He also noticed he had other missed calls.

"What happened?"

"Where've you been? I've been trying to get a hold of you."

Alex stood up and ran his fingers through his hair. He started toward the bedroom. "Asleep. I was up most the night. What's going on? Is Valerie okay?"

"She's fine, but Mr. X may have picked up a lead on Bruce's next move."

Alex stopped. "When?"

"Soon. He hasn't mentioned an exact date in the journal yet, but he keeps making reference to D-day fast approaching. So he's checking every few hours for updates."

D-day? Alex started walking again. He had to take a shower and go talk to Valerie again. He needed to explain the whole thing to her. "Is Valerie still at the hospital?"

Romero was silent for a moment. “No. That’s why I called you earlier. She left about an hour ago. Luke picked her up.”

Alex stopped again, the drumming in his ear starting up. What was she doing? She knew he was watching her now. He gripped the phone. “Where’d they go?”

“To her office. Then she jumped in her own car and went back to her apartment.”

“Her apartment?” For some reason hearing that felt worse than hearing she’d asked Luke to pick her up instead of calling him.

“Yeah, she’s been there for a while now. My guess is she’s getting ready and going to head back to the hospital.”

Alex thought about her wanting to bail before when she’d been upset. He knew she was mad but … “Let me know where she goes next. I’ll be in the shower, so if it’s any time in the next few minutes, just leave a message or a text.”

It really had begun to feel like he was watching now for other reasons than just her protection. He tossed his phone on his bed, trying to get the visual of her and Luke out of his head, and then it hit him. He picked up his phone again. Maybe she did try to call him before calling Luke. Last night when he got home, he tried calling her, and again she hadn’t picked up.

He scrolled through his missed calls. Two were from Romero and one from Sal, none from Valerie.

Since she was back at her apartment, maybe she could talk now. Alex tried her cell phone. After the second ring, he thought of the way things had been the entire time they’d been apart, her never answering or returning his calls. To hell if they were going back to that.

Never again.

To his relief, she answered on the third ring. “Hey.” She sounded down.

“Hey, baby. You okay?”

“Yeah, just tired.”

So was he, but at the moment, he didn't think she'd sympathize, so instead, he asked, "Where are you?"

"I'm sure you already know, Alex. Or did *they* not check in with you yet?"

Well, this certainly wasn't the best time to ask her why she had Luke pick her up instead of anyone else. He was quiet for a moment. "About that, Val, we really need to talk. I know you're upset, but—"

"Alex, I don't want to talk about this, not now. I have too much to deal with right now."

Alex sighed, sitting down on his bed. He wouldn't press, not yet. "Okay. How's your dad?"

"Better. When I left, they were running some tests. If all goes well, he may be released today."

He smiled, finally some good news. With everything going on, the last thing Valerie needed was the added stress of her dad in the hospital. "That's good, sweetheart. I'm glad to hear it." Almost afraid to ask but needing to, he took a deep breath. "So you'll be home tonight?"

"No."

"What do you mean no?" He didn't mean for it to come out so coarse, but this was ridiculous. She couldn't just run back to her apartment every time she got mad. He stood up, unable to sit anymore. "You're going back—"

"I wanna stay with my dad for a few days. The doctor said his lack of discipline when it comes to taking all his medication and his diet are what landed him in the hospital. It wasn't a stroke this time, but the doctor said next time he might not be so lucky. If I have to stay there and help Norma baby him, then that's just what I'll have to do. I don't …" She paused for a moment. Alex heard her take a trembling deep breath. "I won't let this happen again." Her voice broke along with Alex's heart.

He gripped the phone. Damn, he wanted to be there to hold her, tell her everything was going to be okay. He heard her clear her voice. "I have to finish getting ready. I wanna get back to the hospital as soon as possible."

"I'll meet you there."

"No, Alex. There's no point. You'll just be sitting in the waiting room the whole time. You should be at the restaurant or at least getting some rest."

Alex couldn't believe it. Her father was in the hospital, she had a crazed lunatic stalking her, and she was worried about him getting rest?

"When will I see you?"

There was a brief silence, then she spoke. "If they release him today, I'll call you from his house. If he's up for visitors, you can come by."

Alex took an extra-long shower, contemplating everything that he'd just taken in in the last twenty-four hours. There was no way he was going to argue with Valerie about her staying with her dad. If that's what made her feel better, he wanted nothing more. But it still didn't change the fact that Valerie chose to go back to her apartment to get ready rather than come back to *their* place. He still had so many unanswered questions about her and Luke. He was trying to keep his cool, but his irritation levels were already climbing, and this day was just getting started.

***

Sal seemed surprised to see him when he arrived at the restaurant. Since Romero jumped in with him yesterday on the way to the hospital, he had Sal come pick him up. Alex hadn't wanted to leave the hospital. He told Sal he probably wouldn't be in today.

"How's her dad doing?"

"Better." Alex walked to the back office. Sal followed. "He'll probably go home today."

"Really? Romero said it was a stroke."

"Nah, it wasn't after all. Looks like he's gonna be fine." Alex took a seat in front of the computer and moved the mouse around.

After filling Sal in on Valerie's dad, Sal went back to more interviewing. Alex felt a little guilty about leaving all the hiring to Sal, but his mind was too crowded to concentrate on much else. The only consolation was that Sal's anal ass relished making sure they only hired qualified candidates. He liked being the one in charge of hiring.

Alex's dark mood lingered. Everything seemed to annoy him all day from the computer not being quite up to speed to the bus boys laughing a bit too loud out back on their break. By the end of the afternoon, he still hadn't heard from Valerie, not even a text to check in on how everything was going.

He was beyond irritated and ready to snap when his phone rang and it was finally Valerie's name on the caller I.D. Just like that, his mood shifted, and some of the tension seemed to drain. "Hey Val, is he out?"

"Yeah, he's home now." Hearing her voice was even more mollifying.

"Good, I was getting ready to leave."

"Alex, I don't think it's a good idea. He just got home, and he seems a little worn out from this whole ordeal. Maybe tomorrow would be a better."

Alex pinched the rim of his nose and closed his eyes. "Baby, we really need to talk."

"I know, and we will … tomorrow." She added firmly.

He had no choice but to accept. Alex had already alerted Romero of the need to have someone outside Valerie's dad's house through the night.

He drove home slowly, thinking. Always thinking. The more he thought about going another day away from Valerie, the more he was tempted to turn the car around and head to her dad's. His feelings wouldn't be hurt if her dad didn't come out to visit with him. Hell, he didn't even have to go inside. All he needed was to see her, hold her even if only for a moment. Most importantly, he needed to explain himself, damn it. He couldn't have her thinking for even one more night that he'd been spying on her.

Without giving it another thought, he turned the car around. She might be upset that he just showed up, might even ask him to leave. He would if that's what she wanted, but not before she heard him out. Tonight. Not tomorrow.

~*~

Her dad was being stubborn again. Valerie and Norma wanted to settle him in his room and wait on him. The doctors *had* said he needed rest. But her dad wasn't going down without a fight. Norma welcomed Valerie's help. Over the years, they'd developed a buddy system. Valerie played the bad cop while Norma played good cop to try to appease her father when they'd gang up on him. They had to. The man was impossible at times. Like tonight, they were in the living room because he refused to stay put in his bed.

"Look." He said, lifting the handle on the side of his Lazy Boy. His feet went up, and he clicked the television on with the remote. "I did it all by myself. Now go get me a beer."

Valerie crossed her arms in front of her and glared at him. "You're not funny."

Her dad chuckled. "All right, make it coffee."

"I'll go brew some." Norma said, motioning for Valerie to have a seat.

Valerie took a seat on the sofa closest to her dad's chair. "Don't make any for me and make sure it's decaf, Norma."

"Fun police." Her dad muttered.

"You better believe it. And the badge is staying on from here on." She reached over and squeezed her dad's hand. "I mean it, Mister. You're in big trouble."

He waved his other hand in the air. “You can’t stay here and bully me forever. That boy is probably going nuts already with you not around.”

He must’ve seen it in her face because he immediately brought his hand down and squeezed hers. “Things not going so well?”

She shook her head. “Everything’s fine.”

In an instant, the television was off. “I don’t know why you still think you can fool me. What’s troubling you, pumpkin?”

The last thing she needed was to burden her dad with her issues. She was staying with him to make sure he got better, not make things worse. “Nothing daddy, really. Everything’s okay.”

“What did he do?” Her dad dropped the remote on the table next to his chair with a frown.

“You see, you’re already getting upset.” She rubbed his hand.

“Is he still doing the same bullshit as before?”

“No.” She squeezed his hand.

“Don’t think I didn’t notice he hasn’t been around at all these last couple of days. I haven’t seen you on your phone much either. ” He pushed the recliner down and sat up straight. “Did he disappear again?”

“No, no.” She patted his hand. “It’s nothing like that. Sit back, you’re getting yourself all worked up.”

Norma walked in the room. “Everything okay?”

“No.”

“Yes.” Valerie gave him a look. He knew she didn’t like to talk about Alex in front of Norma. “He’s just being stubborn again. I can handle him.”

Norma smiled and shook her head. “Alfred, you best behave yourself.”

“I’m behaving just fine. She’s the one—”

The doorbell rang, interrupting them all. Norma walked to the door and opened it. “Alex, come on in.”

Alex said something Valerie couldn't quite hear. "Don't be silly. You're not disturbing anyone. Please come in."

"Yeah." Her dad agreed. "Get your ass in here."

Valerie shot her dad another look—this time a dagger. "Dad!"

"Well, if you're not gonna tell me what's going on, he better."

Alex nearly took up the entire doorframe. "How you doing Mr. Zuniga?"

"Boy, how many times do I have to tell you to call me Alfred?"

Alex smiled at her then at her dad. "How's it going, Alfred? You feeling better?"

Valerie shifted in her seat. Somehow, she thought she'd be more annoyed seeing him here after she'd made it clear she didn't want to see him tonight. Instead, her heart sped up at the sight of him. How was it possible that she'd been so irritated and hurt with him all day, then he waltzes in here and with one smile weakens her resolve so easily?

"I'm fine. I keep telling these two Florence Nightingales here that, but neither one seems to listen." Her dad sat up at the edge of his seat. "Listen here, what's going on with you two? You playing with my little girl again?"

Alex glanced at her. Norma seemed to sense the need to leave them alone. "I'll go get the coffee." She started toward the kitchen. "Would you like a cup of coffee or anything to drink, Alex?"

"No, ma'am. Thank you."

Alex seemed to wait until Norma left the room to respond to her dad. Before he could, Valerie spoke up. "Dad, I told you. Everything's fine." Valerie stood up. She took a few steps toward Alex with pleading eyes. He *had* to know she wouldn't want her dad worrying about them right now. But she especially didn't want Alex trying to explain his reason for snooping. That's the last thing she wanted her dad to have to think about right now.

Alex reached for Valerie's hand, pulling her gently to him. "Things couldn't be better. In fact," he placed her in front of him, placing his arms around her waist, "I'm not sure if she's told you yet, but I have every intention of marrying her." He kissed her lightly on her temple. "Just as soon as she says yes."

Valerie felt her insides warm. Alex was manipulating the situation. He knew she'd have no choice but to play along with the happy little couple act.

Her dad eyed Alex suspiciously. "Is that so?"

"Absolutely," Alex hugged her a little tighter, pressing his hard body against hers. Her body reacted as it always did to him, trembling ever so slightly.

Alfred sat back in his seat, but he didn't seem quite satisfied. "She told me you asked her to marry her. But are you sure nothing else is going on? She's been moping around all day." His eyes went from Valerie to Alex. "I know when something is bothering my daughter."

Valerie stroked Alex's forearm just so, willing him to understand he shouldn't give in, no matter how much her dad probed.

"Probably just worried about you, sir. She was pretty shaken up."

Norma walked in with Alfred's cup of coffee. The moment her dad's attention was averted away from them, Valerie loosened Alex's hold on her.

"Well, she can stop worrying. I'm just fine." Her dad reached for the cup of coffee and asked Alex to take a seat. He did on the sofa, bringing Valerie with him. Alex had always been comfortable around her dad. Even when she first met him, her dad made Alex come in and talk before leaving with Valerie on a date. Alex seemed to enjoy her father's spunk.

Norma's phone rang, and she excused herself, saying she had to take the call.

Once seated, Alex took her hand in his, resting them both on his thick thigh.

"So you think you're good enough to marry my little girl, huh?"

"Well, I'm not sure anyone will ever be good enough for Valerie." Alex smiled. "But I'll certainly do my best to try and make her happy."

This was the last conversation Valerie thought she'd be having today. Thankfully, her dad asked Alex about how the restaurant was doing. Alex filled him in on it and told him about Sal's plans to turn it into a franchise just as soon as he finished school.

"What about you? Do you plan on finishing school?"

Valerie felt Alex tense up. She knew what a chip on his shoulder he had about not having finished college.

"The restaurant is doing so good, Dad. Alex barely gets any time off as it is."

Alex squeezed her hand. "I'm hiring more help. As soon as we get them all trained and we have enough staff to handle the restaurant a few days out of the week without me, I plan on going back."

Her dad seemed pleased. That was news to Valerie. She wondered how much else he hadn't been sharing with her lately. Thoughts of him spying on her and snooping into her past with Luke rang in her head like a clamoring bell. She tried unclasping her hand from his, but he only held it tighter.

After about a half hour more of talking, Norma came back in the room. "I'm sorry about that. My sister keeps me on the phone so long." She turned to Alfred, phone still in her hand. "Luna wanted me to wish you a speedy recovery."

"Speaking of which," Valerie stood up, and Alex stood with her, "you need to get to bed, Dad. No late nights for you, doctor's orders."

Both she and Norma walked to him to help him up. He waved them both away. "I got this."

Her father excused himself, insisting he didn't need either of them fussing over him. He could get himself in bed just fine. But Valerie insisted on walking with him to his room.

"I'll be back, Alex."

She turned to her father, who was still shaking his head at her, and held his elbow. "Let's go, Mister."

CHAPTER 28

Alex watched, amused at the way Valerie bossed her dad. They disappeared into the hallway, but he could still hear the stubborn man's protests. He ambled around the room, stopping when he came to the table with all the pictures. Her dad still had Valerie's high school senior picture up. That was the year he first met her. Seeing it made him remember how he felt about her even back then. The same as he did now.

He picked up the picture, examining it closer. He traced her lips with his finger. Why the hell had it taken him this long to finally figure out he was crazy about this girl.

"Why are you here, Alex?"

Alex turned around. Valerie leaned against the doorframe to the hallway arms crossed.

He put the picture back down. "We need to talk."

Norma walked in from behind Valerie. "Excuse me, honey, your father needs a glass of water to take his medicine."

Valerie moved, letting her through. They both waited until Norma walked into the kitchen. Valerie spoke in a hushed voice. "I told you not tonight. This is neither the time nor the place."

"We don't have to talk about everything tonight. But there are some things that can't wait."

Norma walked back in the room, holding a glass of water and smiled. As soon as she was past Valerie and in the hallway, Alex spoke up again. "I wasn't spying on you. I swear."

Valerie looked back into the hallway. "How does you watching me for my own safety have anything to do with me and Luke?"

Me and Luke. Alex couldn't even stand hearing her say it. His hand fisted involuntarily. "We can talk about that later, but—"

"No, we will not. What happened between me and Luke is none of your—" she halted when Norma came from behind her again.

"Sorry to keep interrupting, but your father forgot his reading glasses out here."

"That's fine, Norma," Valerie said and started to the front door. "Alex was just getting ready to leave anyway."

Norma grabbed the glasses from the table next to the recliner Alfred had been sitting in. "It was nice seeing you again, Alex. Tell your parents I said hello."

Alex forced a smile, "Sure thing, nice seeing you too."

She turned and walked back into the hallway. With three long strides, he was at Valerie's side. She opened the front door, and he took her hand, bringing her out to the porch with him. As soon as the door closed behind them, he pulled her to him and kissed her. He'd only been away from her a day, and a hunger like no other invaded his entire body. But he restrained himself, instead kissing softly, savoring the luscious moment. She didn't fight him, but after a moment, she pulled away breathless.

Valerie laid her hand flat against his chest. His heart pounded against it, and he knew she felt it. "I need to go make sure my dad doesn't think he's going to be up late reading."

He put his hand over hers on his chest. "I need to talk to you. I'm not leaving until I do."

"I already told you I'm not talking to you about Luke, especially my past with him."

He stared at her, trying not to get worked up again. "And I already told you we *will* talk about Luke later. For now, what I need you to know is I wasn't spying on you. I was having Bruce investigated. He's been stalking you since before you met him. He's the one that was spying on you."

Her heated expression changed. Her lips parted, and she searched his eyes. "He's been writing a journal of sorts. He wrote about the night you and Luke …" Alex didn't even want to say it. She obviously tried to take in what he'd just told her regarding Bruce writing a journal about her, but he saw how uncomfortable the topic of her night with Luke made her. That irritated him. "I just needed you to know I wasn't snooping into your past. I'm trying to find this guy. Romero knew someone who has the resources to look into this kind of stuff, so I hired him."

"I don't understand. He didn't know me until I went out that night and met him."

"He planned it, Z. I'll explain it all later when you have more time. Right now, I just need you to understand this: He's the one that dug up all the stuff about you and Luke. He's obsessed and extremely dangerous. I wouldn't have these people watching you if I didn't believe that."

"But you can't—"

Alex put his finger over her lips. "I can and I will."

No more talking, what Alex wanted more than anything now was to taste her again. If he had to go another night without her, he needed take advantage of the moment before anyone came looking for her. He cradled her face and devoured her mouth again, groaning in delight.

~*~

The phone rang early Friday morning. It was Alex.

"Hmm?"

"Morning, sweetheart, did I wake you?"

Valerie stretched. "Hmm, yeah, but I was planning on getting up early anyway."

"Really? What are your plans?"

She sat up, pulling her legs over the edge of the bed. “I need to raid my dad’s fridge and pantry. I’m cleaning house today. Gotta get some better eating habits for him. But I’m not going anywhere. The only thing I’ll probably leave for is to get him some groceries.”

“You coming home tonight?” He sounded hopeful.

Last night after she’d nagged her dad about not staying up too late reading, she called Alex back. She just couldn’t stop thinking about what he’d said.

Since Alex was having trouble getting any sleep in his empty bed, he was happy to fill her in on all the details. Valerie was grateful he hadn’t brought up Luke again. But she had a feeling he was saving that for a face-to-face conversation. She wasn’t looking forward to it, and she still wasn’t even sure if she was willing to tell him everything. Even though he hadn’t intentionally set out to find out, now that he knew, the details of that night were really none of his business.

When she first decided to stay with her dad for a few days, part of the reason was to get away from Alex. She was so hurt and upset with him. For a moment there, she wasn’t sure if she’d be going back to his house at all. After last night’s talk, she knew she would, but it was too soon to leave her dad. As stubborn as that man was, she knew it would take a few more days to help him make the changes he needed to make. Norma was all for throwing out the bad stuff and stocking up on healthy food. She said she’d been trying forever, but as usual, her dad’s stubbornness was too much.

“No, I really need to be here, Alex, at least through the weekend.”

Valerie stood up. She heard Alex sigh. “I hate waking up without you.”

“I hate waking up without you too, babe. But this is really important to me.”

As disappointed as Alex sounded, Valerie knew he would understand. She’d been glad to hear they were having another big wedding this weekend at the restaurant. It would keep Alex busy, making her feel less guilty. Knowing Alex, since she wouldn't be there when he got home, he'd work late into tonight and be back at the restaurant early tomorrow morning.

"You think maybe you can come by the restaurant today so I can see you?"

"I don't wanna leave my dad so soon, Alex. As it is, I really don't want to go to the market, but I have to."

"And you really think it's necessary to watch him like a child?" Valerie was glad to hear a little humor in his tone.

"Yes, I do. If he's gonna behave like one, then he'll be treated like one." She heard him chuckle. "But you can come by tonight like you did yesterday."

"Oh, I was planning on that. No way am I going the whole day without seeing you." He lowered his voice and murmured. "I just hoped maybe I could be near you … alone before that."

"Oh." She knew what he meant by that. They'd found very creative ways to be *alone* in the past. Her body shivered just thinking about it.

"Yeah, 'Oh.'" She could almost hear the smile in his tone. "Don't worry about it, sweetheart. We'll make up for this later. I promise."

How he could do things to her just with a simple change in his tone was beyond crazy. Once off the phone, she spent the morning digging through her father's pantry as he sat having breakfast. Norma had made scrambled egg whites with turkey bacon, only two slices, some fruit, and glass of prune juice for him.

"You should've been eating like this a long time ago." Valerie scolded her dad, her nose still in his pantry. She'd already gone through the refrigerator. Norma had told her to have at it, that it was high time, making her dad grumble in the process. Valerie pulled out all the high-sodium products. She frowned at the amount they had in there.

"Don't you have somewhere to be?" Her dad complained.

With her hand on her hip, she turned to him. "Obviously this is where I need to be, and I will be once a week. Look at all this." She pointed to the cans of Spam and high-sodium soups on the counter. "You know better, Daddy. You're just being bad. Well say goodbye to all of it." She pulled another can of sardines and shook her head.

"You're crazy if you think you're throwing all that stuff out." He said, raising his fork at her.

"No, I'm donating it to the church up the street. I'll go pick up some stuff to replace these. Good stuff."

Her phone rang, and she glanced at the caller ID. It was Luke this time. She picked it up and answered. "Hey, Luke." She ducked her head back in the pantry.

"You got an interview."

Valerie stood up straight. "I did? When?"

"First thing Monday. I got a whole file here on the types of questions they'll be asking. I can fax it to you."

She bit her lip. "My dad doesn't have a fax machine."

"I can drive by and drop it off if you want."

Valerie thought of the people Alex had watching her. He was already not happy about her breakfasts with Luke. She was sure he'd have questions about Luke visiting her at her dad's. If she knew Luke, he wouldn't just drop them off either. He'd want to come in and meet her dad. "No, hmm. I wasn't planning on going in the office for a few days but—"

"Go!" Her dad said. "I'll be just fine here without you riding me all day."

Valerie scowled at her dad. "You know what? I have to run an errand for my dad in a little bit. I'll stop by and pick it up." She continued to search through the pantry again.

"Do you know what time?"

Three cans of Vienna sausages were stacked in the corner of the pantry. Valerie picked one up, waved it at her dad, and shook her head disapprovingly. "In about an hour, but just leave it on my desk if you have to go anywhere."

"No, I'll be here. I wanna go over a few things with you anyway."

Valerie wasn't sure she was comfortable being alone with Luke so much now, especially since Alex was now under the impression they'd slept together. Well technically they had, but she knew what Alex was thinking. She wasn't even sure he'd be happy about the real version of what really happened that night. Any time she spent alone with Luke now was going to be a rough topic to bring up. There'd be no keeping things from him now that she knew she was being watched. *They* obviously didn't just report back to him with the dangerous stuff. They were telling him every little thing.

She frowned, hanging up. "I'm only going to be gone for a few hours, you hear me?"

Her dad smiled. "Good riddance. So you're going by the market?"

"How rude." Valerie smirked. "And yes, I am. Any special requests?" She started bagging up all the cans she'd be dropping off at the church.

"Chips and dip. I'm watching the ballgame tonight. The kind with the ridges."

She didn't stop her bagging. Her dad wasn't going to stop riling her. She was used to it. "Low-sodium baked chips and no-fat plain yogurt it is." She threw the last can in the bag. His loud groan made her smile. Two could play this game.

***

Valerie checked her rearview mirror. She wondered which of all the cars around her were Alex's guys. Now that she knew how demented Bruce really was and that he'd been stalking her long before she met him, she had to admit she did feel a lot better knowing she wasn't alone.

She didn't bother to dress up. Instead, she purposely wore shorts, a sweatshirt, and no makeup and pulled her hair into a ponytail. Most notably, she wore tennis shoes. Luke had never seen her without her big shoes or dressed down. At this point, she didn't care. In a way, she was hoping he'd be turned off.

Luke locking eyes with her was really getting old. She walked into her cubicle, dropping her keys on the desk and picked up the file that Luke had left there. She had just started reading it when she heard his voice.

"Hey, tiny."

She turned around. Luke leaned against frame of her cubicle, looking down at her.

"Hey."

The smile on his face was bigger than usual. "Wow, Val. I didn't realize you were this short."

She rolled her eyes. "Whatever."

"The last time I saw you like this was the morning after …"

Her eyes were immediately back on the file, annoyed that he'd ever bring that up. "Is this all of it?"

"Yeah, but we need to go over some stuff."

"No, I don't have time, Luke. My dad needs me back."

"But he's better, right?"

"Oh yeah, but I need to be there before lunchtime. The man needs to have his meals monitored like a child. I swear he's been out of the hospital for less than twenty-four hours, and I wouldn't put it past him to try to pull a fast one."

Luke laughed. "I'm glad he's feeling well enough to be sneaky. For a moment there, I thought you might miss out on George Stone this weekend."

Valerie turned to him wide-eyed. "That's this weekend?"

"Don't tell me you forgot."

She placed a hand on her forehead. "Completely, I don't know if I'm going to be able to make it."

"Why not? You said your dad's better. Your stepmom can handle him alone for a few days."

Few days? "That's right. It's an all weekend thing, isn't it?" She shook her head, clutching the file in her hand. "There's no way."

"But it's right here in La Jolla, Val. It's not as if you'll be out of town. If anything were to happen, you're only minutes away. You don't have to spend the night there," his eyes locked on hers, "unless you want to. I never cancelled the suite."

Irritated by the absurd suggestion and more than tired of his uncomfortable stares, she snapped. "Don't be ridiculous, Luke. Of course, I wouldn't be spending the night."

He leaned against the frame of her cubicle with a sheepish smile. "Well, the offer still stands if you change your mind. But you'll still go to seminar, right?"

She picked up the keys from the desk. "I don't know. I'll have to talk to my dad."

Luke filled her in quickly about the man conducting the interviews. He'd worked with him in the past, so he knew about his work ethics and what he expected out of a manager. He wasn't too worried about Valerie making a good impression. He said Valerie had one of the most important things down and that was swagger.

Valerie started to make her exit.

"It's business attire, Val. As cute as you look in shorts and tennis shoes, don't plan on dressing that way for the seminar."

She could feel his eyes on her as she walked past him. Her idea about dressing down had backfired. She responded to that with nothing more than a nod. Somehow, Luke had gone from being bitter about her rejection and getting back with Alex so soon after to flirting again. Spending the entire weekend with him at the seminar wasn't the greatest idea. Even if she wouldn't be going *with* him, it still might encourage the behavior further.

The thing was, now that he had reminded her of it, she really wanted to go. It didn't seem fair. With all the stress she'd been under lately, a weekend of listening to George Stone's inspirational speeches would be bliss. Having to tell Alex about it made her think twice. It would no doubt solicit a conversation about Luke. That was something she was trying to avoid.

She'd worry about that later. Right now, she needed to get to the market. She was determined to stay on top of her dad's health. Like it or not, she intended to keep him around for a long time. If that meant holding his hand through every meal, then so be it.

CHAPTER 29

Alex went up to check the progress of the banquet rooms set up. They were on schedule for the wedding tomorrow still. His phone vibrated on the way down with a text.

FYI, She went to church, her office, then the market. She's back home now.

Romero had texted him a couple of hours ago to let him know Valerie was on the move. He really began to feel somewhat underhanded. The whole thing had started for her safety. In the beginning, they'd only let him know if something was wrong. Ever since his confrontation with her at the hospital, Romero started checking in with him on her every move.

He was trying hard not to read too much into everything. But this morning she'd made it clear she couldn't swing by the restaurant even for just a little bit. Her office was even more out of her way. Did it really take her two *hours* to go to the market?

As tempting as it was to shoot Romero a text asking how long she'd been at the office, Alex held off. He'd get his answers soon enough and straight from the source.

He thought about calling her but then thought better. The day he found out about her breakfasts with Luke, he waited and waited for her to mention it. No way was he having another one of those exasperating conversations with her again. This could wait until he saw her tonight.

Back downstairs, he checked in on the food. The main dish would be *Birria*: the Mexican version of pot roast only a lot spicier. This was a complex dish because it had to cook slowly for twenty-four hours. For a wedding as large as tomorrow's, they'd have to watch it closely.

His phone rang just as he entered the office. It was Valerie.

"Hey, sweetheart."

"Hey, you busy?"

"No, what's up?" He sat down in the desk chair and leaned back.

"My dad's taking a nap, and I was thinking about you."

"You should come by." Just thinking about what he'd do to her made him sit up straight.

"I almost did."

"Valerie, don't tease me." He shifted in his seat; in case anyone walked in, his situation wouldn't be so noticeable. "So why didn't you?"

"I felt bad. I wanted to be here at least one full day since I'll be gone most of the weekend."

"Gone? You coming home?" He sat up, unashamed about how excited that made him.

"Umm, no. I have that seminar to go to. Remember I told you about it, George Stone?"

Alex sat still for a moment, then it hit him. Suddenly there were other parts of his body hard and rigid but not in a good way. "With Luke?"

"No, not with Luke." She replied. "I might see him there, but I'm not going with him."

"What do you mean might, Valerie? He bought the tickets together. His ass will be sitting right next to you the whole time."

"Not necessarily. It's not like a concert. There are no set seats. My ticket just gets me in the door. I sit where I want."

If Luke had even a fraction of a brain, he'd be there, saving the seat next to him for her. That wasn't even what bothered him the most. There was no way Hank or Steve would be able to keep an eye on her in a setting like that.

Bruce was getting ready to make a move. She had to be extra careful.

He stood up. "It's dangerous."

"What? I'm going to be in a conference surrounded by loads of people. The only times he's ever tried anything was when I was alone."

Alex almost growled. *The coward.* "I still think it's a risk, babe. This guy is unpredictable."

"Alex, the place is going to be full of security. A resort that fancy has cameras all over. I highly doubt he'd choose that place to try anything."

He thought about what might've happened to her if Hank hadn't been there and seen Bruce try to force his way into her apartment. Alex had a bad feeling about this. Ever since Romero told him about the D-day entries in Bruce's journals, he'd been plagued with the dread of something really bad happening soon. He just couldn't allow her to take such a chance.

"I don't want you to go, Val."

She was quiet for a moment. "You can't just tell me what to do, Alex."

He felt like punching something. "I'm not telling you." He said through his teeth and took a deep breath. "I'm begging you. I really think you should lay low for the next few weeks until we know what his next move is. I'll get you tickets to see this guy later. I promise."

"Alex, I can't let Bruce hold my life captive." Then she added with even more conviction. "I won't."

Alex paced, frustrated. Valerie's strong will had always been one of the things he most admired about her, but at a times like this, he wished she could be a little more submissive. "Maybe …" He couldn't believe what he was about to say. "Maybe then it is best if Luke stays close by you while you're there. Just so you're never completely alone."

"But I'm never going to be alone in that place. I'm telling you, the place is going to be packed."

Romero rushed in the door, almost colliding into Alex. "I gotta talk to you."

Alex pointed to the phone and held up a finger. "Listen, babe—"

"Is that Valerie?"

Alex turned back to Romero irritated and nodded. "Put her on speaker. She should hear this."

The dread seeped in slowly. He stared at Romero. This wasn't going to be good. He could tell by Romero's anxious disposition. "Valerie, I'm gonna put you on speaker. Romero's here. He wants you to hear."

Romero walked over to the door and closed it.

"What?"

"Just listen." Alex pressed speaker and held it up for Romero.

"We got a date. Shit we got his entire calendar." Romero smiled smugly from the phone to Alex. "Mr. X found it. It has all the dates this guy's confronted Valerie. He has a small V on every one. If we had had this when he attacked her at the apartment, we would have known beforehand because he sets it up in his calendar ahead of time. The next one is Monday."

"Monday?" Both Alex and Valerie spoke at the same time.

"What's going on Monday?" Alex asked.

"I don't know." Romero said. "But all the other dates had a small V in black in the corner. This one has a big V in red takes up the whole square." Romero looked back down at the phone. "You have anything special planned for Monday, Val?"

"No, nothing."

"Think baby. Any properties you showing? Or any events going on?" Alex's own mind raced as he asked trying to think if she'd mentioned anything or if they'd made any plans.

"Oh wait."

Alex's insides were already in knots. Whatever it was, she was canceling.

"I have an interview."

"With who?" Alex asked.

"Where?" Romero added.

Alex heard her sigh. "I didn't want to say anything until I knew for sure. Luke got me an interview with someone from corporate. It's in downtown San Diego. They're looking for someone to manage a second office that will be opening up here in La Jolla. That's what those breakfasts were about. He didn't want to talk about it in the office. I'm the only one he's recommending."

His hand squeezed the phone a little tighter. What else was Luke willing to try to get in Valerie's good graces?

"If I get the position, it means I won't be working with him anymore."

"You're not going." As good as Valerie leaving Luke's office for good sounded, she wasn't leaving his side Monday. Bruce would have to go through him to get to her, and that was final.

"But Luke pulled strings to get this interview for me. Don't you see, I won't have to see him every day anymore. I thought that's what you wanted."

"Not if it means putting you at risk. Reschedule it."

"Alex, I told you—"

"Wait." Romero looked excited. "Valerie, when did you find out about the interview?"

"Just this morning. Luke called to tell me about it."

"Then that's probably when he's planning it. Mr. X said he came across the calendar last night. But the big V wasn't in the calendar until he checked it about an hour ago." He turned to Alex, eyes lit up. "We can set up a trap."

"No way. She's not going anywhere Monday."

"It could work, Alex." She heard Valerie chime in.

"Hell no!" He'd give in to Valerie on a lot of things, but not this. He took her off speaker and brought the phone to his ear. "It's not happening, Z. Understand? You'll be with me all day Monday. Even if it means I have to handcuff you to me."

"Just what gives you the right—"

"I'll tell your dad." Oh yeah, he was pulling out the guns now. If she wasn't listening to him, he was sure her dad would have a thing or two to say about this. He knew that's the last thing Valerie would want her dad to be worrying about. Alex felt a little dirty about the threat, but she left him no choice.

"You wouldn't."

"Try me."

Romero charged him. "Alex, listen to me. This is our chance. You can't be there with her every minute forever. You cancel this shit, and his ass will come up with something else. Let's end this now!"

Alex put the phone behind his back and turned back to Romero's face. "Damn it, Romero I'm not putting her up as bait, so think up something else!"

"You can be there!" Romero stood his ground. "I might have a plan. But if you think this psycho's gonna give up just like that, you're nuts. Let's get him now."

As much as he hated the idea, Alex knew Romero had a point. He brought the phone back to his ear.

"Alex! Are you there?"

"Yes."

Romero stared at him. "Let me and Romero work this out. But we'll talk tonight, okay?"

She was quiet for a moment then, "I'm going to that interview."

"Yeah, I figured that much." He glared back at Romero's dogged stare. "I'll talk to you tonight." He turned away from Romero. "I love you."

"I love you too."

He hung up and loomed over Romero. "This better be good."

***

Romero's plan was actually not half bad. They'd have Valerie park her car in Alex's attached garage Sunday night so that Monday morning Bruce wouldn't see Alex slip in the back seat. Hank and Steve weren't going to be the only ones tailing them. Romero was going to put a few more guys on the job.

He was also working closely with Mr. X, trying to find more details about Bruce's plan. Today he'd be driving down to the building where Valerie would be interviewed to get an exact visual of what they were facing. He said he would plan a place for each of them to park so they'd have Valerie covered from every angle.

Alex had to admit he was a little impressed with how fast Romero had come up with a plan. He filled Valerie in on it last night when he went to see her at her dad's. She didn't seem nearly as apprehensive about this as Alex was. The only good thing was that Alex would be there the whole time. He'd been so immersed in filling Valerie in on the plan and making absolutely sure she would be prepared for Monday he nearly forgot to ask anything about Luke.

His concerns about Luke had lost a little steam, especially after learning about Valerie's plans to leave the office and why she'd met him for breakfast. Even the seminar today had moved down on Alex's list of most screaming worries. He still had this wedding dinner to deal with.

Valerie would be at her seminar all day. She'd be out of there by eight tonight then go back tomorrow in the morning. Hank and Steve were still keeping a close eye on her. Alex wasn't taking any chances, but he felt fairly certain she'd be safe there.

Just after eight in the morning, Alex headed into the restaurant. He had to check on the *Birria* and make sure it'd be ready on time. They couldn't afford to screw this up. The last thing he wanted was to disappoint the old man.

Both Sal and Angel's cars were already there. Angel had only flown back in from his honeymoon the night before, and he was already back at work. Angel was opening, but Sal was supposed to be there tonight to work the wedding. He must've had the same thought as Alex and decided to come in to check on the food.

The delectable spicy scent of the *Birria* hit him almost as soon as he walked in the back door of the restaurant. He headed straight for the kitchen. Sal and Angel were both in there looking into one of the huge pots. Sal turned when Alex walked in and smiled. "Looks good."

"Does it?" Alex welcomed some relief finally.

"Yeah," Angel confirmed. "I feel like having some."

Sal started toward the door. Angel was still picking at the food. Sal lifted his eyebrows at Alex. Damn. The moment of relief hadn't lasted long before having to think about what he had to do now.

Sal tapped him on the shoulder. "You gotta tell him."

Even though this might be something that would hopefully be over on Monday, Alex couldn't chance it. He'd never forgive himself if anything happened to Sarah, and he hadn't at the very least warned Angel.

Some of the cooks had just arrived and started things up for breakfast. Alex glanced around. This might get ugly, so he decided the kitchen wasn't the best place to have this conversation.

"Angel you got a minute? I need to talk to you."

Angel didn't bother looking away from the pot where he'd pulled a spoonful of meat out and was blowing on it. "Sure, go for it."

"In private, it's about Sarah."

Angel turned immediately. Alex knew that would get his attention. If his expression was any indication of what the conversation might be like, he was definitely not looking forward to it.

They walked out back. Angel had already asked what about twice. By the time they were outside, Angel had lost his patience.

"What the hell, Alex. Just tell me."

"Relax, it's not that big a deal." Alex leaned against his truck, wishing he'd put more thought into this.

"So tell me."

Alex inhaled deeply. "All right, the night Valerie's stalker called here, he mentioned Sarah by name."

"What?" Angel looked ready to kill. Alex knew the feeling.

"He mentioned Sofi too. He was just trying to get in my head. Let me know that he's done his homework and knows all about me and my family."

"What did he say?" Angel demanded.

Alex filled him in, giving him more details than he'd originally planned, but that was only because Angel was so damn adamant. They weren't even done talking before Angel was on the phone, checking on Sarah. She was with her mom, and Angel made her promise she'd stay there until he was off.

Though he didn't really think it was necessary, Alex offered to have someone watch her.

"I don't want anyone following her. Just make sure you schedule us to work together until this psycho is caught." He stuck his phone in his holster. "I'll watch her."

Alex tried to reassure him that she'd be okay, but Angel was visibly shaken. Alex understood all too well. He was glad now he'd agreed to go along with Romero's plan. He wanted this thing over with.

~*~

The resort was as glamorous on the inside as it was on the outside. The entire theme was tropical from the enormous saltwater aquarium in the front entrance to the vast assorted plant life that decorated every inch of the hotel. Valerie had been to Vegas several times, and this place almost measured up to some of the more sensational casinos she'd been in.

She walked through the place, feeling excitement build as she glanced around. This was such a welcome retreat from all the stress of the past week. Before she left her dad's house that morning, she made him promise he'd behave. She and Norma went over her dad's lunch and dinner menu. Norma laughed, saying her ears would be ringing when she served him his less-than-exciting, healthy lunch.

Luke gave her the meet-and-greet pass ahead of time in case he was running late. It was a good thing too because he'd been a no show. She wondered if perhaps he'd only gotten her a pass and not one for himself. Had he only said they were both going, to get to Alex? The way he acted that night, she wouldn't put it past him.

The first part of the seminar was everything she'd expected. George Stone didn't disappoint. He was as moving in person as he was in all the books she'd read. His wit was just as quick as in his books even with the impromptu questions he took from the audience.

Valerie was surprised she still hadn't seen Luke. The first break came. They had an enormous set up: bagels, pastries, fruit juices, and coffee. And this was just a break. She could only imagine what lunch and dinner would be like.

She sat at a table with her bagel and coffee lost in thought, George Stone's amazing speech still on her mind. Feeling like she was being watched, she glanced up and saw the guy across the room. He looked younger than she was, but his eyes were very penetrating. She remembered these hard-ass guys back in college, trying to intimidate with their sexy stares much like Luke's, but she was way past that.

He made his way to her table, and she looked away. There had been plenty of times she had to reject guys, and she prepared to be nice. When he reached her table, he smiled. It wasn't a bad smile. He was tall and very handsome.

"Hey, I noticed you the moment I walked in. I haven't heard a word George Stone has said." He reached out his hand. "You're breathtaking. I'm Cesar, what's your name?"

Valerie shook his hand and smiled. "Valerie, and thank you, but I'm practically married."

"Practically? I like that. Means you're still technically available."

"Nope, means she's unavailable, asshole."

Valerie nearly spit up her last bite of bagel. Bruce wore a suit and tie, blending in right along with all the others there to see George Stone. He stood a few inches taller than Cesar, nose to nose. "I appreciate your taste in women, but this one's ALL mine."

Cesar backed off, putting his arms in the air. "I meant no disrespect. I'm sorry." He gave Valerie a quick rueful smile and walked away.

Valerie sat frozen in her chair. Bruce took one beside her, cradling her chair between his legs. "Have you seen the suite yet?"

Her breath was caught somewhere between her throat and her chest. "What suite?"

"The one lover boy got for you? It's pretty cool." He stood up, holding his hand out. "Let's go check it out. This place is going to be on lockdown soon anyway."

"What?" Her heart pounded wildly.

"Moreno's is busy today." He tapped his pocket. "You wouldn't want it blowing up on a day like this, now would you?"

"What are you talking about?" Her heart felt as if it were going to rip through her chest. She glanced at her purse, thinking of the Taser gun and phone that sat in it, then back at Bruce.

His menacing eyes stared at her, pleased. He leaned over, closing in on her face and stopped when she flinched. "Be pleasant, darling. We have an audience—a small inept audience at that, but an audience none the less." He tilted his head. "You always knew this day would come, didn't you?" His eyes twinkled with malice now. "I always did."

"What are you talking about blowing up Moreno's?" She demanded as she stood.

He stood with her and hushed her, leaning in reaching for her hand. "Now, now I'm a reasonable man, Valerie. I'd say I've been very patient. Nothing is going to happen to Moreno's if you just do as I say." He reached for her hand, but she pulled it away. Bruce tapped his pocket again. "It's up to you, Valerie. Take my hand and come with me, or we'll be hearing about the tragedy at Moreno's on the news very shortly. But first," he leaned in close enough so that she could smell the liquor on his breath, "kiss me."

"Go to hell." She hissed, backing away.

He grabbed her hand and pulled her to him. "You're trying my patience." He hissed back then kissed her brusquely. Valerie closed her lips tightly her thoughts going wild with worry. Would Bruce really do something to Alex? She concentrated on staying calm, but at this point, she was close to screaming.

"Let's go."

Valerie grabbed her purse off the table and walked along side of Bruce.

"Good girl. You'll see. Everything's going to be just fine."

There was a commotion near the entrance of the hotel, and Valerie turned to see what was happening. Bruce didn't seem at all interested; instead, he tugged her along, picking up his pace. A security guard rushed past them in the opposite direction. Bodies began to hurry in either direction, and voices started to buzz all around them.

"What's happening, Bruce?" She tugged at his hand, but he held it tightly. "Where are you taking me?"

"Oh, you'll see in just a few minutes. Don't worry about what's happening, Val. It's all part of my plan."

She stared at his evil smile. Alex had told her many times if she ever got caught in a scenario like this to fight her way out no matter what she had to do. Never get in a vehicle with anyone attempting to kidnap her. But Bruce wasn't headed outside. He headed for the elevators.

CHAPTER 30

The energy drink Alex had did nothing to energize him. The past few nights without Valerie, he'd hardly gotten any sleep, and it was really starting to weigh heavily on him. He could hardly wait to have her back in his bed.

Everything was set for the wedding, and they were ahead of schedule. Even the food was coming along very nicely. It wasn't until he was on his way down from checking on the banquet room and he heard Sal paging him over the sound system, that he realized he'd left his phone in the office.

Alex you got a call on line one.

Alex rushed to the phone. Sal wouldn't page him unless it was urgent. The adrenaline immediately kicked in as he picked up the phone.

"This is Alex."

"Hey, Hank's been trying to call you." Romero's voice was troubled.

"Why, what's wrong?" Alex asked his chest already constricting.

"Something's going on at the resort. They're evacuating everyone. Steve saw Valerie leave, holding hands with a man, but it wasn't Luke."

Fear and other unknown emotions bolted through him. "Leave where? In a car?" Sal walked out of the office, and Alex motioned for him to bring him his cell.

"No, they walked out of the dining area where she'd been sitting, having coffee by herself. But listen to me, Alex. He's on to us. He's been on to us for a while. That's why he hadn't changed the emails. The calendar Mr. X found was a ploy. He mocked up a calendar to throw us off. Mr. X picked up his real trail just a few minutes ago. He's been planning this for a while."

Sal handed Alex his cell watching him, aware of Alex's altered demeanor. "Planning what?" He hit the speed dial on his cell for Valerie.

"Getting to Valerie at this seminar."

Alex felt the heat in his veins just as the line clicked on the other end of his cell. "Hello, Alex." Bruce's self-satisfied voice purred.

Alex shoved the restaurant phone in Sal's chest. He gripped his cell phone barely able to contain himself. "Where's Valerie?" His voice so loud Angel rushed out of the office.

"Oh, don't you worry about her. She's in very good hands, Alex. As a matter of fact, these hands are getting ready to enjoy every inch—"

The line went dead. He let out a loud roar from deep down inside as he hit redial again. His vision blurred for a moment. He was going to kill Bruce. Sal was trying to tell him something, but the roar thrumming in his own ears was too loud. The call went to voicemail. Sal grabbed his arm jerking him momentarily back to sanity.

"Romero needs to talk to you, man." He held the phone in front of him. "Calm down and breathe. The cops are already there."

"Tell him to call me on my cell." Alex nearly collided with Angel as he ran into the office to grab his keys from the desk and pulled the gun out of the bottom desk drawer.

His phone started ringing as he rushed out.

"Whoa, whoa, whoa," Sal stepped in front of him. Angel backed him up. "You can't just walk out of here, toting a gun like that. What are you insane?"

"Get out of my way, Sal." Alex growled, the thought of Bruce man handling Valerie nearly blinding him again.

"No, Alex." Sal pushed him hard in the chest. "Calm your ass, already. We're not letting you walk out like this. You're crazy."

Alex's phone was still ringing. In the moment he took to consider answering it, Sal snatched the gun out of his hand. Some of the employees gathered around as if to assist Sal and Angel in taking Alex down if they had to. Alex gave up the gun without a fight and answered his phone.

~*~

The phone flew out of Bruce's hand as he stumbled, falling over the chair beside him. The heel of her shoe to Bruce's temple with all the force Valerie could conjure up had done the job. Somehow, he'd known about the Taser gun in her purse and had disarmed her the moment they stepped in the elevator. He'd even taken her cell phone from her. The only other thing she had on her person was her soft leather purse. She knew that wouldn't make the impact she needed.

From her past experience with him, Valerie knew playing nice was the only chance she had to buy her time. She'd cozied up to him just as they entered the room. He'd been so spellbound when she seductively removed her shoes he didn't even catch that she held on to one of them. The moment he got busy being cocky on her phone with Alex, she took advantage of the distraction, struck him with it, and ran.

Unwilling to take a chance and wait for the elevator, she was now running down the stairwell. Her heart threatened to pummel through her chest. The room had only been on the third floor. She was already halfway down to the first when she slipped and fell hard on her behind. It wasn't until then that she even heard the footsteps coming down fast from the stairs above.

"Valerie!" His voice was crazed. "Valerie, I'm warning you! Moreno's is going down if you don't stop!"

Her heart nearly gave out, and she was tempted to stop, but she thought of what Alex would want her to do in this instance. There was no other option but to run. Struggling to catch her breath, she reached for the rail and pulled herself up. She pushed the door open and ran right into the arms of a firefighter in full uniform.

Startled and barely able to breath, she tried getting past him. She had to get to a phone and warn Alex about the danger at his restaurant. But the fireman stopped her from going any further.

"You need to evacuate, ma'am. There's a possible bomb in the hotel."

"I know who planted it! He planted another one somewhere else at a restaurant!" She said, realizing how frantic she actually was.

The firefighter stared at her wide-eyed. "Come with me."

~*~

Alex tried calling Valerie several times as Sal drove them to the hotel. Romero had already arrived at the hotel. He'd called Alex only to tell him he couldn't get anywhere near the inside. They had the place surrounded with enforcement. There was no way around it.

The only way Angel and Sal had agreed to let Alex leave was if Sal drove him. Even some of the cooks had stepped in to hold him from storming out of there, the damn traitors.

The news updates on the radio about the hotel evacuation only served to further his anxiety. He still had no word on Valerie. The police had blocked off all the streets around the resort. Traffic was a mess. At this point, either he sat patiently or his only chance of getting close was to walk. Since patience had never been his virtue even though they were in the middle lanes of the street, he opened his door and hopped out.

"Where you going?" Sal demanded.

"I'm walking."

"Damn it, Alex. Just wait."

"I can't." He closed the door behind him and leaned in. "Call me if you hear anything."

He hurried across the street and onto the sidewalk, cutting across a few other streets before dialing Romero. "What's the word? Anything new?"

"Nothing on Valerie yet, but …"

"But what?" Alex shouted. This was no time to stall.

"I just heard on the scanner someone's been shot."

Alex stopped sharply. "What?"

"It could be unrelated, Alex. Don't freak out. They haven't even mentioned if it's a woman or a man or how bad it is. I'm still listening."

The other line on Alex's phone beeped. He checked to see who it was, Angel. He was probably just trying to get an update or to give him one about the wedding. He'd have to call him back later. Nothing else mattered anymore. All he could think of was getting to Valerie. If anything had happened to her, he didn't know what he'd do. He hurried almost to a run, the lump in his throat increasing with every stride.

Someone else was calling now. A number he didn't recognize. There was no way he was cutting the only connection he had to finding out about Valerie. He let the call go without answering.

"It's a male that's down, Alex." Romero said then added. "But there are others injured. Hold on."

Alex finally came to the barricade in front of the resort. They weren't letting anyone in. There were dozens of police cars and several fire engines parked along the entrance to the resort. A ton of security and uniformed officers along with plain clothed ones were walking around. The press had arrived as well.

"I need to get in there." He loomed over the security guard at the barricade, still gripping the phone to his ear. "My wife is in there."

"I'm sorry, sir, no one except the police and rescue workers are allowed in at this time." Romero said something, but the siren of an arriving ambulance just behind Alex was so loud he couldn't hear. Just as the ambulance flew by, he heard the beep of his other line again. This time it was Sal. He couldn't know any more than Romero.

"Where are you?" Romero yelled.

"Right in front of the place. They won't let me in."

"I'm gonna answer my other line, Alex. It's Angel for the third time since I've been talking to you. This might be important."

Alex didn't bother to respond. He stared up at the resort, furious with himself. He should've never agreed to let her come to this. He'd known it was a huge risk from the beginning. He should've stuck to his gut, even after hearing about Bruce's bogus plans for Monday. His other line beeped again: that same number he hadn't recognized earlier. Just then, Romero came back on the line.

"Answer your other line. It's Valerie. She's okay."

Alex's breath hitched, and he almost missed the button to click over.

"Hello?"

"Alex, I'm okay. I lost my phone in the hotel, and I couldn't remember your number. I've never memorized it, so I called the restaurant."

The mixture of emotions he felt after hearing her exclaim she was okay was something he'd never experienced in his life. He'd hardly caught anything else she said after that. Something gripped his windpipe, and he couldn't get a damn word out. He sucked in air, finally able to speak, but he strained to get the words out. "Where are you, baby?"

"I'm in the front by all the fire trucks."

A newfound emotion took over. His need to be by her side became overwhelming. Alex glanced around, trying hard to gather the might to speak without choking up. "I'm here too just outside the barricades at the front entrance."

He heard her say something to someone then came back on the phone, "Where? I'm looking for you." Her voice broke. She must've been holding it together also, but she cried now. "They're going to let you in."

Alex started to explain where he was, then he saw her by one of the fire trucks, looking around. She had a phone to her ear with one hand and her shoe in another. She was barefoot and looked so small and helpless. Something gripped at his windpipe again. He waved and called out for her. When she saw him, she ran to him. He pushed past the guard, flicking him aside like a flea. As soon as she was close enough, she jumped in his arms. Alex held her tighter than he ever had, burying his face in her neck.

With a deep breath, he pulled back to look at her face. The hot tears he felt in his own eyes surprised him, but even more surprising, he wasn't embarrassed. He didn't care about any of that. All he could think of was how much he loved her, and he thanked God she was all right. He gulped hard, searching her face. "Did he hurt you?"

She shook her head. "No, I got away when he was talking to you on the phone."

Alex slipped his phone into the holster on his belt, easily holding Valerie still in the air with one arm. He brought his hand back to move the strands of hair away from her face. "Tell me the truth, baby. Did he touch you?" Alex remembered the rough way he'd tried to put his hand on her at the bar the night he knocked him out. If Bruce had so much as put a finger on her, Alex would hunt him down and kill him himself.

Valerie stared at him, the tears beginning to subside. "No, he didn't." She whispered.

He kissed the tip of her nose, still not loosening his hold on her even a bit. "Do you know if they got him?"

She shook her head and leaned her face into the crook of his neck. "They haven't told me anything, except someone got shot."

Alex inhaled her familiar scent: a scent so unique only to Valerie. If he could bottle it, he'd keep a bottle of it on him at all times. "Yeah, I heard about that to." He decided he would worry about Bruce later. For now, he was just eternally grateful that Valerie was okay and out of harm's way. From here on, she'd never be out of sight until Bruce was caught or dead.

His phone had been vibrating in his holster from the moment he hung up with Valerie. Reluctantly, he put her down and answered it. He let Romero in on where he was and told him to update everyone. Then he and Valerie went back to where the detectives were waiting for her.

~*~

That evening, Valerie came home with Alex. He stared at her as she slept, her face against his chest. For days, he tossed and turned, his body yearning, starving for hers. Now all he wanted was to sleep next to her, hold her knowing she was safe. He figured she'd be exhausted, and she was knocked out almost as quickly as she'd cuddled up next to him. It had been such an emotionally draining day for both of them.

Valerie told her story so many different times: first to him, then the detectives. then her father and Norma when they went back to his house. Alex had tired of telling it himself. Everyone had been concerned and eager to know what happened. He'd also heard about the bomb squad evacuating the restaurant right in the middle of the lunch rush. Valerie told Angel about Bruce threatening he'd blow up the restaurant when she called to get his number. Before Angel could even decide what to do about it, she informed him the bomb squad was already on its way. After searching for hours, they found nothing. It was a complete bluff. When questioned by police about it, Bruce denied ever saying anything of the sort.

It turned out Alex wouldn't have to hunt Bruce down. He'd been shot when he pointed a gun an officer. They weren't even looking for him yet. The idiot pointed the gun when the officer tried to stop him from going into the closed-off area. In his crazed attempt to catch up to Valerie, he thought pulling a gun out in a middle of a hotel full of cops would somehow fly.

It wasn't life threatening. The bullet just shattered his shoulder. Alex thought he deserved at least that much. After hours of interviews with Valerie, Luke, and other witnesses, Bruce was not only going to need a doctor but a real good lawyer. The list of charges they slapped him with was as long as his rap sheet. He'd held Luke against his will at gunpoint, gagging and tying him up in the suite's closet, tried kidnapping Valerie, planted a fake bomb at the hotel, and pointed a gun at an officer.

With Bruce still being on probation and having a criminal past, the detectives assured Valerie he'd more than likely be spending the rest of life behind bars. The nightmare was over.

Some things were still unanswered. Alex wondered if he even needed to know why she kept her night with Luke from him all this time. He sighed, caressing her cheek with the back of his fingers. As long as she worked with him daily, it would gnaw at him. They postponed the seminar for another time, so she'd still attend with Luke eventually. He had to know.

He was willing to do anything, make any kind of sacrifice for Valerie. But something like this would eat away at him until he got an answer. He let it go for now, but once the time was right, he'd bring it up again.

~*~

Weeks later, Valerie was still getting calls from detectives for more details about the case against Bruce. What they'd uncovered about Bruce was even more disturbing than some of the things Romero's guy had told them. After being interviewed several times, Bruce seriously believed Valerie owed him the intimacy he'd sought from her. What's more, even behind bars, he continued to believe he would someday get it.

Valerie shuttered just thinking about it. She was safe now. She had to remind herself every time she thought of that. He was locked up, and they kept reassuring Valerie that with every incriminating interview, he was tacking on more and more years to his eventual sentencing.

She had just hung up with the detective and was looking through Alex's refrigerator when her phone rang again. It was Luke. She thought about sending it to voicemail, but then remembered he might be calling with news about the interview. She answered.

"Hey."

"You got it." She could literally hear the smile in Luke's voice.

"What?" She closed the door to the fridge and opened the water bottle she'd grabbed.

"They're only calling two candidates back out of all the one's they interviewed, and you're one of them. And, Val, you were the youngest of all the candidates interviewed."

It had been almost two weeks since she'd interviewed. She'd been one of the first, so she had to wait the longest until everyone else was interviewed.

She smiled, trying not to get too excited. "So what now?"

"They'll call you to schedule the second interview. I can start coaching you on the main things you should know about second interviews and what they'll be looking for tomorrow."

It was a good thing Alex hadn't been there when Luke called. Although he was beginning to get used to her job being different from most nine-to-five jobs, he still got annoyed when she got calls in the evening. But it especially annoyed him when it was Luke.

After hanging up with Luke, Valerie took a long shower. She thought about Luke's coaching. Ever since Bruce's arrest, Valerie had avoided being alone with Luke as much as possible.

She felt terrible about what Bruce had done to him, so she made sure things were amiable between her and Luke. But she kept her distance. Though Alex hadn't asked anything about her night with Luke since the scene he made at the hospital, the mood always got tense when his name came up. Even if she got the position in the new office, the trial was still months away, and she'd be constantly seeing him then.

A couple of times she thought of just telling Alex about it. She hated the tension of Alex thinking she'd slept with Luke and lied about it. Each time she considered telling him and getting it over with, she chickened out.

Alex got home just as Valerie finished dressing in one of his T-shirts and a soft pair of cotton shorts—the kind she loved to go to bed in but usually came right off within minutes.

"Hey." She smiled as he walked in the bedroom.

She picked up her phone from the dresser to check if she'd missed any calls. Ever since her father had collapsed, she'd been paranoid about missing calls from him or Norma.

Alex startled her by picking her up. With his arms wrapped around her, he growled as he took her mouth. He brought her to the bed and laid her down, never once detaching his very active tongue from her mouth. His kiss was hot and hungrier than usual even for him. She felt the immediate erection against her thigh. Her own arousal began to peak. She arched her back, rubbing her hands over his hard shoulders then his back.

Her phone rang, bringing Alex's kisses to a halt. "You wanna get that?" He asked, his lips still on hers.

"No." She was already breathless and burning with anticipation.

"What if it's your dad?"

She stared at his lips. "I get the feeling this is going to be over fast."

"It is." He licked her bottom lip with a wicked smile.

"Then I'll call him back when we're done." She thrust her tongue in his mouth as the phone continued to ring.

Alex's heated eyes glanced down, pulling her shirt up. At once, his mouth was on her nipple. Valerie moaned at the sensation of his tongue. It made her entire body tingle.

Her phone rang again, and Alex stopped. Valerie could feel his annoyance by the way his body tensed.

"I'll turn it off." She offered. "Where is it?"

She'd dropped it when he brought her to the bed. Alex leaned over the side of the bed and picked it up. His hardened expression when he glanced at the caller ID was enough to tell her who it was.

He handed her the phone and pulled himself off her. "Answer it."

"It's probably just about work, Alex. I can talk to him in the morning."

"No." The heat in his eyes now was of a completely different nature than when he'd stared at her earlier. "I wanna know what's so damn important he has to call you after nine. Go ahead, answer it."

Just like that, the mood for the evening was officially ruined. She clenched her teeth but answered the phone, not wanting things to get ugly. "Hey, Luke what's up?"

"I forgot to tell you. I got the email earlier today. The seminar's been rescheduled for two weeks from this Saturday. Make sure you keep your calendar open."

Wonderful. Valerie glanced up at Alex who still stared at her. She'd really hoped it was something work-related—something that wouldn't further the tension she could already feel thickening. "Oh, okay. I will."

Luke was quiet for a moment. Valerie was sure he expected her to be a little more excited or at least have more to say about it. No way was she encouraging any more conversation.

"All right, well I'll talk to you in the morning."

Alex was still staring at her when she hung up. "So what was it?"

She got off the bed and walked to the dresser, turning the phone off as she placed it on the dresser. She didn't even want to see his expression when she said it. "They rescheduled the seminar. He just got the email."

CHAPTER 31

Alex sat there on the bed, still staring at Valerie's sexy little frame in his t-shirt. She put the phone down, but she didn't turn back to him. He got the distinct feeling she purposely left the bed to be away from him when she told him about the seminar.

"When is it?" He tried not to sound annoyed. But he was. Incredibly. The idiot had called at the worst moment imaginable.

"Two weeks from this Saturday."

She still had her back to him. "What's wrong?"

Finally, she turned to face him. "Nothing."

"Then what are you doing over there?" He reached his hand out to her. He just had her under him moments ago, and already he wanted her near him again, annoyed or not.

Something about the way she smiled made him uncomfortable, but she did walk back to him. She was going to sit on the bed next to him, but he pulled her onto his lap, lacing his fingers through hers. Leaning his forehead against hers, he tried again. "What's wrong?"

She shook her head slowly. "Nothing I just …" She bit her lip and then frowned.

"What is it?"

"The night I spent at his house—"

"Stop." Alex straightened up, feeling every muscle in his body go taut. "I don't need to hear about it."

Whether she slept with him or not, he'd never be comfortable with her around him, so it really didn't make a difference.

"I want you to know."

"I don't want to hear about it, Z." If she thought he was going to sit here and listen to her tell him about her night with another man she was insane.

Valerie cradled his face with her hands. "I have to tell you, baby. It's killing me that you think I had sex with him. I didn't."

Alex preferred not to know than for her to lie to him. He swallowed hard, staring in her beautiful eyes. Her touch alone was enough to soften his tensed body, but what she was saying made no sense. "So what? You just fell asleep at his place, and he didn't wake you?"

That made a little more sense. She shook her head, making him squeeze his hand into a fist. He didn't want to blow up at her. "I don't understand, Z. Either you did or you didn't. There's no in between here."

The deep breath she took made him nervous. "I was going to. I won't lie to you. I went there that night prepared to. I still wasn't feeling anything for him—"

"So you decided to sleep with him when you didn't feel anything for him? Bullshit." He remembered Romero saying she'd told Bruce she was in love with him.

Her eyes darkened and eyebrows pinched. "It's true. I was trying so hard to make it work."

"Why, if you didn't care about him?" Alex was aware he was raising his voice, but what she was trying to feed him didn't add up.

She stood up and off his lap. Alex held her hand so she wouldn't walk away. "I wanted to get over you. Okay?"

Alex opened his mouth, but when he didn't say anything, she continued.

"All I could do was think of you and that kiss at the shower when I was with him. I compared everything about him to you, and he didn't even come close. I truly believed that if I could just move on, I'd get over you. Since I hadn't slept with anyone else the entire time I was away from you, I thought maybe that's what I needed to finally get some closure. But—"

"You spent the night." A fact Alex wouldn't soon forget. What she was saying only made it worse. In spite of the fact that she'd just told him she hadn't slept with anyone else while they were apart, she'd spent the night at Luke's, and now he knew she'd gone there to sleep with him.

"Only because I felt terrible about what happened."

Alex searched her eyes, unable to even imagine what she meant by that. "What happened?

Valerie took another deep breath that only furthered Alex's anxiety. "We were making out …" She paused.

Alex's patience was running out. He told her he didn't want to hear about this, and now she was going to drag it out? The visual alone made his blood boil. "Damn it, Z—"

"I called him Alex."

Alex blinked. Valerie looked mortified, her cheeks a bit crimsoned. He pulled her to him, making her sit back down on his lap, still not sure what to say. The fact that she'd been in another man's arms still felt like a kick in the gut. But the thought that she'd been thinking of him the whole time, so much so she'd actually called Luke Alex… He couldn't even begin to imagine what Luke must've felt at that moment.

Without warning, he laughed. Valerie buried her face in his chest, covering the exposed part with her small hand.

"Don't laugh." Her words were muffled. "You've no idea how incredibly awkward that moment was. It was horrible."

That only made Alex laugh even more. He kissed her head, caressing her damp hair. Valerie lifted her head slowly and met his eyes. "So you see. You've never had anything to worry about."

She went on to tell him about how she spent the rest of the evening, telling Luke about her relationship with Alex. And how'd she really believed she was over him until she'd seen him at the shower and found out she wasn't even close.

"The very next time I saw Luke, I broke things off. I owed him at least that much. I knew I'd never get over you. It was stupid to think that by going out with him I would."

Alex couldn't take his eyes off her. He loved hearing her say she'd never get over him. He lifted her chin. "Know what I don't understand?"

She tilted her head. She looked so adorable he had to kiss her. "If you know you'll never get over me, why don't you just marry me already?"

This time she was the one that opened her mouth without any words that followed. She closed it and bit her lip. She tried again and still nothing.

Feeling the annoyance start to build again, Alex spoke first. "Stop trying to come up with an excuse, Z."

The corners of her lips lifted ever so slowly. His heart thumped, and he smiled with her.

"Okay. Let's do it. Let's get married." She smiled big.

Alex knew his eyes must have been as big as saucers. He swallowed hard, barely able to put it all in perspective. Valerie was going to be his wife, entirely his forever. He leaned in to kiss her but stopped. "That phone better be off."

"It is." She giggled.

With that, he leaned back in bed and brought her down with him.

"Mrs. Moreno." He whispered before kissing her deeply.

When he finally let her breathe, she smiled "I like it." She whispered back. "I can hardly wait now."

Alex kissed her, knowing full well she wouldn't have to wait long. He'd make sure of it. First things first. With one yank, he pulled off her shorts.

EPILOGUE

Alex and Valerie walked into the restaurant, holding hands. They'd gone straight to her dad's house then his parent's place from the airport. Valerie seemed much more relaxed after speaking to their parents.

Angel glanced up from the host desk in the front, no doubt expecting to see customers. He did a double take before smiling. "Hey, how was Bermuda?"

"Beautiful," Valerie beamed.

"How's everything here?" Alex asked as he walked by him.

Angel waved a hand at him. "Running smoother than ever."

Sarah was hunched over, reading something at the back bar. Sal, who was on the other side of the bar, glanced up as they walked toward them. "When did you guys get back?"

"Couple hours ago." Alex responded squeezing Valerie's hand.

Sarah turned around and immediately came over to greet them both with a hug. Valerie brushed a strand of hair away from her own face, and Sarah stopped cold. "What is this?" She grabbed Valerie's hand and gawked at Valerie's three-carat diamond ring.

Valerie smiled but didn't answer. She glanced at Alex. Sarah finally looked away from the ring and brought her attention to Valerie's. "Are you guys engaged?"

"Nope," Alex answered for her.

Sarah brought her attention to Alex, now confused. "Then—"

"We're married." He said matter of fact.

Sarah's mouth fell open.

"You're what?" Angel asked, coming around Alex to see what Sarah was looking at. He glanced at Valerie's ring then turned back to Alex. "Tell me you're kidding."

Sarah had her hand over her mouth now. Valerie's hand was still in hers, but her eyes went back and forth from Alex to Valerie.

"No kidding," Valerie finally spoke up. "We got married in Bermuda."

Sal walked over to join the rest of the stunned bunch. He took one look at the ring then at Alex. "Dude, mom's gonna flip."

Alex chuckled. "She did. We just came from there. She was a little upset but got over it pretty quick when I finally agreed to let her throw us a little party. Her and Sofi were already on the phone, making the plans before we even left."

"Ha!" Angel scoffed loudly. "Mom and pop throw a *little* party? Good luck. She'll invite two maybe three *hundred* people."

Alex frowned at that. Sarah finally stopped gawking and let out a squeal. She hugged Valerie again and then jumped up to hug Alex tighter than the first time.

Sarah turned back to Valerie with an accusing look. "You never even told me you were engaged."

Valerie laughed and glanced at Alex. "I was only engaged for a couple days before we left for Bermuda. It was really spur of the moment."

It sure had been. The moment Valerie had agreed, the wheels were spinning in his head. The day after she'd agreed, they both decided they didn't want a big wedding. The only way that was going to happen was if they didn't tell anyone. He worked his schedule around at the restaurant, telling everyone Valerie needed to get away after all the drama she'd been through, bought the ring, and booked the flight. He wasn't about to give her time to change her mind. They'd been married the day they arrived in Bermuda then spent most of the rest of their time there in their suite, honeymooning.

After a round of hugs and a few kisses for the bride from everyone, they sat around the bar for a celebratory drink.

Sarah sat with Valerie, demanding every detail of their small but very romantic wedding. Valerie was doing her best to oblige.

Sal stood behind the bar in front of Alex. "I can't believe you did this. What's with everyone all of sudden? My buddy Jason just got engaged too."

Alex took a drink of his beer. "Really? I thought he was still in school."

"He is." Sal lifted his shoulder. "I guess he just couldn't wait."

"Hey!"

Alex turned to see Romero walk in the restaurant, holding Isabel's hand. "What's the big surprise?"

Valerie told him in the car she texted Isabel to meet them at the restaurant. She hadn't mentioned she told them there was a surprise. He exchanged glances with her, then she gave him a devilish smile. Valerie lifted her finger in the air. Isabel's eyes opened wide. She turned to Alex then back at Valerie. "You're engaged?"

Valerie stood up, shaking her head with a big grin on her face. "We got married."

"Get out!" Isabel hugged her as soon as Valerie reached her.

"Hey, man." Romero shook Alex's hand and clapped him on the shoulder. "How come you didn't tell me?"

"We didn't tell anyone. Everyone just found out. Have a beer. Celebrate with us." Alex turned to the bartender and held up two fingers.

"Man, you Morenos are dropping like flies." Romero took the beers Alex handed him and turned to Sal. "That means you're next, chief."

"Hell no," Sal took a swig of his own beer. "I have too many plans before I even think about settling down."

Romero rolled his eyes before walking toward Isabel with her beer. "Yeah, we'll see."

"What are you talking about?" Sal smiled. "You're probably the next one to go down."

Valerie walked toward them. "Hey, I heard that."

Sal came around from behind the bar and held out his arms. "I'm only kidding. I couldn't be happier for you two. I know how much you mean to this big lug."

He squeezed her a little too tightly, rubbing his hands all over her back and smirked at Alex.

Alex reached out for her hand. "All right that's happy enough."

Sal laughed, letting her go. "You're too easy little brother."

"Funny," Valerie smiled as Alex pulled her to him. "I don't think I've ever heard anyone refer to you as little."

Sal laughed about to say something when Angel walked up behind her and interrupted. "You two sure there's no other reason for this sudden marriage?"

Valerie turned to him, obviously not understanding what he was getting at. Alex squeezed her hand and shoved Angel. "No, ass. But now that we're married I don't see any reason why we shouldn't visit that idea."

Finally getting it, Valerie laughed. "No way. One thing at a time."

Alex laughed and kissed her. They hung around for few more drinks then said their goodbyes. The happiness he felt was a bit overwhelming. Life couldn't be any better.

He'd been more than pissed when Valerie got a call from Luke on their honeymoon. But after hearing the voicemail, it more than made up for it. Valerie had gone on her second interview the day before they left. Luke called to tell her she got the position. Alex would have to put up with her working with him for only a few more months.

Once in the truck, he leaned over and kissed her, "You know, I wasn't kidding in there about us having a baby."

Valerie's mouth fell open. "Alex I swear you're too much. Can we get used to this marriage thing first?"

"What's there to get used to?"

She laughed aloud, putting her hand on his thigh then sliding it up a bit more. Her expression becoming more serious. "I do want to have babies, Alex. Lots and lots of them. I promise. Just not yet."

He'd had her day and night to himself for the past five days straight, and her touch still singed him. "Lots and lots, huh? Sounds to me like we'll need lots and lots of practice making them then." He kissed her again as if he hadn't in ages.

It was a good thing they were married now because somehow he couldn't imagine ever getting his fill of her.

ACKNOWLEDGEMENTS

As always, I would like to thank my husband Mark and my kids, Marky and Megan, for their patience and support. I couldn't do any of this without you guys. Thanks for stepping up and taking care of everything else while I sit in my cave and write my heart away.

To my beta reader and good friend Ivannia. Thank you so much for your feedback on this and for being part of the inspiration to some parts of the story. Thank you for sharing and your complete honesty. I really needed it, and I do think it made the story work better.

To my critique partner Tammara Webber, who I didn't meet until this book was already published but did help me go back and rework a few kinks out. Your input and opinions are invaluable to me. I do feel we've met for a reason, and I am forever grateful and feel very blessed to have you as a critique partner.

I'd like to acknowledge my editor/formatter and beta reader, Theresa Wegand. Thank you for your attention to the finest details and professionalism. Having an editor who not only edits but formats and takes care of all the technicalities is such an enormous help. I feel very blessed to have you on my team as well.

Also, thank you to my cover artist Stephanie Mooney for your added touch to my covers and making them look more professional than the original ones I had.

And last but certainly not least, thank you to the readers. Without you, I would not be living my dream of doing what I love for a living. Your kind words and enthusiasm for my stories are what keep me going and loving the time I spend in my cave. I love hearing from you guys, and it's almost scary how it seems every time I'm feeling a bit discouraged, out of nowhere, one of you will reach out and comment or message me something so sweet that turns things around for me. I thank you all so, SO much!

ABOUT THE AUTHOR

Elizabeth Reyes was born and raised in southern California and still lives there with her husband of almost nineteen years, her two teens, her Great Dane named Dexter, and one big fat cat named Tyson.

She spends eighty percent of time in front of her computer writing and keeping up with all the social media, and loves it. She says that there is nothing better than doing what you absolutely love for a living, and she eats, sleeps, and breathes these stories, which are constantly begging to be written.

Representation: Jane Dystel of Dystel & Goderich now handles all questions regarding subsidiary rights for any of Ms. Reyes' work. Please direct inquiries regarding foreign translation and film rights availability to her.

For more information on her upcoming projects and to connect with her (She loves hearing from you all!), here are a few places you can find her:

Blog: authorelizabethreyes.blogspot.com

Facebook fan page:

http://www.facebook.com/pages/Elizabeth-Reyes/278724885527554